JAIMIE ADMANS is a 35-year-old English-sounding Welsh girl with an awkward-to-spell name. She lives in South Wales and enjoys writing, gardening, watching horror movies and drinking tea, although she's seriously considering marrying her coffee machine. She loves autumn and winter, and singing songs from musicals despite the fact she's got the voice of a dying hyena. She hates spiders, hot weather, and cheese and onion crisps. She spends far too much time on Twitter and owns too many pairs of boots. She will never have time to read all the books she wants to read.

Jaimie loves to hear from readers. You can visit her website at jaimieadmans.com or connect on Twitter @be_the_spark.

Also by Jaimie Admans

The Château of Happily-Ever-Afters
The Little Wedding Island
It's a Wonderful Night
The Little Vintage Carousel by the Sea
Snowflakes at the Little Christmas Tree Farm

The Little Bookshop of Love Stories

JAIMIE ADMANS

ONE PLACE. MANY STORIES

HQ
An imprint of HarperCollins*Publishers* Ltd
1 London Bridge Street
London SE1 9GF

1
First published in Great Britain by
HQ, an imprint of HarperCollins*Publishers* Ltd 2020

ISBN: 9780008330729

MIX
Paper from
responsible sources
FSC™ C007454

This book is produced from independently certified FSC™ paper
to ensure responsible forest management.

For more information visit: www.harpercollins.co.uk/green

Printed and bound by
CPI Group (UK) Ltd, Croydon, CR0 4YY

For readers everywhere.
Aren't books magical?

Chapter 1

It is a truth universally acknowledged that today is the Mondayest Monday ever.

I've been fired. Again.

I trudge home through the afternoon drizzle that's so well timed it's like it waited for me to leave work. I'd left my umbrella behind and was in such disgrace that I wasn't bold enough to go back in and get it. My boss was one angry step away from fire spurting out of his ears. I think the sight of me again would've tipped him over the edge.

The job had been going well too. I'd been there almost a year, and apart from a few warnings about my clumsiness and the odd wage deduction for breakages, being a waitress at a dog-friendly pub within walking distance of my flat wasn't too bad.

That was before this afternoon.

A family out for a walk had come in for an afternoon meal, and as I carried the tray of desserts to their table, the little boy dropped his monkey directly into my path. I stumbled over the plastic toy, instantly decapitating it with my shoe, and the tray slipped in my hands, and like a moment from a cartoon where an unseen crowd in the background do a slow-motion gasp of horror, the child's ice-cream sundae flipped over, doing such an impressive mid-air somersault that if gymnastics judges had been watching, it would've scored a perfect ten. The ice-cream bowl was deposited upside down on the head of its chosen victim like some missile-based hat.

As the child burst into screaming tears – unsure if caused by ice cream on head debacle, murdered monkey toy, or a fair mix of both – the ice-cream bowl continued its pursuit for gymnastic glory by cartwheeling from the child's head to the floor, at which point the family dog leapt from beneath the table and devoured it. As the dad yelled, the mum cried, and the child wailed while ice cream dripped slowly down his neck, the dog clattered the empty metal bowl around the floor, careening into tables, doors, and other diners, dodging any attempt to intercept him with a speed Mo Farah would envy.

When the bowl was eventually wrestled from the dog with only a few teeth marks to show for its adventure, the family were offered their meal on the house and a complimentary voucher, while they bundled their ice-cream-covered child and now some-what pukey-looking dog into their car to rush it to the vet's, lest it had consumed an errant chocolate chip lurking in the ice cream. We watched in horror as they squealed a three-point-turn, the mum in the back seat, trying to haul the dog away from licking the ice-cream-covered child. The dog got so annoyed that he barfed in her lap to show his appreciation. This created a domino effect of vomiting as the child then turned to puke out of the window, and the dad hit the brakes, causing the mum to lean forward and throw up all over the front seat.

And all before they'd even left the car park.

The upshot is that I was on my final warning for clumsiness so I lost my job, and I'm now responsible for the cost of the family's meal, their dry cleaning, car cleaning, the vet's bills, and the vouchers they took despite swearing they wouldn't come back even if every other restaurant in the country was situated in a stagnant swamp and run by zombies. I also got to spend my last half an hour of the job shovelling vomit out of the car park.

Really, it could've happened to anyone. And at least it gave the other diners some amusement as they ate. I did appreciate the little old woman who patted my arm as I collected my things from behind the bar and said, 'Your luck has to change sometime.'

I wouldn't bet on it. Bad luck seems to have been with me my entire life. Everyone has 'one of *those* days' occasionally, but I seem to have them every day. It's a rare event worth marking on the calendar when something *doesn't* go catastrophically wrong.

At least my flatmate's out. I'm grateful for the small mercies as I let myself into the cramped two-bedroom space I share with a twenty two-year-old student whose only hobbies seem to be eating my food, sleeping during daylight hours, and humping a string of scantily clad girls who could do so much better. Him not being here to mock me for losing yet *another* job is the only bit of luck I'm going to have today.

I shrug my damp jacket off and shiver, cold and wet through to my skin from the persistent drizzle that somehow makes you even wetter than heavy rain. I need to go and change, but first – chocolate. I go into the kitchen, open the cupboard that's supposed to be mine, only to find he's eaten my last chocolate bar. I was saving that Wispa for an emergency and it's gone. My fingers curl like claws and I shake them at the ceiling. 'Argh!' I shout to myself, grateful for the empty house.

I start belting out 'Chandelier' in an attempt to cheer myself up as I open the fridge and peer inside, on the hunt for any morsel of food he *hasn't* eaten, thoroughly enjoying the uninhibited singsong despite the fact I have a voice that would make honking geese jealous and can't hit any of the high notes. It doesn't stop me trying though.

It doesn't make any food magically appear in the fridge either.

I'm just hitting the last and highest 'chandelier' in the chorus – the one capable of shattering glass chandeliers even when sung by someone who can actually sing – when I close the fridge door and let out a scream of shock, because my flatmate is not out. He's standing behind the fridge door, laughing silently, with his harem of gorgeous twenty-something women gathered around him looking like they've just stepped out of *Love Island*.

'Is your mum drunk?' I overhear one of them say as they walk away sniggering.

I'm not drunk. I'm also not his mum. I'm nowhere near old enough to have birthed that food-stealing Lynx addict. I might have to agree with her on the singing though. And start doing my hair more often.

My hair elastic chooses that moment to snap, pinging the back of my head and causing my wet hair to drop around my shoulders. No doubt I've walked home looking like I've been lying on my back at the bottom of a bottle of gin too. I should possibly start checking my hair before being seen in public. I sigh and gather it up in one hand, pulling my long hair out from where it's already got tangled around my shoulders, pick up my bag and coat from where I dumped them and trudge upstairs, thinking about facing the drizzle again to go to the shop and get some food in. And some alcohol. Definitely some alcohol.

I unlock my bedroom door and go in, closing it behind me and wanting nothing more than to collapse on the bed and pretend this day didn't happen. I dump my stuff and go to flop on the inviting duvet, but I catch my foot on a power lead and trip over, the movement yanking my laptop, which is plugged into it. I yelp and try to catch it as it starts to fall from the bedside table. I leap forward and thank every lucky star in the universe when it lands on the pillow and I manage to get hold of it before it crashes to the floor.

Maybe I was due some luck today after all. My flatmate hammers on the wall from his room next door at the sound of my yelp, telling me to keep it down.

I roll my eyes and set the laptop back on the bedside table, push its lead in right underneath the bed so no one can trip on it and switch it on to make sure it's not damaged.

I've just lost my job, I cannot afford a computer repair bill as well, and I'm going to need it to start job-hunting tomorrow.

I get changed out of my work clothes while it starts up and sigh in relief from across the room in the middle of pulling on my baggy old jogging bottoms when my usual desktop picture of Belle's library from *Beauty and the Beast* appears on the screen.

I finally flop down on the bed and reach up to open my Facebook groups and see if anyone's got any good book recommendations today. Reading about books is the only way to improve this day. I quickly check my emails first and almost laugh at the one with a subject line declaring, 'You're the winner!'

More spam, no doubt. Despite having a surname that begins with 'Win', I've never won anything in my life. That's why I have to refresh my email screen a few times and rub my eyes to make sure I haven't already fallen asleep and this is just a dream.

Dear Miss Winstone,

Robert Paige here. We've just held the prize draw for the bookshop and I'm delighted to inform you that yours was the ticket that came out of the hat. Congratulations! You have won Once Upon A Page! Please get in touch at your earliest convenience and we'll arrange a visit so I can officially show you around your new property and agree on a transfer date.

Kind regards,

Robert Paige

PS: I'm really glad it was you, Hallie. I think you'll be good for this place!

I take my glasses off and clean the lenses with the bottom of my T-shirt but when I put them back on, the email is still there. And another one hasn't turned up that says, 'Hah! As if!' I know Robert Paige quite well. He's not one for joking around, and it's the beginning of May so he's missed April Fool's Day by a good month.

I let out a squeal and then clamp my hand over my mouth expecting my flatmate to start banging on the wall again, but his music comes on loudly – 'Let's Get It On' by Marvin Gaye, how imaginative – and the headboard starts banging against the wall as one of the two scantily clad girls he was with starts moaning. Have they really got nothing better to do on a Monday afternoon? The light fixture rattles and plaster falls from the ceiling as the banging increases in speed, and I use the opportunity to flop back onto the bed and muffle my scream in the duvet as I roll around in excitement, and clearly overestimate how wide the single bed is, because I roll right off the edge and land on the floor with the duvet wrapped in a knot around me.

Ouch. My still-damp hair has fallen over my face and I pull it back, spitting out blonde strands as I check my computer screen again to make sure it's not all a dream because that would've been certain to wake me up.

The email is still there.

This is actually for real. I've actually won a bookshop. And not just any bookshop – my favourite bookshop in the world. Well, of the ones I've been to, anyway. And by 'the world' I mean the little area of the Cotswolds between where I grew up and where I live now. I haven't ventured much further than that, except on the pages of books. The world is endlessly big when you have books.

How can this be happening? Owning a bookshop has always been my dream, but people as unlucky as me don't get dream jobs. I've always wanted to work with books, but the opportunities are few and far between around here, and the one time there was a job advertised for a bookshop manager, even though I thought the long three-bus daily commute would've been worth it, two of the buses were late on the day of the interview, and by the time I eventually made it, soaked through from the rain and with a broken heel – torn between hobbling in barefoot or limping in one-heeled, they refused to see me because of my poor time-keeping.

I've lost every job I've ever had anyway. What's the point in trying to work with something I love? Reading should just be a hobby, and I should pursue a sensible career in … whichever job I manage to keep the longest without getting fired.

I'd bought the ticket on a cold and damp January afternoon on the way back to the bus stop after visiting my mum and sister – always a good excuse to go into Once Upon A Page and have time for a browse.

Robert Paige was behind the counter as always, sitting in his chair crocheting blankets to send to war-ravaged children in Bosnia, an unusual hobby for an eighty-year-old man, which just made him all the more eccentric and engaging, like the time I'd gone in one day and found him with multicoloured streaks of long fake hair attached to his wiry white locks and sparkly rainbow nails because he'd let a child in the shop give him a makeover.

On this particular afternoon four months ago, he dropped a bombshell – he was retiring. He'd been the bookseller at Once Upon A Page for as long as I could remember, from when I was two years old and my mum took me there to buy the latest picture books, to when I was a pre-teen desperate for the newest Judy Blume, to now – when I still spend too much of my paltry wages on books. He was a permanent fixture in that shop – the kind of friendly old face who makes you feel welcome, who knows something about everything, and would always, always be there. I could never imagine seeing someone else behind the counter.

And then he dropped an even bigger bombshell. He wasn't selling Once Upon A Page – he was giving it away to someone who wanted to take over running it. And to make it fair, in the months leading up to his retirement, he was selling tickets for a prize draw to choose the winner.

At £30 a ticket, and a strict one-per-customer rule, it wasn't cheap. The amount of books I could've bought for that ... I couldn't really afford it, and I thought it was absolutely pointless because the only thing I've ever won in my life is head lice from a boy in primary school, but I don't think that counts. Robert's excitement about his plan was even more infectious than the head lice, and it was impossible not to get swept away on the daydream of somehow being the winner. How amazing would it be to own a bookshop? To get to live and breathe books every day? To get paid for stroking books, arranging books, talking about books, recommending books, and thrusting books into the hands of unsuspecting strangers?

I read book blogs online and am a member of countless Facebook groups, but to actually get to do it in real life, to step out from behind the computer screen and share my love of books with real people? It would be amazing.

I'd dutifully bought my compulsory-purchase-with-ticket book – a cookbook for Mum because I still live in hope that she might actually follow a recipe one day – and handed over money that really should've gone towards the electricity bill, and for a few nights afterwards, I'd gone to sleep dreaming about being a bookseller, about that gorgeous little shop being mine, about me sitting behind that polished mahogany counter, handing out free bookmarks and crocheting blankets for Bosnian children. Well, maybe not the crochet part. Last time I picked up a crochet hook, I got fired from my job at the haberdashery shop for nearly having a customer's eye out.

And then I never thought about it again. Every time I've been in since, Robert's been sitting there with his crochet hook and yarn, and he hasn't mentioned another thing about retiring. I thought he must've changed his mind. And let's face it, I would never win, no matter what. Luck is never on my side.

Until now. I haul myself back up off the floor and perch on the edge of the bed, leaning forward for another look at the email, still convinced it can't be real.

Maybe this is why I've never had any luck in my life. Maybe it was all being saved up for this moment. Maybe fate or the universe or whatever powers that be decided I would have the worst luck in the world, just so on this ordinary day in May, I could win a bookshop, and a new chapter of my life could start.

Once Upon A Page is in the tiny Cotswolds village of Buntingorden, about forty-five minutes away from the rabbit-hutch-sized box someone's had the nerve to call a two-bedroom flat that I currently share with an apparently irresistible twenty-something who barely grunts at me if we happen to be forced to pass in the hallway, smells like mouldy cheese, and never apologises for eating my food, even when I scrawl 'Hallie' all over the packaging, feeling like a college kid sharing a house for the first time, not the mature, adult woman I supposedly am. Waitressing doesn't pay well enough to have grown out of flat-shares by now.

I say a cheery goodbye to the driver as I jump off the bus and skip down Buntingorden High Street the next morning. Skip. I'm thirty-five. I'm not sure what's worse – still living in a flat-share or skipping in public. I've been here many times before because my sister lives in the Cotswold Hills just beyond. There's no traffic through the street, so the bus stop is at the upper end and I walk the rest of the way because it gives me an excuse to go past the bookshop every time I visit her.

The high street looks like it belongs in an award for prettiest high streets in the UK. The honey-coloured stone buildings are tall and the street is narrow as it winds towards the green hills beyond. The cobbled road is smooth under my feet, and the endless fronts of independent shops lined up before me are bright and colourful, with flags bearing logos flapping above their doors, and gingham-patterned bunting in an array of colours criss-crossing overhead all the way along the street. Old-fashioned Victorian streetlamps with modern-day bulbs dot the path, holding up baskets with pretty flowers spilling out. Near the top of the street is the town square, where there's a Gothic fountain burbling away, surrounded by a hexagon of steps, plenty of benches, and concrete planters full of more flowers with bees buzzing around them. Once Upon A Page is directly opposite this little nature idyll in the middle of the otherwise bustling street.

I stand outside the shop window that displays a selection of books for children and adults, surrounded by garlands of artificial green leaves and spring flowers. Robert's goldfish is swimming in a bowl at one shaded side. I breathe it all in for a moment. The smell of coffee from the sandwich deli down the street mixes with the mingled floral scent of the hanging baskets and the indescribable mix of fragrances coming from the candle shop next door. There are bowls of water outside every shop for thirsty dogs, and signs on most doors saying 'dogs welcome'. I'm surprised the street hasn't been used in a movie yet. It exudes a romantic, welcoming, closed-in feeling, like nothing bad could ever happen here.

Once Upon A Page is attached to the only empty shop on the street and the two buildings are connected by a set of steps leading up to a roof terrace that's been closed off for as long as I can remember. The boarded-up windows of the shop next door are out of place on this quaint little road and I turn away from them as I go in the warm blue door with a little bell above it that jingles every time it's opened.

'Hallie!' Robert Paige gets to his feet and sets his half-finished crochet blanket on the counter in front of him as he hobbles over to give me a hug and a kiss on both cheeks. 'Congratulations. I'm so glad it was you. This place can only be run by someone who *adores* books, and I can't think of anyone more deserving.'

It still doesn't seem real. Even as I look around the cosy shop, with its plush grey carpet, miles of wooden shelves full of lovely books, and breathe in the scent of worn leather from the sofa and chairs gathered around a low table in the reading area, and the delicious papery, sweet and musky smell of thousands of books that permeates the air, I still can't believe it. Working in a bookshop is what I've dreamed about my entire life.

'Now, of course it comes with the flat too, and the roof terrace, but the railings up there need reinforcement before you can open it to the public again ...' Robert is saying.

'What?'

'The flat above the shop. It's a teeny little thing but it's served me well. I moved in a few years ago when the commute got too much for me. It's yours now, but you'll have to give me a couple of weeks to arrange for my belongings to be moved out.'

I squeal so loudly that the three customers who are browsing look up from their books in fright, probably thinking I'm here to test the smoke alarms and have started an early fire drill.

A flat too! I didn't even know there *was* a flat above this shop. I hadn't really thought about it. There's an upper floor to the shop, and I assumed the second upstairs window you can see from outside was a storage room. But a flat I can actually live in? Alone? Without a twenty-something lad who thinks a vat of Lynx is an appropriate substitution for showering regularly? It's like all my dreams are coming true at once. I could win the lottery *twice* and it wouldn't be this amazing.

A customer goes to the counter with a pile of books, and Robert pats my hand and quickly hobbles back to serve her, and I watch for a moment as he gets into a deep conversation about the books she's chosen. He seems to know something about each one as he taps the prices into the till and then loads them one by one into a 'Once Upon A Page' branded paper bag. No matter how much I love books, I can't imagine ever being as knowledge-able as he is.

My excitement about taking over this place is tinged with sadness because I'm going to miss him being here. He's like a grandfather to everyone. A friendly, non-judgemental face, which is a welcome sight on the way home from visiting Nicole, her husband Bobby, and our mum, who lives in an annex in their garden. Robert is a purveyor of books featuring single heroines like me who are happy being single and don't need a man in their lives and no one thinks any the worse of them for it. Books with heroines whose mothers are always trying to set them up with inappropriate men. Books with heroines whose dating escapades are enough to put anyone off for life. Books about women who can be single and childless in their thirties and still be happy and fulfilled in other ways, no matter how much my mum believes otherwise and is eternally determined to see me married off, like some Jane Austen novel where I'll be considered a spinster and it'll bring shame upon the family if all daughters aren't married before the age of twenty. I'm not sure my mum has realised we don't live in the 1800s anymore.

I try not to think about the minimum-wage job and crappy flat. I *am* fulfilled. I'm fulfilled by my overflowing bookshelves and my Kindle, bought through the necessity of not having space for any more books in my tiny room of the flat, and not being willing to leave them in the communal living room where Mr Lynx could get at them. He'd probably use them to swat flies or something else unthinkably awful, if he didn't try to eat them. He seems to eat everything else that belongs to me.

I let Robert get on with serving as I go for a wander around the shop, feeling a bit like I'm floating above it, dancing on a cloud, going 'wheeeeeeeeee'. This is really going to be mine. I don't have to add 'fired from pub waitressing job' to my CV and start the demoralising misery of job-hunting again. I can give notice to our landlord. I'm actually going to have my dream job. This is even a step above chocolate taster for Cadbury's or quality control for McVitie's.

I let my fingers trail along the spines tucked into every shelf. Old clothbound hardcovers, new paperbacks, and non-fiction coffee-table books on every subject you can imagine. After the open area at the front, with the counter and the reading area, and the tables to display new arrivals and picks of the week, there are endless aisles of wooden shelving that run up and down to the back of the shop. Shelf after shelf of floor-to-ceiling dark-coloured cherry wood with visible knots, each one holding hundreds of books, so crowded that books are piled in front and on top of the spines facing outwards. The highest places are accessed by *Beauty and the Beast*-style sliding wooden ladders attached to the front of the shelves on runners. I refrain from re-creating the scene where Belle slides along when she returns her book in the opening scene of the old Disney movie. It would not be the first time I've wanted to, and also not the first time I've given it a try when no one's looking.

Once Upon A Page is the sort of shop you could easily lose a day in. You can get lost in the rows of tall shelving, picking up anything that looks vaguely interesting, and before you know it, it's five o'clock and Robert's ringing the bell for closing time, and you've accidentally missed the last bus home, but you emerge with a hotchpotch mix including a book of poetry when you didn't think you liked poetry, a romance novel, a book about the French Revolution, a classic that you should have read but haven't, a travel book about a destination you'll never visit, and a children's book you remember reading when you were younger.

Upstairs is solely dedicated to the children's area. Robert has always been a huge supporter of getting children into reading, and while he's still nattering away with the woman he's serving, I go up and have a look around. It's changed since I was last up here. It's a long, narrow area, with white plastic bookshelves lining the walls, not as tall as the ones downstairs and more spaced out, with room for all manner of picture books to be displayed with their colourful covers facing outwards. There's a set of tiny chairs and tables, on which are a stack of printed colouring-in pages and a selection of coloured pens and pencils, and at one end of the floor, there's a polka dot rug with a load of brightly coloured beanbags around it, all in front of a huge Peter Pan mural covering one wall.

I feel the first little flitter of worry about what I'm getting myself into here. I don't know the first thing about children or children's books, and I have to remind myself that Robert is an eighty-year-old man and is probably not the target audience either, but he manages, probably because of everything he's learnt since he started running this shop, and I can do that too. I can learn. To work in a place like this, to *own* a place like this is all I've ever wanted. Any amount of work I have to put in is worth it.

When I go back down the wooden stairs at the right-hand side of the shop, all the customers have gone and Robert is waiting for me. 'Would you like to see the flat? If you'd rather stay where you are, you can rent it out for a little extra income. There's access around the back as well as through here.'

I almost laugh at the idea of *not* living in it as I follow him between shelves and through a little office at the back. It's sparse for an office, with a desk and chair, a computer that looks like it was technologically outdated in the Eighties, a few filing cabinets along one wall, and a cupboard under the stairs that's obviously for storage because the door's open and there are folded tables and display stands spilling out. He points me through a door that leads to a narrow staircase and hands me a bunch of keys on a key ring. 'Pop up and have a look around so you know what you're dealing with. I fear it may be smaller than you imagine.'

'It could be a toad's armpit and it would still be better than where I'm living now.'

He hovers in the office doorway to keep an eye on the shop while I go up and let myself in the cream door at the top. The flat inside is an odd shape, long but narrow, warring for space with the children's area on the other side of the dividing wall. The front door leads to a small kitchen and living area in one. A door divides that from a bedroom that is barely big enough for the single bed and wardrobe it currently holds, and squeezed in at one side is a bathroom.

The bedroom window looks out on the high street, and I rest my elbows on the sill and pull the net curtains aside. The fountain burbles away in the town square opposite, and I watch a young boy hopping up and down the steps while his mother talks into her phone. I remember sitting there reading on my way back from the library when I was young and so eager to get started on the books I'd taken out that I couldn't even wait as far as getting home.

The sun is shining down, making the water glint with the reflection as the noise of the street filters up, muffled by the thick triple-glazed window. Back across the flat, there's another window that overlooks the green bank of the river that flows past Buntingorden, and a back door that leads down a fire escape and out into a tiny patch of unmaintained garden and then onto the river footpath.

It might be small, but it's *amazing*. It's *so* much better than where I'm living now, and I'm still convinced I'm going to wake up in a minute because how can this be real? The unluckiest person in the Cotswolds has somehow won a bookshop *and* a flat, all in one day. My usual types of days are the ones where you lose your job, flood your flat, and walk in on your boyfriend snogging someone else all in the same afternoon. I've had more than one day like that. More than one boyfriend like that too.

When I'm done, Robert is still standing in the office doorway and looking like he's been on his feet for too long. From the bottom, he directs me around the flat's kitchen to make two cups of tea, and when I take them downstairs, he's sitting on one of the leather sofas in the reading area. It's almost in the centre of the shop, down a bit from the counter and surrounded on three sides by bookshelves. You often see students sitting there to study and people poring over books and furiously scribbling notes.

Robert spreads paperwork across the table in front of him as

I put the two mugs down and one wobbles in my hand, nearly spilling its contents right across the important-looking documents. I breathe a sigh of relief once the mugs are safely out of my hands. That would *not* have been a good start to this adventure.

'This isn't just a big joke, is it?' I ask as he lifts his tea with a shaky hand and sips it.

He laughs. 'I'm not a joker, Hallie. You've been coming in here long enough to know that. The shop and flat above it are yours. It comes with only one condition – that when you are done with this place, whether it's in two months' time if you decide bookselling is not for you, two years when you meet a nice young man and want to settle elsewhere, or in many decades when you've given this shop all you have to give, you will find someone to pass it on to.

'Once Upon A Page must never be sold. Its legacy is in the love for it. *That* is why it's thrived for so long. Ownership is passed from one person to the next, like I'm passing it on to you now. I took over forty years ago from a very dear friend of mine. He had taken over from his father, who had run it for a number of decades, and I believe it had been passed to him from a distant cousin. The chain goes all the way back until it was founded in the 1870s. Each owner has taken over only because they love books and want to share that.

'There have been hard times, but the shop has always survived. From hardship comes greater strength. The roof terrace was the result of a bomb during the war, and the innovative owner at the time chose to make the best of a bad situation rather than give in to despair. He took out the rest of the fallen roof, reinforced the floor, and built a set of steps up to it.

'Once Upon A Page's legacy is in the love of the written word, and you must agree to that condition before we sign any of this paperwork. This is not a property to "flip" or sell to the highest bidder – and believe me, there are high bidders who are *desperate*

16

to get their hands on it – but when you decide to give it up, you must do as I have done and give it away freely. It doesn't matter who you choose; it can be a family member, a friend, a customer, or a stranger, as long as you know they will love it as much as you do, and will agree to being part of the same legacy – to give it away when their time is done.'

I nod. This is a dream job – the *last* thing I want to do is sell it. And it's unthinkable to talk about giving it up already. I can't imagine ever wanting to give it up. This is a gift, something that will change my life, certainly not something to make a quick profit from. 'How did you know everyone who entered the prize draw would be genuine?'

'I didn't. I just had to trust my instincts. I carefully observed who I offered tickets to. When money-grabbers came in enquiring because they'd heard it was up for grabs on some mysterious grapevine, I sent them packing. I firmly believe this shop is special, and that it has a little hand in its ownership. I didn't think it would steer me wrong.'

'You don't have family to leave it to?' I ask gently. I've never asked him about his family before.

'I'm alone in the world, although I believe that anyone who loves books is never truly alone, and that's always been enough for me. I would've loved a family, but it was never meant to be. I lost the love of my life years ago, but don't you worry about me. I have many good friends all over the country and all across the world, both real and fictional. My head is alive with a million characters who have stayed with me over the years, and now it's time for me to fulfil my final two dreams – to let Once Upon A Page live on with someone who loves it like I do, and to retire to the beach in Cornwall. I've wangled myself a flat at an assisted living facility on the southern coast, mere steps from the door to the sand. It's all I've ever wanted for my autumn years.'

His words make me tear up, and I pick up my tea and turn away for a moment to compose myself under the guise of taking

17

a sip. Pure joy gives way to a little nudge of fear. What if I let him down? Beyond a few Saturday shifts in the now-closed local library when I was sixteen, I don't know anything about bookselling, and even less about owning a business. Is passion for reading really enough? It feels like it is at the moment, but I can't begin to imagine how much learning I've got ahead of me.

Like he can read my mind, he pats my shoulder with an age-spotted hand. 'I was in engineering when I took over. I'd never even considered working in retail. I learnt as I went, and it wasn't always a smooth curve, but the rewards are worth it. Seeing customers happy when they finally come across a book they've been searching for. People asking for recommendations and then coming back to tell you how much they've enjoyed something you've recommended. Seeing children's faces light up as they get lost in the magic of a story. It's not always easy – the hours can be long, the constant carrying and stacking of books is physically hard work, and you'll often have slow weeks when you feel guilty for taking even minimum wage for yourself. But this shop has stood here for a century and a half. I can't imagine a world without it. I've always found it worth any hardship that has come my way.'

I kind of appreciate that he doesn't make it out to be all flowers and rose petals. I *know* he's always worked extremely hard in this shop. It seems like he's dedicated half his life to it. I only hope I can be worthy of the gift he's giving me.

'I'm not going to lie to you, Hallie,' he continues. 'The shop isn't in the best financial position. There have been a few … shall we say, lean years? I've feared closure more than once, but Once Upon A Page has always managed to bounce back, and I believe it will again, but it needs someone new at the helm, someone to reinvigorate it.'

Reinvigorate it? Me? I do the opposite of invigorating things. There are straw-stuffed scarecrows standing in fields that are better at invigorating things than me. 'How bad?' I swallow hard.

'You need customers. Lots of them. Something to pull people in. This is a busy little street and plenty of folks walk past, but I mostly rely on my few regular and loyal customers. Without something to breathe life back into this shop … I think we'll be lucky to see Once Upon A Page still open by the end of the year.'

Flipping heck. I knew the shop had been quiet when I'd come in lately, but I'd always blamed it on the time of day because my hours can be quite odd around my shifts at the pub.

'But if I thought that would faze you, I don't think your ticket would've come out of that hat.'

I gulp. It does faze me. He's not just giving me a bookshop – he's giving me a bookshop I have to *save*. Or lose in a matter of months, thereby wiping out a legacy that goes back 150 years.

'There's still time to back out, Hallie …' he offers gently, holding out a pen.

I take it and twist it in my hands, turning it over and over between my palms. 'No.' I push down my fears. This is the most amazing thing that's ever happened to me. It's inconceivable to think of walking away because it'll be a challenge. Maybe a challenge is what I need. My life needs reinvigorating too. Maybe me and the bookshop can reinvigorate each other. 'I love this place. No matter what it takes, it's not going under on my watch.'

'I knew you'd say that.' He signs some of the papers and hands them to me, getting up to go and fiddle with something at the counter and giving me time to scan through the documents. Title deeds and Land Registry transfer of ownership forms. I try to read them but most of the words go right over my head, and I sign the dotted lines he's pointed out anyway.

'Congratulations.' He sits back down and clinks his mug against mine in a toast. 'You're the new owner of Once Upon A Page. How does it feel?'

'Like I could do with a few books on how to run an ailing bookshop?'

He laughs as the bell above the door jingles the arrival of a customer. Buntingorden is always active. We're in a designated Area of Outstanding Natural Beauty, and tourists love the quaint charm of the high street. People come for holidays in the hills of the surrounding area, the scenery is beautiful, there are plenty of rivers and lakes that make popular holiday spots, and the walks are endless and loved by locals and tourists alike.

The customer comes over and asks if Robert's got a book I've never heard of, and he thinks for a moment and then directs him to aisle seven and tells him to look on the third shelf along at the bottom, and I can't help but be impressed that he could know that without looking it up on whatever stock system he uses.

He must notice because he laughs again. 'When you've worked here for over forty years, you'll know the place like a well-read book too … I'll leave you the basic instructions, but I don't want to tell you what to do. This is your bookshop now. I want you to put your stamp on it and do things your way. It's survived for so many years because new people do fresh things and keep it up to date. Your generation understand what people want better than this old fogey does. You can do whatever you want to make sure it stays here for centuries more.'

It makes me feel a bit teary again as he sorts out the paperwork, keeps what he has to file with his solicitor and gives me the relevant documents that I need. I get the feeling he's been preparing for this day for a long time.

He disappears into the shelves and hobbles back with a book from the Nineties about how to succeed in retail and gives it to me as a present because it's the closest thing he's got to 'How To Run A Bookshop', a fictional book that I really wish existed.

He hands it to me with an aged grin. 'I hope the old place brings you as much happiness as it's brought me, Hallie. I have a sneaking suspicion it will.'

It makes me feel more excited than I've ever been before and more nervous too. Everything in my life has always gone wrong and I can't help worrying that this is destined to be the same. It's more than I ever dreamed of and I don't know how I can ever be worthy of continuing the sprinkling of magic this shop brings to our little corner of the world.

Chapter 2

I still can't believe it's mine as I stand in front of the door with the keys in my hand at 8.30 a.m. on a Monday morning two weeks later.

Robert moved out over the weekend and is hopefully safely ensconced on the Cornish sands by now. I came over on Saturday evening to collect the keys and see if I could help, but he had half the village over to cheer him on his way, helping to pack up boxes and load them into a van that one of his friends had hired to drive him down to Cornwall.

Now the flat's empty, Nicole and Bobby are bringing both their cars and helping me to move in tonight after work, although I do wonder if we're going to need at least a month and a fleet of double-decker buses just to shift my books. Mum's already been trying to make me get rid of some, in between squealing, 'Ooh, you'll be just down the road! I can pop in and see you every day! Have you visited that lovely man in the souvenir shop yet? He's single, you know …'

Single men in souvenir shops and moving closer to my mother than strictly necessary aside, I can't help the fizzle of delight as I look up at the building in front of me. The same sandstone bricks as the rest of the street, with it's greyish-blue door and matching fascia above the window frame with 'Once Upon A Page' etched in a fairy-tale-esque font and 'Home to 30,000 books … and counting!' printed in solid letters underneath. It's detached on the left, and the staircase up to the roof terrace is to the right with heavy chains crossing its entrance and a big 'Keep Out' sign blocking it off, while the boards covering the windows of the empty shop next to it stare hollowly back at me.

I put the key into the lock and push open the door of my very own bookshop. The bell tinkles to itself, and once I'm inside, I lock up behind me. Half an hour to get myself sorted before opening time. I could've done with longer but the bus was late. Obviously. Buses are *always* late on the days you most need them to be on time. I put my shoulder bag on the counter and breathe in the smell for a moment, looking at the darkened shelves of all those books, untouched by customers for over twenty-four hours since the shop closed on Saturday night.

When I live here, I'm going to sneak down in the middle of the night and stand silently in a corner to see what happens to the books when the lights go off. It's impossible to believe they stay still, their stories silent inside until someone else picks them up. It would be much more believable to think that they toddle off and go to visit their friends on other shelves, sharing their stories with each other when humans think the world is dark.

I give myself a shake and silently remind myself that I *am* a thirty-five-year-old woman and I should have outgrown fantasies about inanimate objects coming to life at least thirty years ago.

I go to find the light switches inside the office door and flood the shop with light, almost positive that I see a book sidle itself back into a shelf out of the corner of my ey— Oh come on, not the goldfish.

Any movement I saw came from the window display, where Robert's goldfish is still swimming around in its bowl. I crouch down and gently tap my fingertip against the side, and it swims into a castle at the bottom of the tank, only one eye visible through a window as it peers out at me.

Oh no. How could he have forgotten his fish? And to me, of all people. I don't drive, so I have visions of hours on a coach with the goldfish bowl on my lap to return it to Robert in Cornwall. As if the bookshop wasn't enough responsibility, now I've got to keep a fish alive too until we can arrange a way of returning it. Keeping things alive is not my strong suit. I don't know the first thing about fish, other than it couldn't have had anything to eat since Saturday, and after a search that involves running upstairs to the flat and tearing apart the kitchen, I eventually find a tub of goldfish food in the office drawer and sprinkle a few flakes into the oversized bowl. I stand back to watch the orange fish wiggle to the surface and gobble it up. 'I don't even know your name, Fishy.'

I try to get my breathing back under control from the mad rush to find goldfish food, well aware that my forehead must be glistening and not in a good way, and my hair has definitely got a touch of the frazzle about it. I try to smooth it down as I glance at the clock on the wall above the stairs, visible from both floors. 8.58 a.m. How much worse can it get than a late bus and a forgotten fish on your first day? I've had no time to find whatever instructions Robert was going to leave me and no time to get myself sorted and ready for the day ahead. I'd intended to have a walk around and refamiliarise myself with the bookshelves in case anyone asks where something is. I've only ever browsed before, never with the intention of being able to answer queries from customers.

I haven't even had a cup of tea, and if I run up to the flat and make one now, I won't open on time. I weigh up the options and then decide I'd better open the shop, and tomorrow, I'll bring the kettle downstairs to the office. God knows how Robert managed here on his own with no one to take over when he had to pop to the loo or have a cuppa.

The sign on the door is a wooden book with its pages open and the words 'open' and 'closed' etched on either side in burnt calligraphy, and the second I flip it around from closed to open, a man appears.

At first I have a horrible feeling he might be the bloke from the souvenir shop that my mum has somehow bribed to corner me and introduce himself when I can't get away, but his suit looks like it cost more than a yacht and the gelled-back hair doesn't scream souvenir shop.

Well, this is a good sign. Nine a.m. and customers are already appearing.

I pull the door open with a beam. 'Good morning! You're eager. Are you looking for something specific?'

'Indeed I am.' He gives me a smile that shows off predatory-looking teeth and I immediately feel uneasy. 'Your shop.'

'This shop?'

'Drake Farrer, of Farrer and Sons property developers.' He hands me a business card and walks across to the counter, pushing my bag aside as he places his shiny briefcase down and unlocks it with a snicking sound. 'I own the empty shop next door. My company intend to buy this shop too and knock the pair of them down to make way for a new leisure centre.'

I rush after him. 'The shop isn't for sale.'

'No, the shop *wasn't* for sale. Now it's under new management, it's your choice what to do with it. And I advise that it's for sale.'

'You advise? I didn't ask for your advice.' I go in behind the counter like it might give me some authority. Who does this man think he is? I give his briefcase a pointedly annoyed look as I take my bag off the counter and uncover a bullet-point list in Robert's spidery handwriting. Instructions for using the till.

Drake Farrer looks at it with a sneer on his face, like it clearly demonstrates how inexperienced I am. 'Rumour has it that you're not a bookseller by trade, and I'm sure you know as well as I do that bookshops are failing at a rate of a thousand knots in these days of Internet giants and discount superstores. All bricks-and-mortar properties are in trouble, and just like you, plenty of the shops on this high street are only clinging on by a thread. My father and I work together at Farrer and Sons to take over failing shops and make them into something better, and save the owners all that nasty business of going into administration when their businesses inevitably fail. Just like I did with that bakery next door. Bought them out at the last moment, just as they were teetering on the edge of bankruptcy. A *lot* of other businesses around here are in the same position, yours included.'

'The business isn't failing.' I cross my arms and push myself up to stand taller even though I haven't had a chance to look at the state of the shop's finances for myself yet. From what Robert said, it almost certainly *is* failing, but I'm not about to let this condescending man know that.

He shrugs. 'If it's not now, it soon will be. Especially with a non-bookseller in charge. Good thing I'm here to help you.'

He is *not* here to help me. 'Men like you exist only to help themselves.'

'The dear old fogey warned you about me, then?'

'No. Not a word. You warned me about yourself the moment you swept in and decided you had a right to buy my shop.' Calling it *my* shop buoys my confidence and I stand taller.

'All right, maybe we got off on the wrong foot. My apologies. I must've got overexcited to see someone new and pioneering at the helm who might be open to fresh ideas and new approaches.'

That makes me sound like Christopher Columbus, but the only thing I'd like to see him approach is the door on his way out of it.

'I don't think you've realised who I am,' he says before I have a chance to direct him that way. 'I'm not just your friendly local property developer – I'm also your neighbour. As the owner of that ex-bakery next door, I share access to your ugly, unsafe, and probably condemned roof terrace.' He points behind him, towards the set of stairs outside and the empty shop to the right.

'Robert didn't say anything about sharing ownership.'

'Well, you know Robert, always keen on burying his head in the sand, especially when it comes to money troubles. The roof terrace is half mine and the access is shared. You can't do *anything* up there without *my* permission.' His tone of voice leaves me in no doubt that his permission will not be given freely. He pulls some paper from his briefcase, a photocopy of another title deed, and I take it and read it, nodding occasionally like I understand a word that's written on it.

'I had no plans for it.' I try to hold my nerve under his sharp gaze. I haven't even seen the roof terrace, let alone made any plans for it, but the idea of sharing it with him makes a shiver creep down my spine. I put the sheet of paper down on top of Robert's instructions, mainly to hide 'how to unjam the till' from his searching eyes. I get the feeling he's looking around for a weakness he can home in on.

He waves a hand across his shoulder without taking his beady eyes off me. 'I'm also in discussions with several other shop owners about acquiring their shops. We're looking to modernise and update this tacky old street, and Mr Paige has been a thorn in my side from the very first moment I approached him with my ideas, a real old stick-in-the-mud. But you – you're fresh and innovative. You're not stuck in the old traditions like that silly old fool was.'

His hair really is unnaturally shiny where it's slicked back against his head. Like someone's tipped chocolate mirror glaze on him by accident on *The Great British Bake Off*.

'With your shop and mine flattened, picture a shiny new leisure complex in this space. The tourists will love it. We're going to have a big swimming pool, a multi-screen cinema, yoga classes, a spa, all sorts of acupuncture and hot stone massages and all that trendy stuff hipsters love.'

Acupuncture? Well, having needles pushed into my skin definitely seems preferable to talking to him for much longer. 'The majority of people who live around here are elderly. What do they want with a cinema and leisure complex?'

'Well, they have leisure time, don't they? They watch films, don't they? We'll make sure the speakers are hearing-aid friendly and between you and me, there are a few folks around here who could do with a good shower, if you know what I mean.' He waves a hand with neatly trimmed and filed nails in front of his face like there's a whiff in the air, and it would almost be funny if he wasn't so patronising.

'I'm making you an offer you can't refuse.' He whisks another sheet of paper from his briefcase and waves it in front of me. 'Thirty thousand for the building. I don't even want the contents. You can keep all your silly books and relocate elsewhere. That's more than enough to buy another property if you're so committed to the bookshop, and if you're not, then congratulations, you've just won the lottery. Thirty grand in your pocket for doing absolutely nothing. That's an impressive rate of return on the thirty quid you paid for your raffle ticket.'

The fact he knows how much the tickets were makes me even more uneasy, and I have no doubt that he's one of the 'highest bidders' that Robert *did* warn me about. 'Once Upon A Page wouldn't *be* Once Upon A Page if it was anywhere else. This isn't about the money. I'm sorry, Drake, was it?' I purposely pretend I've forgotten his Mallard-like name, even though I get the feeling that Drake Farrer is a name many people on this street are all too familiar with. 'The shop isn't for sale, and it never will be.'

'Ah, the old "this shop has always been given as a gift and its legacy must live on forever" line?'

I glare at him.

'All it takes is one forward-thinking person to be brave and change that ridiculous, outdated concept and think realistically about the future. This isn't about the shop. It's about you. Thirty grand in your bank account for, what, two minutes of work you've done this morning? You could use that to do something you've always wanted to do. Go travelling, see the world … The old boy wouldn't even have to know.'

'I go travelling and see different worlds every day through reading. I've been coming to this shop all my life. It's worth more than money. Books can change people's lives. They can be friends when there's no one else to turn to. They can help people. They can be an escape. They can—'

'Ah, a book*worm*, eh?' He puts unnecessary emphasis on the *worm* part. 'I've got one of *those* in my family too. Honestly, I've never met a bigger bore. Always on about "Have you read this?" and "Have you read that?" nonsense. Trying to get me interested in the most boring plots and talking about fictional characters like they're real people.'

'Do you honestly think insulting fellow bookworms *to* a bookworm is going to help your cause?'

'*Who* has got the time for all that reading? Some of us are too busy *living* to get lost in books for hours on end. If a book is worth reading, they'll make a movie of it eventually.'

I try to school my face into not showing how much of an insult that is. 'But the book is always so much better. Authors spend years researching and writing, and there are so many little touches and details that can't possibly be re-created on film. You miss out on so much by trying to condense a four-hundred-page novel into an hour and a half of screen time—'

He does an exaggerated yawn, and I stop myself because it's pointless. He isn't interested in a word I'm saying. I despise people like him who look down on reading and think books exist solely to fill cinemas further down the line. All he wants is this shop, and he is *not* getting it.

The paper is still dangling in his hand and I grab it and stuff it back into his briefcase, screwing it up in my fingers as I ram it in and slam the top down with a resolute click. 'The shop's not for sale – not now, not ever. I will *not* be the one to break tradition. Thirty grand doesn't tempt me. This is my dream job. It's not up for grabs to the highest bidder.'

'Everybody has a price, Miss Winstone. It's just a matter of finding it.'

A shiver goes down my spine. I'm utterly creeped out by the fact he knows my name *and* it's taken him this long to mention it. Thankfully the bell above the door jingles and a woman carrying a 'Books Are My Bag' tote bag comes in.

'Good morning!' I greet her in my cheeriest voice, sounding shrill because of the change from anger at Drake Farrer to delight at the sight of a customer. The simple fact of not being alone with him makes me feel less edgy than I have until now.

She returns it with a smile and congratulates me on being the new owner.

As she wanders around browsing, I give Drake Farrer a sarcastic smile. 'There's the door.'

He lifts his briefcase from the counter and smiles a wolf-like grin. 'I always get what I want. Persistence is my middle name.'

'That must be very awkward on official forms,' I call as he starts walking away. 'I bet you get questioned about that at the passport office every time you leave the country.'

The bell jingles again as he leaves, and I pull out his business card and tear it up into tiny pieces, vaguely aware that he's outside the window watching me.

'Wolves at the door already?' the customer asks as she walks around the picks-of-the-week table near the counter – a selection of Robert's weekly choices with twenty per cent off.

'Something like that. An actual wolf would've been much more welcome. At least then there'd be a handsome hunter along in a minute to fill its belly with rocks and drown it.'

She laughs and picks up a book from the table and puts it down again, not hiding the look of disappointment.

'You wouldn't happen to know when Robert usually updated his picks of the week, would you?' I ask her.

'Monday mornings, before nine. I start work at half past and always pop in on my way to see what undiscovered gems he's found this week. Sorry, I know it's your first day.'

Great. Another failure. I thank her and promise to have chosen some new picks by tomorrow as I grab a nearby biro and scribble it down at the top of the instructions on the counter. Robert wasn't joking about giving me only basic instructions. Underneath the step-by-step bullet points for using the till, he's put the computer password and log-in details for the accounting software, a list of the book distributors he uses and their websites in order of preference, and overleaf is a load of dates for upcoming local car boot sales to find second-hand books, and a list of how book club members like their tea and coffee when they meet on the last Saturday of every month, and a note telling me to make sure I buy *both* Custard Creams and Chocolate Bourbons for the occasion.

I was expecting slightly more thorough instructions than that. I don't know much about Once Upon A Page's book club, other than the fact multiple copies of Robert's pick for it are displayed on the wall behind me, along with CD copies of the audiobook and DVD copies of the film. I look over at the display. It's *The Boy in the Striped Pyjamas* this month. Oh, thank God. At least I've read that so I can vaguely seem like I know what I'm talking about, and there are two weeks until the last Saturday in May so I've got time to flick through it and refresh my memory. Maybe we can have a book-vs-film chat about it. They do that sort of thing at book clubs, right?

After the customer leaves with a promise to come back tomorrow to see what *my* picks of the week are, I've got time to tidy up and try not to worry about which books I'm going to choose and if I can live up to expectations. Robert's picks were always an eclectic mix of something for everyone.

For now, I concentrate on tidying up because the shop is a mess. The display in the window is dwindling where books have been removed from it but not replaced, and the shelf itself doesn't look like it's been cleaned for a good few months. There are dead bluebottles and spiders knitting fine webs in the corners and although a window cleaner comes to clean the outside of every shop on the street once a week, when I run my finger across the glass on the inside, it leaves a line through the layer of dust.

The goldfish doesn't seem to mind as it looks out, its mouth moving as it watches a Jack Russell dashing around the fountain that's burbling away across the street. Things are quiet at this time of day. There are a few people walking past but none of them come in. It gives me a chance to wander through the shop, and I discover that the dust is more widespread than just the window display, and the only shelves the dust hasn't settled on are the shelves that are so packed and piled with books that there isn't a spare millimetre for dust *to* gather.

Anyone could see that the work was getting too much for Robert, but I'd never noticed how much he must've been struggling to keep on top of things. I only came in once every two or three weeks, and to me, the shop was as charming and whimsical as it always had been, but as I walk around with a different perspective now, as someone who actually has to sell these books to keep people like Drake Farrer from the door, I can see that it needs work. A lot of work. The cleaning is one thing, but there are so many books piled at the front of the shelves that it's impossible to see what's behind them. There are piles on the floor that look precariously close to toppling over, and woodlice keep scuttling back underneath shelves when I get near them.

Upstairs, the children's section is better. It's obviously been refitted fairly recently. The white shelves aren't as tall so Robert must've been able to reach them for dusting easier. Downstairs the walls are all shelving, but up here, they're painted a buttercup yellow, and I pull the net curtains back and open the upper window to let the breeze blow through. The Peter Pan mural is breathtaking. The dark purple of a midnight London skyline with the silhouettes of Peter, Tink, Wendy, John, and Michael flying across it, and the 'second star to the right' quote is painted in big white letters underneath.

I pick up the squashy beanbags one by one, give them a shake and re-plump them as I set them back on the rainbow-spotted carpet. I would've loved sitting here when I was little. The mural is so huge that it makes everything feel magical, like you're really standing there watching people fly across the rooftops of London, a perfect metaphor for the magic feeling you get from reading, especially as a child when you become so immersed in the fantasies that it's like you're really living them. I remember the books I read when I was young like they really happened, like I witnessed the events in them happening to real-life friends, and I have an overwhelming desire to find a copy of *Peter Pan* and curl up in one of the beanbags to read it.

The breeze blows hair from my ponytail into my face and I pull it back and wipe dust off my glasses with the bottom of my Pemberley Manor T-shirt as the bell jingles the arrival of a customer. I run back downstairs, but I can't see a thing without my glasses on, so I trip over my own feet and crash into the banister at the bottom, startling the couple who have just come in.

By ten o'clock, things have started to pick up. Buntingorden High Street is bustling outside, and the smell of roasting coffee and fresh-baked bread from the deli filters in every time someone opens the door. There are three people in here browsing, and I listen contentedly to the rustle of pages as people stand with their noses in books. I've made one sale and almost learnt how to use the till, and also learnt that I haven't got the reflexes not to get my fingers trapped in it yet, which answers why Robert keeps a box of plasters so prominently on a shelf under the counter.

Everyone has been so warm and friendly and welcoming.

Robert's retirement and the subsequent raffle for the shop is a big talking point around here, and it's no secret that today is the day I take over, and everyone who comes in says hello and congratulates me, even though most of them leave without buying anything.

I'm trying to get to grips with the underneath of the counter, which is a lot of shelves full of doodled-on notepads, enough pens to weave a blanket, spare reels of till receipt, and stacks of books presumably put aside for some reason, when the door flies open, sending the bell jangling as a man falls through it. Literally.

He lands with a thud on the floor. The armful of sketchbooks he was carrying go flying, floating down around him like a blizzard of pages. A vase he had with some daffodils in it rolls across the floor, crushing the flowers and spilling water in its wake, and the satchel over his shoulder has opened, sending a slew of pencils, pens, and sticks of charcoal skittering across the room. A customer screams in fright as a pencil sharpener rolls into her shoe.

He pushes himself up on one elbow and looks between the door and the debris scattered around him. 'That went well.'

The deadpan sarcasm makes me snort as I rush over. 'Is that not the standard way to enter a building?'

He gives it some serious consideration while still lying on the floor. 'Depends if you're part of the arse-over-tit brigade. I definitely am. Don't let this fool you – I totally intended to do that. Go arse-over-tit was top of my to-do list today.'

'Are you okay?' I crouch down and my eyes lock onto his blue ones, enlarged by the lenses of his thick black-framed glasses and I suddenly feel unnecessarily hot and flustered.

We hold each other's gaze for a long moment and then he blinks and looks away. 'What, this? This is nothing. It wouldn't be a day that ends in Y if I wasn't falling through something I shouldn't be. Nothing but a bruised ego.' He glances down at himself, his quiff of light-brown hair flopping forwards. 'Maybe a bruised arse and tit too. Or maybe that's still bruised from the

34

parked car I walked into yesterday. To be honest, I don't think even my ego can be bruised anymore – I think it was knocked out entirely decades ago.'

His cheeky grin makes me smile back at him.

'Sorry, everyone,' he says loudly, addressing the whole shop. 'Tripped over my own feet. Again.'

I automatically look at his feet and realise he's wearing odd Doc Martens boots – one blue and one orange. He gets onto his knees and starts pulling coloured pencils towards him while the bell finally calms down enough from its flight to stop jingling.

'I'm so sorry,' he says to me. 'I'm sure that was all you needed on your first day. You can't say I don't know how to welcome people. I might do a little jig next and crash through the window or knock over a display stand to fully complete the horror.'

'Don't worry about it.' I start collecting up the sketchbooks while he shovels art supplies back into his satchel. 'I've fallen through many doors in my time, usually with a coffee in one hand and a white shirt on. You can guess how that ends.'

His laugh is musical and infectious as he crawls across the carpet to grab more pens and pencils, and I'm not sure which to be more impressed by – how far they roll or how many one bag can hold.

I crouch down and start pulling his sketchbooks towards me, smoothing out bent pages as I go, and I can't help noticing the array of pencil drawings in them. 'Is that a ... giant flea?' I say loudly, my volume control gone with the surprise of how detailed it is.

'The drawing, not me.' He finally gets to his feet and holds his hands up to the rest of the customers because the closest two are watching this spectacle with amusement. 'My owners Frontline me regularly.'

It makes me snort again and he looks down at me with a cheeky grin. 'These are amazing. I didn't mean to look, but ...'

'Oh, it's fine.' He waves the hand not still stuffing things back into his satchel. 'They're just scrapbooks, my practice pieces. But thank you.'

Wow. If these are just practice, he must be very talented. It takes all my willpower not to be nosy and delve further into the books. I stack them together and get to my feet at the same moment a customer beckons me over, so I rush across and put them down on the counter while she asks me if we've got the third book in the series she's currently reading and I have to admit it's my first day and I haven't yet found any sort of stock system to tell me what books are on the shelves. It makes me feel useless. I need to get on top of this stuff *quickly*.

The man continues trying to collect up the detritus from his fall, and the customer gives him a wide berth as she leaves without buying anything. I watch with a mix of amusement and sympathy because when he goes to pick up the flowers, the satchel falls forwards as he bends down, walloping him in the head and emptying out again.

He groans. 'I'm beginning to think I shouldn't have got out of bed this morning.'

I can't help giggling as he gives the satchel a look that says it's seriously betrayed him. It's funny when it happens to someone else. Usually it's me walloping myself in the head with things. I go back over and help him gather up the rest of the pencils and art supplies. He really is the strangest-looking man. He's wearing jeans and a long-sleeved blue top with sleeves that are far too long and fall down over his hands, and on top of that is a waistcoat, the kind you'd expect to see as part of a three-piece suit. Instead of a pocket square, there are three pencils sticking out of the chest pocket.

I stand up to give him the handful of pencils I've collected at exactly the same moment he bends down to get them, and our foreheads crash together with an audible bang.

'Ow!' we both say in unison and stumble backwards.

I wince and put a hand to my forehead.

'Oh God, I'm so sorry.' He's got one hand rubbing the back of his head where the bag whacked him and one hand rubbing his forehead. 'This is certainly a first impression you won't forget … unless that bang caused a concussion and amnesia. Do you remember the date and who the prime minister is?'

I laugh. 'I don't think I'll ever forget this date, and the prime minister is probably better forgotten anyway.'

'You're not wrong there,' he says with a laugh. 'And I'm so sorry again. I am a mess of a human being who shouldn't be allowed out in public. Clearly.'

'Don't worry about it. Honestly. I once got my handbag stuck in the doors of a bus as I was getting off, and while I was trying to chase it, I ran headfirst into the bus stop and knocked myself so senseless that the driver had to stop the bus and call an ambulance while thirty bemused passengers looked on. Luckily it was in the days before mobiles recorded video or I'd have been viral on social media by now.'

He grins as he puts the last of his art supplies back into his bag and closes it with a determined click, and I go back behind the counter and watch him pick up the daffodils incident-free this time. He comes across and puts the vase on the counter and arranges the crushed flowers into it. 'Have you got a cloth or something I can use to mop up that water?'

I look around like one might appear from thin air. 'Not without going upstairs and searching for one, and there's no one to watch the shop. Don't worry about it, I'm sure it'll dry in no time.'

'Ah, hang on, I might have a sponge on me.' He lifts the satchel over his head and puts it on the counter, flipping the top back and picking through it.

How many more things are going to be dumped on my counter today? This one is more welcome than the last, though, and I can't help watching the way his gravity-defying hair bounces around as he looks down, his face furrowed in concentration while he starts getting every imaginable item out of the bag and setting it on the counter, from handfuls of pencils, to a water bottle, a flask, smaller notebooks, paints and brushes, and a Tupperware container with his lunch in it, until the counter is completely covered in random items and he finally holds what can only be described as a make-up sponge aloft in victory.

'For blending,' he says when he sees my expression. 'The drawings! Not my foundation. Not that I wear foundation.' He throws his hands up and looks to the ceiling. 'This is going from bad to worse. I should stop speaking altogether and sit in a darkened corner. Things might go better then.'

I can't help giggling again. There are so many days when I've thought exactly the same thing. I try not to watch as he pushes the black-framed glasses back up his nose as they slide off every time he looks down at the wet patch he's trying to soak up with his tiny sponge, but the counter is completely covered by all his stuff, and there isn't much I can do other than watch him. That's my excuse, anyway. He's got a pencil tucked behind one ear, and his straight hair is short at the back and long on top, piled into the haphazard quiff that was probably a lot less haphazard five minutes ago.

Another customer says goodbye as she leaves without buying anything, walking around the tall man, who seems completely oblivious to how much space he's taking up. Eventually he stands back up and suddenly realises what a mess he's left on the counter because he rushes over and starts stuffing things back into his bag. When everything's in except the water bottle, he puts the bag back over one shoulder, wipes the counter down with his hand, unscrews the cap of the bottle and pours some into the vase and rearranges the daffodils, trying to perk them up a bit. I admire his optimism because they look beyond help to me.

'Anyway, hi. These limp, crushed flowers, that wet spot on the carpet, and the possible concussion are to welcome you to the area. And don't tell me I shouldn't have; I assure you I already know.'

'At least the vase was plastic.'

He taps his temple to show his smart thinking. 'Oh, I learnt long ago that me and things made of glass don't mix.'

It makes me grin again because I also don't mix with glass, and I have the scars to prove it.

'So, if you're not going to throw me straight out of your shop for such a dire first impression, hello. I'm Dimitri.' He holds his hand out and I shake it, his long fingers closing around mine, which suddenly feel a lot clammier than they did moments ago. 'You must be Hallie.'

'Dimitri?' I repeat, trying not to show my surprise that yet more people know of me. 'Like the hero in *Anastasia*?'

'I think you mean the crook in *Anastasia,* but yes. I've never had anyone make that connection before.'

'I've never met anyone called Dimitri before.' I've shaken his hand for far too long now and I reluctantly extract my fingers. 'And he might've started off a crook, but he was a hero by the end.'

His cheeks start to redden, so I quickly continue. 'I love that movie. I still sing the first lines of "Journey to the Past" in my head whenever I have to do something scary. I was humming it this morning when I walked in here.'

Maybe I shouldn't have admitted that aloud to someone who I assume is a customer, but there's something about him that's so disarming.

His deeply curved upper lip tips up into a smile. 'Got to admit, it would've terrified me. You obviously have heart and courage that *hasn't* failed or deserted you,' he says, referencing the song, and something inside me does a happy dance at someone else knowing one of my favourite songs. 'And I'm sorry again for the catastrophic entrance. I'm sure that was all you needed on your first morning.'

'Don't worry about it. Like I said, it's usually me dropping things everywhere. On the plus side, for ten minutes it took my mind off how much the shop needs a good clean.'

He laughs as he pokes the water bottle back into his bag and gives the flowers a forlorn look.

'So what can I do for you?' I ask, wondering if I sound as reluctant as I feel because, of all the conversations I've had so far today, this is definitely the one I want to end the least.

'I don't suppose Robert mentioned me, did he?'

'I don't think so. He didn't mention much at all. He even forgot his goldfish.' I point to the bowl on the window ledge.

'Oh, Heathcliff?'

'*That's* his name? Because he's *so* reminiscent of the tortured antihero roaming the moors?'

'He didn't forget him – Heathcliff's the bookshop goldfish. He comes with the shop.'

'Oh, great,' I mutter. 'I'm not good at keeping things alive. I had a houseplant once that, had it been sentient, would've sued me for negligence. And won.'

His laugh turns into a guffaw. 'Heathcliff's been here for years. Children love him. There used to be a whole competition for who could make up the best story about him.' He leans his elbows on the counter and beckons me to come nearer, and when I do, I meet his eyes again and catch a whiff of his woody, smoky aftershave and something goes all flittery in my chest. 'To let you in on a secret, that's actually Heathcliff Number Four after the other Heathcliffs have gone to swim in the big aquarium in the sky, but you can't mention that to any customers under pain of death. Heathcliff is immortal and always will be.' He winks at me. 'There's a pet shop at the retail park on the outskirts of town that provides replacement Heathcliffs whenever the not-quite-so-immortal need arises.'

There's something about him that's so open and endearing. I like him instantly.

'And between you and me, I don't know how to gender fish but given the way he looks at some of the dogs that walk past, I suspect that one might be Mrs Heathcliff. Talk about a randy mare.'

I dissolve into a fit of giggles and he pushes himself off the counter and stands up straight again, and he's so tall that I have to crick my neck to meet his bright blue eyes that are shining with mischief.

'Right, so if a sex-crazed fish wasn't enough to ruin your day, I kind of have a favour to ask that I was hoping Robert would've already mentioned to save me this awkwardness.'

'Go on …'

'I'm working on an update of an old book of Italian fairy tales.' He pats the stack of sketchbooks still on the counter. '*Pentamerone* by Giambattista Basile. It was first published in the 1630s but the edition you've got here is from the 1800s. Do you know it?'

I shake my head.

'Well, it used to be in the library, and when that closed, Robert did a deal with the local council to buy all their books, and the copy I was working from ended up here. And because it's so old and eye-wateringly valuable, and I haven't got a spare two thousand quid to buy it, and Robert always said that because he got it in the bulk deal and didn't pay anywhere near full value, he didn't feel right expecting me to pay so much for something that would've been free to use had the library stayed open, he's very kindly let me come here every day and sketch from it.'

The idea that he comes in every day makes something in my mind overheat. Even with the catastrophic entrance, I can already tell that I wouldn't mind seeing him more often.

'I swear I'm quiet and don't take up much room. Contrary to my entrance this morning. I'd say I'm not usually like that, but honestly, I'm a walking disaster, though I usually manage to contain it in public for short amounts of time.'

His bad luck reminds me of myself so much, and I'm pretty sure it's impossible to say no to someone called Dimitri given how much my nine-year-old self loved *Anastasia*.

'I sit in the reading area, but if it gets busy and other people want the space, I take myself into that corner where the book is kept and sit on the floor.' He points to the far right corner at the back, a little nook of shelves squeezed in under the stairs. It's Robert's Rare and Valuable book section that I've never looked in because, like Dimitri, I also don't have a couple of grand to spare.

'I know I've got such a nerve in asking, and this is your shop now, so of course you're absolutely free to say no. I can find versions online, but they're all abridged modern translations, which aren't the same …' He kind of winces and smiles at the same time like he's expecting me to refuse.

He has a smile that's so wide, it's almost like he's baring both sets of teeth, but in the best way possible.

'Honestly, I have no idea what book you're talking about. I didn't even know there *was* a book of that value here. Go ahead. Do what you normally do. If it was fine with Robert, I'm not going to change that. Besides, I owe you one for the crushed flowers and knowing Heathcliff's name. I thought I was going to be calling him "Fishy" forever.'

He almost bounces on the spot and his whole face glows as his smile somehow gets unbelievably wider, and it's the kind of smile that's *impossible* not to smile back at. 'Oh, I could kiss you.' He looks embarrassed. 'I won't, obviously, because I've already humiliated myself enough for one morning without adding sexual harassment to the list as well. But thank you, and I promise you won't even know I'm here.'

He gathers up his sketchbook, gives the floppy daffodils one final spruce, which does nothing to help their sorry-looking state, hoists his bag higher up his shoulder, and walks off towards the back of the shop, singing Kate Bush's 'Wuthering Heights' loudly as he goes, swaying around and swishing an imaginary floaty dress, which is exactly what I do every time I hear that song.

And Nicole thought working in a bookshop would be boring.

Chapter 3

True to his word, Dimitri installs himself at the end of a leather sofa in the reading area, collects a huge, hefty-looking ancient book from the back of the shop and lays it carefully on the table. He spreads his sketchpads and a collection of pencils and charcoal out in front of him.

I'm trying not to look, but the reading area is just a little way down from the counter and the side not surrounded by shelves is facing me, and every so often, he looks up and catches my eyes with a grin. After the third time of being caught staring, I force myself to get on with some actual work because there are only so many times I can tidy the counter.

Customers come and go, but very few of them buy anything. I'm quickly learning that most people only come in to browse. Between them, I get on with restocking the picks-of-the-week table with new choices. I'm not as well read as Robert was – I'm pretty sure he'd read every single book in this shop and more. I tend to favour romantic comedies, recommendations from fellow book lovers and book bloggers I follow online, and whatever must-reads people are talking about on social media.

It feels a bit disingenuous to choose books I haven't read, but no matter how many thousands of books there are in the shop, if I have to put out ten a week, we're going to run out of books I've read pretty quickly. What a brilliant excuse to read more. And now I get to recommend books to people who actually like books and want to read them. Until now, I've talked about books a lot on Twitter and mostly recommend them to my family of non-readers who look at me like I've got a giraffe growing out of my elbow when I suggest a book they might enjoy.

Walking between the shelves to search out titles makes me realise how badly organised they are. Or, more specifically, they *aren't*. For the first time, I realise that the category labels printed on the front of shelves are meant in the loosest sense only, and while they might once have contained only the books in their own category, now books from all genres have migrated onto every shelf. There is *no* organisation. There used to be a clear divide between new books bought from publishers and distributors and the second-hand books Robert acquired himself, but now the whole shop seems muddled up, and there are ancient copies of Brontë books shoved in between second-hand car manuals and this year's horror releases and thriller books. The stacks at the front of the shelves don't belong to the shelves they're stacked on, and when I think of a book title at random and try to find it, it proves impossible.

Why have I never noticed this before? I've always thought the shop was whimsical and charmingly hotchpotch, and I've always come in here to browse and see what I find rather than with anything specific in mind. How am I going to sort this out? With Drake Farrer telling me bookshops everywhere are failing and Robert talking about closure within the year, how am I ever going to make this better? For *not* the first time, I wonder again if Robert picked the wrong ticket out of that hat. Somehow I have to turn the fortunes of a fading bookshop around. I can't even get my trousers on the right way round most days.

Choosing the week's picks turns into a case of walking down the aisles and seeing what jumps out on the shelves, and eventually I settle on a varied selection – a rom com, a thriller, a Stephen King classic, a celeb autobiography, a YA I read and loved last year, an old Shakespeare, and a classic Jane Austen. I pick up a copy or two of each from the shelves as I go over to the promi nent display and start removing last week's picks, stacking them on the counter while I give the table a quick dust and start setting out my new choices.

'He had that one the week before last,' Dimitri says without looking up from his sketchbook.

I jump so much that I drop the Stephen King book and it lands directly on my big toe. I hadn't realised he was watching me while I was trying so hard not to watch him.

'Oh, thanks,' I say, even though I've gone red at the idea of his eyes on me. 'I don't suppose you know if he kept a list or anything, do you?'

'I doubt it. Robert had a photographic memory and didn't keep lists for anything.'

'Except how the book club readers like their tea.' I wiggle my foot around, trying to surreptitiously shake the pain out of my toe without him noticing.

He looks up and meets my eyes with a laugh. 'Oh, that's not a book club. That's a monthly rugby scrum to see who can eat the most free biscuits and there's a prize for anyone with the juiciest village gossip. Occasionally they get around to books too.'

He doesn't strike me as a book club member, and he must notice my puzzled look, because he says, 'I've been working on this book for a while now. You learn a lot from sitting and observing while pretending you're not listening.'

'I'll bear that in mind.'

'I promise I only use my powers for good, not evil.' He gives me another wink that makes me feel decidedly flushed and I try to compose myself as I take the Stephen King book back to the shelf and select a copy of *The Shining* instead, another 'the book is even better than the movie' classic.

The shop's still empty as I start setting my choices out on the table directly opposite the reading area. 'Do you really come in here every day?'

'Depends. Will you think I live a sad and lonely existence if I say yes?'

Once again, it makes me smile. 'No, I'd think you were a sensible and sane person who enjoys being surrounded by lovely books with characters who are much nicer than real people.'

'Aww. And to think I was worried about meeting the new shop owner in case we didn't hit it off.' He looks up and beams at me. 'I can see that you and I are going to get along well.'

I blush again. Why am I blushing so much around this man? There's something about him that's captivating, from his unusual style to the hair that adds a good few inches to his already tall height. His face is naturally smiley and it makes him seem constantly cheerful and approachable.

I lurk at the table for longer than strictly necessary, watching as he works, his forehead furrowed in concentration, chewing his lip as he skims pencil across paper.

'Are you an illustrator of some sort?' I ask, feeling stupid because it's such a daft question. Obviously he's an illustrator – he's been sitting there sketching for the past hour. He's not an astronaut, is he?

'I'm a children's book illustrator.' He hesitates for a second. 'I suppose I've got a nerve to say that because I haven't had anything published yet, but yeah. I've been commissioned to update this gorgeous old book for a modern translation for modern kids. It's a great set of stories, just macabre enough to appeal to anyone at that awkward age between Disney-style fairy tales and young-adult reads. I saw a gap in the market and a publisher went for it, so here I am.'

I can't hide how impressed I am. 'Wow. It sounds really interesting.'

'Thanks.' He ducks his head and I get the feeling it's not quite as simple as he makes it sound.

I don't want to annoy him with more questions, and I'm glad when a group of three customers come in and start looking around. They're tourists instead of regulars who know it's my first day and they treat me like they would any other bookseller. One finds his favourite books and takes shelfies with them, one asks me for thriller recommendations, and one picks up a book she's seen recommended in a newspaper and asks me if it's as good as they say it is. She buys it, and her two companions pick a couple of books too. It feels a bit like a whirlwind passing through by the time they leave, the bell above the door jingling behind them.

Dimitri's looking at me again. 'It's none of my business, but you handled that like a true bookseller.'

I blush. Again. The thought of his eyes on me makes me feel all fluttery, and the thought that someone who obviously spends a lot of time here thinks I might not be completely useless at this couples with the joy that for a moment there, I actually felt like a bookseller. I actually felt like I can do this. 'Thank you. I clearly need to read more and stay on top of the most hyped books of any given week, which I'm not complaining about, obviously.'

'I would be. The more people tell me to read something and the more something gets talked about, the less I want to read it. I'm stubborn like that.'

'And then you do read it and it's amazing and totally lives up to all the hype and you wonder why you put off reading it for so long?'

'Of course.' He laughs, his whole face lighting up and making me laugh too.

With customers few and far between, I leave him in peace and walk around the shelves again, trying to formulate some sort of plan. There's no getting around how much reorganisation they need. I want them in shelves for each category, new books on upper shelves and second-hand books on lower shelves, arranged alphabetically. Robert must've used the ancient Greek alphabet to organise his stock because I can't find a single shelf that makes sense. I also need some sort of stock list that tells me what books are actually here, how many copies of them we have, and what genre each one belongs to. No one could run a business like this without one, not even Robert Paige. I hope.

'Are you moving into the flat too?' Dimitri says when the shop's quiet again.

I nod. 'Tonight. My sister and her husband are coming to help. Well, if they don't turn and run at the sight of all my books. I don't think they *quite* understand what they're getting themselves into.'

He laughs again. 'That's the main reason I could never move. I'd have to hire sixteen vans just to shift the books.'

We meet each other's eyes across the shop and he smiles. There's definitely something about a man who reads and understands a love of books. 'Do you have family telling you to throw them all out and get them on the Kindle to save space too?'

'Of *course* I do. Non-readers don't understand that some of these books are special. Those old, dog-eared paperbacks were there for me when no one else was. They're *friends*.' He pauses. 'I mean, not literally. I don't think they're actual people and have conversations with them and stuff. Not very often, anyway.'

I giggle, but mainly because he *gets* it. I keep the books I keep because I love them, because they helped me through times in my life when there was no one else to turn to. When I reread them, I want to read that actual copy – *my* copy. *My* friend.

'I've always thought it would be amazing to live in a bookshop. Do you remember that guy who got locked in Waterstones one evening? That would be my idea of heaven.'

He talks with quite a posh English accent, I'm guessing Cambridgeshire or a mix of the Home Counties, and each word sounds polite and refined. I like it. There's something about the way he speaks that makes it sound like he's narrating a fairy tale.

A trickle of customers come through all morning, and between serving them and talking books with anyone who'll listen, I find myself struggling to keep my eyes off Dimitri. True to his earlier word, he's as quiet as a mute mouse and there's plenty of room for others to sit down around him, and I like the way he takes such good care of the old book. He turns pages like he's got white cotton gloves on, and every time he stops for a drink from his flask, he turns completely in the opposite direction to make sure he doesn't spill anything near the valuable old book.

When the clock ticks past one p.m., he leaves the book on the table and his drawings rolled up in the corner of the sofa, and picks up his lunchbox and flask, and waves as he goes. 'Just popping out for lunch. Back in a bit.'

Oh God, lunch. I suddenly realise how hungry I am. I was in such a rush this morning that I didn't think to bring a packed lunch, and I'm used to shift work where you don't need one, and now, of course, I can't leave the shop unattended to go out and get something, and there's nothing upstairs because I haven't moved in yet. At least Robert was kind enough to leave a box of teabags and some milk in the fridge, but every time I think the shop's empty enough to run upstairs and make one, another customer comes in.

I wish I'd asked Robert more questions about the practical side of running this business. He used to manage it completely on his own, with no one to cover if he needed to pop out. Did he close the door with a sign saying back in two minutes? Did he risk leaving it unattended? With both the office and stairway doors open, you could probably hear the bell jingle when the door opened …

It's impossible, anyway. There's a mum and daughter upstairs in the children's section, and a man wandering around down here, and a woman comes in and asks me to point her in the direction of the Regency romance section, and I get a bit flustered because I don't even know if we *have* a Regency Romance section, and I point her towards the Romances and hope for the best.

'Don't go out there, it's a trap. There are people out there,' Dimitri says when he comes back in, thankfully managing to stay upright this time. 'Zero out of ten, would not recommend.'

It makes me smile because I've often felt the same way and spend most of my time hibernating in the flat. I find it impossible not to watch the movement of his biceps as he shrugs the bag off his shoulder and goes to sit back down in the corner of the reading area. Of course he looks up and catches me looking, and I'm not sure which one of us blushes harder as he concentrates intently on getting his books back out and I tidy the counter for approximately the fortieth time today. It will win an award for tidiest counter in Britain at this rate.

By half past two, my stomach is actually cramping with hunger, my bottle of water is empty, and my bladder is full. I can't wait any longer, and for once, Dimitri is the only person in the shop.

'I'm going to make a cup of tea,' I announce, and the sudden words in the silence of the shop make him jump so much that his pencil squiggles across his sketchbook, and I feel so guilty that I offer him one too.

'I'm okay, thanks. Got a flask.' He pats the lid where it's standing on the table beside him.

He's been here for hours. There's no way that tea's still at optimum drinking temperature. 'Is that still warm?'

'Well …' He presses the back of his hand against the metal side of the flask. 'Warmish, I suppose.'

'This is Britain. There's not much worse than a cold cup of tea. I'll get you one. Sugar?'

'One, please. And thank you. I didn't want to impose. You're meant to ignore me and pretend I'm not here.'

Does he have any idea how blue his eyes are? How wide his smile is? He is *impossible* to ignore.

I falter in the office doorway for a second. Even though he's the only person here, if I go upstairs, I'm leaving him unattended in the shop.

'I'll keep an eye and call you if anyone comes in,' he says without looking up. 'It's no trouble. I did it for Robert all the time.' He sketches for a few more seconds and then he does look up. 'And I've just realised that means leaving me alone in the shop and you don't even know me. I'll go and stand outside so you can lock up and let me in again when you come back.' He puts his pencil down and goes to get up.

'No, it's okay.' I stop him because the fact he realises that makes me feel a lot more comfortable. 'You stay. I'll be right back.'

I turn and go through the office before I can reconsider, propping both doors ajar with their little doorstops that are in the shape of an open book. I'm pretty sure you're not meant to leave strangers alone in your shop, but there's something about him that seems infinitely trustworthy, and he clearly knows the shop well and is right at home there. I have no reason to doubt that he regularly watched the shop for Robert too. And if he didn't, well, what's he going to do – break into the till and steal my takings? You can barely get into that till when you *want* to, and I've only taken about thirty quid so far today, and if he wants to ransack the place then good luck to him in finding an un-ransacked part to begin with.

Like Robert knew exactly what would happen, he's also left two plain white mugs and a sugar bowl on the counter in the kitchen, along with the kettle and teabags. I silently thank him for his forethought and wish I'd had some of my own when it came to bringing lunch as I clatter around the kitchen, spilling things because I'm rushing so much.

When I eventually get back downstairs, the shop's still empty and Dimitri doesn't look like he's moved. It feels like I've been up there for hours when it's only been five minutes. I put the mug down on the table near him, at a safe distance not to be spilled on the old book, and go to take my own mug back to the counter, but he stops me. 'You have to stay and drink it with me now.' He rifles in his bag, pulls the lid off another Tupperware container and holds it out to me. 'Cookie?'

I'm so hungry, I nearly burst into tears. And I definitely nearly hug him. Both of which would be Very Bad Things.

The scent of vanilla and chocolate and the buttery biscuit base is so fresh that it's like the chocolate chunks are still melting, and I snatch a cookie with an embarrassing amount of enthusiasm and inhale it so fast that I forget to taste it. He hasn't offered a second one, but I grab one anyway and ram it down my throat with my fist, doing a sterling impression of a baby learning to eat for the first time. He probably thinks I'm practising baby-led weaning minus the baby part.

I sigh in relief as the hunger is abated, and realise he's watching me with an alarmed look on his face. He nudges the container on the table nearer to me, and I gratefully take another cookie, trying to appreciate it this time, rather than swallow it whole and circle the box like a vulture looking for more. Regardless of how hungry I am, they really are amazing cookies. Soft and squidgy, with the perfect amount of gooey chocolate chunks and buttery biscuit. I grab another one as he takes one and nibbles it like a civilised person. 'You wouldn't happen to have forgotten lunch, would you?'

'How did you guess?' I ask guiltily, forgetting that civilised people don't speak with their mouths full.

'Do you want me to go and grab you something? The sandwich deli's at the other end of the road. It'd be no problem.'

God, that's so nice. 'No need. I'm all right now I've stuffed approximately thirty-four of your cookies down my throat. My sister's getting here at five. I'll text her and tell her to bring sustenance. That's so lovely of you though. Thanks, Dimitri.' I feel abnormally touched by his offer. Pure kindness for nothing in return. I didn't think people like that existed.

'Call me Dim. Most people do, and they're *rarely* talking about my name.'

I've only known him a few hours and I can tell he's anything but dim, but I like his self-deprecating sense of humour. When you're as accident-prone as I am, you have no option but to laugh at yourself, and I get the feeling he's the same.

I help myself to another cookie. 'Did you make these?'

He nods as he takes another one too. 'This morning. Couldn't sleep.'

I'm leaning against the edge of the bookshelf that forms the three-sided wall around the reading area, cradling my mug of tea, and when there's only one cookie left, he holds out the box to me. 'Go on, take it. It's amazing to see someone enjoying my baking. I always think the whole point of baking is to share it, and I still keep doing it, even though I don't have anyone to eat it now.'

I want to ask what that means, who he's lost, but the bell tinkles as a couple come into the shop, holding hands, both glowing. 'We've just found out we're pregnant,' the man says. 'Have you got *What to Expect When You're Expecting*?'

I can't chew fast enough not to answer them with my mouth full. I make a series of apologetic noises, but before I can splutter cookie crumbs all over them, Dimitri says, 'Second aisle, fifth shelf from the end, on the right. There's a good selection of pregnancy and baby books there.'

'Congratulations,' I call after them, nearly choking myself on the cookie.

He's trying and failing not to laugh as he hides his face behind his tea.

'You know this place well,' I say when they've gone in the direction he sent them and I've swallowed. 'You don't strike me as a man who spends a lot of time in the pregnancy section ...' I suddenly realise that he could have a wife and six children for all I know.

'I often think I might be pregnant myself.' He pats his quite lovely stomach. 'And the father is Mr Kipling. Or Dr Oetker, or Betty Crocker, or Aunt Bessie, and maybe even Paul Hollywood.'

I burst out laughing so hard that I spill my tea and have to rush over to grab the packet of wet wipes I'd found upstairs from behind the counter and mop it up before it stains the carpet. Scrubbing it puts me at eye level with the dust hidden underneath the shelves where some of the dust bunnies have clearly been reproducing like actual bunnies. 'I never saw how much Robert was struggling. As a customer, everything seemed normal, but I see it now in every inch of the shop.'

'That's exactly what he wanted. He would've been devastated to think that any customers saw how much he struggled with stairs, and could barely get up and down to the flat anymore, let alone the children's section or the sliding ladders.'

And yet, the children's section is easily the most looked-after place in the shop, and I get the feeling that Dimitri does a bit more than just sketching here. 'You helped?'

'If he let me. And not in any official way. Just as a thank-you for letting me use this old book. After the library closed, he welcomed me with open arms, even though I generally just sit here and make a nuisance of myself and can rarely afford to buy anything these days. I'm the type of customer every bookshop dreads.'

He's not the type of customer *I* dread. 'With those cookies, I'm going to roll out a red carpet for you every day. You're welcome here any time. Even without cookies.'

The almost permanent smile on his face gets wider. 'So where were you before? I've heard you're not in the book industry.'

'I was a waitress. I live just under an hour away and worked shifts in the local pub, which was … interesting. Don't get me wrong, most people were families out for a meal who were all lovely and respectful, but a pub is a pub. You get groups of men who get progressively more lewd with every drink and think leaving a tip entitles them to treat you like a piece of meat, slap your bum, stare at your boobs, and call you four eyes when you get annoyed with them. I mean, four eyes, for God's sake. No one's called me that since primary school.' I readjust my glasses self-consciously. I don't know why I said all that. I seem incapable of *not* rambling in front of him.

He pushes his glasses up. 'No, me neither.'

'I lost my job on the day of the prize draw. I've never had much luck with jobs. I've always been fired for stupid reasons, and then the odd time that I have found a job I'm good at and have enjoyed, the company's gone into liquidation or been bought out.' I pause, aware I'm still rambling. 'I just want this to go right. I love books so much, and I love this shop, and what bookworm *doesn't* dream of owning their own bookshop? I'm just kind of in the deep end here. I've never done anything like this before.'

'Well, for what it's worth, I think you're doing a great job so far.' He smiles at me and I get lost in smiling back at him for a moment, and then give myself a good shake.

'I'm not doing any job so far. This shop needs a *lot* of work, and all I've done so far is unlock the door and get bitten by the till.'

'He didn't tell you about the 20p.'

'What?'

'You have to balance a twenty-pence coin on the inner tray, right in the corner.' He stands up. 'Here, I'll show you.'

I follow him over to the counter where he goes behind it and unlocks the till with no hesitation, clearly having done it before. He pulls it open and takes a twenty-pence piece out of the drawer, and steps back to give me a better view. I lean across the counter on my elbows and watch as he balances the coin so it straddles either side of the lower right-hand corner of the inner tray. 'You might think it'll make it unsecure, but it won't. It still locks safely, but now it'll catch on the 20p and give you a few precious extra seconds to get your fingers out of the way.' He pushes the till shut and sure enough, it touches the coin and slows for a second or two before it locks shut. 'Don't worry, you'll get used to it.'

'It's like that plant in *The Little Shop of Horrors*. It's going to start growing with the more blood it gets. It'll be demanding that Rick Moranis feed it before the week is out.'

'So you have good taste in films as well as being a book lover …' He nods approvingly as the pregnant couple reappear from the shelves with *What to Expect When You're Expecting* and two other books on pregnancy and babies, and Dimitri and I swap places so I can serve them.

He goes back to the reading area and picks up a pencil while I put their books into one of our branded paper bags and congratulate them again.

When they leave, I turn back to him. 'Thanks for your help. With the cookies, the pregnancy section, and the till.'

He sips his tea. 'You're welcome. Feel free to ask if you need anything. I'm never too busy to talk to you.'

I like the emphasis he puts on the 'you'. It makes me feel oddly special, which is a nice change because I feel like a mild inconvenience to most people in my life, but I still have to psych myself up to ask the next thing because I don't want to annoy him or pry into his work. 'Okay, one more question because it's been bothering me all day. Where does the giant flea come in? I've never heard of a fairy tale with a giant flea in it before.'

He lets out a peal of laughter and pats the sofa beside him. I go over, the leather of the seats soft under my thighs as I sit down, keeping a safe distance between us, and he reaches across me to pull the book closer. 'This is actually the oldest known collection of fairy tales. It was praised by The Brothers Grimm and Hans Christian Andersen, but it's much darker than their stories. It features the first known versions of Cinderella, Sleeping Beauty, Snow White, and Puss In Boots among others.'

I lean back as he rustles the pages, his long fingers touching them gently, his upper arm brushing my knee where he's leaning over. 'Here, this is the giant flea one.'

I look at the pages of tiny text, just one short story in the book of fairy tales, breathing in the smoky, almost chocolatey scent of the ancient book.

'There's this king who can't find a suitor for his daughter, and when his sheep-sized pet flea dies, he hangs its skin up and sets a challenge – whoever can guess what animal the hide came from will get his daughter's hand in marriage – absolutely certain that no one will guess it was a flea at that size.'

I shift a bit nearer so I can see the book over his shoulder, and his voice is soft and quiet and close to my ear.

'And then an ogre comes along and identifies it, and the king can't go back on his word, so the princess is forced into marrying an ogre. A literal ogre, not the nice Shrek-type.'

'Oh, fun.'

He laughs. 'But it's okay in the end because she gets help from a family of half-giants who behead the ogre and take her back to the castle where she gets to marry a prince and live happily ever after.' He pulls across one of his sketchbooks and flips through it until he finds a pencil drawing of a princess, her white dress covered in red splotches, holding up an ogre's head with blood dripping from it. 'That's what I was thinking of going for, but I'm not sure if it's too graphic or not. The age group we're aiming at is too old to be coddled and possibly still too young for quite so much blood.'

'Are you doing the words as well?'

'No, that's someone else's department. I can't write for toffee.'

I love how posh he sounds, because it's the opposite of how he seems. He seems dishevelled and rambly and endearingly clumsy, but his English accent is lovely, the kind of accent that should narrate audiobooks you spend hours listening to.

'Your drawings are incredible. And so … unusual.' I struggle to find the right word. The couple I've seen so far have got something about them, something magical, whimsical, and special.

'That's another way of saying "no wonder you're thirty-six and haven't got anything published yet,"' he says with a laugh.

'I didn't mean that at all.' I can't tell him that sitting this close to him has made my brain start sounding an alarm, and inside my head is a constant flashing sign saying, *Remain calm. All is well. Just because you're sitting next to a gorgeous man who smells of dark lavender and the fresh wood of newly sharpened pencils, don't do anything stupid like sneeze on him. And for God's sake, don't accidentally spit on him like you did that last guy,* and I can't think of anything other than not dousing him in bodily fluids.

'Do you do anything else?' I ask, because I couldn't help noticing that paints fell out of his bag earlier, along with every other type of art supply imaginable.

'I'll try my hand at anything. I take online commissions to pay the bills and build my portfolio. My last job was creating a logo for a vegan marshmallow company. I like creating things on a blank canvas ...' He hesitates like he's questioning whether to carry on or not. 'You know the Peter Pan mural upstairs?'

'Yeah, it's amazing. I'd never really seen it until this morning, but it's magical. It's my favourite part of the whole shop. In fact, when the shop's closed, I think *I* might sit up there and read.'

He pushes his bottom lip out and tips his head to the side.

'You?' I say in surprise when I realise what he's saying. '*You* painted that?'

'Robert had the upstairs redone and it left a blank space on the wall. He commissioned me to paint something literary in the children's section, so I chose Peter Pan. It's one of my favourite stories.'

'Mine too. I mean, the Disney film version. The book itself is a bit dark, but that scene and that quote are so iconic and magical.' He's still leaning across me to reach the old book of fairy tales so I nudge my arm against his shoulder. 'You're incredibly talented.'

He looks up and we hold each other's gaze. He mouths a thank-you, and I'm not sure if he was deliberately trying to whisper or if he's forgotten how to talk, because sitting this close to him is definitely impairing my motor function.

Thankfully the bell jingles to announce the arrival of another customer and I jump up and go back to my position behind the counter because sitting so close to him is a recipe for disaster in more ways than one.

After that, it's the end of the school day and a steady stream of children and parents start filtering in and drift upstairs, and I listen to little footsteps on the floorboards above me. They're not here to buy anything – apparently it's an afterschool reading club run by parents. Yet more people in the shop who aren't buying anything. Maybe I should rebrand as a library and *that* would be the way to save Once Upon A Page.

I watch Dimitri pull everything he's using closer to take up less space, but when children and parents start filling the sofas around him, he starts putting his things back into his bag, closes the old Italian book and takes it back around the corner to the shelf it came from.

I'm distracted by serving someone, and he makes me jump when he appears in the gap behind the counter. He's still smiling as he leans down so he can whisper instead of shouting over the sounds now filling the bookshop. His glasses slide down his nose and he pushes them back up again. 'I'm gonna go.' His hair flops forwards and he has to shake it back. 'Usually I'd take myself round the back, but if you're moving in tonight, you don't need to be turfing me out at five.'

I shouldn't feel as disappointed as I do. There's been something nice about him being here today, a sort of reassuring presence that's made me feel like I'm not alone, and it's been nice to chat to someone who gets the love of books and doesn't ridicule me for it, and even though it's getting on for half past four and Nicole will be here soon, I'd kind of hoped I'd get to chat to him again once this round of customers have gone.

'Thanks for the cookies and the flowers earlier.'

'I think I'd better take them with me.' He nods towards the pitiful daffodils, which are now so limp that their stems have bent over and their shrivelled yellow heads are touching the countertop. 'Well, it's the thought that counts, right? And as for baking, what do you like? I'll bring something else tomorrow. It's the least I can do.'

I go to protest, but he stops me. 'Okay, tell me what you *don't* like?'

'Carrots. I *hate* carrots.'

'Might reconsider the carrot cake then, although I do tend to agree with you there. Any cake that involves vegetables is not real cake.' He pushes his glasses up again. 'See? It's so much easier to get people to talk about hate than love. Ask anyone about something they love and they'll umm and ahh, but ask them about something they hate and you get an answer in seconds.'

That's so sad. Even as I think he must be wrong, I realise that he's not. People *do* love complaining.

'Dimitri?' I say as he turns to go. 'I'm not going to perpetuate that. I love coconut. And any form of actual nut – hazelnuts, peanuts, almonds, walnuts, the lot.'

'Well, coconut and peanut butter are my favourite things in the world. Something else we have in common.' He lifts an imaginary hat and tips it in my direction. 'See you tomorrow, Hallie.'

'See you tomorrow.' I ignore the little fizzle inside. I have no right to get excited about seeing him, and there's no way he really comes here every day. I've never seen him before. Surely I'd have run into him by now if he's really here that often?

'Bye, Heathcliff!' He plucks the vase of squashed daffodils from the counter and goes out the door just as loaded down as he came in, with an armful of sketchbooks and the flowers held precariously against them. He waves as he walks past the window, and then stops and bends to wiggle his fingers at Heathcliff too, who swims towards the front of his bowl and his mouth movements amp up.

Clearly Dimitri's attractiveness is not limited to the human species.

Gorgeous baking wizard artists and a sex-crazed goldfish. No wonder Robert's got a sign up in the office that reads 'You don't have to be mad to work here, but it helps'.

Chapter 4

Where is that coming from? I open my eyes to the sound of a persistent knocking noise coming from somewhere below. Everything feels weird and different, and I'm on top of the bedcovers with half the duvet wrapped around my leg in such a knot that it looks like I'll need to join the Scouts to learn how to untie it. And I can see, kind of, which means I fell asleep with my glasses on, and they're now diagonally across my face and one of the arms has left a welt across my forehead.

I breathe in fresh bedding and blink up at an unfamiliar ceiling ... Oh my God, the bookshop! And that knocking must be a customer trying to get in, which can only mean one thing. I look around for something to tell me the time, but my usual bedside clock is still in a box somewhere, and my ... where the hell *is* my phone?

The knocking gets more insistent and I scramble off the bed, fall across to the window, shove it open, and stick my head out so fast that the momentum nearly pitches me straight through it.

'Good morning!' Dimitri is smiling up at me from the pavement below.

'Oh thank God, it's only you.' I scrub a hand over my face,

feeling the pillow creases running across my cheeks, and I don't need a mirror to tell what a bird's nest my hair is in. If I stand here for too long, I'm going to have the responsibility of raising a cuckoo.

'You wouldn't happen to have overslept, would you?'

'No.' I screw my face up like I can't work out what he's talking about, despite how glaringly obvious it is that I've just fallen out of bed. 'I was busy. With the … um … bookshop stuff. What time is it?'

'Ten past nine.'

He laughs when I swear.

'Did you know they've invented these nifty little things called alarm clocks?' He calls up with a bright smile.

I give him a scathing look. Well, as scathing as you can be with pillow creases and wonky glasses as you squint at the morning sunlight like it's personally at fault for turning up early. 'And to think I thought you were so nice yesterday.'

His impossibly wide smile gets impossibly wider, and I briefly consider that if I was more awake, I wouldn't have admitted that out loud. 'Stay there, I'll be down in a minute.'

I duck back inside and clonk my head on the window frame.

'Ouch!' Dimitri shouts from below. 'Are you okay?'

'No, I knocked myself unconscious but I expect I'll come round shortly,' I call back.

His laughter reaches my ears as I flail around the bedroom. Where is everything? Why are there so many boxes? Whoever thought it was a good idea to have this many books? I stumble to the bathroom to brush my teeth, and start tearing into boxes to find something to wear. I yank one of my favourite T-shirts on – one that depicts 'Once upon a time' scrawled across a Disney castle – and brush dust off yesterday's jeans because I can't find a clean pair, and I'm still finger-combing my long hair into a side plait as I scramble down the stairs, dash through the shop, and fling open the door to … a completely empty street.

Dimitri's gone. Great. How could I have overslept on my second day?

Moving in did not go smoothly. In fact, the only success of the night was that I restrained myself from braining Bobby with a book for his constant litany of '*Why do you need so many flamin' books when you're moving into a flamin' bookshop?*' Braining him would've been a waste of a good book. Between that and trying to fit boxes of books into a *very* narrow flat, by the time I'd found my bedding, got it onto the bed and fallen facedown on top of it, it was gone four a.m., and setting an alarm didn't even cross my mind. I assumed I'd be so excited for day two of my new job that I'd wake up anyway, and if that failed, then the noise of the street would definitely rouse me.

'That went well,' I say to the empty road.

The tailor from the handmade clothing and alterations shop on the opposite corner next to the town square is standing in his doorway too and he gives me a hesitant wave and a nervous nod, clearly wondering who I'm talking to. I gesture to Heathcliff and mouth 'goldfish' at him, which only serves to make me look like I've got even more screws loose. The man retreats hastily back inside his shop, and I sigh and close the door behind me.

I look down at myself and realise my top is on back to front. I duck behind the counter, pull my arms out and try to swivel it the right way, and at the exact moment I look like I'm in the middle of a game of strip aerobics, the bell tinkles and Dimitri pops his head round the door. 'Hello!'

I squeak and drop to my knees behind the counter to hide.

'I know it's a bit late, but nothing's so important that you have to get dressed in the shop.'

'I'm not getting dressed in the shop, I'm getting *re*-dressed because I couldn't do it properly the first time.' It comes out muffled around the sleeve I'm holding up with my teeth to ensure my bra doesn't pop into view. When I'm satisfied that the top's on safely, I stand up and do a Basil Fawlty-style double take at how close he is to the counter.

'Oh, I'm not complaining.' He waggles his eyebrows and my cheeks burn even hotter than they were before. There's no way he means that as flirtily as it sounds. 'Good morning!'

I groan, but at least he's better than yesterday's opening-time visitor. 'Could you be less chirpy? I'm not used to this time of the morning. I worked evenings before this.'

'Sorry!' he says at the same level of chirpiness. 'Can I be forgiven for bringing these?' He puts a cardboard tray of two coffee cups down on the counter, along with another vase of bright daffodils, uncrushed this time, and his beam shows exactly how proud he is of that fact. It makes me smile as I tear one of the coffees out, mumble something that might be a thank-you, and take a huge mouthful. And immediately regret it because sipping lava would be cooler. I wince and suck air in between my teeth, hoping he hasn't noticed, but he obviously has.

'You look like you need these.' He digs in his bag and pulls out a Tupperware container and pops the lid. 'Coconut and almond bites, with flaked almonds and toasted coconut.'

'Oh my God, you are the best person in the world.'

His smiling face goes the colour of a tomato.

'Oh my God, Dimitri,' I repeat as I pop one in my mouth, the soft and buttery cake-like centre complemented by the crunch of toasted coconut and almond flakes on the outside. 'Have you applied for *The Great British Bake Off*? You could win it blind-folded.'

'You're just being kind, but thank you.' He takes one of the delicious little bites and pops it into his mouth. 'And because I know you haven't had a chance to prepare lunch this morning, I'm going to the deli down the street for both of us at lunchtime.' I go to protest but he stops me. 'It's non-negotiable. Just call me a sandwich-bearing Prince Charming.'

'I've always thought that if Prince Charming was missing

anything in the old fairy tales, it was freshly made sandwiches.' I give him a wink. 'And you've managed to wake me up this morning. Princes are always waking people up in fairy tales.'

'Yeah, but with coffee and a good knocking technique. It's not quite True Love's Kiss.'

'Oh, no, kissing and me first thing in the morning would *not* inspire True Love's Kiss. It would inspire the appearance of an eighth dwarf called Morning Breath.'

He laughs, but all this talk of kissing is a bit much for me with a man *this* gorgeous standing so close. I take another bite to distract myself and try not to make the orgasmic noises I want to at the taste. I'm already embarrassed about the kissing talk; orgasmic noises are not going to help the situation.

He *does* look gorgeous again this morning. He manages to look dishevelled and put-together at the same time, whereas I look like I fell out of bed less than five minutes ago. His light-brown hair is in an impressive quiff again, but it doesn't look like it's styled, it just looks like it naturally stands upwards. His black-framed glasses make his eyes look bigger and bluer than they probably are – they must do, because no one's eyes are naturally *that* bright. He's wearing dark trousers, a T-shirt, and a waistcoat again, and neon yellow socks are peeking out from above one orange and one blue boot.

'Okay, I didn't say anything yesterday because I thought you'd got dressed in the dark and I didn't want to make you self-conscious about it, but now I have to ask. Either you've got a serious problem with the electricity where you live or the odd shoes are a fashion choice?'

He sticks out the foot with the blue boot and wiggles it in my direction. 'I like to be different. And it really annoys the people in my life who want me to conform. It's worth all the odd looks I get for that alone. I'm such a klutz that people are going to look at me anyway, I may as well give them something to look *at.*'

Before I have a chance to comment on how oddly sad that sounds, he cuts me off. 'How'd the move go?'

I groan again as I tell him about the constant moaning about too many books, and totally lose track of time as we both lean on the counter, sipping our coffees, and working our way through the tub of coconut almond bites. I don't realise how long we've been standing there until a customer comes in and I realise how unprofessional it must look.

Dimitri has already put his things down in the corner of the sofa and he goes to collect his book of fairy tales.

'Hey,' I say before he sits down. 'You know a bit about Heathcliff, you wouldn't happen to know how often Robert fed him, would you?'

'Not a clue. Hang on.' He disappears up the stairs, his long legs taking them two at a time, and I listen to the creak of floorboards as he moves around.

'Here.' When he reappears a few minutes later, he hands me a book with a proud smile.

How to Look After Your Goldfish. With an age range of four to six years old. I try to be insulted, but to be honest, I know so little about fish and am so bad at keeping things alive that one aimed at two-year-olds would be more appropriate. 'Now why didn't I think of that?'

'Just call me Prince Charming bearing children's books.' He settles down and gets his art supplies out and spreads his sketchbooks across the table in front of him, while I stand behind the counter reading about how often to feed goldfish, when to clean the tank out, and signs of impending demise. Heathcliff Number Four is *not* going to become Number Five on my watch. I side-eye the daffodils Dimitri brought in. I don't fancy their chances much though.

Again, I try not to watch him as he works. The shop is quiet but a few people come and go, the flip of pages as people flick through books, and readers standing still with their heads bent as they read first chapters before deciding to buy. Or not buy. The amount of people who put the books back and walk out empty-handed is disheartening. I try watching people to see if I can work out why. Do they turn the book over and check Robert's price stickers and can't afford it? Do they like it but think it'll be cheaper on Amazon? Did they just come in to read a certain part with no intention of buying it? How am I going to change things if I can't figure it out?

I realise the window display hasn't changed since I came in on the day after I won the prize draw, and that was over two weeks ago, so I put Heathcliff's bowl on the counter and start clearing the display, leaving Dimitri to keep an eye on things as I run upstairs for cleaning supplies, thankfully left in a labelled box in the kitchen last night.

Between customers, I stack the display books to one side of the counter, knowing it'll be fun trying to find the shelves they came from. There doesn't seem to be any theme to Robert's last window. On one side, he had children's books displayed around Heathcliff's bowl, and the other side displayed the most recent fiction releases and hyped books. Surely something more could be done with this window? It's a good size, a wide shelf set back from a double windowpane that stretches across the front of the shop, and there's plenty of space to use the display stands I found in the office and display books at different levels. Robert left most of the window clear so passers-by can see into the shop, but I think I could use the full window and really utilise the space.

I pull out the faded spring garland that was wound around the edges of the shelf and give it a shake, watching dust float to the floor. This wonderful shop deserves better than this, and I can instantly imagine the seasonal displays I can put here. Spring reads displayed on fake grass, and beach reads displayed on shells and pebbles in the summer. I can scatter autumn leaves in September and fill the display with cosy books, maybe add in

68

some acorns and conkers and branches of autumn foliage. Christmas will be amazing, with tinsel and fairy lights and festive rom coms – my favourite things to snuggle up with on a cold December night.

The other shop windows on the street are quaint and cute, but this one doesn't really say anything or catch the eye of anyone who doesn't usually like bookshops. I once worked in a clothes shop where I got fired for allowing a very large man with a very small dress into the changing room and it didn't end well. How was I to know he intended to try it on and then parade around in front of the other customers as it slowly split stitch by stitch until everyone saw his bare bum? The only saving grace was that the seam ran up the back and not the front.

That shop's emphasis was always on dressing the mannequins in outfits that would catch the eye and pull in people who didn't already intend to come into the shop, and that's what we need to do here too. Draw in people walking past who didn't realise they wanted to buy a book until they saw this window.

It's amazing how quickly the hours pass as I empty the window. I'm still cleaning it when a little boy comes in clutching a teddy bear in one hand and his mum's hand in the other, dragging her with him as he marches up to the counter. 'Excuse me, Miss, have you got any books about monsters?'

I can't help smiling at his exquisite manners. And wishing I'd had a chance to study the children's section because I haven't got a clue what's on the shelves and there's no sign of a stock list of any kind yet.

I figure he's a kid who will appreciate honesty. 'I've got to be honest with you – it's only my second day here and I don't—'

'Now what sort of a bookshop would this be if we didn't have books about monsters?' Dimitri's voice comes from the reading area and he leans forward until he can see around the shelf. 'What kind of monsters are you after?'

'Scary ones!'

'Then you're in luck because there's a whole shelf upstairs dedicated only to scary monsters. It specifically says "No non-scary monsters allowed". You're going to find it on the fifth bookcase along, second or third shelf from the bottom.'

The little boy thanks us both politely and starts dragging his mum towards the stairs, but then stops and comes back to the counter, pushing himself up on tiptoes to talk to me. 'Have you seen our monster yet?'

'You have a monster? Here in Buntingorden?'

'Yes!' He looks more excited than you'd think possible over the prospect of a monster. 'He's called The Stropwomble! If you're new here, you need to know before he eats your brains.'

'Charlie …' his mum warns him.

'He's big and scary,' Charlie says, ignoring her. 'He looks hideous because his skin is all peeling off because he never goes outside, and he sets traps for anyone who goes in his garden, and he eats children for tea.'

'Nah.' Dimitri pops his head round the shelf again. 'Think about it. He's much more likely to eat adults for tea and then have children for dessert. Children are much sweeter. He'd definitely save them for afters.'

Charlie looks like he's giving this serious consideration.

'But you've got a teddy so you'd be safe,' Dimitri continues, nodding towards the brown bear clutched in the little boy's hand. 'Did you know that teddies are warriors? They fight monsters to keep their owners safe. If any monster came near you, your teddy would go into battle. You don't know it but your teddy has got a whole suit of armour hidden away, ready to don the moment you're in trouble. What's his name?'

'Fluffy.' Charlie looks between Dimitri and his teddy in awe.

'Ah, yes, I've heard of Fluffy the Warrior King.' Dimitri tears a piece of paper from one of his sketchbooks and draws a teddy bear in armour swishing a sword around, even getting in the bent whisker of the little boy's teddy with one flick of his pencil. It

70

only takes him a couple of minutes, but Charlie looks like he might explode with happiness when he hands it to him.

'Do you really have a monster?' I ask when Charlie and his mum are safely upstairs and out of earshot.

'I doubt it.' Dimitri laughs. 'You know the posh leafy streets on the outskirts of town?'

I nod. Buntingorden is a village with a few big manor houses dotted around the outskirts – the kind that look like they should have a flag outside when the Queen's in residence, or at the very least be part of the set for *Downton Abbey*.

'One of the mansions there has fallen into disrepair so it looks a bit like a haunted house. No one's ever seen whoever lives there, and you know what people are like. Stories get made up. Kids say it's a monster or a ghost, adults say a vindictive troll, but it's probably just a lonely old man who wants to be left alone.'

It doesn't take long for Charlie to bounce down the stairs and come rushing over to the counter where he slaps three monster books down in front of me. 'Just these, please, Miss.'

I hold back a laugh at how much he sounds like he's just stepped out of a Charles Dickens novel as I tap the prices into the till. He tugs on his mum's sleeve when she comes to pay, and can't grab the books fast enough when I hand them back to him.

'Keep your friend.' His mum covertly points to Dimitri and fans a hand in front of her face. 'If he's not on the payroll, he definitely should be.'

'He's here all the time, apparently.'

She glances back at him and pushes her bottom lip out with a noise of disappointment. 'Clearly we've been coming in at the wrong times, and Charlie drags me in here twice a week. Maybe we need to come in more often.'

'Well, I'm not going to disagree with that, am I?' I say and she laughs.

'And sorry about all the monster talk. He's a bit obsessed with all things monster at the moment.' She nods towards Charlie, who's now showing Dimitri his new monster books. 'He won't stop going on about The Stropwomble of Bodmin Lane.'

'Stropwomble?' I repeat. I managed to hold back a giggle when Charlie said it earlier but now I fail miserably.

'Believe me, the adults around here would rather call him something unrepeatable in polite company, but you know, little ears.' She nods to Charlie, who's now admiring one of Dimitri's less bloodthirsty ogres. 'That vile man is always in a strop about something – he may as well have a name to reflect that.'

I snort again. 'And Bodmin Lane like the moor?'

'Yeah, but don't insult the Bodmin beasts. Angry pumas would make better neighbours than that miserable old twit.'

'That bad?'

'It's like he's set out to ruin the town. He's a grouchy old tyrant who wants everyone else to be as miserable as he is. He complains about *everything*. He got our Christmas tree taken down last year on the grounds it was a distraction to motorists and therefore an accident waiting to happen. He got jack-o'-lanterns banned at Halloween because they were a fire hazard. We'd organised a fireworks display and he got someone on the council to put a stop to that too. He's always writing letters to the local newspaper complaining about this, that, or the other. People swimming in the river, tourists leaving litter behind on the riverbank, and for some reason he's got a right bee in his bonnet about the bunting.'

She points upwards, obviously meaning the strings of pastel-coloured gingham flags that criss-cross the high street. 'Nearly every week, he's writing a strongly worded letter to someone or other about it being dangerous. God knows what he thinks it's going to do. Leap down and slurp up someone's tea, my husband says.'

'You can't live in a village called Buntingorden without bunting,' I say incredulously.

'Exactly! Miserable old twit. He lives in this decrepit old house, his gate's all rusty and chained up with big spikes on top – God knows who he thinks is going to get in. The bunting to take its revenge, maybe. And no one's ever seen him. That's the worst part. He hides behind his anonymity and makes all these complaints but never in person – never to our faces.'

'There's one in every town,' I say, sounding like I'm well travelled and have much experience of living in different places when in reality I've only lived in three places in my life and never outside the Cotswolds.

'Why can't real life be like novels, eh? At least we'd know he'd get his comeuppance and meet an untimely and messy end then.' She thinks for a moment. 'Oh, even better – he'd learn the error of his ways and become a reformed character, wouldn't he? Like Scrooge in *A Christmas Carol*. If only things like that happened in real life.'

After they leave, I go back to my window display. It needs a theme … something summery … Something that a goldfish fits in to … Mermaids! Who doesn't love mermaids, right? I find a beautiful limited-edition copy of Hans Christian Andersen's *The Little Mermaid and Other Fairy Tales* with a baby blue cover and red shells surrounding a red-haired mermaid sitting in a seashell and put it at the front of the window. I'm aware of Dimitri's eyes on me as I dash back and forth to the shelves, trying to hunt out any book even vaguely mermaid-related, and clatter around in the office, digging out the array of acrylic display stands, book holders, and props that Robert's amassed over the years.

I stop as I walk past him, and can't resist peeking at what he's working on – an ogre decorating its house with bones now. 'Hey, you're probably the guy to ask. Do you know what kind of pens I need to draw on glass?'

He looks up with a grin, puts his pencil between his teeth, and starts digging around in his bag, and I can't help watching in amusement as he pulls out an endless array of items. I'm starting to wonder if his satchel is some sort of endless magician's bag because there doesn't seem to be a bottom to it or any limit to the amount of things it holds as he sets item after item out on the table.

'These ones?' Eventually he hands me a pack of pens with 'Glass Markers' written across the front. 'Oh, hang on, I've got these too.' He digs out a pack of chalk markers and gives me those as well. 'Both will work. The markers will need washing off with soap and water and the chalk ones won't last as long but can be wiped away. Try 'em both and see which you prefer.' He meets my eyes with a soft smile. 'For the window?'

'I'm going for a mermaid theme, with Heathcliff and all. I thought I could draw some scales around the edges or something …' Saying it aloud makes it sound worse than it did in my head, although I'm touched that he doesn't mind me borrowing the pens. I'd only intended him to tell me what was best to order from Amazon, I didn't expect him to have any on him.

'Sounds good. I've always said Robert could make better use of that window.'

'Thanks.' I feel a little jolt of pride that he agrees with me. Dimitri clearly knows a lot about this shop, and him thinking the same as I do makes me think I might not be that far off base after all.

It all goes well until I actually start trying to draw mermaid scales at the edges of the window. This whole drawing back-to-front thing so it looks right from the outside is no easy task. That's my excuse, anyway. It looks nothing like mermaid scales. A tin of baked beans poured over the window would make more accurate mermaid scales than this.

'How's it going?'

'Oh, please don't look.' I groan. Of all people you want assessing your terrible attempt at artwork, an artist is *not* one of them.

I hide my face behind my hands as Dimitri steps up behind me, so close that I can feel his body heat, and I fight the temptation to lean back just a tiny bit.

His eyes scan over my attempt at prettifying the window. 'Well, at least you used the chalk markers so we can wipe it off.'

That says it all, really.

He laughs. 'I thought you were going for mermaid scales. Why have you drawn puddles all over the window?'

Well, puddles are a step up from baked beans. 'Because even with a book cover with a mermaid on it in front of me, I can't figure out how to make them look right.'

He grabs a cloth from the counter and comes back to wipe the glass clean. 'Can I try?'

Our fingers brush and we both hesitate for a moment, neither of us moving as I hand him the pink chalk pen, my fingertip pressing into the side of his, and then he looks away and somehow folds himself onto the empty shelf and sets to work.

'I was intending to expand them out from each corner to fill the space, and then join them along each edge, like a frame around the window.'

He makes a non-committal noise, and a customer goes to the counter, so I put the pack of chalk markers on the shelf beside him and go to serve her. She's buying a stack of romantic comedies, and we have a chat about the pros and more pros of Sophie Kinsella's books, and she somehow hasn't read *Can You Keep A Secret?* so she goes back and finds that one too and adds it to her pile, and I've got a massive smile on my face as I ring up her total and load the books into a bag. It's my biggest sale so far. If I could get a few more customers like her, we might have a chance.

When I look back, Dimitri's stopped drawing on the window and is sitting there grinning at me. 'You were made for this.' He shakes his head. 'I mean the bookselling, obviously. No offence but you weren't made for drawing mermaid scales on windows.'

'But you were. Wow.' My mouth is agape as I get out from behind the counter and go back to the window. 'How did you *do* that?'

Extending from each corner is an ombré mermaid's tail that

starts pink and fades into purple and then turquoise for the perfectly flicked fins that look like they're diving down into each angle of the window. Instead of more scales joining the four corners, there are waves up each side and a line of shells along the top and bottom, all outlined and shaded in pastel colours.

'I've only been chatting for ten minutes,' I say in awe. 'All right, I get a bit carried away when it comes to romantic comedies, but this is …' I trail off because I can't find the words to do it justice. 'So you can give Mary Berry a run for her money in the kitchen *and* make Van Gogh weep. Can you plumb a sink, retile the roof, pilot an aeroplane, and charm some snakes on your way back too?'

'Oh, stop it.' He blushes again.

I like how easy it is to make him blush. 'You're helping me instead of doing your own work again.'

He clambers off the window ledge, holding on to the wall and stamping his foot to get pins and needles out of his leg, and something in my chest floods with warmth when he looks up and meets my eyes. 'Believe me, it's my pleasure.'

For one moment, I think he's going to hug me and we stare at each other awkwardly for an embarrassing amount of time, until he ducks his head. His quiffed hair flops over and then bounces back as he stands upright, and I find it impossible to take my eyes off him, especially when his meet mine again and the glint in them is just a little bit more sultry than cheeky.

'Excuse me, I wonder if you could help me?' The woman standing behind me makes me jump so much that I nearly topple over. I hadn't even heard her come in. How can I have been so lost in Dimitri's eyes that I'd even missed the bell tinkling? 'I can't remember the name, but I'm looking for a book that's been made into a TV show where they all wear red.'

'*The Handmaid's Tale*,' Dimitri and I say in unison.

The lady smiles in recognition of the title, and Dimitri's face crinkles in concentration for a moment before he says, 'Aisle two, under Dystopian Fiction, which is on the third bookshelf along, four shelves from the top.'

The lady looks as impressed as I am. 'Ooh, he's clever, isn't he?'

'He is,' I say as he looks up and meets my eyes again with a grin, and she hurries off to follow his directions.

'Wow,' I say in surprise. 'You know this place absurdly well. How long did you say you'd been sketching here?'

'I didn't.' He rubs at the back of his neck. It doesn't seem like he's going to elaborate, but I hold his gaze, and eventually he looks away. 'A while. It's a *big* book.'

'I've never seen you.'

'I lurk.'

He doesn't seem very lurk-y. As far as I can tell, he sits in the reading area and takes up a not-small amount of space when the shop's quiet. I'm surprised I haven't noticed him before given how much time he seems to spend here. He is not the sort of man you *don't* notice.

'I try not to get in anyone's way,' he says when I don't look away. 'I told you, I go and hide in the Rare and Valuable aisle when things are busy. I treat this place like a library and Robert's been kind enough to let me – I'm not going to take up space that valued, *paying* customers might want.'

The customer places a copy of *The Handmaid's Tale* on the counter and I rush back to serve her, which distracts me from Dimitri and his intricate knowledge of this shop.

'Thanks for your help,' the customer says, turning to direct the words towards Dimitri too. 'My friend says the TV show is utterly gripping but I refuse to watch any adaptations without reading the book first.'

Dimitri gradually shifts closer to the counter as she starts talking about films versus books and various adaptations. She's clearly under the impression that we both work here because she keeps turning to involve him in the conversation too.

When she leaves, he starts rifling through my small selection of mermaid books that are piled on the counter waiting to be positioned in the window. 'There are more in the children's and YA section. I'll go and have a look.'

When he comes back downstairs with another four books in his hands, I'm still staring at the empty shelf. I've put some of the clear Perspex stands in, but the bare shelf looks dull and boring in comparison to the amazing artwork on the glass. 'You don't know if Robert had any props or decorations, do you? I've had a look round the office but all I can find is a box of Christmas decorations. You wouldn't expect Christmas decorations to have a sell-by date, but these ones have definitely passed it.'

'And they would, of course, be just the thing for a mermaid-themed May window. Nothing says "spring days" like tinsel and mistletoe.'

His deadpan sarcasm makes me laugh as I take the books and thank him for finding them.

'And no. I think there's an autumn garland to match that manky old spring one knocking about somewhere, but Robert was never big on windows. He worked on the basis of trying to take care of existing customers rather than attempting to attract new ones. He thought word of mouth was his biggest draw.'

'Why can't I do both?'

'You can. This place needs to be invigorated and re-energised. You seem full of energy and, er, vigoration … vigoratedness? As you can tell, I *rock* at the English language.'

I can't help laughing at him. 'Well, I can honestly say no one's ever told me that before.'

He laughs too, and our gazes stay locked until he shakes his head and points through the window. 'There's a little craft shop down the street that used to do things like shells for about a pound per bag. You could always nip down and have a look.'

'I can't leave the shop,' I say, only just starting to realise how limiting it is to be alone here. 'And you can guarantee that they have the same opening hours as us so I won't be able to go after we close.'

'I don't mind keeping an eye on things while you nip out for a minute, but I also understand that you don't know me or trust me and won't be offended if you say no.'

I quickly weigh up my options. On one hand, he's right, I don't know him or trust him, and there's got to be something in the mythical rulebook of owning a shop that says leaving said shop in the care of a stranger is a terrible idea, but on the other hand, he's *lovely*. And he's a baker. There's something about people who bake that makes them seem like inherently good people. Why do people bake if not for the sole purpose of making other people happy and creating something that will bring others joy? He's been nothing but kind and helpful, and he obviously knows the shop extraordinarily well.

'That'd be great, thanks.' I take a tenner out of the till, feeling like I'm stealing even though using the takings to buy things for the shop is okay, and go out the door before I can reconsider.

The pavements are bustling with tourists as I walk down the cobbled road, dodging dogs on leads who have stopped to chew up biscuits they've been given by shop owners or to lap from the water bowls outside. One of my favourite things about Buntingorden has always been how dog friendly it is. I pass the flower shop, the antiques shop, the souvenir shop, the toy shop, and the retro sweet shop, before I come to a little craft shop I've walked past many times but never been in.

Inside I spot the bags of shells that look like they've come straight off a beach and grab two. I take a bag of smooth grey pebbles too, and on my way to the till, I see packets of crepe paper and grab one in a dark blue ocean-like colour, and quickly pay and walk back to Once Upon A Page, wanting to leave Dimitri alone for as little time as possible.

When I get back he's behind the counter where I left him, and he looks up from flipping through one of the mermaid books I'd left out.

'That doesn't look like your usual reading matter,' I say, nodding to the iridescent pink cover as he closes it.

'I used to read this to Dani.' There's something off in his voice, like he's trying to hold back a wobble, and the smile that's been on his face almost permanently since I met him is missing. 'My sister,' he clarifies as he stands up straight and shakes his head. 'But that was a long time ago. What did you get?'

I show him my haul as I take it across to the window and dump it all on the sill. 'Did you sell anything?'

'One copy of *The Da Vinci Code*. You went out at exactly the right moment because the guy wanted to talk, talk, talk about Illuminati conspiracy theories. You owe me one for fielding that.' The smile he gives me doesn't look anywhere near as wide as his usual smile, and his fingers are still rubbing over the embossed cover of the mermaid book.

I think I owe him a bit more than one. He's been ridiculously helpful. 'Thanks, Dimitri.'

'You're welcome.' He pushes the pink book underneath the stack and comes out from behind the counter, and this time when he looks up and grins at me, he's his usual smiley self. 'Can I help?'

'Don't you have ogres to draw?'

He glances towards the reading area and then back at me. 'Ah, this is much more fun. My giant fleas can wait.'

A customer chooses that moment to walk past and is unable to hold in a snort of laughter when he overhears, which sets both Dimitri and I off too as he helplessly tries to explain the context.

I lay the blue crepe paper out so it covers the shelf, set the pebbles at the front underneath the window, crumple more paper into balls and line them up behind the pebbles to create a wave. Or not. When I go outside to see what it looks like, it looks like crumpled paper. I wrinkle my nose as I peer in, trying to work out the best way to arrange it or if it's a daft idea and should be scrapped immediately.

As I stand there trying to figure out the best thing to do, Dimitri appears in the window brandishing a stick of glue and a paintbrush with white paint on it. I watch as he glues a few of my paper balls together and arranges them across the pebbles. He starts dabbing white watercolours at key areas of the paper balls and when he's finished, it *does* kind of look like a wave crashing onto the beach. If you have a good imagination.

When I go back inside, he carries on painting and rearranging while I set out shells on the shelf and put some of the Perspex stands into position, saving a shaded space for Heathcliff.

'What are you up to tonight?' Dimitri asks as we stand side by side at the window, arranging the children's mermaid books around Heathcliff's bowl and putting the YA and adult ones higher up on the stands to separate them. 'More moving in?'

'No, I'm going to open the accounting software on that pitifully old PC and do the thing that business people call balancing the books. All my stuff is here now. I can unpack boxes at any time, but I really need to tackle the shop's finances so I know exactly what I'm dealing with.'

I don't tell him about Robert's words when we signed the paperwork, or Drake Farrer's visit yesterday and how much he spooked me with his talk of failing bookshops and dying high streets, and how he made it seem like common knowledge that Once Upon A Page is on its last legs and it's only a matter of time until it goes under. I can't let that happen, and I can't begin trying to prevent it unless I know exactly what I'm dealing with.

'And I thought my night of tea, toast, and reading was boring.'

Tea, toast, and reading sounds a lot better than the type of books I've got to face. 'This is the terrifying part. Selling books, talking about books, rearranging books in windows ... Ooh, ordering new books from distributors and publishers ...' I get momentarily sidetracked by the idea of budgets and shiny new stock. 'That's the fun part. But I have no idea about the business side of things. I need to know what kind of position we're in. I've already got vultures sniffing round the door; I need to know if there's any flesh left for them to rip off our carcass.'

'That's a remarkably macabre metaphor.'

'Well, not everyone can be as endlessly cheerful as you.'

'Ah, thank you. I think there's very little to be miserable about in a bookshop.'

I can't help smiling at him. 'I think you might be one of the greatest philosophers of our time. What other pearls of wisdom are you hiding?'

'There is no day that cannot be improved by a jar of Nutella and a spoon.' He thinks for a moment. 'And if in doubt – Jaffa Cakes.'

I burst out laughing and he grins. 'It's okay, you can use them as inspirational wall quotes if you want, I won't mind.'

I leave him displaying the books in the window when a non-buying customer stops on her way out and compliments it. 'It's nice to see someone making use of that window. My daughter loves all things mermaid. I'm going to bring her by at the weekend to have a look.'

I thank her, and as she leaves, Dimitri hands her one of the display shells. 'Here, take her a shell as a reminder.'

The lady grins as she looks between me and him and then tucks it into her bag. 'Thank you, she'll love that.'

'Sorry, I've just realised I'm giving away your display pieces without asking,' Dimitri says as the bell jingles behind her.

'Are you kidding? That was really sweet of you. She might come back and actually buy something now. And you've just painted me the best window this shop has ever seen – you can do whatever you like. Take money from the till and bathe in it if you want. Although it would be a very shallow bath, and *very* unhygienic ...'

He cuts me off by laughing. 'I love this place. It's a privilege to sit here and work every day. The least I can do is scribble a bit of chalk on your window occasionally. This is a special little shop. It doesn't feel like work here, it feels like home.'

He's definitely got a point there.

Chapter 5

Usually the universe is not on my side. Usually the universe is on the *opposite* of my side, especially when it comes to things like rain on the day I've forgotten my umbrella, the wonky table in a restaurant, or the wobbly legged trolley in the supermarket, but today, after the horrendous look at the shop's accounts last night, Once Upon A Page is sent an exceptionally busy day, like the retail gods of Buntingorden are smiling down upon us.

A group of ladies come in the morning and attack the Catherine Cookson and Sagas shelf, and then in the afternoon, a coach load of tourists on a Cotswolds sightseeing trip are sent off their coach at the top of the high street and picked up again two hours later after they've browsed every shop on the street.

According to the accounts I looked through last night, this is the busiest day Once Upon A Page has seen in years, and another 365 days like this might be my only chance of getting back into the black, money wise.

Dimitri was around this morning but he quickly disappeared when the group of ladies recommissioned the reading area as a gossip station. He went out for lunch and returned with a sandwich for me too but I barely had time to thank him for it before more people asked questions and wanted serving. This afternoon, in the midst of the tourists, I saw him pick up his things and go to return his book, but I had so many queries and customers that I missed him leaving, and I feel ridiculously sad at not getting to say goodbye.

The mermaid display has been decimated by people spotting the books from outside and coming in to buy them, and I haven't had a chance to find any replacements yet. It's only my third day in this job, but by the time the last customer leaves at ten past five, I can't shut the door behind her quickly enough. Buntingorden is a traditional little town. We've got no late opening hours and there's still a law against Sunday trading, so every shop on the street opens at nine and closes at five with no exceptions, and it's not unusual for some to close for lunch as well.

I lean against the door and try to get my breath back. I didn't even realise that bookshops had days as busy as this, and while I'm not complaining in terms of money taken especially after that look at the accounts last night, it does make me wonder how Robert ever coped. And the day doesn't end here. I want to go upstairs, flop down on the bed and sleep for a hundred years or until a handsome prince wakes me up, but I have to tidy up the chaos left by so many customers, restock the window display and the picks-of-the-week table, and if all the customer queries and questions I've been unable to answer today have taught me anything, it's that I desperately need to do a stock take and rearrange every shelf so they reflect the categories that are actually written on them.

The group of old ladies kept bringing car manuals and war memoirs and DIY how-to books up to the counter and saying, 'These shouldn't be in with the Sagas, love.' They were trying to be helpful, but now I have two piles of books behind the counter and no idea of where they're supposed to go.

I run upstairs to make myself a restorative cup of tea, quickly tidy up the window display and restock the picks-of-the-week table, which is going down fast, and then I face the shelves.

The past two nights have been a bit hectic after closing time – Monday with Nicole and Bobby turning up, and then yesterday I had to learn how to cash-up at the end of the day, balance the money in the till against the receipts, and attempt to make head or tail of Robert's accounting software. I've got so caught up in banking that it's easy to forget I'm doing something that's always been my biggest dream.

This *is* my dream job, no matter how much work it needs. Books have always been my escape from daily life and now they *are* my daily life, and it makes me want to skip around the shop and sing 'I Have Confidence' like Julie Andrews running down the lane in *The Sound of Music*. This is my chance to turn it into the bookshop of my dreams, like starting from scratch with a blank palette. And no matter how convinced I am that something is going to go wrong, I have to throw my all into this. Opportunities like this are rarer than once in a lifetime, and I'll regret it forever if I don't give it everything, even if it does fail. Usually I hold back because I'm sure things will go wrong, but I can't with this. It's a new start.

'I own a bookshop,' I say to myself as I climb the ladder to the top shelf of the autobiographies section, full of dusty hard-backs that no one ever buys because the paperback has come out since and includes an extra chapter, or the Kindle version is 99p, whereas Robert was expecting to get £12.99 for even the most z-list of celebs' ghost-written ramblings. This is the sort of thing that can go – at least to the new sale section I'm creating to free up valuable shelf space. I lean my body weight on the ladder as I start piling the heavy books into my arms, feeling old and out of touch because I've never even *heard* of half these celebrities.

'If it's taken you this long to realise ...'

I scream at the unexpected voice in the empty shop and jump so much that I fall off the ladder, clinging to the sides and trying to lower myself down with all the grace of an octopus on an ice rink as the books go clattering to the floor. I quickly assess myself for injuries – just pride this time, thankfully – and despite the shock, I can't help smiling when I see who it is. I *knew* he'd have made a point of saying goodbye, no matter how busy it was. My heart is pounding with the shock of his sudden appearance and how good he looks even as the sight of his ever-present smile loosens something in my chest. He's wearing a long-sleeved teal T-shirt with the sleeves rolled up to his elbows, and there's a silvery-grey tie around his neck, loosely knotted at mid-chest for presumably decorative purposes only because a business tie doesn't go with the casual top at all. He has a lightness about him, a joy that makes things seem brighter than they are.

'First rule of working in a bookshop – always check for strays before you close up.' He bends down and collects up the dropped books, choking on the dust they've released. 'Sorry, I didn't mean to startle you.'

'It's all right, I should have known to stay away from ladders.' I hold my arms out for the stack of books he's picked up. 'What were you doing back there? Hiding?'

'I didn't realise the time. I don't wear a watch, I can't see the clock from back there, and I could hear you chatting to customers. It didn't occur to me that it was so late until it all went quiet.'

I don't know why I asked him that – what do I think he's doing? Hiding for nefarious purposes? The words *nefarious* and *Dimitri* don't belong in the same sentence – he's the smiliest, chattiest, furthest thing you could get from nefarious.

'You were saying you own a bookshop?'

I'm *so* glad he overheard me talking to myself. Luckily I didn't get as far as the inspirational pep talk I was about to give myself. 'No, I mean, I really own it. I'm not looking after it while Robert's away. I'm not taking care of it until he comes back. It's not 'our' shop – it's actually mine. And if I want to keep it then things have got to change. I might not know much about selling books, but I do know something about loving books, and this – .' I indicate the shop around me – 'is *not* a book lover's paradise. Look at the state of these shelves.'

Dimitri's eyes follow the hand I throw out towards the shelf in front of me, nearly dropping the pile of autobiographies again.

'I think quirky was Robert's choice of words.'

'Chaos would be mine. Unmitigated disaster would be a close second.'

'Some words do spring to mind.'

'Which ones?'

He mulls it over carefully. 'Piss-up, brewery, organise.'

His turn of phrase makes me giggle, but I force myself to be serious. 'Something's got to change, because I still believe in bookshops, and I don't believe all the fear-mongering about the printed page dying out and bookshops falling in their thousands. Every year you see more and more positive reports about independent bookshops thriving and print sales increasing. Busy days like today prove that. There's so much potential here, but Once Upon A Page isn't living up to it.'

'So what are you going to do?'

'Some of these books have been on the shelf since I was a little girl. The shop was founded in Victorian times and I'm pretty sure that we've still got some of the original books. They're not rare and antique finds, they're just *still* here. That's not good stock turnaround. We've got old books, new books, used books, signed books, and ex-library books all muddled in together. We've got books that have been handled by customers so much that they're in terrible condition now. We've got every genre muddled on every shelf. To say that the whole lot needs sorting out is an understatement. There are thirty thousand books here. Someone came in today and asked me if we had something, and I opened my mouth to answer but no words came out. I mouthed at her helplessly like I was doing an impression of Heathcliff until she thought I needed medical attention and went away. But the only possible answer was … how the hell should I know?'

I look at him, aware that I haven't stopped for breath in quite a few minutes, and he nods in agreement, listening seriously.

'So firstly I need to know what's on the shelves. Geri was still in the Spice Girls when the last stock take was done. Seriously. I finally found it in the office last night. It's handwritten and dated 1998. And secondly, the customers need some way of *discovering* what's on the shelves, so they need to be completely sorted out and alphabetised because *no one* has a clue what books we've got or where they are if we have got them.' I glance at him. 'Except you, apparently. You don't happen to know what alphabet Robert used to organise his stock, do you? Because it certainly wasn't the regular one.'

'I think he'd worked here for so long that he knew the place off by heart and knew where every book was.'

'I know what I love about bookshops. I know what I loved about *this* bookshop years ago. I just hadn't noticed how much it had faded from what it used to be.'

'Robert struggled in his later years. He knew all this stuff, but he lacked the motivation and strength to sort them out. I think it's what pushed him into retirement in the end. He knew the shop was going under and he knew he didn't have the years left to fix it, so he chose someone else who could.'

I blush at the vote of confidence. Not many people in my life think I can *do* anything.

'You know the shop's going under too?' I ask, wondering why it seems to be common knowledge for everyone but me.

He considers it for a minute before answering. 'I spend a lot of time here. I see the number of customers Robert has – or *doesn't* have. It doesn't take a genius to work out that when you make that much of a loss for that many years, it can't continue for much longer.'

His words make a shiver go down my spine, not the usual tingle that he's been responsible for in the past few days. 'This shop is my dream. I'm not going to let it go without a fight. I've never had anything worth fighting for before, but this place *is*. I'm not going to step aside and let some smarmy property developer knock it down. I'm going to turn things around.'

Even as I speak, I wonder where this confidence is coming from. I expected to be a wibbling wreck in the face of the accounts last night, but each red minus sign made me realise that I'm closer than I thought to pleading with the horrible Drake Farrer to take the shop off my hands, and I am *not* going to let that happen. I can't afford new stock and fancy gimmicks to get people in, but I *can* make this shop the best it can be with what it already has – books. Lots of books.

'So what are we doing then?'

'We?'

'Well, you're going to let me help, right? I don't want to go home yet – there's something magical about being in a bookshop after closing time.'

I like how easy-going he is and how he seems to find something positive at every turn. There's something about him that makes me want to step back and appreciate things.

I hand him the stack of biographies back with a grin. '*We're* sorting out each shelf one at a time. My laptop is on the counter with a blank spreadsheet open on the screen, and *we're* painstakingly putting every title, author, genre, publication date, and number of copies into it, which *we're* going to update on a weekly basis with what's been sold so we've got some hope of having a clue what's actually on these shelves, and we're also creating a sale section and an unsellable section. There are so many old books here that I can't possibly expect money for. I thought I'd give them away for free, or maybe do that thing where people hide books around town for others to find …'

'That's a fantastic idea. I was at a hospital in London with Dani a few years ago and she found one hidden in the children's ward. It made her day. She read it and then we went and re-hid it for someone else to find.'

'Then we'll do that.' I watch him, wanting to pry for more info, but he quickly takes the books across to the counter.

'Where are you putting the sale section?'

'Over there.' I gesture towards an empty space near the picks-of-the-week table. 'There are two spare tables in the cupboard under the stairs, they'll fit together, and I'll load them with these books that have been sitting here for donkey's years and clearly aren't going anywhere: £2 for hardbacks, £1 for paperbacks. It'll clear shelf space, shift some books, and bring in more money than they're earning by sitting up here gathering dust.'

After clearing another three shelves, I run upstairs to get some cleaning products and a duster, and when I come down, Dimitri has dragged the two tables out of the office and is clipping them together as I climb back up the ladder and start cleaning the shelving, daydreaming about how I can make this place my own.

'How did the book balancing go?' he asks, bringing me out of the reverie with a crash. 'Was your first look at the accounts as bad as I suspect it might've been?'

I hold my hands up like they're scales and then dramatically drop one down so it clonks onto the shelf. 'Not well. I'm not good with numbers and figures so I'm not even sure I'm reading them right … but I think "struggling" would be the word of choice to describe the shop …' I trail off as I realise how unprofessional it is to talk to a customer about my business woes

Like he can read my mind, he says, 'I'm not an ordinary customer. You can talk to me. I studied business at uni. I know a bit about figures and stuff …'

I think about it for a moment. On one hand, it's no one else's business and I *should* keep it to myself because it's my problem, not his, but on the other hand, I want someone to know. Since Monday, I've felt adrift here, thrown into the deep end to learn as I go, and I *am* completely out of my depth when it comes to the business side of things. Robert left his new address, but no phone number so I can't keep hassling him with questions, and

I've got no one to turn to. My sister thinks I'm mad for taking it on, the only use Bobby has ever found for a book is when a wonky table leg needs balancing, and the only part of my life that my mum's interested in is who I'm going to marry. She was pleased about my win solely because 'business owner' will look more attractive to potential matches than 'waitress'. And there's something about Dimitri that I just like. He's positive and cheerful, and that's something that's been missing from my life for a while now.

'Robert was barely making a profit. The occasional good week was the only thing keeping him afloat, and every bit of his earnings seem to be tied up in paying business rates and public and premises insurance. His only expenses were second-hand books from car boot sales and electricity for the shop. He must've been paying for his own essentials like food and bills from his savings because he hasn't taken a wage in years, and he hasn't bought any new books in months.'

'He never worried about anything. He thought that there was no point stressing about a bad week because the next one would be better. He lived by the mantra that one way or another, everything would be all right in the end.'

'Yeah, but it won't, will it? Not if everything stays exactly as it is. Things are failing.' I glance at him and then back at the dusty shelves in front of me. 'Fast.'

'Once Upon A Page might be on its last legs, but it's not sunk yet. There's still a chance to pull things around, and you're already making the best start possible. We can do this, Hallie.'

I appreciate his blunt but cheerful words, and his use of the term 'we', like we're somehow in this together. Having support, a gorgeous friendly face who seems to know what he's talking about, buoys my confidence in my ideas for this place. 'So, business studies?' I ask, because he seems like the furthest thing from a businessman.

'It was a long time ago. Before I realised that life's too short to do something you hate. I'm not that person anymore. Now I just draw pictures for a living.'

'What's your ultimate dream?'

'To have my own gallery. And to have a book published.'

'Well, you're well on the way with *Pentamerone*. You're going to do a book signing here when it comes out, right? When's the release date?'

'We're not that far along in the process yet.' He suddenly seems awkward and clammed up, and I wonder if I've been too nosy.

He's quiet as he piles more books into his strong arms, and I find myself distracted by the way his biceps flex under his teal shirtsleeves as he takes the stacks across to the counter.

'What's your favourite book?' I ask because *something* has got to get my mind off his biceps. And forearms. And the curve of his chest, and how just a hint of collarbone shows above the rounded neckline of his T-shirt …

He gasps in mock horror. 'You can't ask me that! That's like asking a parent to pick their favourite child. I could do you a top thirty, but you'll be collecting your pension by the time I've decided on it.'

It makes me giggle and something in my chest floods with warmth. He's so much like me, and I love that he 'gets' loving books. If I asked my family that question, Nicole would say the last book she heard of but hadn't read just to get me off her back, Bobby would say 'The Highway Code' because it's the only book he's ever read without a secondary school English teacher breathing down his neck for an essay afterwards.

'Well, I was thinking we should start doing personalised recommendations – you know, those little cards on the shelf in front of the book with a note from the bookseller saying what they enjoyed about it? I've been noticing that picks of the week are popular. People come in to discover new books rather than with something already in mind.'

'And you want recommendations from *me*?'

'If you wouldn't mind writing out a few notes about books you've enjoyed, I'd love to display them. Customers want recommendations, and you love books and obviously have excellent taste.'

He looks up at me, holding my gaze as a smile twitches his lips. 'Wouldn't mind? I'd be *honoured*. No one ever asks me for book recommendations.' The smile he's been trying to hold back lights up his face. 'Can I sign them off as the bookshop's resident artist?'

I grin. 'You can sign them off as the prime minister's poodle if you want. I can't recommend a whole shop of books by myself, and I'd love for you to be involved. If people like the idea, I was thinking we could extend it to customers too. I've had two people come in over the past few days, not knowing Robert's left and wanting to tell him how much they enjoyed a book he recommended, and it's got me thinking. You know how you feel when you finish an amazing book, and it's kind of a happy sigh and immediate desire to tell someone, *anyone*, how good it was? I always like going on Amazon and reading the reviews to see if other people enjoyed it as much as I did. And I always want to write one, but I can't articulate how much I enjoyed it and it just comes across as fan-girly and obsessive. People want to tell people when they've enjoyed a book. I was thinking we could have a stack of little cards and if anyone mentions that they've enjoyed something, I could ask if they fancied writing a little note to highlight it to others …'

He's stopped in the middle of taking a stack of books from me, his arms frozen in mid-air, and he's grinning like I've announced the secret of getting free chocolate every day for life. 'That's a fantastic idea. That's exactly how I feel when I finish a great book and I have no one to tell. It'd be great to come in the next morning and write a little bit about it. You'll have to stop me rambling though. I do have a tendency to go on a bit … I don't know why I'm telling you that – you've obviously noticed … I say *while* rambling … I'm going to shut up now.'

94

Apart from how utterly adorable he is, the main thing I've taken from that conversation is that he must be single. Why does it make a little sparkle run through me? Why do I care if he's single? As if he'd be interested in me. He's *gorgeous* and talented and lovely. I'm clumsy and flustered and so far away from looking for a relationship that I may as well be in Outer Mongolia. I do better in relationships with fictional book boyfriends only. Real ones have never worked out for me. I've never felt a spark like the ones I read about. The only time I ever did feel chemistry with anyone ... well, that didn't work out either. I've decided that men are better on the page. Love doesn't happen like it does in books, and I'd rather get my happily-ever-afters that way, because it never happens in real life.

'Kids would love it too.'

It takes me a moment to realise he's not talking about fictional book boyfriends and has gone back to the index card idea.

'It would make children feel important if you asked them to recommend whatever book they read last. Anyone who loves books generally loves talking about books.' He takes the books from my arms, puts them on the table and then comes back. 'You're good at this, Hallie. I don't mean to overstep the mark, but you clearly doubt yourself sometimes, and I just wanted to say from the perspective of an outsider that Robert absolutely picked the right person.'

I blush and my throat closes up, unsure if I'm about to burst into nervous laughter or embarrassing tears. Or both. 'Thanks,' I croak at him.

He takes another stack of books from me. 'So, after that totally unfair question, it's my turn to ask – what's your favourite book?'

'Ah, see I defy the laws of being a book lover because I do actually have one that's really special to me – just a little bit more special than the rest. *Tiger Eyes* by Judy Blume, do you know it?'

He shakes his head.

'My dad died when I was twelve, and a few months later, I was in a charity shop with my granddad. He'd gone to try something on, and I was sitting in front of the bookshelf – obviously, it was always my favourite place in any shop. It was right by the till, and this random woman got her change, came over and handed me a pound coin, and told me to buy myself a book. I remember being really touched by the kindness of strangers.

'Anyway, I loved Judy Blume books. I'd devoured all the ones my school and local library had and my granddad had given me book vouchers for my last birthday, which all went on Judy Blume books too, and I found one on the shelf in the charity shop that I'd never heard of before. It was 65p, and I know that because I've still got the same copy with the original price sticker on. I don't think I even read the back of it, just bought it with the money this lovely stranger had given me, and it felt like fate. It was like the book had found me at exactly the moment I needed it most.

'It's about a girl called Davey who's just lost her dad and how she's coping with the grief and emotions. Her mum takes her and her little brother to stay with an aunt and uncle that she doesn't know, and she goes climbing in the canyons of New Mexico even though they tell her it's too dangerous. She meets this mysterious boy called Wolf whose own father is dying and they help each other through the grief. She's reckless and angry at the world and the empty canyons represent the vast hole in her life.

'It was the first time I'd ever recognised myself in a book. It was the first time I realised that books could be written about people like me. I understood Davey, I climbed into the canyons with her, I met Wolf, I discovered I wasn't alone in the way I was feeling after my dad's death. I felt isolated from my friends at school because they didn't know what it was like, but I clung to that book and read it over and over again, sobbing into it every time because the book "got" it. Davey got it. It made me feel less alone. It was the first time I'd ever read present-tense narration and it transported me there. The style really captured me.'

I pause to take a breath because I've been rambling for so long, and when I look down from the ladder, Dimitri's smiling at me. 'What?'

'This is why books are so important. It's why kids should be encouraged to enjoy reading – because books can change lives and make people feel not alone when they most desperately need it.'

'Have you ever read a book that's *so* special you don't want to tell anyone about it? You just want to keep it to yourself so it's all yours? My sister wasn't a reader and my mum had very specific tastes and I never told them about that book because I didn't want them to ridicule it. It was *mine*. And with the lovely stranger giving me money to buy it, it was like my dad had somehow sent it to me, and I didn't want anyone else to have that.' My eyes are filling up the more I talk about it, and I turn away to scrub a particularly stubborn spot on the shelf.

I know he can hear the wobble in my voice, but I appreciate that he doesn't make a big deal out of it. 'No wonder you always wanted to be a bookseller.'

'I volunteered in the library when I was sixteen. I always wanted to be a librarian, but libraries were closing left, right, and centre when I left school – it wasn't a viable career path. I thought about trying to get into publishing but most publishers were London-based and moving there was too scary, and this corner of the world always felt too small to pursue it in any other way.' I watch him as he goes over to type in the titles of every book so far chosen for the sale section. 'How about you? What's your story? How did you get into drawing? Actually, it feels wrong to say that because what you do is not just drawing. You're an *artist*. How do you get into the world of illustrating children's books?'

'Do you want the superficial, flippant answer that I always give, or do you want me to overshare?'

'Oh, overshare, always. Usually at inappropriate moments in front of inappropriate people.'

'I'd agree, but that would imply that I actually talk to people.' He laughs, but I like how introverted he seems. He's a bit of an enigma, really. He seems happy and cheerful but also sad and contemplative sometimes. He talks to customers and gets involved with questions but it's easy to see that he's uncomfortable when the shop's busy.

'I was terrible at school. The only things I was good at were art and reading. My father forced me into studying business at uni, but halfway through I quit and got into an art school in Oxford, and after I graduated, I worked on a series of graphic novels. Do you know *Death Note*?'

'I've seen the films. The original Japanese ones were amazing. I flicked through the anime in a bookshop after I watched them.'

'Well, they were a bit like that – the art style and the weird, otherworldly, eerie tone. I got a literary agent and then a publisher signed me for all three …'

I go to congratulate him because that's an amazing achievement, but his tone isn't a happy one, and he's already said he hasn't had anything published.

'My little sister was ill all her life. She had a form of cancer when she was a toddler, and had a leg amputated at four and an arm at six. My mum was her carer. She had everything under control. My sister was in remission for a long time. She could get around in her wheelchair, but she also had a learning disability that meant her mental age was a lot younger than her years. She went to a special school and things were great for a while, and then my mum died. She went out one night and never came back. She had a van that was modified for Dani's wheelchair and it flipped over on a roundabout not far from our house and she was gone. So I stepped into her role. I moved back home and became my sister's carer. Family comes first and Dani needed me. I tried to keep up with the deadlines but I couldn't do it. I lost the publishing deal and eventually the agent. So for the past seven years, I've been living my mum's life and caring for my sister. Not long after Mum died, the cancer came back and Dani couldn't beat it this time. She died last year. Since then I've been alone, trying to find my way in the world again ...' His voice breaks and he turns away.

It's probably a good thing I'm still up the ladder, because if I was any nearer to him, I doubt I'd be able to stop myself giving him a hug. Instead, my fingers grip on to the side rails so tightly that it's a wonder the wood hasn't started splintering. I haven't found the right words to say before he speaks again.

'Sorry, I didn't mean to dump all that on you. It was such a big part of my life that I can't explain how I got to this point without mentioning it.'

'What about the rest of your family? Didn't they help?'

'I've got an older brother but he wasn't interested. He'd rock up once every few months and take her out for a couple of hours, giving me a fun chance to catch up on housework. My dad's still around but he and my mum were divorced, and it was an *ugly* battle. Things with my father are ... complicated. Before my mum died, I hadn't been home for a really long time because of that.'

'I'm sorry.' I feel inadequate because I don't have the words to tell him how awful it sounds and I daren't vocalise how much I want to give him a hug.

'So no, it was just me. We read together because she loved to read. I drew pictures because her eyesight was failing and she struggled to imagine the images described in books and the middle-grade books she was into by the end didn't come with pictures. That's how I found *Pentamerone*. She loved fairy tales but was too old for kids' ones and too young for YA or adult books, so I went on the hunt for something darker than Disney and more original. I baked because Dani loved to get involved. She could have mixing bowls on her lap and stir with her good arm. Every morning she'd give me some random flavour combinations and I'd try to find something to bake with them by the end of the day. So there you go. That's why I love how much you enjoy my baking. It's something I find relaxing and de-stressing, but I always did it for someone else to enjoy, and something's been missing in my life without having anyone to share it with.'

My fingers are actually cramped from how tightly they're curled around the wooden ladder. I always say the wrong thing so my natural reaction in a situation like this is to go over and give him a hug, but there's no way that would be appropriate. 'Thank you for telling me,' I settle on eventually, because I get the impression it's not something he talks about easily and I want him to know I realise that. 'I love hearing people's life stories. You know when you're on a bus and a random old woman sits next to you and starts chatting and by the time you get off, you know all about her childhood, where she met her husband, how he proposed, what their wedding was like, where she worked, where her children live, and what her grandchildren's favourite games are? Most people try to avoid that woman, but I love it.'

'So I'm a nattering old woman? Thanks.' He gives me a grin, and it makes us both giggle, but this time, there's a hint of vulnerability under his smile. It really hits me how much people can hide behind a smile. Dimitri is so happy, easy-going, and cheerful. I would never have guessed he'd been through anything like that.

'I love stories. I love learning about people and getting glimpses into their lives. Like those inscriptions you find written inside the cover of second-hand books – I love making up stories about the giver and receiver of those books. Sometimes the messages can be so heartfelt that you wonder how anyone ever had the heart to chuck the book out.'

'Robert always used to say the same thing.' He nods when I look across at him in surprise. 'He dealt with a lot of second-hand books and he always used to read those dedications and say, "How could anyone want to get rid of this? Doesn't it mean anything to them anymore?" I thought they'd decrease the value of books he was trying to sell, but he thought it was a sign of how loved a book had been. He was always reading them out loud and trying to get me interested.'

I watch his brown hair flop forward as he leans over the counter, typing the titles into my laptop before he puts each book on the sale table. He must still be struggling with so much grief, but everything about him is light and happy, and he makes everything seem brighter just by being here.

'How can you be so positive?' I ask before I realise I'm going to say anything. 'I mean, after everything you've been through, I'd expect you to be sad and angry at the world ...'

'I always believe that something wonderful is about to happen.'

It stops me in my tracks, knocking me off-guard because it's such a lovely sentiment. A view of life that I *don't* have. I don't think like that. I'm always waiting for the next sucker punch, predicting the next thing that will go wrong, counting down to the next embarrassment, the next accident, the next time I wish the ground would open up and swallow me whole. 'Yeah, but ... to you?' I shake myself. 'Usually wonderful things only happen to other people.'

'Says the girl who's just *won* a bookshop ...'

'Present circumstances excluded, obviously.' I tell him about how I believe my luck somehow collected up in a stagnant pond until it overflowed like a sparkling waterfall in that once-in-a-lifetime moment when Robert picked my ticket.

'But that came out of the blue. You never saw it coming, and suddenly, your life changed in an instant. That's exactly what I mean – we never know what's around the next corner.'

'In my case, it's probably a bus waiting to mow me down,' I mutter, even though I have no right to complain about my luck at the moment, and I can't exactly moan about my life to someone who's just shared these tragedies in his life and is somehow still smiling. It must take a certain kind of person to give up their own life, deal with their own grief, and still step into the caring role he took over. I can't imagine the kind of courage and self-lessness it takes to do that, especially alone.

I move from top to bottom of the shelf, keeping the few auto-biographies that might still be popular, and moving downwards, sorting celebrity lifestyle, coffee-table books, and other famous-in-some-way authors into piles of fiction, non-fiction, second-hand, and new. It feels like quite an achievement to complete one of the tall cherry wood shelving units and leave it clean and smelling of lemon-scented polish, and with two empty shelves to transfer other books onto and clear some of the haphazard stacks on the floor.

Time seems to move faster here. It's not even seven p.m. yet, and between us, we've started on the stock take, dusted a *lot* of books and cleaned up shelves that hadn't been cleaned in far too many months. And we've made a start on filling the sale table. When I ask Dimitri if he wants to go home yet, he laughs like it's the most absurd question he's ever heard, and I try to ignore the little thrill because I don't want him to go home yet either.

I slide the ladder along, still unable to believe that this magical place is mine and sliding ladders along shelves of books is part of my everyday life now. I move on to the 'Classics' shelf and call out to Dimitri to add a new section to the spreadsheet. On the top shelves are forgotten editions of everything from Shakespeare plays to Jane Austen, the Brontë sisters, and Charles Dickens.

'*Great Expectations*.' I pull the battered old copy out. 'My first ever Dickens book. Everyone in school hated having to read this in English class, but I loved it. I identified a worrying amount with Miss Havisham. I always thought I'd end up as a sad, lonely old bat, wearing a wedding dress and only one shoe. Although, to be fair, stopping all the clocks would be a great excuse for always being late.'

'Me too.' He laughs. 'With the loving it in school bit, not the identifying with Miss Havisham bit.'

'We've got at least three versions of *Wuthering Heights*.' I pull them out one by one and blow dust off each different cover. 'Do you think I should start reading them aloud to Heathcliff to teach him about his namesake?'

'Yes, I think reading to fish is totally normal. It's bound to catch on, especially if you do it in public in the middle of a crowded shop. People will definitely *not* think you're nuts,' he calls back, making me laugh.

'These books are still popular. They shouldn't be hidden away up here.' I lovingly stroke a dusty, battered copy of *Pride and Prejudice*. 'And now we've got *Pride and Prejudice and Zombies* in with them. That doesn't belong with the classics.'

I dust each book off and stack them onto the empty shelves beside me so I can clean each section before I put them back, dusting each book as I pull the classics down from the uppermost shelf they've been relegated to.

'Aww, *Les Misérables*.' I pull out the Victor Hugo classic and clutch it to my chest. 'I love this book. All right, it's a bit long-winded and in the middle of monumental battle scenes you get three chapters on the history of the Parisian sewer system, but I felt like a rebel manning the barricades when I read this for the first time. I could also sing you the musical word for word, back to front while standing on my head. But I won't. Because you don't deserve that, and I don't need any more problems here when I cause all the window glass to break.'

'I love the musical. I confess to never reading the doorstop of a book though.'

'It's brilliant – it adds so much depth to the musical.' The spine is cracked from being read, and I run my fingers over the red, white, and blue cover, a version I've never seen before, and open it to look at the copyright page for a date. 'Aww, would you look at this?'

There's a handwritten note inside the cover that reads:

My dearest Esme,

Victor Hugo was correct when he said that the power of a glance is underestimated in love, and yet, what other way does love begin? You lit up my life from the very moment I laid eyes on you. One glimpse of you was all it took, and I believe, my dearest mademoiselle, that I am a little bit in love with you.

Forever,

Sylvester

'Those are Eponine's last words when she finally confesses her love to Marius before she dies,' I say when Dimitri appears at the edge of the aisle. 'Isn't that the most romantic thing ever?'

I hand the book down to him from the ladder. 'This must be how he told her he loved her. How lovely is that? I'd have married him on the spot for that.'

Dimitri snorts as he reads the message, but I can easily imagine how Esme must've felt upon opening that book. What a lovely way of telling someone you love them. Did she already like *Les Mis*? Did he just think she'd like it? I would *love* a guy to buy me books, and to write such a heartfelt, meaningful message ... Why can't there be men like this in my life? Men who buy books and write declarations of love inside are sorely missing from my doomed love life. In fact, I've never met a man who didn't question the number of books I had, never mind buying me more.

'Very sweet.' He hands it back to me. 'Very defaced.'

'This edition was published in 2005.' I run my fingers over the biro message. 'This could've been the very start of their relationship. They could be married with children by now. Oh my God, they could have named their children Enjolras and Courfeyrac and Combeferre.'

'A whole *barricade* of children. Robert would've loved your enthusiasm. Like I said, he was equally enthusiastic about messages in books.'

'I wonder if there are any more. According to the accounts,

he'd been buying a lot of used books lately.' I run my fingers along the spines until I find one that looks particularly well loved and open the cover in anticipation. Nothing.

I take another one and find a random scribble inside that can't possibly mean anything, not even in Hieroglyphics or Wingdings. Inside a copy of *The Amazing Adventures of Kavalier and Clay* are the words '*love, Dad*' and I find a copy of *War of the Worlds* by HG Wells with the words, '*Congratulations on finishing your GCSEs, I bet you never want to see this book again!*'

I hold on to one of the ladder rungs and lean out to look at the shelves around me. 'Don't you think that's a *lot* of books with messages inside them?'

He shrugs. 'It's a second-hand bookshop. Well, a bookshop that deals with both new and second-hand books. You know what I mean. You're always going to find some used books have scribblings in them.'

'Yeah, but … that's like an unnatural ratio?'

He takes a copy of *Vanity Fair* from the shelf, opens it and holds up the blank pages inside the cover. 'See? Nothing.'

I don't know what I'm expecting really. I've always had a thing about messages written in books. They feel special somehow, like they bear traces of their readers' lives. A glimpse into a stranger's life, a view into something that was once important to someone. The giver and the receiver. Whenever I see them, I wonder about who wrote them and who they gave them to. Were they lovers, friends, or family? Did the giver spend hours feeling out the perfect book to purchase? Was the receiver pleased? Did they read it? Did they love it? Did they think, 'Why the hell has this person chosen such an awful book for me?' Did the gifter's choice affect their relationship in any way? Did the giftee start wondering if there could be something more between them given how well the other person knew their taste in books – or did they start questioning their relationship because the giver clearly didn't know them at all?

Dimitri pushes *Vanity Fair* back into the snug space on the shelf, and that's another good point – some of these books are packed so tightly that it's the equivalent of a gym workout to squeeze them in, and you can't pull one out without it taking two or three on either side with it. Robert didn't seem to realise that there can be a balance between loving books and a customer-friendly shop. I mentally add it to the endless list of jobs in my head – take at least one book out of every shelf so browsing is actually possible.

'Oh, for God's sake. The organisation of these shelves just gets worse. There's another *Pride and Prejudice* down here.' I lean down to pull it out of a lower shelf that's full of thrillers and four shelves below where the rest of the classics are.

'Aww, that was my mum's favourite book,' he says.

I know he's not impressed by the mutilation of innocent books, but I can't resist a peek inside the cover to make sure. 'Oh wow, listen to this.' I read out the gorgeous message, written in age-blurred blue biro on the title page. *'To the man who brought joy back into my life, you will forever be an even better Mr Darcy than Colin Firth!'*

'My mum loved Colin Firth,' Dimitri interjects. 'She was obsessed with that BBC adaptation when it came out.'

'Thank you for giving me a reason to get up every morning. I would never have learnt how to smile again without you. "We are all fools in love."' I read out the quote from *Pride and Prejudice*. *'I love you more than words can ever express. Always forever, Della.'*

'My mum's name was Della …' Dimitri says slowly. He holds both hands up towards me and I wordlessly put the book into them.

'This is my mum's handwriting.' He runs his fingertips over the words on the title page like they might disintegrate at any moment.

The hairs on the back of my neck stand up. I've never under-stood the saying of feeling like someone walked across your grave before, but I suddenly feel a chill and a shiver goes down my spine. 'Your mum wrote that?'

'She must have.' He shakes his head, looking lost for words. 'And this was her copy. Or, I mean, it's got the same cover and it looks well read enough. I never noticed it was missing from her library, but it must be.'

I like how posh he sounds in calling bookshelves a library. Unless his mum had an actual library, obviously, and who has their *own* library other than The Beast? 'To your father?'

'Hah.' He lets out a sarcastic burst of laughter and then composes himself. 'There's no way this was to my father. My father's never read a book in his life and he's *proud* of that. Also, that lamppost outside has got more romantic bones in its body than my father has. This couldn't possibly be to him.' He stares at the message for a long few minutes. 'It's definitely romantic, right? I'm not imagining that, am I? I mean, comparing him to Mr Darcy and mentioning Colin Firth, who she *loved*. This is not to a friend, right?'

I bite my lip, unsure of what to say. 'It doesn't sound like it,' I venture, aware of the implication if his mum was writing romantic notes to someone who wasn't her husband. 'You said your parents were divorced … It could've been after that?'

'That was only a few years before she died. This looks older.'

It does, he's right there. The biro has sort of fused with the paper so it's completely flat, there's none of the usual indentation you get after writing with biro. 'Maybe it's not as old as it looks,' I say, even though I don't believe myself any more than he does.

'It's okay. This is a good thing. Whoever it was, it means she had someone else. Someone who made her happy, which my father did *not*. She deserved happiness after what she went through with that man. She deserved someone who loved her and appreciated her. If she had that with someone else, maybe it explains why she put up with my father for so long. She handled him with … serenity and detachment. Maybe this is why – because she was happy elsewhere.'

I'm desperate to ask him what the story with his father is, but apart from him being a relative stranger and it being none of my business, he looks lost in thought, still staring down at the book in his hands.

'Whatever this was, it must've been going on for years. It sounds like she was head-over-heels in love with him. She was very practical and sensible. She wouldn't have written something like that unless she meant it, and she wouldn't have fallen in love that deeply in a short amount of time. And my father would've gone mad if he'd found out. She must've taken huge risks to see someone else, and my mother was not someone who took risks.'

'Love makes you do things you wouldn't normally do.'

'And how did it end up here? Whoever she gave it to … gave it away? She couldn't have been that important to him then, could she?'

'It doesn't have to mean anything. And it's quite old … Something could've happened to the owner and his family got rid of his books. It could've been thrown out accidentally. Something could've happened between them – a row and he threw out all her stuff. You know, the old-fashioned version of deleting someone from your phone and blocking them on social media? Relationships can end, no matter how much people care for each other. He could've been devastated after she died and found all reminders too painful …'

'And you say I'm the one who always looks on the bright side …'

It makes me laugh and release my grip on the ladder, appreciating the giggle in the middle of such a serious moment.

He holds the book to his chest. 'Can you … can I put it in the office? I don't want it to be sold.'

'You can have it, Dimitri. It's yours.'

'No. I feel like it ended up here for a reason. Like it was meant to be here. Like we were meant to find it. I mean, what are the chances? There are thirty-something thousand books in this shop and you come across one with a message written by my dead mother. It has to mean something. And I think it should stay here until we find out what.'

'I told you there was an unnatural ratio of dedications in these used books ... *Now* do you think there could be more?'

He looks up at me with that ever-present smile pasted firmly back on his face, his blue eyes twinkling again. 'I guess we're going to find out.'

'We?' I say for the second time this evening, trying to hide a smile because I already know what he means.

He grins. 'I'm involved now. And so are you. *We're* going to take an inventory of this whole shop and *we're* going to find out who the man in this note is. Together.'

'How on earth do you think I can help with that?' I say, even though I had no intention of letting him do it on his own. I was going to get involved whether he liked it or not.

'I don't know. But you found it – that's got to mean something. I've still got all my mum's stuff. I'll see if I can face having a look through it and finding out if there's anything about this mystery man.'

Despite his smile, his voice shakes when he mentions looking through his mum's things, and I'm glad I've stayed up the ladder because those few rungs between us are the only thing stopping me hugging him, and *that* would've been even more inappropriate than the way I found myself watching his biceps move as he put those tables together and lugged around books, and I can't help feel a little thrill at the idea of spending more time with him.

Chapter 6

I haven't been able to get Dimitri's mum and her mystery man out of my head all night. It's so romantic – the kind of love story I've always imagined finding in one of those handwritten dedications, the kind of tale I've always made up but never believed could actually happen. I've never even told anyone how much I love looking inside second-hand books for those secret messages, knowing Nicole would ridicule me and my mum would tell me to get my head out of the clouds and look for a real man.

The only man I'm interested in seeing the next morning is Dimitri. I'm up early, which is a miracle in itself because I'm *never* up early, and there's a little flutter in my stomach at the thought of seeing him. I'm even looking forward to his cheery 'Hello!' as he pokes his head round the door. Usually I'm utterly against people who can be cheerful in the morning and feel they deserve the wrath of a thousand miniature Satans, but it doesn't apply with Dimitri.

By half past eight, I've drunk two cups of coffee, eaten more Cornflakes than is probably legal *and* managed to get the timing between dry and soggy right which is a miracle in itself, and now I'm pacing the aisles, plucking random second-hand books from the shelves and snapping their covers open like I'm trying to catch the messages inside before they go into hiding. I don't have much luck though – I only come across quick dedications like 'with love' and 'enjoy', but nothing that could be considered declarations of love or special wishes.

I'm still convinced there's an unnatural ratio of second-hand books with inscriptions in them though. Almost every one I pick up has got something written inside it, even if it isn't anything important, and my eyes are peeled through every one, trying to catch a glimpse of Della's distinctive looped writing, wishing I could find another one, something that answers the mystery that copy of *Pride and Prejudice* has stirred up. It would be amazing to greet Dimitri this morning with an answer to who the mystery man is or how that book ended up here.

Heathcliff is eating his breakfast of fish food flakes, so I wedge the door open with the book-shaped doorstop, and lean against the doorframe, watching the street waking up around me, like I see other shop owners do most mornings.

The air is heavy with the scent of fresh-baked bread and freshly brewed coffee from the deli, and bees are already buzzing around the flowers in the hanging basket on the Victorian-style lamppost near my door. I deadhead some of the faded pink petunias in it, shout good morning to the lady from the chocolate shop next door to the tailor, and my eyes wander to the steps leading up to the roof terrace. I know Robert said it needed repair, and Drake Farrer having part ownership of it doesn't fill me with joy, but I haven't even had a chance to go up there yet. I close the shop door behind me and dig the keys out of my pocket, jangling through them until I find one with 'roof terrace' written on the attached tag.

The staircase is criss-crossed with heavy chains holding up a hefty 'Danger: Keep Out' sign. Rust flakes off as I find the padlock locking the chains to the railings and push the key in, but it doesn't move when I try to turn it. The padlock's near the bottom

111

so I bend down to get a better grip on it and twist the key, but it's stuck.

It's probably one of those padlocks that are supposed to never rust. Promises like that are guaranteed to never work when they're in my vicinity. Like non-stick frying pans or easy-peel price stickers.

I try to at least get the key back out considering it's attached to my keyring and I can't leave the entire set of shop keys dangling out here all day. This is not the breezy stroll up to the roof terrace I'd envisioned when I came outside.

'Come on, you rusty thing,' I say through gritted teeth as I throw all my strength into it and give it one final pull, and at exactly the same moment, a voice says, 'Hello!' It makes me jump so much that my movement obviously catches the lock just right because it releases my keys and the momentum makes me go careening backwards and straight into Dimitri. Who is carrying a tray of two coffees. No. Who *was* carrying a tray of two coffees.

I look down as coffee soaks through his light blue shirt and navy waistcoat, and runs down my jeans, making me feel like I've wet myself. The cups are upside down on the floor and Dimitri's strong arms are around me, holding me up. In any other circumstances, this would be a not entirely undesirable position.

'That went well,' I mutter. It's become some sort of catchphrase for my life, especially when Dimitri's involved. On the plus side, it doesn't give me a chance to think about how *glad* I am that he got a full view of my oversized bum wriggling around as I fought with the lock.

Instead of pushing me back up, his arm slides around my waist and he dips me like we're about to go in for a Hollywood kiss. 'And people say I don't know how to sweep a girl off her feet.'

I come over all flushed, and it's not just because of the hot coffee running down my legs. He has *no* problem in the sweeping-off-feet department, and part of his charm is that he has no clue how charming he is.

He laughs as he tips me back upright and looks down at himself. 'I'm so glad I chose a pale shirt this morning. It's like I *knew* I was going to get coffee spilt on me today.'

'I think everyone who puts light-coloured clothing on in the morning knows, on some level, that they're going to get coffee spilt on them.'

I love the way his eyes get incrementally more twinkly as a smile spreads slowly across his face. 'Well, luckily, I'm well versed in the hazards of light-coloured clothing and carry a spare black T-shirt with me at all times. Do you mind if I pop inside and change? And you ... um ...' He waves a finger politely towards my crotch and I look down to see that my dark brown wet patch is spreading, and now I look like I've wet myself *and* like I'm in desperate need of an Immodium.

'Do you want to go up to the flat and get changed in the bathroom?' I ask as I let us into the shop and close the door.

'No, you carry on. You need it more than I do. Heathcliff won't mind me changing in here.'

I snort and choke at the same time, like all parts of my body are having a competition between themselves to do the most undignified thing possible in front of the most gorgeous man. Heathcliff might not mind but the idea of Dimitri changing is a bit too much for me. 'Are you kidding? Heathcliff's got a real thing for you. It'll make his day.'

'Or scar him for life. If you have to go and get Heathcliff Number Five today, you can't blame me.' He winks at me. 'I'll pinch one of your wet wipes from behind the counter though to make sure I don't smell of coffee all day.'

I toss him the packet and traipse up the stairs holding my dripping jeans up off the carpet. Obviously I was wearing my lightest-coloured stonewash blue pair today. I stick the kettle on, and after the fastest wash-down in the bathroom, I find a pair of black trousers – probably safer – and make two cups of coffee to make up for the spilt ones.

At the bottom of the stairs, I stop so abruptly in my tracks that I nearly have the second coffee-related incident of the morning. Dimitri's bare back is to me, and he's got a black T-shirt over his head and his arms up as sinewy shoulder muscles work to pull it down. If the thought of him changing was too much for me, the actual sight of it has caused my whole body to go into emergency override mode and although I should turn away and give him some privacy, I'm rooted to the spot, transfixed by the sight of all that pale skin dotted with freckles and his strong, muscular frame.

I'm so lost in thought that I don't notice I'm staring until the coffee mugs in either hand drift towards each other and hit with a clink that reverberates through the shop, making Dimitri jump. Heathcliff, who was also transfixed by the sight in front of him, gives me what can only be described as a fishy death glare.

'Oh God, I'm so sorry,' I stutter. 'I didn't … I was just going …' I gesture vaguely back where I came from, sloshing coffee around in the mugs to a dangerous level.

It's an understatement to say I can't form a coherent sentence as he pulls the bottom of the T-shirt down around his hips, straightening it until just a sliver of skin is showing, and I think I moan in disappointment when he tugs the plain T-shirt down and covers that too.

'It's fine, I'm done. And thankfully a very attractive pug walked past the window which took Heathcliff's attention, so he didn't keel over in shock either.'

I laugh, but the T-shirt has knocked his hair skew-whiff and I have never wanted to touch something more in my life.

He ruffles a hand through it so it sticks out in all directions and leaves it, looking adorably dishevelled as he cleans his glasses on the bottom of his T-shirt and puts them back on again.

My face is still burning red from the visual of so much skin, and I'm amazed by how hot a simple black T-shirt can look. He managed to escape coffee on his jeans, but he looks different without his shirt and waistcoat combo. Hot rather than quirkily sexy. *Really* hot. Even with the ever-present pencil behind his ear. I have never before considered how sexy a pencil behind the ear can be.

He comes over to take one of the coffee cups out of my hand and clinks it against mine in a toast. 'Good morning. Shall we start over?'

'I think that's a good idea,' I say, touched by how laid-back he is. He doesn't even seem annoyed that I spilt coffee on him *or* made him lose two cups of not-cheap coffee from the deli.

'So what were you doing before the thing that didn't happen? Exploring the roof terrace?' His glasses steam up as he takes a sip.

I nod. 'It would make an amazing reading space, but Robert said it needed repair. I was trying to see what I'm dealing with, but the first thing that needs replacing is that rusty padlock. It tried to absorb my key by osmosis.'

'Ah, WD-40's what you need.' He flips open the satchel and plunges his hand in, rooting around inside.

No way does he have WD-40 with him. 'And you just happen to have …'

He pulls out a blue and yellow can and thrusts it into the air in victory. 'I've got just the thing.'

Literally just the thing. 'What *don't* you have in that bag?'

'A giraffe?' he asks like he's not even sure himself, although I wouldn't be at all surprised if there was a strong possibility that his satchel did indeed conceal a giraffe.

It makes me giggle so much that it distracts me from him coming nearer.

'Before I go outside and try it, I don't smell of coffee, do I? I think I got it all off, but you can never be sure.'

He's standing near enough for me to sniff him. And actually expecting me to. My cheeks burn red again and I'm starting to think that red-faced and stuttery is my natural state of being and it's unusual when my cheeks are normal-coloured.

He definitely does *not* smell of coffee. I can feel my heart rate speeding up with how good he actually does smell. The powdery scent of the baby wipes, some sort of spicy clove aftershave, and the ever-present scent of pencil lead and shaved wood. 'No,' I choke out and have to take a sip of coffee to calm down.

'Good.' He doesn't notice my embarrassment as he takes the keys off the counter and walks towards the door. 'I've been curious to see what the roof terrace is like for ages. Robert never unlocked it. The stairs were too steep for him and he thought it was too dangerous to send anyone else up there.'

'Luckily, I'm not as health and safety conscious as he was.' It's still too early to open the shop, so I follow him outside and watch as he squirts the oil into the lock, jiggles it around a bit and then pushes the key in. It turns easily and the rusted padlock finally creaks open.

Between us, we untangle the chains and lift the 'Keep Out' sign away, and Dimitri steps back to let me go through first, so he's got a perfect view of my oversized bum as I walk up in front of him, and I think he's seen enough of that for one day. Chivalry isn't dead, but sometimes it should be. If he gets any closer, my giant wobbling bum will certainly finish the job and suffocate it for good.

The stone steps going up one side of the building are narrow, separated from the empty shop next door by a wobbly metal banister that was painted white once but is now covered in peeling paint revealing patches of rust. The metal fence continues all the way up and encircles the roof terrace as a safety barrier, although the wobbliness doesn't make it feel very safe at all. At the top of the steps, the space is paved with slabs in different shades of brown from caramel to honey-coloured, perfectly matching the bricks of the surrounding buildings. Some of the slabs are lifting around the edges and some bounce when you step on them.

'Wow,' Dimitri murmurs, stepping up behind me.

He's got a point there. To either side of us are the roofs of the surrounding buildings – to the right, the block that Drake Farrer owns, and to the left is the scented candle shop. We walk to the edge and look out over the river that crosses the street at the upper end and runs behind Once Upon A Page. The grassy banks are a popular walking spot but empty at this time of day, green grass and flowing water meandering along until it disappears into the hills on the horizon.

'It's beautiful up here,' I say, although I can see why Robert closed it. There are three sets of metal tables and chairs that look like they've spent a good few years being repeatedly rusted by rain and bleached by sunlight, and when I put my hand on the railing along the back, it wobbles and the paving dips underneath my feet.

'It's so romantic,' Dimitri says. 'You can imagine someone getting down on one knee and proposing up here.' He gestures towards the trees waving along the riverbank. 'The trees blowing in the breeze, the splash of the river, the trickle of the fountain from the street ... The wonky paving sending them flying like a seesaw the moment their knee touches down ...'

It makes me laugh, but I can honestly say that proposals were not my first thought upon seeing the terrace. 'You don't strike me as the romantic type,' I say, even though there's something inherently romantic about the tall, quiet, and handsome artist who lurks mysteriously in bookshops sketching ... well, giant fleas in his case, but you can't win 'em all.

'I'm better off alone. I've lost too many people to let anyone else in, Hallie.' He looks over at me like he owes me a personal explanation and then looks away again, his eyes on the point in the distance where the river disappears under a viaduct and into the hills. 'Relationships have never worked for me. I had a couple when I was still living in Oxford but none that lasted. Since I moved back here after my mum died, I couldn't bring that grief into a relationship, and then the responsibility of looking after my sister … it would've been too much to expect someone else to get involved in that. And since then … my life's been torn apart by grief. I can't take my heart being broken by love too.'

Even with everything he shared last night, I can't imagine him feeling like that. He's so endlessly cheery, and yet in some moments, I can see something quieter and hurting in him, and I take a step closer so our hands are next to each other on the railing.

'I still believe in love though,' he says. 'I'm not completely dead inside. I'd just rather read about it in books.'

'Have you ever been in love?' I ask, not even sure why I'm asking. It's not like it's relevant to me – I have no luck in relationships and I'm not looking for another one. Neither of us are interested in relationships. That's good. Something else we have in common.

'No.' He's quiet for a moment. 'Have you?'

'I thought maybe I was once, but I've never felt the way characters in books feel. I've never felt that fluttery feeling, that urge to just be near someone, that comfort of sitting doing nothing with someone. There's never been someone I'd do anything for or who would do anything for me, or anyone I felt I could share everything with.'

'What happened to Mr Maybe?'

'He fell in love with someone else and cheated on me for over a year. Eventually the woman he was seeing got fed up of being strung along and got in touch to let me know what was going on. But at least he proved that happily-ever-afters only happen in books and I'm better off getting my romance strictly from printed pages and the Kindle screen forevermore.' My foot presses against one of the cracked terracotta planters around the edge of the roof terrace. They still hold the dead twigs of what were once trailing wallflowers that twisted through the railings and dangled over the edges of the building, but now there's one solitary cabbage

118

white butterfly trying to find some nectar in the weeds that have made it their home.

'Aw, I'm sorry.' He knocks his shoulder into mine, making the railing wobble again. 'You can't give up though. Fairy-tale love is still out there somewhere, the kind that will make Colonel Brandon pale in comparison.'

Even though I love *Sense and Sensibility* and Colonel Brandon in particular, I don't believe him. The whole point of books is to experience something that is never meant for us in real life, but the gentle steel and sincerity in his voice makes me feel even wobblier than the railing itself. 'How can you still be so positive?'

'There will always be hopes and dreams to keep us going. There will always be something to look forward to, even if it's only the knowledge that things will get better. There will always be love. To look for, to hope for, to dream about. Maybe not even romantic love. A job you love, a friend you love, an animal, or a thing, or even a book that will improve your life. There will always be something good coming.' He nudges his shoulder into mine again and repeats, 'There will always be love.'

I'm surprised by how much my throat closes up and my nose burns with the familiar sting of tears. It's such a simple sentiment, but there's something so uplifting about it.

I swallow hard. 'If you ever want to do a line of inspirational prints or greeting cards or something, you could sell them in the shop. That's exactly the sort of thing people would buy.'

'Seriously?'

I nod, because I was kind of half joking and kind of not-joking-at-all at the same time.

'I'd love to do something like that. Something with a literary, bookish twist. You'd seriously let me do that?'

'Yes, yes, and a thousand times yes.' I can never resist an opportunity to quote *Pride and Prejudice*. 'Your artwork is *incredible*. I'd be honoured to stock it. I've been thinking about it anyway. Bookshops don't just stock books anymore – they have to diversify. I've had three people ask me where I got the book-shaped doorstops from and if they were for sale in the past few days. If I could get hold of something like that, and other gift-type things – mugs, keyrings, pretty pens and stationery. No one can resist a notebook, and tote bags are really popular. Any sort of bookish gifts.

'If you did some greeting cards, or prints mounted on card, we could get some pretty tissue paper to wrap them in, and display them on a stand of their own. Make everything affordable in a way that boutique gift shops aren't. Summer holidays aren't far away. There are going to be things like teacher thank-you gifts to buy, and of course, it'll be brilliant later in the year for Christmas ...'

I trail off, glad to have someone to share the idea with. I'm sure literary merchandise is a good way of pulling in non-readers or attracting customers who might not otherwise come in, but I still feel like I'm out of my depth and too new to this to be making huge changes to the shop, and still waiting for the moment it all goes wrong. And then there's the budget to think about. All this stuff is a great idea, but I have no idea how I'm going to afford it.

'It would be amazing. I could really use the money, and it's an absolute dream to have my stuff on display, on sale, and I've got so many ideas ... Ahhh!' He leans over the railing and shouts in joy at the empty riverbank, then turns back to me, slides his arms around my waist and picks me up, the loose paving clunking up and down under his feet. My arms encircle his shoulders and he pulls me tight against his body and spins us around.

I curl my fingers in his unkempt hair, laughing into his shoulder at the uninhibited glee as I get a little bit lost in the scent of hair wax, charcoal, and his woody, spicy aftershave. His breath moves the hairs at the back of my neck. My fingers curl tighter into his thick hair and my arms tighten around his shoulders. There's something about being in his arms that makes everything feel like it will be okay, and in this moment, nothing else matters.

It's a struggle to force myself to think clearly. 'What about your deadline? You must have one ...'

'It can wait.' He puts me down on a wobbly paving slab and something flashes across his face before he grins at me. 'And there you go, now I've got the initial awkwardness of inappropriately hugging you out of the way, we can hug anytime and it won't be awkward.'

It makes me smile as I finally take my hands off his arms, grateful to him for defusing my awkwardness with his own awkwardness until we're in such a jumble of awkwardness that it doesn't matter who started it. I want to say something witty and flirtatious, like how he can hug me anytime he wants and it isn't inappropriate at all, but I end up feeling a bit fluttery and stuttering out a mumbled agreement.

'What do you think about doing bookish characters and quotes from their books? Like *Alice in Wonderland*, *Narnia*, *Breakfast at Tiffany's* ... I mean, as long as the copyright's in the public domain and everything. Or famous quotes about reading and being a book lover.'

'You know what, I trust whatever you're going to come up with. Your attitude to life is what makes me smile. Just make them *you*, Dimitri, and they'll be brilliant.'

His face is so red that someone's going to post a letter in him in a minute.

'So all giant fleas and ogres then, yeah?' His smile is infectious in the best way possible, and I find myself feeling lightweight and giddy just by being close to him, and I know he's joking because he *cannot* stop smiling, and I'm suddenly so glad I said it. I'd been thinking about it since he drew that teddy for the little boy, but never in a million years thought he'd go for it, or that he'd have time given the deadline he must be working to for his publisher.

'Hal … I don't mean to be patronising and obviously it's nothing to do with me, but can the shop afford all that merchandise?'

I don't know whether to be offended that he thinks I can't manage my own retail budget or touched that he cares. And he's not exactly wrong. The shop *can't* afford it. 'I'm going to use my own credit card.' I try to sound authoritative, like I know what I'm doing. 'The shop is stuck in a vicious circle. Round and round we go – not making enough money so not being able to afford new stock. Changing the window displays is going to sell a couple of extra books a week, maybe. Reorganising every shelf will make it easier to find things, but it's not going to magically turn our fortunes around. It needs a boost, a stock injection, something to break the cycle and get new people in through the door.'

He goes to say something but I cut him off. 'I know it's not a good idea, okay? I know I should probably apply for some kind of business loan that I don't understand, but it'll only be for a while. When the shop starts making money again, I can take a proper wage and afford to pay it off. I've failed at every job I've ever had, Dimitri, I can't fail Once Upon A Page, no matter what it takes.'

'You're *not* failing it. You've only been here a few days. You're on exactly the right track. But Robert wouldn't want to see you get yourself into difficulties.'

'It'll be fine.' I hope he can't hear the wibble in my voice. 'Don't worry about it.'

I know he wants to say something else, but he stays quiet.

It's still not quite opening time, and it's even more peaceful up here than it is on the street below and walking down that is as relaxing as a massage in a spa with hot stones and whale noises. Up here, there's nothing but the chirping of spring songbirds, the splash of the river and the rustle of the leaves reaching to us from the trees on the riverbank while a swan glides along the water.

'Did you find any clues in your mum's stuff?'

He shakes his head. 'I had a look, but … my house is complicated. It's kind of left as it was. I started going through my mum's stuff after she died, but it upset Dani too much. She wasn't mentally capable of grasping that Mum wasn't coming back, so I left it. And now she's gone too and I've got her stuff to sort out as well and … it's a lot to face. I'd rather hide in bookshops and draw giant fleas.'

He makes it out to be a joke, but it's easy to see that it isn't funny. Without thinking, I shift my hand closer to his on the railing, not quite sure why either of us are holding on to it in the first place because I don't think it's stable enough to do anything in the event of a fall, and he shifts along incrementally so the sides of our hands are touching on the cold metal bars.

He shakes his head. 'How about you? Did you come across any more secrets hidden in book dedications?'

'Plenty, but none were significant.'

'You've been looking then?'

'Of *course* I've been looking. Did you really think you could leave me unattended in the shop overnight and I *wouldn't* look? Er, not that I wanted you to attend me or anything. That didn't sound right. There was meant to be absolutely no attending by anyone for either of us …' I realise I've made an innocent statement that he wouldn't have given a second thought into some sort of weird innuendo and embarrassed both of us. I glance down to the ground. It's not that far. If I jumped, I'd probably only sustain a broken ankle or two. It would be less embarrassing than this and would get me away from his beautiful blue eyes faster. 'I'm going to shut up now.'

He's laughing so hard he looks like he's about to fall over, but it still feels like he's laughing *with* me, not at me. Knowing he's prone to rambling himself somehow makes me feel better, like it's normal, like he gets it. 'What were your mum's other favourite books?' I ask, mainly to distract myself from how much I like his smile and his laugh. 'If *Pride and Prejudice* was her favourite, it stands to reason she might've shared some other books with the mystery man. We could start there?'

'She loved Virginia Andrews, but I couldn't tell you which one was her favourite. Other than that … I don't know. I'll have to look at the romance shelves and see if I recognise any other titles. She was always such a romantic. I always asked her how she could possibly be romantic with a man like Dad, but now I know. Finding that message last night answered so many questions I've always had and never knew I needed an answer to.'

In the distance across the river, a chapel bell chimes nine times.

'I need to open up,' I say, although the need is not that urgent judging by the quiet street below, but what is urgent is how much I'm going to hug him if I don't walk away right this second.

As we reach the bottom of the steps, a customer appears out of nowhere and tries to go in the locked door. I rush to open it for him and toss the keys back to Dimitri, who stays to put the chains and 'Keep Out' sign back across the stairway.

'Any ideas what you're going to do with it?' he asks when he comes back into the shop where the man I let in is rifling through the sale table with reckless abandon.

It's only 9.01 a.m. and the sale table has been much more popular than I anticipated.

'I don't know. It's not even mine. The property developer who owns the empty shop next door has got half of it, and he made it clear that he won't give me permission to do anything up there.'

'Drake Farrer?' Dimitri's face falls.

'You know him?'

'Most people in Buntingorden know Drake Farrer and most of them wish they didn't. I didn't realise *he* was the one who'd been hassling you.' He pushes his glasses up and pinches the bridge of his nose.

'He left me some sort of deed about the roof terrace.' I crouch down and rifle around the shelves underneath the countertop until I find where I buried it under a pile of books so I could pretend it didn't exist.

Dimitri takes it and scans over it, looking like he might actually understand it, which is more than can be said for me. 'He's got his solicitor to put a dividing line in at the stairs, so you're free to use your half, but you'd have to block off his half, and the access to it is shared between you, so opening it would require his permission.'

'How do you understand that?' I say more to myself than to him because he never fails to surprise me. 'It looks like gobble-degook.'

'I know a bit about property law. I studied it for a while. You could still use the roof terrace, it'd just need a *lot* of logistical planning.'

'And I'd need to get a builder or an architect or someone in, wouldn't I? They're going to cost more money than I have, and whatever profit the shop makes *has* to go back into buying stock and improving the shop itself. The roof terrace would be a lovely addition, but it's not safe and it needs more help than I know how to give it, and that's without whatever issues Drake Farrer will cough up. He wants this shop – he's not going to give me permission to make it better, is he?'

'Hal, about Drake Farrer ... There's something you need to—'

The sale table man limps up to the counter, struggling under the weight of all the books he's carrying. I tap their prices into the till and Dimitri leaps in to help pack them into the man's reusable shopping bags.

'Thanks,' I say after the customer leaves, constantly impressed by how kind Dimitri is. I barely know this man, but I feel like if I asked him to nip up to space and collect some moondust, he'd be straight on the phone to NASA.

'You're welcome.' He picks up the deed and hands it back to me. 'You need someone to buy that place next door and turn it back into a bakery. They could go halves with you then and share the space. It would be incredible to sit up there with cake and tea and read a book.'

His words conjure up a daydream of a warm spring day, a comfy chair up there, the scent of May blossom from the trees on the riverside, a good book and a gorgeous cake ...

We meet each other's eyes and smile, both clearly having the same daydream, except in mine, I'm sitting there with him, on a bench with his legs in my lap as we read each other passages of our favourite books and eat something he's baked ... When I snap back to reality, he's drifted so close that he's leaning on the counter and our arms are touching again, and I stare at them for a moment like I can't quite work out why.

He blinks like he was lost in a daydream and suddenly startles and pushes himself upright and pulls his arm away from mine. 'I'm going to grab *Pentamerone* and make it look like I'm working, but really I'm thinking up inspirational quotes and literary images to put on greeting cards.'

He's almost bouncing as he disappears into the shelves, and I can't help smiling at his enthusiasm. I'll be so *proud* to have any of his work on display here.

Customers start to trickle in and the sale table is quickly emptied, and the cash in the till has started to add up from lots of cheap books being sold, as opposed to few expensive ones.

Every time I look up from serving someone, I look over at Dimitri, and every time he looks up at the exact same moment and meets my eyes, and we smile at each other across the shop, and there's something so calming about his presence. I never did very well in shop floor jobs because I got too flustered when there was a queue. One time on the checkout at a DIY shop, a young couple in a hurry came up with forty tester pots of paint, and I had to scan every one of them individually while the man shouted at me to scan one and alter the quantity. While I was trying to explain they were all different brands and different prices, another man with a large trolley full of plants joined the

126

queue and started loudly telling everyone how much of a rush he was in, and then another woman with an armful of wallpaper came along and told him to shut up by saying, 'Don't rush the poor girl, she's obviously new.' I'd been working there for over a year, but I got so flustered with all of them watching me that my hand jerked and I knocked over a tester pot and, like dominoes, the whole lot went sliding onto the floor and smashed into an impressive number of pieces. I got fired, but all those shades of purple and blue made it the prettiest accident anyone had ever seen.

Maybe it's because it's a bookshop and things are naturally calm here. Or maybe it's because I know Dimitri's over there, silent support, and if things are busy, I have no doubt he'd jump in to help.

Apart from the customers who take random books from the shelves, wave them in the air to get my attention, and then call, 'Is this one on sale, love?' despite the fact there's a very clear notice on the sale table saying only books on this table are included, it's a good and busy day, but for once I'm counting down the hours until closing time, until Dimitri and I are alone again and taking stock of books and what other messages we might find.

Chapter 7

'What is this again?' I push my fork through the unidentifiable goop on my plate.

'Lasagne.' Mum says it like it's obvious.

It is not obvious. I have strong doubts about it being lasagne. And about it being edible.

Nicole and I share a glance. It's an unwanted reminder of every childhood teatime we shared. There are probably some benefits to living near your mum, but her cooking isn't one of them.

'Mum, you didn't use a pouch with "Whiskers" written on it, did you?'

Mum thwacks my sister good-naturedly with a tea towel. None of us are under any delusions about her cooking abilities, but at least she hasn't given up trying. That's what she always says anyway. Nicole and I wish she'd given it up about thirty years ago.

Bobby's working late, so Mum forced me to come over to Nicole's for a family tea. Actually she coerced me with promises of getting a takeaway. We do not have a takeaway.

I decide to be brave and try a bit of the goop. Isn't there supposed to be pasta in a lasagne? If there is, God knows where she's put it. One of my mum's favourite time-saving cooking tricks is to remove vital ingredients that take too long. Nicole and I spent our childhood being given 'macaroni cheese without all that fuss about a cheese sauce' so we just had the macaroni with a bit of cheese grated on top. Fish finger sandwiches without the fingers – tuna between two slices of bread – and Cottage Pie with a box of Micro Chips 'to save all the fuss of mashing potatoes for the topping'.

'I cut up some pasta bows and stirred them in,' Mum says. 'Save all that bother with those lasagne sheets.'

Nicole gags. My teeth crunch on a bit of the pasta – it's a shame she didn't think to *cook* the pasta bows before she added them to the goop.

I could be eating cookies with Dimitri right now. He was all set to stay and do more of the stock take and hunting for dedications, and he seemed so disappointed when I said I had to go out instead, and I keep thinking about him. Should I have invited him? Mum wouldn't have minded even though it was supposed to be a family dinner. Oh, who am I kidding? *Minded?* My mum would be dancing down the street if I brought a man to dinner. She'd have got her megaphone out to announce it and started selling tickets to the neighbours to come and witness this rare event.

What am I thinking? This goop is addling my brain. I could never, ever bring Dimitri to meet my mum. He's my age and he's single. She'd have him in handcuffs and signing a marriage register within three minutes of opening the door. No, scratch that, she'd never let us get as far as opening the door – she'd have met us at the end of the street with a wedding dress and two rings.

'Now tell me all about this job.' Mum shovels goop into her mouth, clearly having lost all her taste buds over the years of terrible cookery. 'Have you met anyone yet?'

'A lovely woman stopped for a chat yesterday. She'd read all of Marian Keyes' backlist and wanted something similar. We chatted for ages and she bought a selection of Cecelia Ahern,

Sophie Kinsella, and Jojo Moyes. And I recommended one of my favourite books – *See Jane Date* by Melissa Senate – and she bought our only copy and promised to come back and let me know what she thought. It was great to chat to someone who likes the same kind of books as me,' I say, knowing full well that she means anyone of the male persuasion.

'If you're not careful, I'm going to make you dessert as well.' She tries to glare at me, but using her cooking as a threat always makes us laugh. 'You know what I meant, Hallie.'

'No, I haven't met anyone.' It's not exactly a lie. I can't tell her about Dimitri. She will literally move into the shop and hassle him for every minute of every day. And it's not like there's anything between us anyway. He's just a friend. A very lovely, very hot friend. With the best smile I've ever seen, eyes that brighten up any room, and quite possibly the sexiest naked back in the universe. If sexy backs are a thing … Oh God, I have to stop thinking about him.

'Well, have you at least updated your occupation on all the dating sites to "business owner"? It sounds much better, you know.'

'I'm not on any dating sites.'

'No, but I'm on them for you. You get a lot of potential matches. And a lot of unsolicited photos of nether regions.'

'Mum! You can't be looking at dick pics on my behalf.'

'You're welcome to look at them yourself. If you'd run your own accounts on these sites …'

I sigh because I've told her I'm not interested a million times, in dating *or* dick pics, especially dating men who *send* dick pics, but she won't have it.

'I just like to point and laugh,' she continues. 'The ladies in my knitting group pass my phone around and we all have a good giggle about it. None of us can understand why it's the men with the smallest appendages who seem the most keen to take photos of them.'

'Mum!' I groan again.

'We're thinking of knitting a selection of willy warmers to send them for Christmas. The poor chaps must be freezing with all that whipping it out so often.'

Nicole's choking on her 'lasagne' – air quotes audible – and I've given up on trying to figure out if Mum's serious or not.

'Maybe it's a good thing anyway,' Mum carries on.

'The dick pics?' Nicole and I pull a face at each other.

'You working in the shop, silly.'

'Because I love books and I love that shop and owning it is an actual dream come true?' I say hopefully, because I know she'll mean it in some romance-skewed way.

'Oh, well, that too, I suppose.' She sighs, like the books are a pesky afterthought spoiling her plans. 'But when you get men in looking for relationship books, you can ask them out. Save them the trouble of self-help books in the first place. You should move the relationship self-help section to right near the counter so you have a good view of any potential matches. Just think, if you were to fall madly in love, they wouldn't even *need* to buy the book, so it'd be a great money-saving measure as well.'

Great. Just what you want to be to a potential partner – a money-saver. 'Well, it's a good job that my purpose is to *sell* books then, isn't it?'

'You could sell them something else.'

'The *Kama Sutra*?' Nicole offers. '*How To Please A Woman In Bed*? *Fifty Shades of Grey*?'

'Ooh, I've got a great chat-up line for you.' Mum clears her throat. 'Men are from Mars, women are from Venus, and *I'm* free at eight o'clock.' She winks at me and continues before I have a chance to protest. 'You have been doing your hair and make-up every day, haven't you? It won't do to be scruffy – you never know who could come in. A handsome tourist, a millionaire after some old rare edition, a single—'

'Someone who's not so shallow that they can't see beyond my

hair and brand of foundation?' I say to distract her from the fact that far from appearing on the shop floor poised and primped every morning, it's a rare occurrence that I manage to get down there fully dressed, and I should mark it on the calendar as a special occasion if I've managed to run a brush through my hair too.

She sighs again at the tone in my voice. 'I wouldn't keep going on about it if you gave some of the dates I do find for you a chance. What was wrong with that nice gynaecologist I set you up with?'

'He wasn't a gynaecologist. He was a gynaecological cosmetic surgeon and he spent the entire date listing all the ways he could make me look better *down there*. When the waitress came over, he offered her a twenty-per-cent off voucher, and then over dessert, he finished off with a rousing top ten list of the best vaginas he'd ever seen. And I'd ordered the banana split, which suddenly looked a lot less appetising in the way it was, you know, split down the middle with a lot of cream in it and red fruit around the edge. They have vaginal overtones at the best of times and his monologue didn't help the situation. Any man who can spoil dessert is not for me.'

'Were you more upset about that or about the fact that he *didn't* offer you a twenty-per-cent off voucher?' Nicole asks. 'Maybe he thought you'd need so much nipping and tucking that he couldn't possibly afford the discount.'

I poke my tongue out at her. 'Oh believe me, across the table of the pub was the closest he was getting to any part of me, especially *that* part. The only thing in his favour was that he was marginally better than that undertaker Mum set me up with.'

'It's a perfectly respectable job,' Mum scolds.

'Oh, I know it is, but he spent the entire date trying to sell me a funeral plan.'

'He was only trying to plan ahead.'

'Funnily enough, I don't want to spend a first date planning ahead to my death. It was morbid, and made me wonder what he had in store for me if he was so certain I'd be imminently dead.' I drop my head into my hands. 'Why am I talking like I voluntarily went on dates with these men? I worked in the pub and you sent them in to ambush me, and you had a deal with my manager so he'd make me sit down with them while I was still on shift so I couldn't get away.' God knows how she bribed him with jars of her home-made apple jam, which is just about the only thing she's ever made that hasn't poisoned someone. It's the amount of brandy in it that gets people drunk on one slathering across a piece of toast that makes it so popular, I reckon.

'What about that lovely dentist I set you up with?'

'You didn't set me up with him, Mum, I went for my six-monthly check-up.'

'Yes, but I'd been the week before and confirmed he was going through a divorce. I mentioned you were single and he mumbled something about a conflict of interest in dating patients, but obstacles can be overcome in the face of true love. All you had to do was ask him out. You could always have started going to another dentist.'

'It'd be easier to get a seat on the next space shuttle to the moon than it would to get a new dentist these days,' I mutter.

'Well, a visit to the moon is about as realistic as all those silly romance books you read. They've given you unrealistic expectations when it comes to real men.'

I groan and put my hands over my ears. 'Oh, not this again.'

'I'm just saying that not all men are going to be handsome, rich, and brooding like Mr Darcy. They're not all going to sweep you off your feet, or lend you money for nice scarves like Luke Brandon. They won't always leave you vast amounts of money and trips to Paris like Will Traynor, or notes from beyond the grave like that handsome Gerard Butler in the film of *P.S. I Love You*. Sometimes eyes don't meet across a crowded room and spotlights don't illuminate each other while stars glitter and angels sing. You can't expect that—'

'I don't expect that.' I don't know why I'm bothering – I've already said it 8,954 times in the past couple of years. She didn't listen any of the other times, so I don't know why today would be any different.

'You expect men to behave like characters in books.'

'No, I *wish* men behaved like characters in books. They don't – that's the problem. It doesn't mean I've got unrealistic expectations – it means I don't want to date a guy who wants to do cosmetic surgery on my hoohaa or a funeral director who's planning to murder me. Most of the men you sent into the pub seemed to want to be anywhere but there and definitely wanted to look at women who were anyone but me. I can only imagine the amount of gossip you must know about people to have blackmailed them into it in the first place.'

'I only had to show them a picture. That nice one of you at Nicole and Bobby's wedding. You look quite pretty when you do your make-up and leave your hair down.'

'Last time I left my hair down, I accidentally got too close to a candle and set myself on fire!' I glare at them both for laughing. It wasn't funny at the time. Well, not until afterwards. When I'd cut the singed hair off. 'And are you seriously going around showing random men my photo? I'm surprised you haven't stuck up posters on every lamppost with those tear-off strips on the bottom saying "ring this number if you'd date my daughter".'

Mum sits up straighter like this is the best idea she's ever heard.

'Mum, no!' I say quickly while Nicole doubles over with laughter. 'And you …' I turn to my sister. 'You can get that photo off her. No wonder she's attracting lunatics. I'm wearing a bridesmaid's dress and clutching your bouquet with a slightly deranged look on my face after too much Prosecco at the reception. I look like some kind of desperate Bridezilla!'

'Are you kidding? Mum trying to find you a boyfriend is the

best entertainment I get all week. It's not as much fun now you don't work in the pub and get coerced into actual dates with them though. What's she going to do now – send them in to buy a book?'

'Oh, now that's—'

'No!' Nicole and I both say in unison.

'No more dates, Mum, please. No more single men. No more photographs of me. No more online dating sites. I don't have unrealistic expectations. If anything, my expectations are *too* realistic in that every relationship I've ever had has been an unmitigated disaster at worst and a crushing disappointment at best. Something always goes wrong. And enough things go wrong for me alone; I don't need to strike someone else down with my bad luck too. Besides, I have the shop now, I need to concentrate on that, not on men.'

She mutters something about too many romance books.

'And speaking of romance books, I'd better be getting back.' I push my chair out and look down at the three-quarters full plate of 'lasagne' left on the table. 'That was, er, delicious, as always.' My stomach lets out a loud rumble to contradict my lie, either because it's still hungry or because it's threatening to object to the few spoonfuls I did eat.

At least I pass a chip shop on the way home.

'Oh, don't go yet,' Nicole says. 'She'll start on me about when Bobby and I intend to have a baby if she hasn't got your love life to keep her occupied.'

No wonder she was so keen for me to come over tonight. With Mum living in her own annex at the bottom of their garden, Nicole and Bobby are under her constant scrutiny *and* subject to each new recipe experimentation.

'I'm only trying to help you both.' Mum pushes her bottom lip out. 'I'm a good matchmaker and I'd make an excellent grand-mother, and I live here so you'd have free childcare on tap!'

Nicole rolls her eyes like she's heard that argument as many times as I've heard about my unrealistic expectations from reading too many romances.

'Why are you so eager to get away anyway?' she asks me. 'You've only been here an hour, and there's chocolate cake for afters. Shop-bought!' she adds quickly, making us all dissolve into giggles again.

I push the 'lasagne' away and sit down again, unable to resist the temptation of cake. Why am I so eager to get back anyway? It's not like Dimitri's still going to be there. It's just me, going through books on my own, which has become a far less attractive prospect without him there to help. I suppose I could tackle some of the boxes in the flat that I still haven't unpacked because spending my evenings sorting books with Dimitri has been a far more attractive prospect, but if it's a choice between boxes and cake, the cake wins every time.

'We've found messages,' I say when Mum's sat back down after serving up a suitably big slice each and covered it with extra cream to make up for the lasagne disaster.

Mum's ears prick up. 'Who's we?'

Trust her to pick up on the important parts of a sentence. 'Me and the goldfish. Heathcliff.'

She looks sceptical. In all fairness, Heathcliff isn't exactly pulling his weight in terms of shop chores, but he's a big hit with customers. Kids love watching him, especially at feeding time. 'Are you sure there's not a man waiting for you?'

'Why would there be a man waiting for me? That's ludicrous. As if. And even if there was, it's nearly eight o'clock – the shop's shut.'

'What messages?' Nicole asks, getting us back on track.

I tell her about the notes inside books and the unusual amount of books with dedications written inside their opening pages. By the time I've finished gushing about how romantic some of the messages are, she looks like she's about to fall asleep.

'No maps marking out buried treasure? Because that would

136

be cool. And useful.' She sounds unimpressed by my tales of sharing love and romance through reading. 'None of them signed by authors or special editions or anything? You could make a bit of money out of those.'

Typical Nicole. 'It's not about making money. These books are special. I want to know where they came from, who wrote them and who they gave them to. They meant a lot to someone once – both giver and receiver.'

'Well, clearly not that much or they'd still be on their own bookshelves, wouldn't they? Not lounging about in some mouldy shop.'

'My shop's not mouldy!'

Mum interrupts before I can protest any further. 'You should track some of these men down and see if they're single. I mean, that Esme one – if she didn't want him, you'll have him. He likes *Les Mis*, and so do you, so you'll have something in common – what more do you want?'

'Well, firstly, I want their relationship to still be going strong and happy. Secondly, we have no idea what year that was written in. All we can decipher is that it's in biro so it was sometime after the invention of the biro pen. The mystery Sylvester could be dead by now. He could be ninety years old. And thirdly, what makes you think I'm so desperate that I'm going to track down some random man who once wrote in a book and throw myself at him? Whoever or wherever he is – I don't want him, I want him and Esme to have lived a long and happy life together.'

I try not to get annoyed, but I just want someone to get it. Like Dimitri does. All right, he was a bit disbelieving at first, but since we found that note written by his mum, he's been getting as involved as me. We've checked every copy of every Virginia Andrews book in the shop – there was nothing, but both of us have still been opening every book with a fizz of excitement, hoping for some mysterious message from some random stranger across the decades.

I should have known Mum and Nicole were not the people to understand that.

Books are magical in that they can transport you to another time and place, introduce you to people you come to know as friends, in both characters, authors, and now in real people who, at some point in their lives, have chosen each book as carefully selected gifts for someone they cared about. My family will never understand that books contain whole worlds to get lost inside, like the people who wrote those messages knew and wanted to give that gift to someone else. And I want to know more about them.

Chapter 8

'Will you marry me?'

'Well, I'm flattered, but …' Dimitri fans a hand in front of his face like he's about to swoon. 'This is so unexpected. It's all moving so fast.'

'Not you, you idiot.'

He grins at the affectionate insult as I hold the copy of *Jane Eyre* up and tap the cover page. 'Someone proposed in the book.'

'Wow.' He comes over to take it out of my hands and his glasses fall down as he looks at the neat writing. 'Do you think she said yes? Or he, seeing as there's no clue about who actually wrote it?'

'Hopefully. I mean if you love books, maybe this book in particular …' I reach across and close the book in his hands, running my fingers down the front of the pink cover with a woman's silhouette on it. 'Whoever it was must've chosen this book for a reason. Maybe it was her favourite, or his; it must have been significant. You wouldn't propose in a random book, would you? And for someone to go to this much effort … Of course they said yes.'

'Why is it here then?'

I stop mid-cover-stroke. 'You mean, why isn't it still lovingly ensconced on their family bookshelf where the happy couple get it out every so often and reminisce about how wonderful their relationship has always been and maybe show it to a few precious munchkins while a handsome dog looks on from a furry rug in front of the hearth?'

'Something like that.' He laughs. 'You've got to admit it's the kind of thing you'd keep. Unless you'd split up and hated each other.'

'And you're meant to be the cheery, optimistic one between us.'

'I'm realistic when it comes to love.'

'There are plenty of reasons it could have ended up here unintentionally.'

He raises an eyebrow and crosses his arms, clearly waiting for an answer.

'It could have got lost in a house move,' I say.

'When they moved to a bigger house to accommodate their growing brood of treasured moppets and handsome dogs?'

'Exactly! Or some well-meaning friend could have sorted their bookshelves for them and chucked it without knowing its significance.'

'Maybe one of them was reading it as they drove along the motorway with the window open, and whoosh, a gust of wind rips it out of their hand, never to be seen again. Or maybe it was pilfered by a particularly well-read squirrel.'

I narrow my eyes at him for the sarcasm. 'Maybe they took it to the wedding to share this incredibly romantic proposal with all their friends and it got left behind at the venue.'

'Do you really think it's romantic?'

'Of course.' I answer like it's a trick question. 'Don't you?'

'Well, it's a bit impersonal, isn't it? He hasn't even written her name or signed it or anything. There are no sweeping declarations of love, not even a paltry "I love you". It's so generic that you could use it to propose to the milkman, and if he turned you down, you could have a crack at the postman instead.' He thinks about this for a moment. 'Although why anybody'd be proposing to all these random men who bring things to your house is a bit weird … I think I might have got off track here. Besides, if it's her favourite book, she's undoubtedly already got a copy, so he should've kept the money he wasted on another copy and put it towards a nice meal out and got down on one knee in the traditional way.'

I giggle at his rambling reasoning, but despite my reluctance to believe that a proposal in a book could have ended anything but happily, he's got a point. Well, maybe not about the milkman and the postman, and some people aren't naturally wordy, like this straight-to-the-point proposer, but this *is* the sort of thing you'd hang on to for sentimental reasons, unless the proposee said no or the marriage wasn't a happy one.

I sigh and put a tiny little heart sticker on the base of the spine – my new method of marking out which ones have messages inside them – while Dimitri enters it into the laptop in the office. I can't take them all off the shop floor but I can't lose track of which ones have got something written in them. They feel important, special somehow, like I might need to find them again one day.

The books with messages hidden inside their covers are endless, and in the past few days of looking, we've found everything from well wishes to family recipes to declarations of love. I'm desperate to know where Robert got his second-hand books and if he knew that quite so many of them had words inside, but something tells me this is no accident. Dimitri keeps saying that Robert loved finding old messages inside used books, and I know from my own experience that he preferred second-hand books to new ones because of the life each book had had before it reached him. He liked books that had been passed around, their stories shared between friends and families, and often talked about it when I came in and he had his latest delivery spread across the counter while he priced them up.

Dimitri hands *Jane Eyre* back to me. 'Don't worry, I'm sure there are plenty of reasons their proposal book could've been thrown away and they're too busy living happily ever after to notice.' He says it with the same tone he'd use to suggest the Loch Ness Monster was thinking of setting up a nest on the roof terrace, but I appreciate his attempt to humour me.

Instead of the waistcoat today, he's wearing jeans and a grey T-shirt with a pair of brightly striped braces across his shoulders, although they seem to be solely for decorative purposes and don't appear to be bracing anything as his jeans are held up perfectly well by a belt. My eyes have wandered to Dimitri's lower half again, and it's not good. Heathcliff can get away with it; I cannot.

It's two minutes to nine, so I go over and open the door. The sun is shining and the fountain is burbling away across the street. The flowers in the hanging baskets are starting to trail over the edges and the gentle breeze rustles their green leaves. I prop the door open to make it more welcoming and go back across to the counter. There's a stack of books with messages in them piled up at one side, an open Tupperware container of coconut lemon bars and a cup of coffee each, which he risked buying again even after the disaster last week.

'These are so good.' I pop one of the small rectangular bars into my mouth.

He doesn't look up from the book he's scanning through, but a smile spreads across his face as he pushes his glasses back up his nose for the fortieth time, and I love how much he loves other people enjoying his baking.

'Nothing in that one.' He closes the book and puts it back on its rightful shelf. The reorganisation of the shelves is a long and arduous process, far worse than I thought it would be because there are simply *so* many books to move around, and rarely space to put them in the right places and nowhere to put the ones we've taken out. And there's the small matter of how we keep getting waylaid by the messages scrawled inside covers and on title pages.

'Yeah, but look at this.' I pull one of the books off the pile beside me and open it, leaning on the counter to flick through the copy of Mary Shelley's *Frankenstein*. The words inside look like they were written in quill and ink, and it's the kind of fancy handwriting that you'd expect to see in a letter closed with a wax seal. I read the message aloud. '*Remember what I promised you. ~ Reginald.*'

Dimitri leans across the counter from the other side and reads it upside down. 'Hmm. Vaguely threatening.'

I smack at his arm and he grins and takes another coconut lemon bar from the container before he moves his coffee out of the way, turns around and hoists himself up to sit on the counter, and I like how at ease he is here. His back is facing me and he leans back on his hands so he can see the book from my angle and I push it forwards and lean further across so my shoulder is touching his side.

'It's old. The writing and the book,' I say. This edition is from the 1930s, and the ink is faded and the page edges are brown with age, the clothbound green cover threadbare and frayed.

'It's crazy how much I want to know what this means.' He picks up his coffee cup again and sips it. 'Who is Reginald? What did he promise? *Who* did he promise? Was it a promise or a threat?'

'Oh, come on. Look at his handwriting. It's like something out of *The Phantom of the Opera*.' I nudge my shoulder into him, nearly making him spill his coffee. 'Even his handwriting is romantic. No one writes like this anymore.'

'I didn't know handwriting was the defining factor in identifying a psychopath.' He looks down at me with a raised eyebrow, but he's smiling as he shakes his head. 'Besides, this book is about a man who dug up graves and raided morgues to collect body parts to sew together as a new person. His "promise" could be that this is what's going to happen to the receiver if they don't do whatever he's demanded.'

'Nope. I'm not having that. Frankenstein's monster wanted love; he wanted to be accepted for what he was. He didn't fit in. This Reginald is clearly telling the receiver that he has promised to love and accept them for all their flaws, come what may. He's promised to give them the unconditional love that the monster always craved.'

He's smiling when he looks down at me this time. 'God, you are so …'

I look up and meet his twinkling blue eyes even though I'm looking over the rim of my glasses so he's a bit blurry, we hold each other's gaze for a long moment, and it's like the air between us is sparkling.

But that's probably just my dreadful eyesight.

Even so, I can feel my smile getting wider as his does, spreading slowly, making everything look more twinkly and—

'A man!' Mum's squeal comes from the doorway. 'I *knew* there was a man!'

'Kill me now.' I drop my head down onto the counter and hiss urgently at Dimitri. 'Run. Save yourself while there's still time. Your legs are long – she'll never catch you.'

I look up and rub my fingers across the head I clonked down too hard and I've now got the corner of the book imprinted in my forehead. 'There is no man, Mum. You're imagining him.'

'Well, I've got an *excellent* imagination. You are *gorgeous*.' She approaches Dimitri. 'Are you single?'

He looks slightly alarmed as he jumps off the counter. 'Yes. And planning on staying that way.'

'Oh, now that's no attitude to have at your age. A handsome young man in the prime of your life.' She turns to me. 'Is he the "we"?'

'What?'

'We! The we!' She sounds like she needs the bathroom. 'When you said "we" last night, I knew it wasn't about the fish.'

He looks at me and waggles his eyebrows. 'So you've told your mum about me.'

'No. I have categorically *not* told my mum about you. There's nothing to—'

'She doesn't need to tell me! I'm a mum! I read between the lines!'

'No, you make up lines that aren't there and then read words that aren't there either. There *are* no lines to read between. He's a customer.'

'I saw that look! That is *not* a customer look. And you're sharing baked goods. *Everyone* knows the way to a person's heart is with baked goods.'

'Go out the fire exit,' I hiss at him again. 'I'll throw a blanket over her while you make your escape. If that fails, jump from the roof. It's the only way.'

He's laughing. He's actually laughing. He thinks I'm joking.

'No wonder you were so eager to get away last night. *Now* I see why.'

'He wasn't here then. The shop was shut. Besides, I don't even know him. He's just walked in. In fact, he was just telling me about his wife, weren't you?' I try to wink at him to get him to agree, even though he's already told my mum he's single.

The look on Mum's face makes me wonder if she was standing outside the door for a few minutes and we didn't see her. I've got to admit that with Dimitri sitting as close as he was, we could've been in Morocco and I wouldn't have noticed with the warmth from his body pressing against my shoulder and the earthy scent of his woody burnt lavender aftershave all around. She's a bit over the top, but even she wouldn't approach a customer in the way she's approaching Dimitri.

She's cornered him and is about a centimetre away from pinching his cheeks.

'Mum! Personal space!' I shout, momentarily distracting her and giving him a chance to duck out of the way.

'Well, it was lovely to meet you, Mrs Winstone, but this customer had really better be getting on with his work.' His bag and sketchbooks are already on the sofa in the reading area, and he starts towards the shelves to fetch his Italian book.

'Polite!' she squawks.

He does a sort of mix between a curtsey and a bow as he backs away, his glasses sliding down his nose again.

She points in the direction he's gone and mouths 'wow' at me, then she comes over and pinches one of the coconut lemon bars from the open box and pops it into her mouth. Her eyes widen in delight and she mouths 'wow' again with her mouth full.

'Please leave him alone,' I say. 'There's nothing between us, and he's quiet, he doesn't need—'

'Then he needs a girlfriend, doesn't he?' She's in the reading area before I can stop her. She lifts the cover of one of his sketchbooks on the table and starts rifling through it.

'Mum!' I put my hands on my hips. 'You can't do that! It's not your—'

'Ooh, he's very good, isn't he?' She flips a few more pages. 'Although quite an odd subject matter. Why is there all this parsley? Why's this ogre wearing a dress?'

'That's apparently the oldest known version of Rapunzel.' I start trying to explain some of what Dimitri's told me about his subject matter. 'This girl's mother stole some parsley from an ogress's garden, so as punishment, the ogress imprisons the girl in a tower, but she's rescued by a handsome prince climbing up her long hair.'

'Oh, now the ogre's being eaten by a wolf.' She shudders and lifts another page. 'Couldn't he draw some cute fluffy bunnies instead?'

'Don't you find cute fluffy bunnies awfully boring, Mrs Winstone?' Dimitri reappears with the huge Italian fairy-tale book under his arm. He doesn't seem even vaguely annoyed that she's invaded his privacy by inviting herself to look through his work.

'I didn't mean it in a bad way.' At least she has the decency to look guilty. 'Your talent is exceptional. And look at your lovely blue eyes. Oh, with eyes like that, you could draw a dustbin lorry and I'd think you were the most talented man I'd ever met.'

'I'm not sure having blue eyes is a discernible talent or how they relate to his work, Mum.'

She ignores me. 'What's your name?'

'Dimitri.'

She gasps like a fly's just gone down her throat. '*Anastasia* was Hallie's favourite film when she was younger.'

'Oh, I wouldn't say it was my *favourite* …' I pick up a book and briefly consider how hard I'd have to hit myself on the head to cause a severe enough concussion for my memory to stop recording for a while.

'Yes, it was. Don't you remember?' She holds her hands up like they're on the shoulders of an invisible man and starts a one-woman waltz around the shop while caterwauling a version of 'Once Upon a December' when she's clearly forgotten what the lyrics actually are, until she crashes into the sale table and sends books skittering to the floor. Unless they've hurled themselves off for mercy lest she start trying to partner them up too.

Dimitri, the perfect gentleman, puts his book down and offers her his hand and properly waltzes her across the shop while humming the real version of 'Once Upon A December', spinning her around like a budget *Strictly Come Dancing* with pink leisure suits instead of spangly dresses and absolutely no sign of Tess Daly.

When he stops, she clutches a bookshelf for support and fans a hand in front of her face.

I kneel down to gather up the books she sent flying, trying not to think about how lovely he is to indulge my mum like that, and how attractive he looks in a waltz pose, or how much I'd like to dance with him. Dancing is usually something I avoid at *all* costs because I have the coordination of a slug that's just fallen out of a beer trap.

He's even lovely enough that he comes over and crouches down beside me to help pick up the books.

'Do you have any idea what you're doing?' I whisper. 'You're unleashing a demon. We're going to need pentagrams and salt circles to stop her now. She's *never* going to leave you alone. Or me, for that matter. We're going to have to leave the country. How does Iceland sound? We could start a new life in Iceland. No one would ever have to know.'

He puts his head down on his knees because he's laughing so hard, even though I'm only half joking. Tears of laughter are forming in his eyes and I give him a gentle shove, but he overbalances and falls over onto his bum, his hair flopping forward and springing back up again as he laughs even harder, and the sight of him sprawled on the floor makes me start giggling too.

Mum looms over us, clearly wondering if coffee was the only thing in our cups. 'Don't you think this is a nice photo?'

She holds her phone down so he can see it, and I try to snatch it out of her hand but she dodges far more easily than a seventy-year-old should be able to. 'Mum! Don't show him that!'

He looks up at it from the floor. 'Oh yes, it's very nice. If slightly deranged Bridezilla was the look you were going for.'

He looks over and winks at me and I frantically do a 'cut' motion. If Mum catches him winking at me, she'll probably need to be taken home by ambulance.

She pulls her phone back with a huff and stomps away. 'That's what Hallie always says. She must've told you to say that.'

'No, not at all. She just looks like a desperate Bridezilla lying in wait to ensnare a husband.'

I laugh but it's not like he's saying anything that's untrue. 'I was going to help you up but now I think I'll leave you flailing about on the floor.'

It makes him laugh even harder. 'I do seem to have spent an abnormal amount of time lying on the floor in this shop.'

Mum's mouth forms an 'o' as she tries to work out what *activity* we've been up to that's put him on the floor.

He pushes his bottom lip out and I hold my hands out, squeezing his as he slips them both into mine and lets me pull him up.

'She hates having her photo taken.' Mum's frantically scrolling through her phone for a better picture. 'How about this one?'

'I was six! And you took that photo to show how bad my chickenpox was!'

'Very cute.' Dimitri has the decency to barely glance towards the photo she holds out. He reaches over to grab his coffee cup and uses the distraction of Mum lost in her phone to go and sit down on the sofa and start getting art supplies out of his bag.

He is severely optimistic if he thinks that's going to be enough to get her to leave him alone.

Sure enough, she puts her phone away as soon as she clocks that he's moved, and the sofa lets out a whoosh of air as she plonks herself down next to him.

'Mum, why don't you come and have a look at the recipe books?' I say, knowing my mum and recipe books make a recipe for only one thing – disaster. 'We've got a great one about single meals for *one* person. That you only cook for *one*. And don't need to share with other people because they're only for *one*.'

'She has unrealistic expectations of love, you know,' she says to Dimitri.

'It comes from years of being told we were going to have spaghetti bolognese for tea only to be served plain spaghetti with a dollop of ketchup on top.'

She ignores me. 'It's from all those books she reads. All those handsome men running about on the moors or sweeping ladies off their feet. She's still waiting for Mr Rochester to walk in.'

'I'm really not.' I look to the door, imploring not Mr Rochester but a great wave of customers to pour in and shut her up. The shop remains quiet. Even Heathcliff seems to be interested in my mum's conversation. Any mention of the moors perks him right up.

'And all those contemporary Romances where the hero and heroine are so utterly perfect for each other and everyone sees it but them until some horrible misunderstanding tears them apart, but then at the end, he does some big, fancy gesture to prove how truly sorry he is, and they live happily ever after.'

'But that's the point of those books,' he says gently. 'People read them as an escape from reality. A chance to believe that life could be a fairy tale just for a moment. Everyone knows it's not real. If it was real, no one would want to read them, would they?'

He looks at me across the shop and his mouth tips up into a smile when our eyes meet.

'I don't think it's a bad thing to believe in magic,' he continues. 'To believe the world could be a little bit better than it is. And it's definitely not a bad thing to want to meet someone who makes you feel like that. Isn't that what everyone should hold out for?'

My whole body floods with warmth, and if my mum wasn't here, I'd go over and throw my arms around him for that. It's exactly what I've always wanted to say to Mum when she starts on about my unrealistic expectations but have never found the right words for. As she *is* here, I have to settle for smiling at him. I could never even consider hugging him. She would literally keel over in shock.

Mum goes to answer but nothing comes out.

Dimitri has superpowers. That's the *only* possible explanation. No one has ever, ever rendered my mum speechless before. Ever.

'She's thirty-five!' Mum splutters eventually. 'The biological clock is ticking.'

'I grew up with parents who were unhappy. Believe me, Hallie deserves to be happy and single rather than married to someone

150

solely to fulfil expectations of what other people perceive to be perfect life goals. That's not having unrealistic expectations, that's wanting to be happy.'

God, he's perfect. In a few gentle sentences, he's politely shut my mum down and eloquently worded everything I've never been able to say.

He looks up at me again and I can't smile any wider at him. My face is hurting from how much I'm smiling, and I can't take my eyes off him and the way his eyes shine as he smiles back at me.

'Dinner!' She suddenly squeals so loudly that he visibly jumps and I jump so much that my hand hits the counter with such force that it makes me jump again.

'Mum, no. Dimitri's a nice guy, he doesn't deserve that.'

'Well, I do eat dinner ...' he starts.

'No!' I try to plead with him using only my eyes. 'You don't understand what you're getting yourself into. What Mum calls dinner is *not* food.'

'Now I've got knitting club on Monday,' Mum starts. 'My felting workshop on Tuesday, I'm down at the allotment on Wednesday, and it's Nicole's week for working late so this Thursday's out, and Friday is Nicole and Bobby's date night ... Would Thursday week work for you?'

Is it good or bad when your mum's social life is a hundred per cent fuller than your own?

'Thursday week it is,' Mum cries after Dimitri's told her he's free at any time.

'He's busy on Thursday night.' I rub my bruised hand. 'He's going out with his wife and children, aren't you?' Has someone accidentally hit my mute button? 'His *multiple* wives!'

'Now don't you bring anything, I'll cook. What's your favourite food?'

I look at Heathcliff. 'Can you even see me?' I say to the goldfish. 'Have I become invisible?'

He doesn't answer either. Or look particularly interested in whether I'm invisible or not.

'Pizza?' Dimitri looks warily between me and my mum like he's not sure whether it's the right answer or not.

Pizza. I count all the ways pizza could possibly go wrong until a light bulb moment strikes. 'How about we bring a pizza?'

'Pish posh. I'm not letting this gorgeous man suffer *takeaway* pizza. A good home-cooked meal is what you need.'

I groan.

'Home-made pizza sounds great,' Dimitri says. He *really* doesn't know what he's letting himself in for.

Mum reaches over to pat his cheek. 'Oh, you are kind. It's been many years since I heard that from either of my girls.'

'There's a reason for that,' I mutter.

Thankfully a couple of customers choose that moment to come in, and I'm so grateful for the distraction that I'd go and hug them if it wouldn't scare them away. One of them is a man who might be single – well, he's about forty and he's on his own. Usually that would be enough for my mum to corner him and enquire – but she doesn't move from Dimitri's side.

He's started showing her some of his drawings and I overhear him telling her about the greeting cards he's doing and the bookish gifts I'm going to be stocking, and as long as they're on a neutral topic that's not my love life, I decide to stay out of it. The more I try to drag her away, the more convinced she'll become that there's something to drag her away *from* and the more determined she'll be to stay and find out what.

With Dimitri talking, Mum looks more interested in the shop than she's ever been. He's animated when he speaks, his smile lighting up his face, his hands gesticulating wildly in between leaning over to draw tiny sketches to show her examples of what he's talking about. My mum is not an easy woman to handle, and seeing him chat to her and actually look like he's enjoying it is positively heart-melting.

Chapter 9

'How can you even make inventorying thirty thousand books fun?' I say after closing time the same night.

It's one of many nights Dimitri's insisted on staying to help, and I know there will be many more nights like this in front of us, but I'm not complaining because he's walking around with an open book laid across his head like a hat, his hair sticking out in all directions from underneath it, for no discernible reason other than to make himself look like an adorable idiot.

'It *is* fun,' he says simply. 'They're books. We get to see them, hold them, and stroke them. There are plenty of people who would kill for this job.'

Which is true. And no matter how much I love it, it still seems like a mammoth task. I still look at the endless shelves and piles in front of us and wonder how we'll ever get through them all. But I like how nothing seems like a big deal to him. Not even my mum.

The shop's been busy today and this is the first chance I've had to broach the subject with him. 'I'm sorry about my mum earlier.' I look up from where I'm kneeling on the floor in front of the Cosy Crime section.

'You don't have to apologise. She's amazing.'

'I didn't mean for you to get dragged into it. I didn't think she'd come in. She's got a few favourite authors and she'll sometimes read things her friends recommend, but she's so busy with all the various clubs and groups she goes to that she doesn't have time for reading.' I try to wrestle a book out of the shelf where it's wedged in so tightly that I'm one step away from going to find a crowbar. 'She's the one who introduced Nicole and Bobby about ten years ago, and since then she's been convinced that she's missed her calling in life as a matchmaker, and that her sole purpose is to find the perfect man for both her daughters. She's only succeeded with one so far, but she certainly hasn't given up trying with me. She can't help herself when she sees a single man. She did the same with my ex-flatmate at first, and he was twenty-two years old and came with a crispy Lynx coating.'

Dimitri snorts so hard that the book falls off his head.

'Thank you for being so nice to her. She's a bit overbearing. Overwhelming. She could be described in a lot of ways, most of them beginning with "over". She really struggled after my dad died and started joining all these clubs to keep herself busy. After Nicole and I had both moved out, she was getting too lonely in the house, so when Nicole married Bobby and found a house with an annex in the garden, it was the perfect solution for her to move in there. As you'll find out when she gives you the grand tour ...'

'Hal, honestly, it's fine. It was nice to meet her. She's lovely. She was interested in my work and complimentary about my baking.'

I don't tell him that, knowing my mother, her interest in him was all about assessing him for husband suitability, and he undoubtedly passed her test with flying colours and a gold star. No, the coconut lemon bars would've earnt him at least *two* gold stars. 'And don't worry about dinner next week, I'll tell her you've been bitten by a radioactive bat and gone down with rabies or something.'

'Are you kidding? I'm not missing this for the world.' He cocks his head to the side and thinks about it for a moment. 'Although radioactive bats do sound fun. Do you know any?'

His earnestness makes me giggle, until he says, 'Besides, it's pizza. What could go wrong with pizza?'

I look up at him, not trying to hide my look of pity. 'Oh, you poor, sweet, innocent man. You have *no* idea. If she makes pizza, it's going to be topped with anchovies, pineapple, and grass cuttings from the lawnmower. You do realise that, don't you?'

'She was saying she likes seasonal ingredients …'

'Yeah, except she chooses the ones that you *can't* eat. Never mind the violas and nasturtiums, she goes for tulips and lily of the valley. And if she offers you a mushroom in the autumn, never *ever* take it. Despite her assertions, she does *not* know which ones are edible. Bobby can attest to that – he once spent a night in hospital having his stomach pumped after a particularly hefty portion of her mushroom carbonara.'

He laughs like he still thinks I'm joking. 'It'll be fine. I'm looking forward to meeting your family. I've heard a lot about them.' He doesn't add that a solid 99.99 per cent of it was heard this morning as my mum wittered on and on at him. 'I've got some of my father's vintage wines. I'll bring a bottle and, what, meet you here and we'll walk over?'

I nod, still desperately thinking of ways to get out of it. Faking your own death can't be that difficult, right? Emigration is also a definite possibility. Maybe I could become one of those yachtswomen who sail around the world on their own. Or an astronaut. The ocean might be dodgy because she could still hire a boat and follow me with a line of single men behind her, like The Pied Piper of Hamelin in dating terms, but she'd never make it to space.

'It's been so long since I had a family dinner. I'm honoured that she asked me.' His voice wobbles and for just a second, it's like I can physically see his loneliness surrounding him. He clearly isn't close to what's left of his own family. He's mentioned his house being empty and every night when I suggest it's time to call it quits for the day, he's reluctant to go.

He covers it with a smile in an instant, but I feel guilty for trying to put him off.

'It's just …' I stutter, unsure of what to say. 'I just want you to be forewarned that what you think is dinner and what my mum thinks is dinner are two different things. And on the plus side, we pass a chip shop on the way back so the night won't be lost if the pizza is up to her usual standards.'

'We could take some books.' He nods towards one of piles balanced precariously on my desk in the office.

'My mum might try to cook them.'

He laughs again. He *really* doesn't know my mother well enough. 'I mean for hiding. In the dark of the night and all that. We could go and be book fairies.'

I laugh at the mental image, but it makes me feel all warm inside too. I've never thought of it as being a book fairy.

The idea is to replicate what I've seen other towns doing online, and put books inside a waterproof bag and hide them in spots around town for other people to find, along with a note saying to enjoy it and re-hide it for someone else to find, and with a mention of where it came from.

'You really want to help me with that?'

He opens the book and puts it back on his head, spins in a circle, and does a bow, causing the book to fall off and clatter to the floor. Luckily it was one of the ones for the recycling bin anyway. 'I want to help you with anything. *Everything*. I love being here. I love that you haven't chucked me out yet.'

'I feel like I should be paying—'

'Don't finish that sentence.' He interrupts before I can mention anything about the awkward niggling feeling I've been having about how much he's doing to help me and expecting nothing in return. He's spending more time here than a full-time employee would, and I haven't forgotten what he said on the roof the other day about needing the money.

'I already have a job. I'm helping you as a friend, not because I want anything out of it.'

'I know, I just mean … You can't be getting much work done. When's your deadline for your publisher?'

'Don't worry about it. I've got ages yet.'

He also clearly doesn't want to talk about it anymore.

'It feels like things are starting to take shape.' It's an obvious attempt to change the subject as he hands me down a stack of books taken from other shelves that belong in the Crime section, and I pass him back a few Romances that clearly don't.

He's not wrong. It does feel like we're making progress as we methodically work along the bookcases organising the categories, cleaning each shelf and dusting each book, and putting titles and authors into the computer database. I've set up a half-sized narrow shelf inside the door, and Dimitri's doodled a 'Free to a good home' sign, because the books are in far too bad a condition to sell, or hide around town, but someone might still enjoy them. It's only the *really* bad ones that are heading to the recycling bin. The sale table is filling up again, and in the office is a mixture of books for children and adults that aren't quite in good enough nick to sell, but still deserve to be read and enjoyed.

'I keep thinking we should have a Facebook page and add it to the bottom of each note with the books we hide,' I say. 'Nicole keeps saying it would be good advertising, and even though it's not about that, it would be nice to ask people to tag us when they find one. We could even ask other people to hide unwanted books and post clues about where they're hidden … Get the whole community involved, and start our online presence with a boost. Robert mentioned that he'd been trying to build an online presence – he just didn't mention that he'd been trying to build it on Myspace. So I'm going to start again. We're going to have a website and offer an option to order online. I follow loads of bookshops on Instagram, so we're going to do all the modern social media, not a Myspace account that was outdated in 2003, complete with flashing neon gifs and Tom as a friend.'

'I think that's a great idea. We should post pictures of the shelves, the window displays, new arrivals when you order them, picks of the week, those mugs and bookmarks that came in earlier ...'

The mention of them makes me feel like an ice cube is slowly sliding down my spine, because a very large credit card bill came in with them, and if they don't sell, I don't know how I'm going to pay it off.

'Anything that gets people involved and makes people care about the bookshop. Or even realise there *is* a bookshop here. You know when something's stood in the same place for so long that people sort of walk past it without really seeing it? Robert's raffle draw got a bit of attention from the local press, but the local people who actually shop here should know that you're moving with the times.'

I like that he agrees. I value his opinion a lot. He's exactly the type of person I need to appeal to. I push the last of the books he handed me into their newly created spaces on the sparkling clean bottom shelf, and he holds his hand down to pull me up.

'Any more secret messages?' I ask.

With a huge grin on his face, he wordlessly hands me a copy of *The Hunger Games*, the striking dark cover untouched and the spine pristine. I carefully open the first page and read the inscription. In the messy, uncoordinated handwriting of someone who I'm going to guess is a teenage boy, are the words:

Vickie, my hand is shaking because I've never told you how much I like you. I keep hanging around with you and trying to make you laugh and every time you laugh, I fall a bit more in love with you. I keep hoping you'll notice me. I mean, I know you notice me as a friend, but I wish you'd see me as more than that. I would do anything for you.

~ Tommy.

'That's so sweet,' I murmur, instantly picturing a lovesick lanky teenager at the peak of awkwardness around girls, confessing his love for a friend in the front of a book he must've thought she'd like. 'This hasn't even been read. How sad is that? I mean, he went to all that effort and Vickie didn't even read it. It doesn't look like she even opened the cover.'

'Rejection's hard at that age. He must've been devastated.'

'Maybe she didn't reject him. Maybe she was a very careful reader …' I say, knowing full well that no one is *that* careful a reader. Dimitri and I have done the most damage to this book by peeking inside the front cover. It's immaculate. 'Maybe he plucked up the courage to tell her without giving her the book. Or maybe she already had a copy …'

'Or maybe he gave it to her and she peeked inside and laughed in his face.'

'Why are you so positive about everything except for love? How can you say the beautiful things you say about believing in anything that makes the world better but still be so pessimistic about these messages?'

'Because either people aren't as sappy as I am, or they don't want these books anymore. These are the kind of sentimental keepsakes that can't be replaced by Kindles. To end up in a second-hand bookshop, they must've been thrown out, so it doesn't exactly suggest the relationships were long or happy ones.'

'But aren't you desperate to know?' I clutch the book and hold it up. 'I know you want to find out about your mum's mystery man, but aren't you desperate to know what happened between Vickie and Tommy too? Did his declaration of love work or did she not even read it? How about Esme in *Les Mis*, and Frankenstein's monster and his promise? Don't you want to know what became of them?'

He looks at me with a raised eyebrow. 'Why do I get the feeling that anything other than "yes" is the wrong answer?'

'Glad you agree.' I mark *The Hunger Games* with a tiny heart sticker at the base of the spine and add it to the box that I've currently got the YA section in while I move it downstairs. There's no way teenagers want their books lumped in with picture books and toddlers sitting at the tables upstairs finger painting and colouring in, so all the YA books we've found strewn around other genres are currently waiting for a shelf of their own. And everyone knows YA books aren't just for teenagers, so there's a much better chance of adults finding wonderful books they wouldn't otherwise have looked at if I can squeeze them in between the romantic comedies and the fantasy books.

I turn my attention to the next shelf, the start of the horror books, which also contains a lot of sagas, women's fiction, and cookery books that have been put back in the wrong places. Although, with my mum and cookery books, horror is admittedly the right section. We've been trying to tackle the piles of books on the floor first because everywhere is so stacked up there isn't even space to slide the ladder along and reach the upper parts of some shelves.

I pick up a copy of Henry James's *The Turn of the Screw* and open it. 'Oh, look at this. Someone's written a baby's birth announcement. Hadley. Born 19/9/09. 6lbs 2oz. How sweet is that?'

I hand the book up to him and he looks between the cover, the writing, and me, with a confused look on his face. 'Do you not think this is an odd choice of book to write it in?'

'A horror? Maybe it's what they were reading at the time?

Maybe it was the only thing a proud grandma or granddad had to hand when the call came through telling them about the birth?'

'Have you read it?'

I shake my head. 'I don't like horror books. I think the world is horrible enough as it is. I read books to escape to somewhere nice. I remember watching the film with Nicole late at night when Mum had gone to bed after expressly forbidding us to watch it because it was too scary for our young minds.'

'So you know it's about two seriously creepy children? A governess starts work at the spooky old house and her job becomes protecting the children from the evil spirits that want to get at them, but the children are arguably creepier than the ghosts and certainly don't want to be protected from them. The writing is maze-like and everything's left ambiguous, but this book freaked me out when I was little. I grew up in a house not unlike Bly Manor, and after reading this, every time I looked up during a storm, I expected to see a ghostly face at the window. This was on the banned shelves of my mum's library, but me and my brother used to sneak in and raid them. Why would you write a baby's birth announcement in a book about evil children?'

'I doubt it even crossed their mind. They were probably so excited they just grabbed the nearest thing. Or maybe they were *really* proud parents and wanted to share their baby's birth with *everyone*. They could've written it in all their books for all you know.'

'Maybe it's a warning. This book is very much about not being taken in by beauty. The governess is captivated by the children because they're so beautiful. She doesn't understand why people keep saying they misbehave and why they've been expelled from school when they're so eerily perfect. Maybe it's a way of saying horror can be hidden by even the most beautiful of façades.'

'For someone who is so unerringly positive, you can be really dark sometimes, you know that, don't you?' I ask, feeling myself smiling involuntarily. What I really want to ask is more about his upbringing and if he really grew up in a manor house and if he's as posh as his lovely English accent sounds.

He looks up at me with his usual smile. 'I also overthink things, as you can tell. I'm sure there's absolutely nothing *Omen*-like to this *at all*. At least the baby wasn't called Damian.'

I'm giggling as I reach up to snatch the book out of his hand because he's just winding me up now. 'Oh, stop it. You're nowhere near as funny as you think you are.'

'I'm just saying. They obviously didn't have high hopes for how that baby was going to turn out.'

I mark the spine with a heart sticker and slide it into a space on the horror shelves with the other 'J' authors. There's still a *long* way to go on the alphabetising work.

Dimitri crouches down beside me and takes a marriage manual from between the Joe Hill and Susan Hill books. 'Now there's one that belongs on the horror shelves.'

'You believe in love,' I say incredulously.

'I believe in the hope of love. As something to look forward to. A hope to cling on to. My only actual experience of relationships is that they end in misery. And I did specify that it doesn't necessarily mean love in a romantic way.' He opens the book and holds it out in front of me. 'Look at this.'

I read the inscription.

Best wishes on your wedding day, Tracie and Dean
Follow this guide and love will be by your side.
Laugh and love and you'll be forever young and forever happy.
  All my love, ~ B

'How sweet,' I say. 'What a lovely wedding gift.'

'A novel came out a couple of years ago about a woman who chopped up her husband and ate him. B could've chosen that instead.'

I narrow my eyes at him until he nearly overbalances from

laughing so hard. 'At least it's not written in a "How to get away with murder" book. I'm not sure I can take any more weird book choices tonight.'

I can't help laughing. He's trying to wind me up but his eyes are shining and the harder he tries not to smile, the more he does.

'Oh, stop it,' I say again as I put my hand on his knee and give him a playful shove.

He squeaks as he topples over and grabs my arm, dragging me down too, until we're both sprawled on the floor laughing, like a deranged game of Twister, with my head somewhere near his knee and my arm wrapped around his calf and his other foot under my elbow.

'Left foot, yellow!' he calls out, and I start laughing. 'All we're missing is a Twister mat. I'm going to have to stop crouching down near you. It rarely ends well.' He thinks for a moment. 'Although ending up in compromising positions on the floor of a bookshop is not the *worst* way I've spent an evening.' He nudges his foot gently into my side as we try to untangle ourselves.

'Now what could be compromising about this?' I say as I get onto my knees and hold a hand out to pull him up too. I'd be lying if I said it wasn't an excuse to slip my hand into his and feel his elegant fingers close tightly around my mine. I pull him up but the momentum sends him crashing into me and I end up on my back with him on top of me, his chin pressing into my upper boob area.

'I have no idea.' He looks pointedly down at my chest and then back up at my face and my whole body flushes as his eyes focus on my lips and his body weighs heavier on mine. His eyes darken and his tongue wets his own lips and my arm tightens around his back, holding him to me rather than pushing him up like I should be doing.

'Dimitri ...' I murmur, reaching up to tuck his hair back, my fingers curling into thick, straight strands and using the grip to pull him closer, and the movement is enough to shock us both out of the trance we seem to have fallen into. He scrambles backwards and, ever the gentleman, holds his hand out to pull me into a sitting position.

He picks up the book that's got lost somewhere in the melee, and leans across me to take a heart sticker and put it on the spine. 'Now, see, I'd love to know if this marriage worked out. It would be a great advertisement for the book if it did.'

I straighten my glasses and try to concentrate on picking up one of the book piles we knocked over, but an idea has popped into my head and every thought is currently centred on it.

'I'll go and put this with the non-fiction.'

'Hey,' I say as he goes to walk off. 'Do you realise what we've found here? Young love, marriage, and a birth, and that's just tonight. Every milestone in life can be shaped by books.'

'It shows how special they are. Books stay with you in a way that TV shows and films don't. Every one of these messages proves that.' His smile is soft and his words are quiet and meaningful. 'It's been a long time since I met someone who agreed with that.'

I come over all flushed because he makes me feel exactly the same way, and every time I talk to him, it's like a breath of fresh air – like I've found what's always been missing from my life. Someone who understands me.

'What if we did find out?' I blurt out the thought that appeared at his mention of the marriage before I can rethink saying it. 'Whether the marriage worked out. What about Vickie and Tommy too? What about Esme in *Les Mis*?'

He leans against the shelf and crosses his orange boot over his blue boot. 'Go on …'

'What if we've found these messages for a reason? What if we could bring some much-needed joy to Buntingorden? What if the reason we've found these is because we're supposed to reunite the people in them?'

He looks like he's humouring me, but now the idea is there,

I can't get it out of my head. All these books with messages in them. Romantic messages. Special messages. Messages that don't seem like they belong, unwanted, in a second-hand bookshop. Robert was always talking about the unique magic that existed in Once Upon A Page. I always thought he was just a soppy old book lover, but what if he was right? 'What if these messages are hidden away in here for a reason and now we're supposed to put them back out into the universe and share some of that unique magic that books invoke?'

'Well, I *am* starting to believe it can't be coincidence that almost every second-hand book in this shop has a message inside it …'

'Exactly! This little bookshop is full of love stories and they deserve to be shared. I feel like we found them for a reason, and now it's up to us to find out what it is. Don't you think it would be fantastic to find some of the writers or receivers of these notes?'

'It'd be incredible, but how, Hal? We have no idea where these books came from or when the notes were written …'

'The answer to most things these days – the Internet.' The fact he hasn't immediately dismissed my idea buoys my confidence and I scramble excitedly onto my knees, re-knocking over the stack of books I've just picked up. 'We need to build our online presence, and this could be how. This is something unique to Once Upon A Page – something that makes us different. We put these notes online. Photograph the books and their inscriptions and post them on Twitter, Facebook, Instagram. See if we can get them to spread far and wide … See if anyone recognises them.'

'The words needle and haystack spring to mind …'

'I know, but we have to try,' I say, because there's something special about this shop and all the hidden inscriptions inside its books – something that deserves to be shared with other bookish people who will think it's as special as I do.

Chapter 10

It's ten to one on Saturday afternoon when Dimitri suddenly jumps up from the reading area and starts shoving pencils back into his bag and gathering up his sketchbooks. 'Oh God, I've forgotten the book club!'

Never mind that, *I've* forgotten the book club. I glance at the display of *The Boy in the Striped Pyjamas* on the back wall of the shop. I hadn't realised how much it had diminished over the past week or so. I know I've rung up a few copies, but it didn't even occur to me they were for the book club.

'Are you getting up to help me?' I frantically search around under the counter for where I put the list of teas and coffees Robert left me.

He lets out a laugh so hard that he starts choking. 'No, I'm going to hide. You know that song by Meatloaf, "I'd Do Anything For Love (But I Won't Do That)"? The original lyrics were probably "the Saturday afternoon book club at Once Upon A Page in Buntingorden", but they thought "that" was more succinct for the final version. Did you get biscuits in?'

'No.'

He freezes in his tracks and his eyes grow impossibly wide. 'Please tell me you're joking.'

'I'm sure they can cope without—'

'Give me money from the till. I'll do an emergency supermarket run. *Quick!*' He's practically vibrating on the spot as I fumble around until the till opens and I take a tenner out of it. 'Will this—'

He grabs it out of my hand so quickly that he nearly takes a couple of fingers with it. 'Your life won't be worth living if you've forgotten the biscuits! Can you put my stuff away?' He shouts from outside the window as he's running down the road. He suddenly stops and doubles back. 'Hallie, CHAIRS!' he yells before running off again.

All this over biscuits? Surely they could've done without? All right, I haven't exactly stocked my cupboards lately, but I'm sure I could've found a bar of chocolate or two for them to nibble on, or maybe some cheese and crackers … Well, I don't have any crackers, and I suppose offering them pieces of cheese would've felt a bit like feeding a herd of mice, but I've never seen anyone get so wound up over biscuits before. And this is Britain – if there's one thing we're going to get wound up over, it'll be biscuits.

I mutter to myself as I go over and pack pens, charcoal sticks, erasers, sharpeners, and approximately 48,283 pencils back into his bag, stand the sketchbooks in and go to return *Pentamerone* to its usual shelf under the stairs. There are a few chairs stacked in the office so I drag them out and set them up near the reading area, but there's nowhere near enough for all the names on the tea and coffee list, so I go and grab some of the kids' ones from upstairs too, frantically wishing I'd had time to prepare. Book clubs are supposed to have questions and intelligent discussions led by a leader, and although I've read the book, it was years ago, and I intended to flick through it again to refresh my memory before this afternoon arrived, but now I've got no chance.

Dimitri comes dashing back in with an armful of packets of biscuits, which he dumps on the counter along with a clatter of change. I look at the selection in bewilderment. There is literally a packet of each Great British Biscuit rolling around on the countertop, from Rich Teas to Malted Milks to Custard Creams.

I pick up his bag. 'Here's your—'

'Thank you.' He grabs the bag from my hand, his fingers lingering on mine for just a second too long. 'I'm not here. Good luck – you're going to need it.'

And with that, he's gone. Disappeared into the shelves where he hides when it's busy, not giving me a chance to consider that touch or how much he seems to be over-reacting to a few old people coming in to chat about a book they've recently read.

I can still hear him panting from the run as the first group of old ladies enter, all clutching the blue-striped book, and I take their momentary distraction at the window display as a chance to surreptitiously grab a packet of Chocolate Hobnobs and shove them to the back of a shelf behind the counter. If there's an event that requires this amount of biscuits, I'm going to need a Chocolate Hobnob to myself, although I don't know what he's so worried about. It's a book club. What could possibly go wrong?

Oh, God, they're everywhere.

When I go upstairs to make drinks, I have the brilliant idea of writing the names from the list Robert left onto Post-it Notes and sticking them to each mug as I make it rather than trying to remember which one is which, and by the time I've taken the risk of carrying a full tray of mugs down the stairs, there's a woman called Pauline behind the counter serving a customer, another one trying to sell a young student on the merits of Jilly Cooper, an old man having a snooze in the reading area, and another old man with a grandson who's trying to show him how to use an iPad while the little boy looks like he's swiftly losing the will to exist.

Every chair has been occupied and every inch of sofa and table in the reading area is overtaken too.

There is biscuit carnage on the counter. And the tables in the reading area. And the sofas. The Bourbon Creams are nearly gone, and that's without cups of tea to dunk them in. The rest of the packets look like they've been torn into by a troop of famished hyenas, and the constant squawking babble in the shop is also reminiscent, and I glance out the window, wondering if we've accidentally turned left and ended up on the African savanna and we're about to see herds of wildebeests and prides of lions sweeping past while giraffes nibble the bunting overhead.

There's a vacuum cleaner in the office and I briefly consider getting it out and leaving it running full time and just sort of swishing over everyone's clothes each time they move to suck up some of the biscuit crumbs that are currently being trodden into my carpet. That wouldn't be terribly rude, would it? 'Another Fruit Shortie? That's fine, just have a quick swoosh with Henry first. Thanks.'

I have to look away from the carpet. It's stressing me out too much.

'Hallie!' they squeal in unison when I appear, waking the snoozing bloke with a jolt.

Old ladies swarm around me as they come over to hug me and introduce themselves, and by the time they've all taken their cups of tea and settled themselves back into their chosen chairs, I'm feeling distinctly oxygen deprived. I'm also terrible with names. There's a Hilda and a Tilda and there might even be a Milda. No, that sounds like something you'd be bleaching out of bathroom corners, I must've got that wrong. There's a Pauline and a Francine, and Barbara's married to Percy who's definitely got the right idea about having a Garibaldi and going back to sleep.

'Did everyone read the book?' I ask.

No one answers. No one heard me. They're too busy gossiping about their neighbours' gardens and whose what is flowering and who looks like they've sabotaged someone else's hydrangeas. I've never been in a room with twenty old ladies before, but hydrangeas seem like an unnaturally popular topic of conversation.

I repeat myself, and this time they do hear, but making my presence known was a mistake. I'm immediately surrounded by the Tilda, Hilda, or Milda, and questioned on my age, relationship status, and whether I've got my eye on anyone in the village as they start drawing up a list of Buntingorden's most eligible bachelors.

'Ooh, have you met the chap who runs the souvenir shop?' Hilda cries, and a chorus of agreements follow. They are basically my mum in surround-sound.

Somehow the packet of Gingernuts has remained unopened and Tilda or Milda tears into them, accidentally breaking the wrapper and scattering biscuits right the way across the low coffee table in front of the brown leather sofas, breaking as they land, and the ladies set upon the broken smithereens like hungry birds when you throw a handful of seed out on a snowy midwinter's day and more crumbs fly around, worse than that time I made the mistake of buying glittery wrapping paper.

'Speaking of gossip, did you see that letter from The Stropwomble of Bodmin Lane in the paper this morning?' Tilda or Milda says. Maybe it was Vilda? No, that's a brand of mop, isn't it?

'Complaining that the swans are too noisy, for goodness' sake,' Pauline says. 'Swans are the most silent bird in existence.'

'And last week it was starlings. Too many starlings, he said. Trying to get people to sign a petition to ban starlings from Buntingorden. I put out extra food for them just to spite him.'

'Whatever will it be next?' Barbara says. 'Complaints that the dawn chorus comes too early? Petitions to stop badgers having pedicures? Death to all earthworms?'

'Oh, not him again,' I mutter, my mind going back to the little boy called Charlie and his stories about the monster of Buntingorden.

Of course, of all the things I've tried to say so far, *that's* the one they choose to hear.

'Have you met him?'

'No, but I've heard of him. I hate people like that – people who can't find anything better to do with their lives than complain and spoil things for everyone else.'

A collective sigh shakes the room. 'No one's ever seen him, you know,' one of the ladies says. I should get name badges made up because I've got so muddled that I can't remember her name.

'They say he's a hideous monster, disfigured and cold to a world that's turned its back on him,' another one says.

'You sure that's not *The Hunchback of Notre Dame*? He hasn't got a couple of talking gargoyles, has he?' My sarcasm goes straight over their heads.

'He's this nasty, evil presence. Whenever something nice happens in Buntingorden, you can be sure that he's lurking in the wings to find a way of ruining it. The whole town would be so much nicer if he wasn't here.'

'And look at that house on Bodmin Lane. It used to be so lovely, and now it's all crumbling and overgrown, and he's got this great big iron fence with barbwire on top. I think he killed the previous owners and took over the place and that's why he never comes out, because he's a murderer on the run,' Tilda says. Now I remember her name because of the brand of rice.

'A fugitive!' Someone else claps.

They sound abnormally excited by the prospect of a murderous fugitive in town, while I wonder if I've accidentally stumbled into an episode of *Midsomer Murders*.

'We were hoping you'd have met him. He likes to complain about everything – we thought he was bound to have come in and complained about the bookshop.' Milda, the biscuit crusher, sprays crumbs as she talks.

'You've still got bowls of water outside for thirsty dogs, and you let dogs inside. He's always writing to the local newspapers complaining about how unhygienic it is,' says the man who's given up on his iPad and is watching his grandson playing on it now.

'I love dogs. Who *wouldn't* want them inside? One of the nicest things about this village is that it's dog-friendly and you can't go far without meeting a dog to scruffle. It's not uptight like other high streets where dogs aren't welcome. It's great considering we're in the middle of a touristy dog-walking spot.'

'And that roof terrace.' Hilda ignores my monologue on the benefits of allowing dogs in. 'You had that open the other day. There's no way he would've let you get away with that. I wouldn't have been surprised if he'd come straight over to demand you close it at once.'

'It was open for ten minutes,' I say incredulously. 'How would he know about that? How do *you* even know about it?'

They ignore me. 'You can bet your best socks that he's written to the council complaining about it. You'll probably get a letter from them soon saying they've received a complaint.'

'And your window display,' the one called Barbara says. 'It's very pretty, but he's always writing letters to the local newspaper whenever something changes on the street. He'll say that's a visual hazard or an invitation to thieves because it blocks some of your visibility.'

I glance at the mermaid window. It's about time I changed it, actually. Dimitri's chalk scales are being accidentally rubbed off by hands reaching for books in the display, and my selection of mermaid-themed books are getting thin on the ground. 'That's not fair. Why would anyone complain about it? It doesn't affect him in any way.'

'He would've called it an eyesore. He's done it with every shop – written to the council complaining about the things on display in their window.'

'That's awful. My friend did those scales – they are *not* an eyesore.' I feel ridiculously protective of Dimitri's artwork.

'Ooh, that gorgeous young chap who sketches here?' Tilda asks, but the question is obviously rhetorical because a wave of 'oohs' and 'ahhs' sweep through the group at the mention of him.

'Oh, if I was thirty years younger,' one of them says, kicking off a squabble with her neighbour who has the gall to suggest that fifty is more accurate.

'I want to set him up with my granddaughter but he's never here on Saturday afternoons,' another one adds.

'He's *delicious*,' Milda says. 'And single too, you know?'

'Is he? I had *no* idea.' My voice goes high and unsteady, even though there's something adorable about a group of old ladies thinking he's the best thing since chocolate was invented.

'Are you going to ask him out?' Tilda says. 'I think you'd make a lovely couple.'

A chorus of agreements follow from everyone else in the group. I know my face has gone red, which is kindly pointed out when one of them squeals, 'Ooh, you must like him – you've gone red!'

I sincerely hope Dimitri can't hear any of this from his hiding spot.

Percy sits up long enough to say in a deep, booming voice, 'Hush now, you're embarrassing the poor girl,' before going back to sleep. I suspect he might be faking it to get out of book club.

I decide it's well past time we stopped talking about gorgeous men who sketch here and pick up a copy of *The Boy in the Striped Pyjamas*. 'So how did you all get on with this month's read?'

The sooner we can get on with the book club discussion, the sooner I can get those crumbs hoovered up.

'A refill!' Tilda shouts.

'Have you got any more biscuits?' Milda asks.

More biscuits? They're not having my Chocolate Hobnobs, and they've wolfed down nine packets already. No wonder this is only a monthly occurrence. I'd have to buy shares in McVitie's otherwise.

I take another round of orders for tea and coffee and leave them muttering about my pathetic lack of biscuits. It's almost like they know I've got one hidden and are trying to sniff it out.

By the time I get back downstairs with more drinks, I've lost them again as Hilda holds court with a story about her postman's canary. Even Heathcliff is hiding inside his aquarium castle, and he's usually all over a bit of gossip. Even a Shih Tzu walking past outside isn't enough to tempt him from his hiding place.

'Shall we get onto the book?' I say loudly. I'm sure I can hear Dimitri's laughter echoing out from the shelves under the stairs.

They all turn to look at me.

'I read it years ago. I remember not liking the sound-a-like words, even though I see the innocence the author was trying to convey, and I thought Bruno was unrealistically dense to not realise what was really going on. But that ending. That's an ending I never, ever saw coming, and I've never forgotten it since. What did you all think?'

I get a chorus of 'oh, yes, that' and 'excellents, goods, and greats'. I'm ninety-nine per cent sure that not one of them has read it. And if they have, then they definitely didn't come here to discuss it.

A customer makes her way through the biscuit crumbs with a couple of hefty Shakespeare plays and I go behind the counter to serve her, and there I stay, wishing I could risk a Chocolate Hobnob without being seen. The other old man goes to sleep on the sofa and the grandson with the iPad turns up the volume on whatever game he's playing, so the soundtrack to the afternoon is a series of bloop-bleeps as he shoots down pixellated aliens, and a whole slew of gossip about people I've never met.

At five to five, they all put their cups down in unison, pop their books back into their handbags, gather up their coats and cardigans, which have been strewn an impressive distance across the shop, and start filing out. Hilda drags me out from behind the counter and envelops me in a hug. 'Lovely, Hallie. Just as good as Robert ever did it.'

Each one follows in her footsteps with a hug and a variation of the same thing. 'Better, even. More biscuits to choose from.'

'See you again next month.'

'Don't forget to put June's book up on Monday. We'll all be in for a copy.'

'Can you get the double-pack of Custard Creams next time?'

'I wouldn't mind some Jaffa Cakes. Ooh, how about a packet of Fig Rolls?'

I can still hear them discussing various biscuits as I shut the door behind them and flick the book-shaped sign to 'closed.'

I let out a breath that feels like the first one all afternoon. I see why Dimitri went into hiding.

I go through to the back half of the shop and duck around shelves until I get to the little corner under the stairs where Robert stored rare or valuable books. I knock on the edge of the shelf like it's a door and put my head round it. 'They've gone – you can come out now.'

It's a short aisle with shelves down either side and one across the back wall, and Dimitri's sitting in the corner, surrounded by cushions, reclining against the back shelf with his head resting on the right-hand shelf. *Pentamerone* is on the floor beside him and his sketchbook is open on his knees as he draws.

He looks up at me sleepily. 'No, I can't, because that would require moving, and I'm way too comfortable to move.'

He does look comfortable. And I'd thought the sofas were looking a bit bare because he must have every cushion from the reading area.

I lean against the shelf. 'So when you said it wasn't a book club, but a monthly biscuit-eating contest ... Why didn't I take you seriously?'

He gives me a soft smile. 'Some things you have to learn for yourself. A rite of passage, like your first Stephen King novel or the first time you find out a bandicoot is a real animal or discover it's not really Christopher Plummer singing in *The Sound of Music*.'

To be fair, my first Stephen King novel was a lot more enjoyable than my first Once Upon A Page book club, although equally terrifying.

'Word to the wise though – do *not* buy Jaffa Cakes next time. Robert did once. They were here for three days having the "cake or biscuit" debate. And don't buy Jammie Dodgers, the chewiness leads to all sorts of denture-related pandemonium.'

I really hope he's exaggerating.

He looks so relaxed that he could fall asleep, different to the usual way he sits hunched over his sketchbooks on the table. His eyes are heavy lidded behind his thick glasses when he looks up at me again and pats the empty cushion beside him. 'Come and sit here.'

I gesture towards the shop. 'I have to clean up.'

'Hallie.' His voice is gentle but firm, and I don't need any more persuasion.

I get an idea and point at him. 'Hold that thought.'

Steadfastly ignoring the biscuit crumbs, I dash upstairs and make two cups of tea and snag the hidden Hobnobs on the way back.

Dimitri's face breaks into the widest smile I've ever seen when I reappear at the shelves. I've always thought a smile lighting up a face was a myth, a trope that romance authors use to convey happiness but I didn't think it was something that actually happened. 'You're a star, thank you. I was just thinking how much I wish I'd nicked a packet.'

He pulls *Pentamerone* under his legs to make space for me, and knowing how clumsy I am without me needing to say it, he takes both cups off me and sets them carefully in the space at the front of the shelf he's leaning against, and holds his hand up to help me down.

I'm quite capable of sitting down without assistance, but I don't miss an opportunity to slip my hand into his and lower myself onto the cushion beside him, and he produces another one from seemingly thin air and I stuff it in behind my back, surprised to find it's comfier than it looks down here. It's not exactly roomy though, and I'm sort of tipping towards him on the uneven cushions. I wriggle around a bit, but one arm is already pressed against the shelf to my left and the other is pressed against his.

He neatly undoes the packet of Chocolate Hobnobs and offers me one first – ever the perfect gentleman. We both manage to take one out without spilling a single crumb, which is quite a feat for two people who are so uncoordinated, but I'm not sure I can handle any more biscuit-related mayhem today.

'For what it's worth, I thought you did a great job. I silently applauded your efforts in trying to get the conversation back round to the book. And if it's any consolation, I thought *The Boy in the Striped Pyjamas* was excellent and totally agreed with what you said. It's been years since I read it and that ending has never left me.'

'And to think I was worrying that I hadn't had time to swot up on the book.' Our hands brush as he passes my cup of tea over, holding the hot mug itself so I can take the handle. 'So let me get this straight – they buy the book, either read it or don't read it, and then come here once a month on the pretence of discussing it but really just to eat biscuits and gossip? They're supporting the shop, but as a biscuit-eating and tea-drinking establishment.'

'I wouldn't knock it. That's a good amount of books you sell each month, and no one cares what they're about. I reckon you could have a book about painting walls and they'd still buy it to read about which ones dry first. I *do* think they read the books, but they only get around to talking about it when they run out of biscuits and village gossip, and with at least twenty busybodies on site, they *never* run out of village gossip, although the biscuits don't stand much chance.'

'Even though I'm seriously questioning your loyalty for going into hiding …' I nudge my shoulder against his. 'Thank you for doing the supermarket run. I see how it would've been an unforgivable offence not to have biscuits.'

'Aw, I'm sorry. I'm not very good with being surrounded by people, but I didn't want to abandon you entirely.'

I look up at him, his hair falling across his forehead, looking floppier than usual, reflecting how relaxed he is. 'You're a real introvert, aren't you?'

He considers it for a moment. 'I'm used to being on my own. When my sister was alive, she was self-conscious of how she was treated in public, and when the treatment started up again, she lost her hair and was terrified of running into girls she knew from the time when things had been better and she'd been able to go to school, so we rarely went anywhere apart from hospital appointments and the library. And since then …' He takes his glasses off, blinks up at the ceiling, and puts them back on again. 'I must sound so dull. Until Robert took pity on me and let me come here, I was basically a hermit.'

The mental image makes me grin. 'You are way too clean-shaven to be a hermit. Did you have a beard?'

'I dunno, you couldn't find it under all the hair that had grown Cousin Itt-style to my feet.'

This time it makes me laugh out loud, and he beams at me with just enough hesitancy behind his smile to make me not *quite* sure he's joking.

'You don't sound dull at all,' I say. 'You sound …' Perfect. Gentle. Like a guy who's been through more than he ever lets on. 'It sounds like my version of heaven. Peace and quiet, and books.'

'And plenty of tea and biscuits.'

'Naturally.' I pull my head back to look up at him, and for one surreal minute, I think he's going to kiss me. He bites his lip to stop the tremble in it, and his head lowers almost imperceptibly. I can feel the brush of his hair against mine, the fine blonde hairs covering his muscular forearms graze my arms, feeling like

178

burning beacons where our arms are touching, and then he turns away and picks up his cup from the shelf and the moment is lost. I pick up my own cup of tea and take another biscuit, sploshing it in with reckless abandon and regretting it when one half glugs sorrowfully to the bottom of the mug. That'll teach me to dunk biscuits without due care and attention.

I want to know everything there is to know about his life, but he seems quiet and introspective, and not like he wants to talk about it. My eyes fall on the open sketchbook in his lap. 'Why does that woman have a goat's face?'

'There's this poor man with twelve daughters who he can't afford to feed, so a giant lizard offers to raise his youngest daughter in exchange for giving him great wealth. The daughter is raised in a palace and eventually falls in love with a king and marries him, but when she leaves, she doesn't thank the lizard so he turns her head into a goat's head. As you do.'

'Well, you would, wouldn't you?' I giggle.

'They're not all as disturbing as they look, I promise.' He puts his sketchbook aside and pulls the old storybook onto his lap instead. 'Here, you'll like this one.' He turns some pages and runs his finger across the lines of text on the aged paper and starts reading aloud, a story about three princesses marrying three princes who have been enchanted into the form of animals. I lean closer to him to follow the words he's reading, but the text is tiny, and it seems like the most natural thing in the world to rest my head against his shoulder, and I'm surprised in a good way when he lowers his head and leans it against mine too. I feel the smile spreading across his face, the quietness of his words and how I feel every breath against my hair.

It only takes him a few minutes to read, and when the story finishes with a typically fairy-tale-esque dragon slaying, the curse being lifted, and a happily-ever-after, I should probably lift my head, but I don't, and he makes no attempt to move either.

'Did you just read me a bedtime story?' I speak in a whisper because speaking normally will sound like a shout in the empty shop.

He lets out a soft laugh. 'I don't know what time it is, but it can't even be six o'clock. We can't go to bed yet.' He instantly stiffens and tries to backpedal. 'I've just realised how bad that sounded. I didn't mean we should be going anywhere near a bed together, I just meant ...'

I reach over and pat his knee, the nearest thing I can touch without having to move. 'I know what you meant,' I say, even though I'm so comfortable down here that I could happily fall asleep with him.

'You must think I'm mad to like this stuff. I find the evolution of fairy tales fascinating, and how they're something that's survived for centuries in different forms and they still appeal even to this day. There's something so innocent and hopeful about them, particularly Disney ones. Even the oldest of those films are over eighty years old now, and children still grow up with them. They're timeless. It feels ... I don't know, kind of special to go back to these original tales and try to update them for a modern world.'

'These stories are wonderfully weird.' I look at the brightly striped socks with penguins all over them showing above the ankles of odd-coloured boots that are on the opposite feet this time. Wonderfully weird, just like him.

I try to think of any other person I've ever known who would sit on the floor of a bookshop and read centuries-old Italian fairy tales aloud to a fellow adult, and somehow make the simplicity of sharing biscuits and drinking tea into the best evening I can ever remember.

'Have you met whoever your publisher has got updating the text? I mean, you must be working together on it. What if you hate the translation the other person comes up with?'

'It doesn't really work like that and I'm sure you don't want to hear about this. Another Hobnob?' He holds the packet out, and if I wasn't enjoying his company so much, I might've thought twice about the oddly abrupt subject change, but chocolate biscuits are enough to distract anyone without adding Dimitri's aftershave that's like the fresh wood of walking through a forest where they've just been felling trees to the mix.

'I feel like a kid again,' I murmur against his shoulder, not keen to move any time before Monday.

He rubs his head against mine gently. 'Me too. I love being here. Everything feels better here. It's like being surrounded by different worlds, different lives, and whatever you're going through, you know there are stories here about people who have been through different things and always found a way to overcome them. I find that comforting somehow, even though they're only fictional.'

'I think books have a unique power. A way of transporting you to a place or time that makes you use your imagination, instead of just showing you, like a film does. I've used them as an escape all my life.'

'Me too. I was a shy, dorky kid who didn't make friends easily, and I turned to books for a better world, and now I'm a shy, dorky adult who doesn't make friends easily and I still turn to books for better worlds. I've never felt like I fitted in anywhere, but it didn't matter when I was reading about characters who didn't fit in either. That's why I love coming here. I've always felt at home when surrounded by books.'

Hearing him describe himself like that makes me want to hug him, but we're too cramped together, and it's probably best I don't anyway. I settle for tilting my head and pressing the side of my jaw against his shoulder. 'Same,' I whisper against his shirt. 'Shy, clumsy kid who never knew what to say to make people like me and always ended up choosing the wrong thing. I was bullied at school so I used to hide in the library every lunchtime. I'd snaffle my packed lunch on the way up the stairs and then have a whole fifty minutes every day to read. I found some of my favourite books there. I read all the Judy Blumes over and over again, all the Point Horrors and Point Romances, and my favourite was a two-book series by Dyan Sheldon about a girl who fell in love with the ghost that haunted her bedroom. I used to lie awake at night wishing I had a hot, motorcycle-riding ghost haunting my house.'

I can feel his smile against my hair. 'Me too. Well, maybe not about the hot ghost, but yeah. I was bullied too for being tall and awkward and stuttery, and I hid in libraries too. My mum used to take me every week when I was little and the librarian always used to tell me off for trying to sneak out more than my allotted four books and an extra four on my mum's card too.'

'Kids are cruel,' I murmur, because the idea of him being bullied for everything I like about him makes me want to pull him into the tightest hug and sort of clutch him to my bosom like some old matronly Mrs Doubtfire character, even though my bosom is nowhere near ample enough and I've never once referred to it as a bosom before in my life. I don't know what's got into me lately. I must be being possessed by the spirits of all these old book characters. I'll be pulling up my stockings and going Morris dancing while moaning about my varicose veins next.

'Adults are worse.'

My breath catches because his voice is flat and quiet and without any of its usual timbre, and I kind of want to pull back and look into his eyes and tell him he's wrong, but he's not, is he? Adults can be the cruellest of them all, and they're old enough to know better, and somehow that makes it worse. And if I move, it might be weird to put my head back on his shoulder again so I don't want to risk it yet.

Like he can tell how melancholy that sounded, he takes a breath and seems to rally himself. 'Thank God for books, eh? Every big event in my life has been marked by books. I remember what I was reading at the time, or what was recommended to me, or what was bought for me. My mum was a huge reader and always believed in marking occasions with books. Whenever something good happened, she'd take me to a bookshop to choose whatever one I wanted. Do you remember the school book fairs?'

'Oh my God, the book fairs.' I'm glad he can't see my face because I'm currently the spitting image of the heart eyes emoji. 'My mum's most hated week of the term, and my most anticipated. There was something so special about those big metal cases being wheeled into the assembly hall. It's one thing secondary school was always missing – no Scholastic book fairs.'

'Mind you, we would've been a bit old for them by then, wouldn't we?'

'Oh, I don't know. I made my mum get me a Funfax from the book fair when I was eight and I thought I was the coolest kid in class. The best thing ever was filling in all your details and spending all your pocket money on those little books to put inside.'

He laughs. 'But you remember it as a pivotal part of your childhood. That's what I mean. Everyone's life is shaped by special books. I grew up with Enid Blyton's tales from The Wishing Chair to the Famous Five, and The Faraway Tree to Malory Towers, and then onto teenage books, and smuggled adult books that were supposedly too old for me.'

'I loved Enid Blyton, especially Malory Towers. Malory Towers was the Harry Potter of our generation. You know, the boarding school that everyone wanted to go to, full of characters that everyone wanted to be friends with?'

'I went to boarding school. Believe me, it's not all it's cracked up to be.'

'Really?' I tilt my head against his shoulder. Boarding school has always struck me as a thing for frightfully posh people and Dimitri doesn't seem like that at all.

'Yeah. When you're young and loving life in the local primary school and all your friends are here, and then suddenly you're being driven across the country and dumped in this strange environment with all these new people and rules and rich kids who *really* don't like you. My brother already went there and he'd taken to it like a fish to water, but he's different from me. I'd begged my parents for months not to make me go there, but like everything else with my father, what he wants is all that matters.'

'I'm sorry,' I say quietly, surprised by the bitterness in his voice.

'No, I'm sorry. I didn't mean to say any of that. There's just something about you that makes me want to talk. Suffice to say it's not all wizarding spells and house elves, although I wish Harry Potter had been around in our younger days. I would've been *obsessed* with it as a pre-teen. I mean, I was obsessed enough as an adult, but …'

I wasn't surrounded by book lovers before I won Once Upon A Page, and something as simple as someone who understands my love of books and grew up at roughly the same time I did, reading the same things that I loved … there's something so special about it.

My mind drifts as I sit there with my head on Dimitri's shoulder, thinking about all the books I've loved over the years, both of us occasionally sharing titles and opinions, from the classics of *Great Expectations* to the magic of *The Lion, the Witch, and the Wardrobe* series by C.S. Lewis, and how enchanted we both were by the idea of finding a whole new world through something as ordinary as a wardrobe, and the crushing disappoint when none of *our* wardrobes led to Narnia.

'Should we move?' he says when silence has fallen. 'It's not that I want to, but I'm going to fall asleep in a minute and my biggest fantasy is spending the night in a bookshop, so if you're not careful, you're never going to get rid of me.'

'Worse things have happened.'

'Mmm.' He mumbles an agreement and reaches a hand out blindly until I catch hold of it and slip my fingers between his.

He squeezes tightly and pulls my hand against his leg, holding it there. 'I'm really glad we met, Hallie. It feels like I've known you forever.'

'Me too,' I whisper, my voice sounding as unsteady as I feel.

This doesn't just happen. Gorgeous men don't fall into the shop you're working in and sweep you off your feet – not in real life, anyway. And yet I feel distinctly unstable and like my legs are metaphorically going from under me. He's *perfect*. And perfect men like him don't exist, so there must be a catch. His words make my stomach roll and goose bumps rise all over my body. I still feel light-headed from his aftershave and wobbly from the proximity and how right it feels to sit here holding his hand and leaning against him, and it would be so easy to kiss him. And I want to.

I swore off relationships long ago. Things had never worked out, even before Mr Maybe, and he was the final straw in my disastrous love life, but for the first time in many years, it feels right with Dimitri. Everything feels right and in my experience that can only mean one thing – it's not.

'We should get up.' Tension shoots through him as he seems to sense the precarious situation we're in. He starts moving with a jolt, shifting back upright from where we've slumped against each other, closing *Pentamerone* carefully and sliding it back into the empty space on the shelf as he sits up and pitches himself forward onto his knees and then feet.

He turns around and holds his hand out, and I look up at him with a disappointed grin, because I could easily fall asleep down here too, but it was a lot more comfortable when he was beside me.

'You get the chairs; I'll get Henry out of the office.' I go to protest but he cuts me off with a threat of upturning what's left of the Hobnobs packet.

I slip my hand into his and let him pull me to my feet. A man who hoovers. A man who *helps*. A man who is such a gent that he could've stepped from the pages of a Jane Austen novel in a top hat and tailcoat.

That's worth getting up for, even though there has to be a catch, because men like that don't exist outside of the printed pages that surround us.

Chapter 11

'I bought you something,' Dimitri says when I let him in at half past eight a few mornings later. I've noticed he's been coming earlier and earlier every day, which is fine because I've been getting down to the shop floor earlier every day too. It's impossible to lie in bed ignoring the alarm clock like I used to when there's the prospect of seeing him and finding more messages hidden in books.

'Well, made you something. Call it a prototype for the art prints I'm going to sell here. I thought I could do them about favourite books, with an image and a relevant line, and I could offer bespoke ones that people could order if they wanted a really individual gift for someone special …'

I'm unable to stop myself smiling as I pile more books onto the counter from the window display I'm in the middle of emptying. I love how much he's getting into this. I thought someone of his talent and a soon-to-be published author would be above handmade prints for a little bookshop.

He pulls an A4-sized canvas frame out of his bag, puts it on the counter and unwraps the cloth protecting it, keeping the reverse side turned towards me. I reach out to turn it around and he pulls away like a jolt of static electricity has sparked as our fingers brush.

And I can't hide the intake of breath. It's the most *beautiful* drawing I've ever seen. A mix of watercolours and charcoal depicting a scene from *Tiger Eyes* by Judy Blume, my favourite book. There's the silhouette of a girl sitting on a rock overlooking a canyon, and the words '*Cuando los lagartijos corren*' written across the orange-to-mulberry ombré sky above her.

I burst into tears.

They're the words that Wolf says to Davey in the book to give her hope to hold on to, something to look forward to when he goes away. It means that he'll see her again in the springtime 'when the lizards run'. They're words I repeated to myself in my head many times in the difficult years after my father died, despite the fact we lived in the Cotswolds and there were no canyons and certainly no lizards.

And he has no way of knowing that and yet somehow, he knows that.

Horror floods his face. 'Oh God, I'm so sorry. I shouldn't have. I *knew* I was overstepping the mark because you said it was personal to you and you didn't share it with anyone and I had no business—'

I jump out from behind the counter and throw my arms around his neck, pulling him down for an enforced hug while I try to furtively swipe my hands across my cheeks and not snivel in his ear. 'You are the kindest, loveliest, most thoughtful person I've ever met in my life. That's the most beautiful picture I've ever seen.'

'I've never wanted anyone to like something as much as I wanted you to like that.' His whole body sags with relief and we both stumble, glad there's a bookshelf there to stop us hitting the deck.

'It's not just that. It's *you*, Dimitri. That's the nicest thing anyone's ever done for me. You read the book just for that?'

'Are you kidding? I read the book the second you mentioned it. Do you honestly think you could mention your favourite book and I *wouldn't* read it?'

Every part of my body is shaking with the effort of trying to hold back yet *more* tears, and I force myself to reluctantly pull away from the hug. There's something about this man that makes it impossible not to hug him.

'Thank you.' It doesn't seem sufficient for everything I want to say. The fact that he's read my favourite book and somehow managed to take from it the most beautiful image and the most significant words that meant so much to my younger self ... A simple thank-you is nowhere near significant enough. 'You're so incredibly talented. You pick out simple things that invoke emotions – love, hate, fear, horror. Every time you show me something, I can never find the right words to tell you how special your work is.'

It would be so easy to lean up and kiss him. My hand reaches out and I *nearly* touch his face, slide my fingers along his smooth jaw. My eyes are glued to his mouth, the way his tongue wets his lips and he swallows, and—

There's a hammering on the door that makes us both jump so hard that it's like someone's installed a trampoline in the floor.

I spin around to see an unwelcome figure standing outside.

'It's ten to nine. We're not open yet,' I call just to be awkward.

Drake Farrer moves from the door to the window, looking in as he taps the glass and then taps his wrist. Talk about impatient.

I have every right to be petty and not open the door until nine, but I don't want him coming in and making a scene if there are customers about, and I feel safer with Dimitri here than I did on my own.

I sigh as I go to open the door. I intend to hold it ajar and refuse him entry, but the second the key has turned, he's got hold of the handle and shoved it, making me jump out of the way as the door swings open.

He stops to wipe his feet on an invisible doormat – a gesture that feels like an insult, like he's trying to imply the shop is far below his usual standards.

'Miss Winstone,' he leers, inviting himself in and striding across to the counter. 'And Dimitri. What a surprise.'

The smarmball adjusts the buttons on his wool-silk suit as he casts his eyes up and down Dimitri like he's something he's found stuck on the underside of a school desk. He sounds like he'd be more surprised to find milk in a milk bottle, and about as impressed if there was an angry hornet swimming around in said milk. A swarm of angry hornets, even.

'Farrer,' Dimitri says in a voice that's not his own. 'Hallie said she'd been having trouble with vultures. Now I see what she meant.'

Drake laughs a horrible, false laugh. 'Oh, I think birds of prey are the least of Hallie's troubles, don't you? What with *you* hanging around like the stench of a blocked drain and the dreadful state of this place.' His eyes fall on my empty window display. 'At least she saw fit to take that mermaid trash out of the window. I bet that didn't bring in any customers. No one likes mermaids anymore, do they?'

'What do you want?' I snap before he has a chance to insult my shop any further. Of all things you can insult, mermaids are not one of them.

'Merely a follow-up, Miss Winstone, to see if you've decided to come to your senses yet.' His snake-like eyes leave Dimitri and swivel to me as he steps up to the counter and puts his briefcase down on it. I don't know why I'm so offended by the gesture. Dimitri puts his bag on the counter all the time. I dump stuff there all the time. It's the only surface in the shop that's not stacked with books – things get put on it. But everything Drake Farrer does seems like it's carefully chosen to undermine me. 'I must admit I'm surprised to see you're still open. I didn't expect you to last more than a week. Still as old and stuffy as ever though. I thought you'd have tried to clean the place up a bit by now. What's that I can smell? Is it mould?'

'No, it's not. It's—'

'It's the books. The paper, ink, and glue break down over the years to release chemical compounds that produce a sweet, almost vanilla scent.' Dimitri sounds calm and collected, whereas I feel bristly and uneasy in Drake Farrer's presence.

'My, how interesting.' Drake does a fake yawn and slides a business card from his open briefcase. He holds it out but I refuse to take it. Unperturbed, he lays it on the counter and pats it instead. 'Thought you might need another one. I'm sure you *lost* the last one I gave you.'

I like the way Dimitri stands to his full height and folds his arms across his chest. He's hovering, like he's not sure whether this is anything to do with him but also like he can tell that I feel better with the moral support.

'You can tell your guard dog to stand down.' He glances at Dimitri. 'I'm actually here to apologise. I realise I may have been a bit hasty before in coming on your first day before you'd had a chance to examine the shop's accounts. My intention wasn't to put you on the spot, but merely to let you know that when you *did* have a chance to see how spectacularly your business was failing, you would know there were options. May I enquire just how spectacularly it *is* failing?'

'It's not fail—'

He lets out a low whistle as his eyes roam the shop. 'I see you've not yet ordered in any new stock, presumably because you can't afford to.'

His eyes fall on the canvas Dimitri's just given me that's propped up against the till until I decide where to hang it and he raises a cruel eyebrow. 'If you've been reduced to selling such items, business must be even more dire than I imagined.'

'How dare you—'

Dimitri places a hand on the counter and speaks without taking his eyes off Drake Farrer. 'Don't let him wind you up, Hal. He's doing everything he can to get a rise out of us. It's what he does, and he *hates* it when people see through that.' He gives him a sleek, completely false smile.

Drake Farrer ignores him. 'On the contrary, Miss Winstone, I'm trying to help you. I'm even prepared to up my offer. Here we go.' He pulls a sheet of paper from the briefcase and dangles it unnervingly close to my face. 'Five grand up from last time. And as before, you can keep your contents and your *staff*.' He gives Dimitri another obnoxious look. 'I merely want your building. But I must impress upon you that this offer expires with my patience. If you leave it until things are falling apart and then *you* come to *me* and beg me to take it off your hands, the offer will be much lower, and by that point, it will be easier and cheaper to have a nice bonfire for stock removal.'

His eyes slide to the sale table. 'I see you're already having to offer discounts. Oh dear, it doesn't bode well, does it? You are simply unable to compete with chain stores who sell their books for a pound or two.'

'We don't have any of them in Buntingorden. This is the only bookshop.'

'Well, there's the Internet, isn't there? When I build my leisure complex, I'll offer free Internet access so no one will ever need stuffy old shops like this again.'

'You've found a new site for it, have you?' I try to match the saccharine tone in his oily voice. 'You certainly won't be having this one.'

'I thought you liked Buntingorden, Miss Winstone. Don't you *want* to see this street be the best that it can be? Don't you want our little village to thrive with all the extra tourism?'

'Soulless leisure centres won't help with that. Quirky independent shops full of oddities and charm are what people come here for, and the walks and the scenery. Our little higgledy-piggledy buildings are part of that. Sticking a big shiny new building in will take away from the charm, not add to it.'

'Well, it's certainly full of oddities.' He casts his eyes towards Dimitri again.

'At least it's not full of snakes,' I snap. Forget staying calm. How dare he come in here and be so horrible? And what the hell has he got against Dimitri?

With the amount of gel holding down his abnormally shiny hair, it's no surprise that insults slide off him like water on wax, and he continues like I haven't spoken. 'I told you that my father and I are in the process of acquiring other shops on the street. If *you* were that one person to be brave and go against stuffy old tradition, the other shop owners would take *your* cue and follow *your* lead. If you make the first move and sell your ridiculously outdated building and unsafe roof terrace.'

'If they haven't already, they're doing something right,' I snap. He's like a slippery politician, but worse. 'What I don't understand is why you think marching around insulting people *and* the things everyone loves about this street is going to help your cause. No one is going to sell to someone with such disregard for everything that's good about Buntingorden.'

In my head, I'm crossing every possible crossable body part that I'm right. He already owns the empty place next door – if more shop owners give in and sell their businesses to him, surely it's only a matter of time until he gets everything he wants?

'In my opinion, business owners such as yourself deserve and respect honesty. Buntingorden's quieter than it has been in years, and you're not exactly batting customers into a single-file line as they swarm outside the door, are you?'

'We're not open yet.'

'Exactly why you'd expect them to be queuing outside.' He looks over his shoulder to the empty doorway, open because he didn't close it behind himself. 'Oh dear, what a pity.'

I glare at him.

'I'm merely stating fact, Miss Winstone. No matter how many packets of biscuits your book club consumes, you're still only selling a very limited number of books.'

How on earth does he know about that?

'And the fewer books you sell, the fewer new books you can afford to buy, so your stock remains as stale as it currently is and you get fewer and fewer buyers because there's nothing new for your few loyal customers *to* buy, and you end up going into your personal savings account to fund new stock, but you have to sell it at a discount because it's cheaper to buy online, so you don't break even on what you've spent, and you get further and further into debt, both business and personal now, until you're facing financial ruin and there's no way out.' He gives me the sort of smile you'd expect to see on an eel. 'It's simple business, but of course, you're not a businesswoman, are you?'

Well, he's definitely wrong about me dipping into my savings. Mainly because I don't have any, but still. He doesn't need to know that.

'Or maybe you'd be like Robert, living on his savings and never taking a wage for himself. Dedicating his *entire* life to a shop that gave him nothing in return. And if you've spent years doing a string of minimum-wage jobs that you've struggled to hold down, maybe you wouldn't have any savings, so maybe you'd have to start using credit cards and loans you can't pay back, and I think we all know the interest rates on those can get astronomical very quickly and debt can spiral out of control before you know it.'

How could he possibly know about that? He seems to know my entire life history *and* far too much about the shop's finances and Robert's accounts. Is he really just guessing? Am I that much of an open book? The only other person I told about Robert not taking his own wages is … I glance up at Dimitri beside me, currently glaring at Drake Farrer like a snarling hellhound who wants to feed him to carnivorous ducks.

194

Nah. It's just coincidence. Drake Farrer is used to reading people, and everyone around here knows my name from the write-up in the local newspaper about the prize draw. He must've been googling me and putting pieces of info together. I'll switch my Twitter profile to private later.

'Or I can offer you thirty-five *thousand* pounds for this worthless, crumbling building,' he carries on. 'You can get on with your life like this never happened. Be brave, Hallie.'

Him using my first name sends a horrible shiver down my spine. 'I think it's time for you to leave.' I put my hand on his business card and slide it back across the counter towards him. 'And take this with you. I won't be needing it.'

He smiles that smug condescending smile but doesn't take the card. 'I'm sure you won't. You can simply google Farrer and Sons as and *when* you need us. Unless your Internet's been cut off by then because you can't pay the bill, of course. I would imagine bills get harder and harder to pay when you're not making any money.'

He finally snaps his briefcase closed and removes it from the counter. As he turns to leave, his eyes fall on the shelf of 'Free to a good home' books inside the door, and he strides across to it and picks up a battered old copy of Roald Dahl's *Charlie and the Chocolate Factory*, holding the corner between thumb and forefinger like he might catch something from it. 'This is terrible business sense. Giving things away is not going to put any more money in that cranky old till of yours.'

I try not to show how spooked I am that he even knows how cranky my till is. As soon as I get a chance, I'm going to check for hidden cameras. 'And what would your suggestion be, oh wise businessman? They're damaged. I can't sell them, but they're perfectly readable. Someone might still enjoy them.'

'Put them in the bin like a normal person.'

I can't hide the shiver at the idea of putting a book in the bin. A book has to be in an absolutely *dire* state for me to chuck it out. 'So you think it's better to toss something out rather than let someone enjoy it for free, do you?'

'I hope you're not planning on doing that nonsense you see on social media where they're hiding unwanted books all over the place for other idiots to get all excited about finding some kid's manky discarded books.' He puts the copy of *Charlie and the Chocolate Factory* down on the front of the shelf, not even bothering to put it back where he got it from. 'It's littering. That's what it is. It could even be termed fly-tipping. If I found any books hidden around here, I'd rip them up and deposit them swiftly in the bin. Save the planet and all that.'

Hidden cameras. There've got to be hidden cameras in here somewhere. How else would he know I've got a stack of books in the office ready to package up and hide?

I refuse to show how shaken I am by how much he seems to know. 'Well, aren't you a lovely human being?'

Dimitri snorts at the sarcasm in my voice, but Drake Farrer smiles. 'Just remember, Miss Winstone, when you come begging me to buy you out so you can pay off your debtors before the bailiffs come knocking, my offer won't be nearly so generous. Then we'll see which one of us is the better person,' he says as he glides through the open doorway.

'Be right back.' Dimitri pats the counter, and yells, 'Farrer!' as he rushes out the door after him and lets it bang shut in his wake.

I go over to the window and peer out to see Dimitri's caught up with him outside the empty building next door, and there's some sort of heated conversation going on. Drake Farrer's back is to me, but even his back looks smug and condescending, like it's somehow better than other people's backs, but I've never seen Dimitri look so serious. He's got a naturally smiley face, his eyes are bright enough to always have a hint of cheekiness in them, and his mouth is always curved upwards like he's permanently seconds away from doing something naughty. But now he's practically snarling. Every hint of his usual smile is gone, his hands are curled into fists, and even at this angle, I can see his teeth are clenched.

I'm pretty sure I catch the words 'leave her alone', but I'm not sure if I'm eavesdropping or lip-reading.

Am I touched that he's so protective or annoyed that he thinks I need him to stand up for me? I appreciated him being there because I didn't like the way Drake Farrer made me feel when we were alone, but do I need him to chase after the man and fight my battles for me?

'What do you think?' I say to Heathcliff as I lean on the empty shelf and press my forehead against the glass to get a better view of the two men.

Heathcliff's busy watching a French bulldog on the opposite side of the street who's giving him 'come hither' eyes, and looks like he's about to jump out of his tank and attempt to get hither.

Dimitri looks like he's three seconds away from lamping Drake Farrer one, and I'm quite surprised by this chivalrous Jane Austen hero-esque side. No one's ever fought my battles for me, and it kind of gives me a warm feeling inside that someone wants to, even though I'm far from a damsel in distress and the mere sight of me would make actual damsels even more distressed with my tomboyish dress sense and aversion to both skirts and high-heeled shoes.

I scramble backwards and nearly send Heathcliff's bowl flying when the two men part abruptly and Drake Farrer strides off in the direction he came while Dimitri turns back to the shop.

'Sorry about that.' By the time he comes in, his easy smile is back in place.

I pretend to be tidying the stacks of books I've taken out of the window display, not wanting it to be quite so obvious I was watching them.

'He pestered Robert for years, but I thought Robert handing over the shop would be the end of it. He obviously sees you as fresh blood. You've got chalk mermaid scales on your forehead.'

Great. That doesn't make it at all obvious I was watching. I rub my forehead with the back of my hand and try to surreptitiously wipe it off on my 'It was a dark and stormy night' Snoopy T-shirt, knowing I probably look like a Labrador that's been caught with its head halfway down the kitchen bin. 'Do you know him well?'

'No … Not really … Hallie, there's something I should …'

'I've never met a man who makes me feel so uneasy,' I grumble. 'I'm going to check for hidden cameras later. I don't understand how he knows so much about this place.' I take a deep breath and then blurt out the stupid thought that won't leave my head. 'Unless you've told him.'

'Me?' His voice is high with indignation.

'He knows Robert hadn't taken a wage for months, Dimitri. And about the books we're going to hide. And the book club, and the till. And on that first day, he knew a lot more about the shop's finances than I did. And so did you when you asked me about the book balancing. You weren't surprised when I told you how bad things are.'

'And you think he couldn't have found any of that out in another way? You don't think he's observed Robert serving customers on the till and walked past on a Saturday afternoon to see the book club tearing into biscuits, or that he's projecting what he knows from the ex-bakery and the trouble they were in? He's a property developer. It's his job to stay on top of the financial situation for this area. He's making wild guesses and has hit a couple of lucky targets, that's all.'

It does make sense. I know it does. There's just something in the back of my mind that niggles occasionally.

'He's trying to spook you. Things are going well since you took over, Hal. You have to trust me on that. The books on the sale table are boosting the income and doing a lot better than they would be gathering dust on the shelf. We're gradually getting the stock sorted out. People *are* coming in because of the window.' He nods towards the now-empty display.

'There's still not enough money in the till to order the few thousand quid's worth of new stock this shop needs. I'm spending money on mugs and notebooks and tote bags – things that *aren't* books. And I *have* used my own money, just like he was hinting at. Without rent to pay, I thought I could stretch to it this month, but he's right – all I need is one unexpected bill to come in and I *will* be in trouble. Am I going about this all wrong?'

'No, but that's exactly what he wants you to think. I watched him do the same with Robert, but he got nowhere because Robert had been doing this for forty years and had seen it all before. Farrer's homed in on you being new at this and is trying to make you doubt yourself. Don't let him. He doesn't know the first thing about running a bookshop *or* about what the people of Buntingorden want, because it's certainly not a leisure complex.'

'Why does he think a leisure complex is better here than anywhere else? This is a tiny Great British high street full of "ye olde worlde" charm. A leisure complex is the *last* thing that would suit this area.'

'It's a hotspot for tourism. A lot of people come to visit the countryside. He's trying to grab the crowd on rainy days when walking is unappealing.'

'This is England. It's almost impossible to go out in the countryside without getting caught in the rain. That's half the fun of being British. Besides, have you *heard* the sound the rain makes pattering on the roof terrace? There is nowhere better to spend a rainy day than a bookshop. Why does he want to wipe out everything that's charming about this street and make it shiny and modern and undoubtedly painfully expensive to get in?'

'Because Drake Farrer gets what he wants. Robert refused him. Every other shop owner on this street has refused him too. The only thing he's managed to get his hands on is the empty place next door because the owner got into financial trouble and needed someone to bail him out.'

'What if he uses it to drive us out? He could do anything he wants with it. He could move a discount bookshop in. He could turn it into a nightclub. He could open a sewage works in it.'

'I don't think he'd get planning permission for a sewage works,' Dimitri says with a laugh.

I pick up the canvas picture and walk over to the back wall, reaching up to hold it central above the display books.

'I wish I was in a financial position to be able to buy it. I'd turn it into an art gallery with a little gift shop that sells artwork, sculptures, and stuff by local artists. Doing these greeting cards has made me realise how much I miss that aspect of art. I believe young artists don't get enough support and encouragement so I'd have a section dedicated to their work. And I'd open a cake and coffee bar in the corner and go halves on the roof terrace with you so people could take their goodies up there and sit reading.' He shakes his head. 'But I'm struggling to get by as it is. I can't even dream about that sort of thing.'

It's not the first time he's mentioned money worries, and I want to pry and push further, but he's been unwilling to talk about it before, and it's not like I can offer any help.

I pull a chair out of the office and climb on it to clear the books on the highest display shelves and make room for the canvas I'm still holding up on the wall. 'Dreams can come true. I'm living proof of that. And there ...' I stand the canvas on the shelf and tilt it slightly so the wall is holding it up. 'Your first piece is officially on display. First step to a gallery.'

He's beaming as he looks up at it. 'I can't believe you like it enough to display it so prominently.'

'Are you kidding? I *love* it.' I look down at him from the chair, trying to gauge whether he *is* winding me up or not. 'For someone who's about to have a book published, you have a strange lack of confidence in your work.'

'I'm weird, you know that.' He holds his hand up to help me down and I grip it as I step off the chair, coming to a wobbly halt with my chest pressed against his body.

It takes all I have to stop myself adding 'and that's what I love about you'. It's not right to say that to him even though I don't mean it in a romantic sense. I mean, he's *lovely*, and he's adorably charming, and just weird enough to make me feel normal in my own weirdness when I'm with him, and like he won't judge me for being clumsy and awkward, and getting excited about stupid things that other people don't care about, like book release dates, pre-orders popping onto my Kindle at midnight, notebooks that are too pretty to write in, and tote bags with handles long enough to slip over your shoulder *and* fit a decent amount of books in.

I blink up at him as his hand slides to my waist to steady me, even though I'm fairly sure I don't need steadying right at this moment. Although I do usually need some form of steadying so maybe it's just pre-emptive steadying. His eyes are dark and seductive rather than bright and twinkly and his head dips towards mine and I push myself up on my tiptoes on autopilot. I let out a shuddery breath, the proximity to him obviously making me forget how unstable I am on tiptoes because far from the sensuous kiss I imagined, I overbalance and fall against him, knocking him over too so we both stumble and crash into the counter.

He shakes his head like he's trying to clear it and pushes a hand through his hair, manoeuvring us until we're both safely on two feet and he can politely extract himself. He doesn't say anything about the almost-kiss.

'So what am I drawing on the window this time?' He steps away and nods to the empty display like he can tell what I'm thinking and is determined to derail the thought from its track.

'You really wouldn't mind?' I try to recalibrate myself and pick up Heathcliff's bowl and carry it across to the counter even though I'm feeling more unsteady now than I was while standing on the wobbly chair. 'I was thinking of doing a fairy-tale theme this time around.'

'How about Pen—'

'No giant lizards, bloodthirsty ogres, overgrown fleas, or anything else horrible from *Pentamerone*.' It makes us both giggle, easing the weird tension and making it like that never happened. 'I mean real fairy tales – we could pop in some for kids, and then intersperse them with modern-day fairy tales for adults and some great YA retellings.'

'So how about an enchanted wood?' He pulls the pencil from behind his ear and points it towards the window, showing me roughly where things would go. 'Trees on either side with branches dangling over, red and white mushrooms and a couple of bunny rabbits and hedgehogs along the bottom, and then some fairies flitting around the upper half?'

'That would be amazing.'

He grins. 'Who needs a gallery to display their work when they've got a shop window and a pack of chalk markers?'

Chapter 12

That evening, we're message hunting again. Well, Dimitri calls it 'doing the inventory' but I think of it more as seeing what other secrets these books are hiding.

'Listen to this,' Dimitri calls out from the Health & Lifestyle section two aisles over. '*It's great to see you looking so well after everything you've been through. Thought you might like this in the next chapter of your life.* It's in a book about switching to a plant-based diet. I wonder what she went through? I wonder if going plant-based helped her recovery?'

'It obviously wasn't a well-received gift if it ended up here,' I call back, pre-empting his next words.

'On the contrary, it looks well read. She must've got something out of it.'

'You're very chirpy tonight. All that glitter paint you used on the fairies' wings must've got to you,' I say, because he's always the first to remind me that these books wouldn't be here if they were still wanted.

Glitter-addled or not, the design he's painted for me is spectacular. Green leaves tumbling from tall trees on either side of the window, an array of woodland creatures and toadstools dancing along the bottom, and fairies with sparkling wings flitting under the canopy. The reflection of the real sunlight makes their glittery wings glisten. We've filled it with a selection of old Ladybird classic books, YA fairy-tale retellings, and adult books with a hint of whimsy about them – the perfect enchanted forest.

I hear him peel a heart sticker off the crinkly backing paper and there's a clunk as he slots the book back onto a higher shelf. We're tackling shelves separately tonight and only meeting when we take the next pile of titles over to the counter and put them into the spreadsheet on my laptop before putting them alphabetically back into the shelves where they belong, which are rarely the ones they came from. Every day in this shop surprises me more and more by how much of a muddle it's in. How has Robert stayed in business all these years? How has any customer ever found *anything* before now?

I hear the thuds as he pulls more books out of the shelves and the flip of pages as he goes through them. I try to concentrate on the Contemporary Fiction section in front of me, but Dimitri is distracting, with his insistence on smelling every book and the way he's humming musical theatre songs to himself. Everything seems so much easier when he's here, even the seemingly endless shelves of books that aren't where they're supposed to be and how many paper cuts my fingers are covered in.

'We've got a treasure map!' he suddenly shouts, making me jump so much that I crash into a pile of books and send it sprawling to the floor. 'This is not a drill! We've got a treasure map!'

'In what?' I call out.

He appears at the edge of my aisle holding up a book depicting a blue and yellow map and a one-legged pirate. '*Treasure Island*, obviously. Look at this!'

He brings the book over and shows me a map drawn on the inside cover and spread across the front page too. It looks like it was drawn by someone very young, with a big 'X' in red pen and annotations in a child's handwriting that say things like 'the oak tree' and 'four paces past the bridge' and 'at the swan's nest'. Apart from the X, there's not much that even identifies it as a treasure map, but Dimitri's practically bouncing on the spot, his eyes gleaming like *he's* a little boy who's found a treasure map. 'What's *Treasure Island* doing in the Health & Lifestyle section?'

'Well, pirates *arrrr* a life choice, aren't they? Ahoy, me hearties! It's the *Jolly Roger*! Shiver me timbers! Avast ye, matey!' He bangs on the shelf three times. 'Grog, grog, grog!'

His innocence and excitement is palpable and I can't stop myself giggling. He has *no* concept of how adorable he is. 'If this kid is as young as his writing looks, isn't *Treasure Island* a bit dark for him to be reading?'

'Or he could be a criminal mastermind who's disguised his writing to *look* like a child's so everyone dismisses it. This could be ...' He trails off as he studies the map. 'This could be *here*! Look at this, this is Buntingorden.'

I go over to him as he holds the book out to show me. 'Look, this is the river.' His finger runs along a wide space between two lines. 'This old oak tree is right at the end of the path, just before the wooden bridge over the pool where kids go swimming in the summer. When you cross that, you come to a spot where the swans used to nest, and that X is at the base of the crab apple tree where the river goes under the viaduct and disappears into the hills.'

I squint at what he points out, but it looks like lines and squiggles to me. 'I think you need a child's imagination to work that one out.'

He grins, obviously proud of this fact, and I can't help smiling again. His adult joy at childlike things is something sorely missing in this world.

'We're going to find this. Have you got a shovel?'

'It's nearly dark. And no, I haven't. I've never lived in a flat with a garden – why on earth would you think I own a shovel?'

His face falls before he quickly perks up again. 'I'll bring one from home and we'll go tomorrow.'

'It's a wild goose chase.'

'Okay, maybe we'll find some wild gooses. Geese. Maybe *they'll* be so excited about the prospect of treasure that they won't mind my complete butchering of English grammar. You know what I mean.' He closes the book and clutches it to his chest as he backs away towards the office. 'This isn't going back on sale until we've found it.'

'You're mad as a hatter.' I watch as he lovingly places the book front and centre of my desk, grabs a pen, and writes 'shovel' on his arm as a reminder, but there's something about his excitement that makes me feel excited too, and makes me think about that childlike sense of wonder that disappears as we grow up, and how amazing it is to meet someone who's not afraid to believe in fairy tales.

He sweeps back out of the office, and I go back to where I was and pull a copy of *Love in the Time of Cholera* off the Literary Fiction shelf. I open the cover, not expecting there to be anything written inside, and stop in surprise.

'Dimitri,' I say before he gets back to the Health & Lifestyle section. 'Have you seen the film *Serendipity*?'

'Rom com?' he asks, and I make a noise of agreement as he pops his head back round the edge of my aisle. 'No, why?'

'It's about two people who meet in a twist of fate and feel a connection, but they're both in relationships with other people, so they decide that if it's meant to be, they'll find each other again. They send two items out into the universe with their names and numbers on them so if they ever make it back into the other's hands, it'll be a sign. His on a five dollar bill, hers written inside the cover of *Love in the Time of Cholera*. Look at this.' I hold up the book to show him the name and phone number written inside this copy of the same book.

'Mindy,' he reads it and the numbers aloud. 'You think we've accidentally stumbled into a rom com?'

'I don't know, but it's a bit weird, isn't it?'

'Movie prop they didn't need after filming that somehow ended up here?'

'No, it's a different name. Kate Beckinsale's character is called Sara.'

'Shall we ring it?'

'Noooo.' I laugh, shake my head, and feel a flitter of excitement inside me at the mere suggestion. 'Of course we're not going to ring it. That would be ... I don't know. Invading someone's privacy? It has nothing to do with us. It's weird and ...'

He takes my hand and pulls me towards the office. He uses his foot to kick out the chair at the desk for me to sit down, and uses his other hand to lift the shop phone and plonk it in front of me with a pointed clunk. 'We're going to ring it.'

'It's probably a phone sex line. They're probably going to charge me ten quid a minute to realise it's an advertisement for lonely old men to get their jollies off and their phone bill up.'

'If you thought that, you wouldn't look so excited.' He lets go of my hand to pick up the receiver and place it in my empty palm, then he holds the book open on the page. 'Put it on speaker phone.'

My fingers are shaking as I dial the number and I have to grip the receiver extra tight because my palms have gone all sweaty. 'It's probably old,' I say as it rings out. 'No one's going to—'

'Brandon?'

'No. Er, is that Mindy?' I stutter out. A little thrill has gone through me at the name – she's obviously expecting someone to call. 'This is probably the weirdest phone call I've ever made. I work at a bookshop in Buntingorden and we found your number inside a copy of *Love in the Time of Cholera* ...' I go on to tell her a bit about the shop, the way almost every one of the second-hand books has a message written inside it, and about how finding her number reminded me of *Serendipity*.

'No one ever calls this number *or* knows that film, and yes, that film is exactly why we did it.'

'We?'

'His name was Brandon. I met him fifteen years ago and barely a day has passed since when I haven't thought of him. This is the first time anyone's ever called this number.'

'So this is for real?' I tap the desk in excitement. 'This is a real-life *Serendipity*?'

'You could call it that,' she says, a laugh in her West Midlands accented voice.

'Will you tell us what happened?'

She hesitates, but I can almost hear the moment she decides she hasn't got anything to lose by sharing her story. 'I fell off the bus and into his arms. I was loaded down with shopping while getting off, and he was the first in the queue to get on. There was ice and snow around and the bus step was wet, and he caught me when I slipped, and we had that magical movie moment, you know? The one where you lock eyes and you just *know*. It took my breath away, and it wasn't just the adrenalin of the fall. He insisted on taking me for a coffee to make sure I was all right – I was fine, of course, I just wanted to go for a coffee with him. And the coffee led to another coffee and we ended up wandering around Bristol city centre for hours because neither of us wanted the day to end. We even went ice skating, like they do in the movie. We were both attached to other people, but I couldn't get this idea of fate out of my head. It felt like it was meant to be, but it also felt too perfect, you know? Things like this don't happen in real life, and with hindsight, I can see I was waiting for the punchline.'

'Oh, I know that feeling.' Dimitri and I share a glance.

'So I had this idea of doing what they do in the film and sending two items out into the world with our names and numbers on them, and I happened to have that very book in a pile waiting to go to a charity shop. It seemed like a sign. He wrote his on a five-pound note. And, of course, the old fivers have been retired now, so his is lost forever. Him one day finding that book is my only hope.'

'Ah, I'm sorry to disappoint you that it was just us.'

'At least I know it's still out there. That's something. I don't even know if he'd still be looking … I'm kidding myself, aren't I? It's been *fifteen* years. He must be married by now, and me, daft beggar that I am, still carrying around an old flip-phone from the early Noughties, keeping it charged and in credit because this is the only number he'd have. I didn't think to future-proof my phone number at the time, but like everyone else, I've gone through at least ten phones between then and now as technology moves on, but the number I put in the book was the phone I had at the time. I thought it would be a matter of weeks until we found each other again because it felt so … meant-to-be. I know I should give up, but I'm still waiting for the day he phones. Because some part of me still thinks he will.'

'He *will*,' I say. 'He has to. That's such a romantic story. You can't have a moment like that for that to be *it*.'

'That's what I keep telling myself.'

'Have you tried to find him online?' Dimitri asks.

'A few years ago, after Twitter and Facebook took off, I put up a post hoping he'd see it somehow. It got a few shares and retweets but it didn't come to anything, and the more years that have gone by, the more stupid I've felt for still holding a candle for this man I spent one day with so many years ago.'

I reassure her that it's far from stupid and that he could be doing exactly the same wherever he is, and I promise that I'll ask the name of any potential buyers who go to pick up this book.

'Isn't that the most romantic thing you've ever heard?' I say to Dimitri as I put the phone down and keep watch on the receiver like it's going to spring up and start doing the Argentine tango at any moment.

'It's a shame no one predicted fivers being retired and phone technology advancing.'

'That makes it even more romantic. Star-crossed lovers, near misses, fate stopped by the advancing of time and technology. It's both really sad and incredibly romantic.'

He leans down, puts his arm around my shoulders and squeezes me into his side. 'You say I'm childlike to believe in fairy tales, but *you* still believe in love stories and happy endings. You say love doesn't happen in real life but you still believe it does.'

'Yeah, for other people. Not for me.'

'But it *will*.' His voice has the same conviction I had when I told Mindy that Brandon would phone her. 'You deserve a thousand handsome princes sweeping you off your feet.'

'Ew, no, the shop would be far too crowded. Just one would do. If they existed outside of fairy tales.'

'Anything's possible.'

I reach up and rub his upper arm where it's still around my shoulders, creasing the soft cotton of his thin grey top. 'What if we find him?'

'A thousand real-life non-fairy-tale princes?'

I laugh. 'No. Brandon.'

He releases me and stands upright. 'Go to a bank and ask them if we can examine every single five-pound note they've had returned?'

'No, I mean, put out an appeal on social media. Not just a couple of photos like we did the other day, but run a proper appeal to track him down. You know those shareable graphics people post when someone's lost their wedding ring on the train or a child's left behind a much-loved bear on the bus? Put up what little info we know, place, date, maybe a photo of Mindy if she'd be up for it. Ask people to share it far and wide.'

'And just hope that he runs across it?'

'Well, if it's meant to be then he will, won't he? Mindy could be the love of his life. He could've told everyone about their magical meeting that day. Someone could see it and recognise the story. I could get in touch with the local newspapers too. They might be willing to run it as a story. And some of those news sites that run quirky stories. This has the potential to go viral. It's romantic and interesting – I already care about these two finding each other again, and others will too.'

'And what if we do find him and he's married? What if we find him and he's a complete and utter wanker?'

'Trust you to keep things realistic,' I say with a grin. 'And what if he's absolutely lovely, still single, and still looking for her too?'

'I guess we'll find out when we find him. Because we *will* find him. I have total faith that when you put your mind to something, it's going to happen.'

'Thank you.' I can't help smiling at the compliment, because it's wonderful to hear that, even if generally the only thing I'm good at is knocking things over and making a mess.

Not many people in my life have ever had confidence in me, and it's bewitching to meet someone who does.

Chapter 13

'Shut up!' Mum whacks the smoke alarm with a broom, which only serves to make it squeal even louder. 'What is wrong with you? It's only a bit of cheese, for goodness' sake. Nicole, why is your smoke alarm so oversensitive?'

'It's not oversensitive, it's reacting to a kitchen filled with smoke.' My sister waves an oven tray in front of her, trying to disperse the fumes.

'The cheese is *on fire*, Mum. That might have something to do with it.' I flap a tea towel around.

'Stand back!' Bobby comes in with the fire extinguisher.

'Oh, now that's just overkill. It was only a few flames and they've gone—'

She's cut off by a *whoosh* as Bobby coats the oven with white powder, putting an end to the sizzling as half a block of cheese fuses itself to the bottom of Nicole's oven, and yet more probably toxic fumes fill the tiny kitchen.

'I do hate that smoke alarm,' Mum mutters to herself. 'It's always going off at me. I don't know what's wrong with it.'

Dimitri is standing in the open doorway, using his coat to either flap fresh air in or burning cheese fumes out, I'm not sure which.

'It's trying to save my oven, which you've destroyed. Again. We've only just replaced our last oven because it couldn't cope with any more cooking disasters.'

'Bit of bicarb and vinegar once it's cool and it'll be as good as new,' Dimitri says, and judging by the state of the blackened cheese dribbling from the oven door, frozen mid-drip by the fire extinguisher powder, I admire his optimism.

'A man who can give you cleaning tips!' Mum squawks, looking up from the still-sizzling crumpled shard of charcoal she's trying to resuscitate. 'What a keeper!'

I'd say I was embarrassed for this to be his introduction to my family, but it's his own fault for suggesting the pizza, although he wasn't to know that my mum's idea of pizza was a tortilla wrap cooked in the oven until it's lightly cremated and as rock hard as one of those steel ninja throwing stars and about as sharp, then spread with ketchup and put back in the oven with half a block of cheese grated on top, which promptly slides off and melts into the oven itself, causing caustic fumes, which my mum insists on cremating even further with the oven on the highest temperature, until it's so hot that the influx of melted cheese actually catches on fire because it can't *get* any hotter without spontaneously combusting.

Bobby goes to put the fire extinguisher away – never far with my mother on site – and open all the windows to air the place out.

'Shall we sit in the garden?' Dimitri suggests. 'It's a lovely evening.'

It's very polite of him not to mention that sitting in the house is impossible because smoke is still billowing throughout the living room and kitchen, and everyone's eyes are stinging and watering from the fumes.

Nicole and I brave the haze to make everyone a plain, safe, non-cremated cheese sandwich. Mum picks up the bottle of wine Dimitri brought and drags him to sit on the wicker garden set

213

nestled on Nicole's patio, looking out across the neatly mown grass, surrounded by borders of colour-schemed flowers, and towards Mum's annex at the end, overhung by a flowering cherry tree.

'This is very posh!' Mum reads the label on the bottle before glugging some into five glasses.

By the time we get outside, Bobby's joined them and is sitting back watching while Mum makes Dimitri play twenty questions, which he fields like a master. Without being rude or abrupt, all she's managed to get out of him is that he doesn't have any pets or a girlfriend, and it's like some kind of Jedi mind trick where he's dodged the questions without anyone realising.

He's definitely got some kind of magical powers, because by the time Nicole and I have carried out plates of slightly smoky-tasting cheese sandwiches, and I fear the smell of burning cheese on metal will follow me like a cloud around my hair forever, like that swarm of wasps that took a liking to my ice-cream cone on the beach one summer, he's telling Mum about the messages in the books, and how he's drawn up a few shareable graphics with photos of the book cover and message, and how we've put our campaign to find Brandon online. So far it's had a couple of thousand retweets, even more shares on Facebook, and multiple comments saying how sweet it is and how much they hope we find him. I've also put up posts about Esme, Vickie and Tommy, the promise in *Frankenstein*, the baby's birth announcement, and some of the other notes we've found, figuring if we're getting extra social media traffic on our new Facebook, Twitter, and Instagram accounts, it would increase the chances of those note writers seeing it and getting in touch too.

By the time he's finished talking, Mum, Nicole, and Bobby, who is critical of anything to do with books, are all leaning forward in their seats listening intently, and it makes me think again about making these notes public somehow. If talking about them can make even these three care, we might be on to something.

'Why are you looking at each other like that?' I say when Dimitri's finished talking and has started eating his sandwich, which is probably a bit of a stretch from the home-cooked meal he had in mind. I keep catching furtive glances between Nicole and Mum, aborted nods and gesturing with nothing but their eyes.

Nicole shakes her head but Mum sighs wistfully. 'I've never heard anyone talk about books the way you do, Hal.'

Dimitri goes red and I choke on my cheese sandwich, resulting in Bobby having to thump me on the back.

'Now, if we could just find you a nice boyfriend who didn't mind your *collection* ...' She calls my sagging bookshelves a collection because it sounds better than 'obsession' or 'addiction to buying more books when you already have so many, you could read twenty-four hours a day until your ninety-eighth birthday and you still wouldn't get through them all'.

'Now, how about that friend of my friend from cheesemaking class I was telling you about? He's still single.'

'Mum, he's a vicar!' I roll my eyes. It's not the first time she's brought him up. 'And he's pushing sixty!'

'Well, how about that nice young chap you used to copy your maths homework from in school? Have you been on Facebook to see if he's available?'

'He's married to a man named George.'

'Oh, I know – Joyce's son! He's single again.'

'Mum! He's single again because he was widowed last week!'

'Exactly. You want to get in quickly before someone else snaps him up.'

'No, I don't. I don't want to get anything in anywhere at any speed. You just want me married off to someone with a willy and a heartbeat, and I'm starting to think the heartbeat is not a deal-breaker.'

It's Dimitri's turn to choke and Bobby gets another round of back-thumping in, although I'm not sure why, because it doesn't help.

'Well, I wouldn't need to if you had *someone* interested in you, would I?' She looks pointedly at Dimitri, who drops his gaze and gives his sandwich more attention than any sandwich has ever deserved.

Mum starts wittering on about something that happened at the allotment, and Dimitri keeps catching my eyes and holding my gaze every time we look up. He seems relaxed and smiley, and I like how comfortable he seems around my family.

I don't miss the way Nicole's watching us and keeps exchanging glances with Bobby while Mum's carrying on obliviously.

Mum's actually acting like she's forgotten he's there, which could be termed a miracle akin to walking on custard and then a swift batch of water into wine when there's a single man in the vicinity. Usually they're like a flashing beacon and her radar homes in on them and ignores everything else until they agree to whatever she wants just to make her leave them alone, like you do with those double-glazing salesmen who knock on the door and keep going with their marketing spiel, no matter how many times you tell them you're seriously considering moving into a molehill and have no need of windows. She's snagged a few of those men and tried to set me up on dates with them in exchange for window quotes too.

But she's different with Dimitri. He slots right in like he's meant to be there. I bite my lip as I watch him following Mum's conversation with more interest than Nicole, Bobby, and I put together have ever given her tales of papier-mâché club.

Before she can get into what happened at glassblowing class, we're attacked by a swarm of midges as dusk falls, after a thankfully shop-bought lemon meringue pie for dessert.

It's now absolutely freezing inside the house with every window and door open, but Mum drags me into the kitchen to help with the washing up, while Nicole is on her knees on the kitchen floor, praying to the gods of kitchen appliances and throwing baking soda and vinegar into the oven with reckless abandon.

'Did you see that wine? I've heard of the chateau where that was made – that stuff costs a *fortune*. He must be from money.' Mum plunges her hands into the washing-up bowl.

'Mum!' I say in horror, which has nothing to do with the fact my eyes are *still* smarting from the oven disaster. 'A – his financial situation is nothing to do with you, and B – I don't think he is. He said it was from the collection his father left when he moved out.'

'Oh, he's from a broken home. He needs someone to mend him.' She gives me a conspiratorial wink.

'He doesn't need mending. He's perfect as he is.' I know it's another mistake when Mum's head whips round so fast, she must've broken some sort of light-speed record.

Amazingly, she doesn't say anything, but a smile spreads gradually across her face. 'I think he's lonely.'

'I think he's lonely too,' I say, forgetting myself for a moment. You don't make admissions like that in front of my mum – she'll have him enrolled in crochet club and on the waiting list for an allotment before the week is out.

'I think Mr Anastasia is pretty much perfect.' She clatters a plate onto the draining board with such force that it almost breaks in half. 'What's his surname, anyway? I need to google him.'

'I … don't know. Is that weird?' I think about it for a moment and then suddenly realise what she's saying. 'Wait, no, it's not weird, it's good because you are *not* allowed to google him.'

'It *is* a bit weird,' Nicole says.

'It's never come up.'

'Haven't you added him on Facebook yet?' Mum asks. 'He was saying you're doing all that social media stuff together. I'm going to find him on your friends list and add him. He said he wanted to keep up to date with the knitting group.'

I'm pretty sure he never said that. And I'm pretty sure he's not on Facebook either.

I look through the door at him and Bobby sitting in the living room. He looks relaxed and completely at home, nattering about the architecture of European buildings, Bobby's favourite subject, and I'm kind of impressed that even Bobby gets on with him, because Bobby doesn't like *anyone* apart from Nicole.

'Is it weird that I don't know his surname?' I say, surprising myself because I hadn't realised I was going to share the niggling feeling I keep getting that he's holding something back. 'I don't even know where he lives. He's vague about the book he's working on and he doesn't seem to be on any form of deadline. And there's this property developer who keeps coming in and knows a creepy amount about the shop when the only other person who knows those things is …'

'Maybe it's just because Bobby likes him, and the chances of Bobby enjoying someone's company are about as likely as the chances of me achieving sainthood,' Nicole offers, ignoring my worries.

'Maybe I've been too trusting because he was Robert's friend, but every time I'm with him, all my doubts go out the window.' I've still got enough sense to stop myself before I say anything more, like how those doubts are swiftly replaced by thoughts of his lips and his eyes and his smile and those freckle-dotted muscular shoulders I caught a glimpse of that day he was getting changed … Mum would have a field day with an admission like that.

'You're trying to sabotage yourself,' Mum says. 'You always do it when a relationship's going well.'

'No, I don't.' It takes me a moment to realise what she's said. 'And there is no relationship, Mum. He's just a friend.'

'Friends don't get that upset when I try to set their female friends up with vicars. I was only trying to make him jealous and let him know that there are other prospects out there for you if he doesn't act quickly.'

I don't tell her that an elderly vicar, a happily married gay man, and a recent widow are *not* prospects.

'Did you see how happy he looked when you said you weren't interested?'

'No.'

'Well, he did. And he's just like you, Hal. Shy and with an odd taste in clothing.'

'You still own a shell suit!' I protest even though she's not trying to insult him. 'His shyness and slightly awkward weirdness are exactly what I like about him.'

'So you *do* like him.'

'No. I mean … no. Gorgeous men don't just fall through the door of your shop and sweep you off your feet. You're always going on about my unrealistic expectations but this is the most unrealistic of them all. He's not …'

I look through the open door again and this time he catches my eyes and his mouth curves into a smile that makes the butterflies inside me start zipping around with such force that I nearly drop the plate I'm wiping up. 'This doesn't happen in real life. My luck already changed once with the shop, and lightning doesn't strike twice. Unless it's actual lightning and I'm outside carrying something metal. But that's beside the point. There has to be a catch.'

I look back at him and he hasn't taken his eyes off me even though Bobby is still talking to him. 'Somewhere. Hidden. Really, really deep.'

Because I could never be so lucky that someone as amazing as Dimitri is really as amazing as he seems.

'That was really fun,' Dimitri says as we approach the shop. 'Your family are amazing.'

'Well, you're still on speaking terms with me – that's more than I expected after an evening with my mum.'

'And I still have both my eyebrows. That's more than *I* expected when those flames started coming out of the oven.'

My phone beeps with a Facebook notification, which it's been doing a lot since we put some of the notes online, and I can never resist checking it instantly in case it's something important. 'We've been tagged in a photo,' I say as I wait for the page to load and then scroll down in confusion when a picture of two twenty-somethings clinking glasses in a brightly lit restaurant appears. 'I don't know what—' I read the post. 'Oh my God, it's Vickie and Tommy on their first date!'

'What?' His eyes widen.

I shove my phone at him. 'Vickie saw our post and remembered finding the book in her school locker! She already had a copy at home and thought it was a mistake and left it on a bench for someone else to pick up. She never opened the cover!'

I watch his face light up as he reads the caption on the photo.

Ten years late, but I finally found out why there was a copy of The Hunger Games *in my locker in Year Eleven.* She's reposted our photo of the note and tagged the shop's page. *Luckily still FB friends with this guy and finally plucked up the courage to tell him I was head-over-heels for him and still am! Thank you, Once Upon A Page!* #FirstDate10YearsLate

He hands my phone back with a smile that's almost as bright as the Victorian streetlamp we're standing under.

'Tell me this isn't magic! Somehow that book found the right person, because of something *we* did, even so many years later. And look at how happy they look! This is *amazing.*'

He leans his head against the lamppost. 'Oh, I don't think it's the *book* that's amazing, Hal.'

I know there's hidden meaning in that sentence and a weird awkwardness shoots through the air between us, interspersed only by my flashing red cheeks. I shove my phone back into my pocket and kick awkwardly at one of the cobblestones.

'Hallie, can we …' He stops himself, alternately pressing his lips together like he can't work out what to say and worrying at his bottom lip with his teeth. 'I mean … I don't …' He sighs in frustration at not finding the right words, but it's okay because I don't know what they are either.

Eventually, he pushes himself upright and takes my hand as we carry on walking.

He doesn't say anything, and I don't either as his fingers slot between mine. I'm busy hoping my palms aren't too sweaty.

I reluctantly let go when we get back to the shop and I have to dig out my keys to unlock the shop door, hovering awkwardly while I debate whether I should invite him in or not. I've still got a lot of tidying up to do after the customers today, and I don't want him to see the state of the shop and think he's got to help, and my flat upstairs hasn't really been unpacked yet and I'm still getting most things out of boxes so I'm not overly keen to invite him up there either … but I don't want him to think I don't want him to come in *or* to think that inviting him in insinuates something more …

'I should be getting back.' He puts an easy end to my deliberating. 'Thank you for letting me be part of your family for a little while. It was great. Even the fire extinguisher part.'

He's smiling as he looks down, hesitating, like he can sense my reluctance to let him go *or* invite him inside. His teeth chew his lower lip and his eyes are fixed on my mouth, and for a long, awkward moment, I'm certain he's going to kiss me goodnight. He's got a cleft chin with a deep gap in it that I want to settle my thumb in and let my fingers stroke his face, and I so nearly reach up and do just that, and it's only my fingers curling around the doorframe that stops me.

Well, and the death glare from Heathcliff, who's watching us through the window. I'm pretty sure he would not support anyone other than himself kissing Dimitri.

'Goodnight,' he murmurs so quietly that I might've imagined him speaking, making it sound like the sexiest word anyone has ever said. His smooth skin is so close to mine that I can sense how his sharp jawbone would feel against mine, and my eyes close involuntarily as his lips press against my cheek and stay there for seconds that stretch out like minutes, the smell of his herby and oaky aftershave almost outdoing the loitering burnt-cheese fumes.

My hand finds its way to his upper arm and my fingers curl into it, trying to hold him near, to let him know that as pecks on the cheek go, this is by far the most intimate one I've ever had, and if he wanted to stay there all night, that would be fine with me.

He suddenly comes to his senses so hard that it makes him jump, which in turn makes me jump, which startles Heathcliff who zooms into the castle at the bottom of his tank.

'Er, yeah. I'd better ...' He quickly takes a step back. 'See you tomorrow, Hal.'

I stand in the doorway and watch as he walks away, his shoulders slumped and his hands shoved into his pockets. He crosses the street and walks past the fountain, stopping to look back and wave before he turns onto one of the narrow back roads that lead out of Buntingorden.

'That went well,' I mutter to Heathcliff as I go in and lock the shop door behind me. I dump my bag and jacket on the stairs up to the flat, and give him his third helping of fish food today before I face the shop. It's been a busy day. I lost an old lady in the Sagas section and didn't find her again until long after closing time, so we were late leaving and didn't have a chance to clean up.

There might be a sense of magic in the air here, but it's a shame that it doesn't tidy itself when my back is turned.

I pick up various books that have been left on the floor or shoved into the shelves upside down, back to front, or otherwise, and collect up children's books that have migrated downstairs and bundle them in my arms to go back up. I gather books that have been taken out, browsed, and put back in the nearest empty spot regardless of the fact it wasn't the spot they came out of, and finally the shelves look tidy enough to drag Henry out of the office and give the carpet a hoover.

I want nothing more than a hot shower and a cup of tea and some chocolate biscuits, so I swish around quickly, sliding across the grey carpet smoothly until the foot hits something under the Non-fiction Travel shelves. I get down on my hands and knees and slide my hand through the gathering of dust bunnies until my fingers close around a book and pull it out.

'*Anne of Green Gables*,' I say to Heathcliff as I brush dust off the cover, an old copy depicting a girl with her red hair in plaits, wearing a blue dress and holding her hat on as she stands on a bridge over a brook. 'I remember my grandma reading this to me.'

Heathcliff looks about as impressed by that as he looks at having finished his food and not being given any more.

I open the cover anyway, even though I'm not expecting to see anything inside the dusty and forgotten book, and instantly gasp and choke on the dust I've accidentally inhaled.

I recognise the looped writing, the neat curve of each word. It even looks like it might have been written in the same biro as the one in *Pride and Prejudice*. The hairs on the back of my neck stand on end, and I get the feeling that if I turned around, there would be a ghostly figure standing in the corner with wispy fingers reaching out towards me, although I'm pretty sure that's my imagination running wild.

I wipe my hands on my trousers and trace the words with my fingers, trying to glean information from them.

To my love,
 Oh, the adventures we've been on, both real and fictional. The lives we've lived and places we've travelled to, when the only non-fictional adventure is the one of falling in love. Thank you for giving me the life I've always dreamed of.
 I can't wait for more endless days walking by the river and sharing our dreams.
 Always forever,
 Della

That feeling of magic sparkles again, like if I looked up at the right moment, I'd catch fairies flitting between the shelves and books closing their own covers as they finish sharing their stories for another day. I want to call Dimitri back and show him, but I don't have his phone number or any idea where he lives or how far he'd have got by now if I tried to catch up with him. And after that awkward parting, maybe it's best to leave it for tonight.

Even with all the looking, all the searching inside every book we pick up, I never *expected* to find another note from his mum. I'm almost convinced I'm imagining it and when I look down at the book again, the page will be blank.

It isn't. And it feels like I was supposed to find it here tonight, alone, even though I'm fairly sure I've already cleaned under that shelf and it definitely wasn't there then. It seems like it's trying to tell me something. I just wish I knew what.

Chapter 14

'It's not even eight o'clock!' I stick my head out of the bedroom window and squint down at Dimitri in the burning morning sunlight.

'I know! Thought we'd get an early start!' He whacks the shovel he's holding into the pavement and raises his other hand, containing a tray with two cardboard cups of coffee in it. 'I also have pistachio crinkle cookies.'

'Good. Because never mind digging up treasure, we'd have been going to bury *your* body if you hadn't brought coffee and baked goods at this time of day.'

'Never mind that, there are books to hide and treasure to be found,' he calls after me as I pull my head back inside the window and risk a glance in the mirror to see quite what a state my hair is in. I cringe at the sight. One day I might learn that sticking my head out the window first thing in the morning when gorgeous men knock is not the best idea. Today is not that day.

I flatten it down with my hands and go back to the window to toss the shop keys down to him. 'Let yourself in, I'll be down in a minute. Dimitri …'

I wait until he's looking up at me before I speak, trying to make eye contact even though mine are still half-stuck together.

'There's a book on the counter for you. You need to see the inside of it.' I duck back inside before he can question me. I don't want to shout out the window for the whole street to hear about his mum and the second book I found, but I haven't been able to stop thinking about it all night.

By the time I make it down the stairs, washed and dressed in my favourite 'And they lived happily ever after …' T-shirt and jeans, he's sitting on the counter with the book open in his hands, his fingers stroking the aged pages.

'*Anne of Green Gables* was her favourite book as a child,' he says when I come in. 'I should have thought of looking for it.'

It was one of my childhood favourites too, even generations apart from Della. I loved the whimsical story of the resilient, curious, and feisty orphan and longed to spend a day in Avonlea with her, picking apples, drinking tea and raspberry cordial, having a picnic at the Lake of Shining Waters, and wandering through the forest to see the beautiful autumn leaves.

'This is really special,' he says. 'A glimpse into a life I didn't know she had. Thank you for finding this.'

It seems an odd thing to thank me for. 'I didn't. It found me. It was just sitting there under a shelf.'

'Robert always said this shop had a way of delivering the exact book you needed at the exact moment you needed it.'

'Maybe that was his stock system – a customer walks in and asks for something, and lo and behold, it hurls itself from the shelf to land at their feet? It's certainly a more feasible explanation than anyone actually understanding Robert's method of organisation.' I go over to the counter and lean against it beside where he's sitting, deliberately pressing my elbow into his thigh as I sip my coffee and pop a pistachio crinkle cookie into my mouth, the cracked sugar on top giving way to a buttery, nutty middle that melts on my tongue. I watch him gently turning the pages of *Anne of Green Gables*, completely lost in refamiliarising himself with the story of Anne and Diana and Gilbert. 'Are you okay?'

'Yeah.' He lifts his glasses and rubs his eyes with the back of his hand. 'I remember her reading every word of this book to me when I was little. I remember her reading it to my sister over and over. And seeing it again is like being eight years old and entranced by Anne's adventures and imagination. It's that …'

'… Unique magic books have in transporting you to a different time and place?'

'Exactly.' His wide smile makes his sad eyes twinkle again. 'Shall we go? I need some fresh air.'

I *love* that he's not afraid to admit that. There's something so refreshing about a man who openly talks about his emotions. I finish my coffee and reluctantly put the lid back on the container of pistachio cookies and then pick up my tote bags, sliding one onto each shoulder. He puts *Anne* into the office and does the same, picking up the copy of *Treasure Island* as well and grabbing his shovel from where it's leaning by the door as I lock up behind us.

We've got two tote bags each full of books to hide around town. They're sealed up in waterproof bags with a note reading: *You're the finder of this book. We hope you enjoy it! Please feel free to take it and read it or leave it for someone else to find. You can keep it for as long as you like, and when you're done, sign and date the inside of the cover and re-hide it for someone else to enjoy. And don't forget to hide any books that you'd like to pass on as well! Feel free to take pictures and post clues and let everyone know about your book hunt on our Facebook page ~ Once Upon A Page, Buntingorden.*

I don't think it will help business, but I've been following groups on social media who do this in their own towns, and it's become really popular. It's mostly children's books, but why should children have all the fun? Dimitri and I have got two tote bags each – one children's books and one adult books – all of unsellable shop stock, but still perfectly readable. I've already started posting about it on the Once Upon A Page Facebook page and encouraged other people to get involved too. We could have a town full of books. Books lurking around every corner. It would be amazing, and anything that encourages *anyone* to read has got to be a good thing.

Outside, the morning air is fresh and warm with enough of a breeze to keep it pleasant. Even though the sun has been up for a while, it still feels like a sunrise is not far behind.

Dimitri yawns and stretches, the movement of his arms causing his burgundy shirt with foxes all over it to rise, showing a sliver of pale skin at the base of his back, and my breath catches at how much I want to run my fingers along it. I force myself to look away and shrug one strap of my bag off and start getting books out. I lean one against the corner of Once Upon A Page, leave one around the side next to the closed-off staircase up to the roof terrace, and tuck one behind a drainpipe on the other side in the little gap that separates the bookshop from the candle shop to the left. I snap a photo of each one ready to upload as a clue later.

I stand one in the hanging basket swinging from the lamppost outside the shop, being careful not to damage any flowers, and then we cross the cobbled street to the fountain and town square. Dimitri leaves one on each bench, while I stand one under the lip of one of the steps in a hexagon around the fountain, and we both tuck one in next to the flower troughs on either end and partially obscure them with trailing aubretia and busy Lizzies.

When we leave the fountain area, I'm happy to follow Dimitri's lead about which way to go because I don't know the village well enough yet, having spent most of my time in the bookshop since I arrived three weeks ago. There are other shopkeepers around, and I ask permission to hide a book at the edge of their buildings and peeking from the corners of their outside displays, and everyone is so supportive of the idea. I'm pleasantly surprised that no one seems to share Drake Farrer's attitude.

We leave books tucked into hanging baskets and sitting on

windowsills as we pass the chocolate shop, the sweet shop, and the many handmade gift shops that make up Buntingorden High Street. We stop to inhale the smell of freshly roasted coffee outside the deli. When we get to the end of the street, we turn onto the grassy paths behind the buildings that lead down to the river, Dimitri swinging the shovel beside him as we walk. The grass is wet with morning dew and the longer edges are sparkling as they reflect the spring sunshine high above us. With the slight hills and dips in the uneven ground, he holds his arm out to me, and I shift both half-empty tote bags onto one shoulder so I can get closer to him. I've wanted to hug him since I walked down the stairs this morning and saw him reading his mum's second message, and I settle for slotting my arm through his and sort of holding it against me.

He squeezes my arm against his side, and it gives me the courage to suggest something that's been floating around in my mind since the dinner at Nicole's house the other night. 'I don't think the notes should stay hidden.'

'What do you mean?'

'I don't know. You talking to my family the other night got me thinking. They got so involved and invested in the stories of Esme, and Vickie and Tommy, and Mindy and Brandon, and none of them have ever been interested in books. They haven't been interested in me owning the shop or this new career I've got, but the stories of those notes got their attention. If they can draw in even non-readers, it would be brilliant to share them with people like us. People who love books and care about books and remember the days before Kindles when spines were flexed, page corners were turned down and paragraphs were run through with highlighter pens.'

I can see the effort it takes for him to arrange his face into a frown. 'If you ever mistreated books like that, you and me are going to have to have a serious conversation about where our relationship is going.'

He probably feels the physical jolt of surprise that goes through me at those words. Where *exactly* is our relationship going? I mean, I'm sure he didn't mean it in *that* way and it's just a figure of speech, but it sends a simultaneous shot of butterflies straight into my belly at the thought he wants it to go in *any* direction.

Eventually the false frown becomes too hard for someone so naturally smiley to maintain and he laughs, not seeming to notice the burst of butterflies swishing around inside me. I feel so fluttery that I'm certain he must be able to feel them through my fingertips on his warm forearm.

'How?' he asks gently, not immediately dismissing the idea.

'I don't know. Like the campaigns we've already put on social media to try to find the people mentioned in the notes, but we put them all in one place, photos of all the book covers and the notes inside, and form an online collection of all these lost love stories we've found. If we could get BuzzFeed or one of the other sites that shares viral news to mention it, ask for retweets and shares on our social media pages … Our Twitter account's got a couple of hundred followers now, and only about half of them are creepy men who want me to send them money.'

There's a low hedge surrounding a garden at the back of the flower shop, and I stop and go over to slide a book under it. As I walk back, I lean another one against the carved stone base holding up a birdbath on the path edge. 'It's our unique thing and having the books all hidden away, lost in the shelves like they aren't anything special seems wrong. I want to display them. I want to make them a reason to come and visit Once Upon A Page. I think there's importance here. History. People might be interested in them. Other people might enjoy reading them as much as I do.'

'Like an art installation?'

'Exactly. We could have a big open day and invite people down to see it. I could ask local newspapers and tourism websites if they're interested in reporting on it. I know we haven't found all the notes yet and there's still over half the stock left to go through, but we could add to it whenever we find new ones to keep it fresh, and we could make a real thing of finding the people in these notes. Like Vickie and Tommy. How amazing was that? That these two people reunited because of us – because *we* solved a years-old misunderstanding all because of that book. They could go on to fall madly in love and live happily ever after. They could be each other's *one*, and they would never have known if it wasn't for that book resurfacing. How many more are there like that?'

'It's brilliant. *You're* brilliant. This will create such a buzz. The little bookshop of lost love stories. A unique selling point. Something that makes it stand out. Something that will make people remember it – and you want people to remember it when they're next thinking of buying a book. This is *you*, Hal. You love those messages; you love thinking about whoever wrote them, whoever received them, whoever threw them away. This is what you've been saying all along – and this is a chance to find out.' He nudges his elbow into my side. 'Although I still think it's all because you want to find Esme.'

I grin because he can see right through me. 'Hers is the most romantic thing I've ever heard. Sylvester was *so* in love with her. I want to prove to myself that love is real and that men don't write something like that if they don't mean it … It was the start of a relationship. It *has* to have lasted. They have to have lived happily ever after, like Marius and Cosette.'

'Who lived happily ever after because they were the only characters who didn't die.'

I smack his arm lightly where my fingers are still curled around it.

'I think it's a good idea.' He talks slowly, obviously putting thought into every word.

I can finish the sentence for him. 'But the books have been thrown out, obviously no one cares about them, no one's sentimental, et cetera?'

He laughs. 'Well, maybe there was a spate of burglaries where the burglar broke in and just took sentimental books from the shelves rather than all that cash and jewellery nonsense. It's as viable an explanation as any for how they got here if they're such valued, treasured books. All right, Vickie and Tommy was a misunderstanding and finding that book led to them reconnecting and who knows where else it will lead, but they *have* to be the exception, not the rule. If these books were wanted, they wouldn't be on your shelves. Even Esme's.'

I let go of his arm to dodge across and lean a book against the trunk of a hawthorn tree that's covered in white flowers, and the almond scent of May blossom fills the air around it.

'What about your mum's notes?' I hook my arm back through his. 'Do you want to put them online too? See if we can find out who the mystery man is. If he died and his estate was sold off, his family might recognise the books and come forward ...'

He's quiet as we walk, for so long that I think he's not going to answer. 'I'd like that. My father won't be happy if he finds out, but I can feel how much she loved whoever she wrote those notes to. They're special. Whoever he was obviously meant a lot to her. They shouldn't just be forgotten.'

'You never talk about your father.'

'There isn't much to talk about. He works a lot. He sits in his office judging people who diverted from the plan he had for them.'

'People who switched their university courses from business studies to art?' I ask carefully, squeezing his arm a bit tighter than necessary in an attempt to let him know that I'm not trying to pry. Well, not much anyway.

'Pretty much. Like I said, he's always been a fair-weather father. And my weather's always been rainy.'

It's an odd metaphor, mainly because everything about him is so sunny, and I'm not really sure what to say in response because everything sounds overly sappy or inappropriate. 'You're the epitome of sunshine.'

'Thank you.' His voice breaks and he can't hold back a smile at the same time, like when it's bucketing down and somewhere on the horizon, there's a burst of sunlight and a rainbow.

'Have you got any inklings about your mum's mystery man?'

'None. But I wouldn't know. I didn't live here then. I hardly ever came back after boarding school. My relationship with my father had already broken down. I never forgave him for sending me there and not realising I wasn't like my brother and I wouldn't thrive in that environment. Coming back reminded me of how happy I'd been here and how I no longer fitted in with the friends I'd had here, so I stayed away. I only came back after Mum died. I wouldn't have a clue who she spent time with.'

I squeeze his arm so tight that he'll probably need a plaster cast by the end of this walk. 'Maybe it's The Stropwomble of Bodmin Lane.'

He laughs. 'Trust me, it's *not* The Stropwomble of Bodmin Lane.'

The atmosphere suddenly feels charged between us and it would be so easy to pull him to a stop and reach up and hug him, and it feels like we both know it wouldn't end at hugging.

I extract my arm from his and go across to the bright green wild raspberry bushes that separate the public river walk from the edges of a farmer's fenced-off field. They're covered in white flowers that will become juicy red berries later in the season, and I have to say 'excuse me' to a bee and nestle a book in the top of a bush.

We've reached the path along the edge of the river now, empty at half past eight in the morning apart from a flash of blue and orange as a kingfisher skims along the river and darts into the water.

Dimitri stops and shrugs the tote bags off his shoulder and readjusts his fox shirt. 'Right, Little Miss Non-Believer, you hide the rest of the books, I'll find the treasure.' He winks at me as he starts loading the last few books to hide into my bag, and folds his empty ones up gleefully. 'Empty bags for all our loot. And at least we're not far from the shop, so you can run back for more while I guard the vast amounts of treasure we're going to dig up.'

I can't help grinning at the childlike joy on his face. There's something so innocent about him, so uncomplicated, and his outlook on life is enviable. Don't we all want to get excited over a child's treasure map in a book, like we would have before growing up stripped us of wonder and saddled us with cynicism?

I listen to the gentle lap of flowing water, low because we haven't had much rain lately. A swan glides near us, checking to see if we've got any food before disappointedly sailing away again.

'It's going to be a murder weapon.' I try not to think about how much I can't resist Dimitri's smile as he pulls *Treasure Island* from his pocket, practically vibrating on the spot as his index finger follows the lines of the biro-drawn map.

'It's going to be some sophisticated criminal who knew no one would ever look at a child's map in a pirate book.'

'It'll be a map marking the location of a buried body.'

'A million pounds!' He thinks for a moment. 'No – *two*. One each!'

'Oh, maybe it *is* the body. We're going to be knee-deep in skeletons any minute now.'

We pass the oak tree and I go across to lean a book against its trunk, and then put my foot on the lower bough and reach to tuck one into a juncture of branches at eye level. My feet splash into dew-damp grass when I step back down.

'Gold bars!' He swings the shovel in one hand and holds open the copy of *Treasure Island* in the other, and I keep dashing off to tuck books into hidden spots along the walkway, leaving one on a picnic table, one on a bench, another on a large flat stone that birdwatchers use as a seat.

'A gun.'

'A time capsule!'

'A genie's lamp with an evil genie in it.'

'A "Welcome to Earth" box for aliens!'

'An *actual* alien. Cramped. Slightly murderous.'

'A magic wand that actually works!'

'The loot from a diamond heist being monitored by the FBI.' Despite how difficult it is to think up outrageous suggestions to counteract his positivity, I'm giggling by the time we cross the wooden bridge over the river, a deep pool below us where people swim in the summer. I leave another book at the post on the corner.

We pass the place where the swans used to nest and follow the bank on the opposite side to the crab apple tree at the edge of the water.

Dimitri looks up at the huge, gnarly tree, its twisted branches laden down with pink-tinged blossom and the first spray of the green leaves that will cover it in summer. 'This is it. X marks the spot.' He holds the book out, his finger on the red X. 'It's this side.'

He hands me his phone and the book as he taps his shovel against the grass a few times, trying to decide where to dig.

'You're not going to find anything,' I say as he presses his foot on the top of the shovel and drives it down into the earth.

'Oh, ye of little faith.' He takes care to slice the top layer of grass off and set it aside so it can be put back afterwards with minimal damage, and then digs up a couple of shovelfuls of earth, being careful to avoid the tree roots.

'It's just a kid's imagination while reading a book about treasure. Who *wouldn't* make up their own—'

His shovel makes a clang as it hits something that is definitely not mud or root, and he looks up at me with exhilaration on his face. 'You were saying?'

'It's probably where someone's buried their hamster.'

He lies down on the wet grass and plunges his hand into the

235

hole, using his fingers to knock away earth and move aside the tangle of tree roots. 'It's metal.' His face screws up as he reaches for it, trying to get enough of a grip to pull it out. 'Quite small. Not big enough to hold any gold bars.'

He hasn't stopped smiling since he pulled *Treasure Island* out, and even now, lying on the ground with dew soaking through his clothes and both arms up to their elbows in earth, he looks radiant. I don't think he's even remotely interested in finding wads of cash down there. I don't think he'd care if it was a box of crayons. He's just experiencing the joy of a treasure hunt.

He makes a series of noises as his hand closes around whatever is hiding down there and he loses his grip a few times before finally easing it out one centimetre at a time.

It's a battered old tin with mostly rusted pictures of seed packets on the front and hinges that look like they're barely hanging on.

Dimitri's so excited that when he opens his mouth, all that comes out is a series of noises, and I can't help grinning at him. Even if he is about to prove me wrong. Or find that it *is* somebody's dead hamster.

He lays it on the grass and kneels in front of it, and I crouch beside him as he tries to open the corroded tin, fused together by rust. It creaks and scratches as he carefully works the lid from the tin and lifts it off like a precious artefact.

The hinges are so rusty that they split with the first hint of movement and his fingers hover above it before he lifts something gently from the box. 'It's a car! Isn't that amazing? Look at the age of this.' He cradles the rusty, muddy thing in his palm – a little metal toy car, with a hint of red and blue scraps of paint peeking out from under the rust and mud that's seeped inside the tin. 'It's got to be 1950s at least. *This* is the sort of thing we have to put online. Can you imagine being the little boy who buried this? To come across it again sixty-odd years later?'

'I doubt he still wants it,' I say, even though it is pretty impressive. I don't know anything about the rust patterns of metal or old toy cars, but it certainly looks like it's been down there for the best part of a few decades.

He tucks the car back into the tin, handling it like it's made of glass. 'We should be getting back – it must be late.'

The time! I'd totally forgotten about the time. I quickly check my phone – five to nine. It'll take longer than that to walk back. Let's hope there isn't a queue of irate customers lining up for me to open the door. There's a first time for everything.

I notice the Twitter app on my phone has got a glowing red dot beside it, indicating a new direct message. I put Dimitri's phone, the copy of *Treasure Island*, and the old tin down on the grass so I can read it while he carefully refills the hole and lays the turf of grass back where it came from.

And then it's my turn to squeal. 'Brandon's just direct messaged me! And he's looking for Mindy too!'

He cries out too and in the midst of the excitement, it flits across my mind how nice it is to have someone to share my excitement with, but the thought is quickly replaced by more excitement.

He holds his arms open, and despite the fact he's soaking wet from lying on the grass and he's got soil up to his elbows and there are shards of tree root stuck to his foxy shirt, I leap on him. We're one step away from doing the lift in *Dirty Dancing* but with far less grace than a pair of sozzled squirrels, but he catches me easily, holding me to him with his arms rather than putting his muddy hands on my T-shirt, and I wrap my arm around his neck and read the phone screen over his shoulder.

'*I've been looking for this book for YEARS! My best friend saw your post and recognised the similarities between it and what had happened to me years ago. I'm still single, I've never forgotten her, and like John Cusack in the film, I look in every copy of this book I find. I email sellers on Amazon to ask them if their copy has a name and number written inside. I was devastated when the old fivers were retired, knowing she'd never find mine.'* I squeeze him tightly. 'Isn't this the most amazing thing?'

'Wow,' he murmurs. 'I did not expect that.'

I'm not sure if he means the DM or me hitting him with quite such force.

'Hal, this is amazing.' He draws the middle *a* out and spins us around, but the tree roots spidering out into the riverbank around us are an unexpected hazard, and he catches his foot on one, sending us both sprawling towards the river.

I scream and somehow have the forethought to throw the phone that's still in my hand onto the grass to avoid drowning it, as Dimitri crashes down into the water with me on top of him, creating a splash that can probably be seen from space and is definitely going to register on the Richter scale, and earning dirty looks from the swans further up the river who swiftly scarper.

Even in spring, the water is freezing and I squeak as it soaks through every inch of my clothing. I scramble off him and stumble upright on the stony riverbed with water flowing around my ankles.

'That went well.' His hair is surprisingly long when it's wet and his face is almost completely obscured by the long brown strands, dark with river water. He holds his hands out in front of him and examines them. 'At least it washed some of the mud off.'

He always finds something positive in every situation, and the way he's just sitting there in the water, looking completely unfazed and trying to blow away the wet hair that's glued itself to his face is so cartoon character-esque that it sets me off giggling.

From my not-at-all-wobbly upright position, I hold my hands out, and he slips both of his into mine and lets me pull him to his feet.

Maybe it's the shock of the cold water or the adrenalin of the fall but something is making this seem much funnier than it is.

'Why are we laughing? I'm cold, wet, I'm standing in a river,

I've got a bruised bum, and I don't care about any of it.' He's laughing too as he takes his glasses off and tries to dry them with the bottom of his wet shirt, which only serves to make them wetter.

I go to put my foot on the shallow bank and get out, but he pulls me back, and before I know it, his arms are around me from behind and his lips are on my cheek. 'Have dinner with me?'

I turn around in his embrace and he looks completely uninhibited and just as surprised to hear the words as I am, like his mouth has run ahead of his brain.

I reach up and brush wet hair off his forehead. 'Did you hit your head when you landed or something? After last time?'

'Yep.' He grins like he physically can't stop grinning. 'But just you and me this time, and it'll be me cooking. And it won't be pizza. Or whatever the hell that *thing* that came out of your sister's oven was because it certainly wasn't pizza. It's just … I know you know I've been holding back, and there's something I want to show you. Saturday night?' He reaches his dripping hand out like it's asking the question on his behalf.

I slip mine into it and squeeze it in response. 'Sounds perfect.'

And despite the fact we've both got too much to carry to hold hands, he doesn't let my hand drop, and I can't get the smile off my face as we drip back towards the shop, long after opening time, despite the fact we're both soaked, cold, and muddy. Nothing matters beyond the smile on his face and the joyful looks he keeps giving me, and the butterflies inside me feel like they're the size of the disgruntled swans we pass by, and I can't help wondering how I ever got so lucky – to win the shop, to find the notes, or to meet Dimitri.

Chapter 15

I shouldn't be nervous about having dinner with Dimitri. I've had lunch with him almost every day and breakfast with him regularly since I got here, but this invite feels different – special, somehow. He hasn't specified but I assume we're going to his house, which he never talks about, and since the river incident, he's been asking me what my favourite savoury foods are because he's only ever brought me sweet things until now, and quite frankly, by seven o'clock on Saturday night when he's arranged to meet me at the shop, I'm a bit of a wreck.

After I closed at five, Nicole pulled up in her car with a boot full of industrial-sized make-up cases and a back seat full of garment bags, and now I have a good three-quarters of Boots' nationwide stock adhered to my face and I'm wearing one of her dresses – a silky thing with blue and green stripes that melt into each other like the dress melts against my body and makes me feel svelte and slinky when I am neither of those things. It's the sort of thing I'd never even consider buying because it's far too nice and I would undoubtedly ruin it.

Nicole's already given me the name of the local dry cleaners and pointed out the tailor across the road, lest I do exactly that.

I intended to carry on checking books for written messages

while waiting, but I keep opening them and putting them back on the shelf and not remembering if there was a message inside or not, so I give up and pace the floor in my ballet flats that Nicole assures me do *not* belong with this dress, but even I drew the line at wearing heels. *No* situation is that desperate.

It's seven on the dot when there's a knock on the shop door, and I love that someone as dishevelled as Dimitri is also such a good timekeeper.

I take a deep breath as I turn the key and open the door, wondering why I feel so nervous. It's Dimitri, for heaven's sake. I've seen him every day since I got here. I've stuck my head out of the window and yelled at him first thing in the morning. *Nothing* could be a worse sight than that.

'Hello!' He greets me with his usual happy greeting and holds out such a huge bunch of multicoloured tulips that I can barely see him behind them.

'Wow. Where did you get these? They're beautiful,' I say because they're so unusual and obviously handpicked. He still hasn't learnt that I'm not good at keeping things alive. I glance at Heathcliff happily swimming around in his bowl. He must be some sort of miracle fish to still be alive a month after I got here.

I hold the flowers by their stems and turn back to look at him. Neither of us tries to hide our eyes widening in shock at the sight of each other.

'Wow.' He takes my hand and pulls it up to his mouth where he kisses the back of it. 'I'm sorry, I'm here to meet Hallie. Do you know where she is?'

I wallop his hand. 'You're not funny.'

He *is* gorgeous though. He's wearing dark suit trousers and a matching waistcoat over a shirt that's the exact same shade as his eyes, making them look impossibly bluer. I've always loved a man in a waistcoat, and I love Dimitri's odd fashion sense of wearing one with non-traditional waistcoat outfits, but tonight … If I wasn't already overheated from nerves, I'd be overheated from the sight of him. And his aftershave, which is like a walk on the beach on a hot summer's day with the waves lapping at your feet. Salty and orangey but still with a hint of something as dark as charcoal and as warm as wood.

'Flipping heck, Hal. I'm leaning on the doorframe because I think my knees might go if I try to stand upright. Do you have any idea how beautiful you look?'

If Santa ever wanted a new suit, he would take my cheeks to his tailor for a colour match on the fabric, but no matter how hard I try, I cannot stop myself beaming. What girl *doesn't* want to hear that?

'Thank you,' I mumble, my mouth suddenly as dry as particularly parched dust. 'You too.'

His hair is neatly done up in a strong quiff, and sort of curled in at the top to make it look a bit shorter than usual. As much as I love his usual haphazard look, I'm glad that he thinks this night was worth making an effort for too, because I thought all the make-up and the dress might've been overkill.

'Sorry, I had to sell my car last year. We'll have to walk.' He goes to run a hand through his hair but stops himself before he dislodges it, and it makes me feel better that he's nervous too.

'That's okay, it's a gorgeous evening. Just let me put these in water.'

One of the vases from the last lot of flowers he brought me is still in the office, so I run upstairs to fill it with water and plonk the tulips into it, fluffing them up a bit like people do when they put flowers in water, although I haven't the first clue what I'm doing.

He holds his arm out when I finally step out the door and lock it behind me, and I slip mine through it gratefully.

'Where are we going?' I ask as we cross the street and go around the burbling fountain and down a lane that leads onto the main road out of Buntingorden. Despite the wide pavement, he insists on walking on the outside like the gentleman he is.

242

'You'll see.'

One thing I never appreciated about Buntingorden before I moved here was how pretty it is. Even the main roads have a cosy shut-in feel with wide verges full of greenery interspersed with patches of wildflowers, and tall trees with weeping branches that overhang the spacious pavements. There are road signs to watch out for wild deer, and each road we turn down looks like the kind of fairy-tale street where you might find Snow White living in a cottage at the end of it or Cinderella doing housework with the help of some friendly birds.

He's quiet as we walk, and I get the feeling he's nervous, but I can't work out why.

It's only when we turn into a quiet road with nothing but the occasional mansion set back from the pavements that I notice the name on the sign. 'Bodmin Lane?' I say in surprise. 'Do you live around here? Do you know The Stropwomble? Oh God, is he one of your neighbours and all the time people have been slagging him off in the shop, you actually know him?'

'Something like that.'

We come to what is undoubtedly the house that everyone's been talking about with black iron railings that must be at least ten foot high, with spikes on top and barbwire wrapped throughout them. The front gate looks rusted shut, and I try to see through the gaps between the railings to get a glimpse of the house, but the garden is overgrown with welcoming things like stinging nettles and brambles. Dimitri extracts his arm from mine and reaches out to take my hand instead, his palm clammy when I slip mine into it. He tugs me around the side of The Stropwomble of Bodmin Lane's house.

'Where are we going? Are you, like, on his staff or something?' I get the feeling that my questioning is making him more nervous, so I decide to be quiet and trust him, wherever he's taking us.

Past the thick railings is a crumbling red-brick wall covered in ivy leaves, scrambling from the pavement to the top, sending its roots into every crack in the brickwork, and Dimitri leads me around the curved wall, off the main pavement and onto a tiny, unworn path that even the bravest of dog walkers wouldn't venture down. I keep trying to see into the garden, but the wall is as high as the spiked railing tops, and although there are holes in the deteriorating brickwork, none of them are big enough to see through.

Dimitri doesn't let go of my hand as I follow him down the narrow path, overgrown on either side by yet more brambles that threaten to snag Nicole's dress if I'm not careful.

We walk around another curve in the broken wall surrounding what must be an absolutely immense garden, and eventually he stops and moves aside what can only be described as a sheet of ivy, uncovering a battered wooden gate set back in the brickwork, completely obscured from view. It looks damp and is mouse-chewed at the bottom, but the four shiny padlocks look almost new and leave me in no doubt about how welcome visitors are.

Until he lets go of my hand, fishes a jangly keyring from his pocket, and starts undoing the locks.

'We're going in?' I say in surprise as adrenalin floods my body. Of all places I expected Dimitri to be taking us, this wasn't one of them, and from what I've heard of The Stropwomble of Bodmin Lane, he's right at the bottom of my list of people I want to meet. 'We're *sneaking* in? He's not even going to know we're here, is he? I didn't take you for an adrenalin junkie. Where are we going for our next date – bungee jumping?'

I realise in that instant that it *is* a date. *That's* where all the extra nerves have come from, probably for both of us.

He crouches down to undo the last lock, and I start frantically trying to make myself look presentable. If I'm about to meet the most hated man in Buntingorden, the least I can do is smooth my dress down and de-frizzle my hair.

He gathers all the padlocks in one hand and pushes the gate, holding it open for me to go through, and then turns around and starts attaching the padlocks to a matching four locks on the inside of the gate. He must sense me watching him because he looks up from what he's doing. 'This isn't as bad as it looks. It's to stop anyone getting in, not you getting out. You can have the keys if you want, but I don't feel safe here without the gate locked.'

I trust Dimitri, I tell myself. He's lovely and kind and thoughtful. He's not up to anything nefarious. I look around the garden instead to distract myself from why we're coming into a place so obviously keen to keep us out and clearly not very hot on the idea of us leaving either. Inside the gate is a wide concrete path leading to a huge Gothic mansion, complete with gargoyles, broken turrets, blackened windows, and metal door hangers that I half-expect Jacob Marley's face to appear in.

Far from Snow White or Cinderella, of all the fairy-tale characters I expected to find at the end of this walk, this looks more like somewhere Jafar or Rasputin would live.

Beside me, the outside wall continues inside, closing off a piece of the overgrown garden with a well-worn path around it, and while Dimitri's still doing up the last lock, I follow it round to an open doorway and peek inside.

'A walled garden!' I say in surprise. And not just a walled garden, but a walled garden filled with the most beautiful beds of flowers. Roses, daffodils, and every colour of tulip you can imagine. There are pansies and giant snowdrops, and baskets hanging from a wooden frame that criss-crosses the open ceiling. 'This is where you got the tulips from. And the daffodils.'

He appears next to me, takes a key from his keyring and hands it to me. 'Here. You take it. I don't mean to make you feel uneasy. You're free to go anytime you want.'

I don't know what's going on, but I *do* trust him, and the fact he's willing to give me the key to the gate is touching. It means he's aware of my feelings and of how a man locking a gate behind a woman could be perceived. Instead of taking it, I take hold of his hand and close his fingers around it, trying to let him know I trust him without saying the words.

He smiles, but instead of putting it back on his keyring, he goes back to the gate, lifts a stone from the path and slips it underneath, making sure I'm watching exactly where he puts it.

I walk back to the concrete path that leads up a ramp towards the doorway, like a yellow brick road to the entrance of this sad old castle, and this time when he holds his hand out, his fingers are shaking. I slip my hand into his again, wondering what this is all about.

At the woodworm-ridden wooden door, scarred by what look like burn marks licking up from the bottom, he pulls his keyring back out and undoes a heavy-duty set of three locks and uses his shoulder to shove the gigantic wooden door open.

'Come in.' It sounds for all the world like he's inviting me into his own house.

I stand in the grand entranceway and look up at the ceiling in awe because it's so far up that I have to tilt my head back to see it, and it looks like it should've been painted by Michelangelo. Or possibly was.

But awe doesn't feel like the right description for this place. It's awe-inspiring to look at, but a sense of sadness permeates every inch of the building. There's a wide double stairway to one side, but the tall ceilings above it are decorated with spider's webs, and dust motes float through the air as the evening sun glints across the building. There are stone pillars with cracks circling around them like a pattern, and the tiled floor beneath my feet has got corners of tiles missing, others with chips out of them, jagged broken lines running through them, and blackened grouting.

'The living room's better,' he says. 'This way.'

I should probably push him, but I also feel that there's a fragile peace between us, and my pushing him will break some part of it, and I get the sense that he needs to explain in his own time.

I follow him down a cold hallway until he pushes open the creaky door of what must be the living room. Inside, it looks like the scene of a forgotten film set from the 1920s. There's a threadbare damask carpet covering scratchy concrete floors, and big leather sofas and armchairs from more than one mismatched furniture suite. There's an unlit coal fire in a hearth on one wall and a cracked chimney breast extending into the room. A wide bay window beckons from the opposite side, and I walk across to it, dodging varnish-peeling coffee tables and footstalls that I half-expect to turn back into a dog when the curse is lifted from the castle.

I stand at the grand window and look out through streaked glass, taking in the immense garden, the sharp iron railings that we saw from the road that looks miles away with the amount of stinging nettles, brambles, and other unidentifiable weeds that have taken over the huge plot of land between here and the gate.

'You live here?' I look back at him and he nods. 'But this is where the monster of Buntingorden lives, right?'

He nods again.

'So what are you trying to tell me? It's not you, is it?' I say jokingly, and the unexpected chuckle that bursts out of him seems to make him relax.

'No, it's not me.' He takes a few steps towards me, and I turn back to look out the window, trying to work this out because I get the feeling he wants me to put two and two together for myself.

'Then why does everyone think he lives here?'

He puts his chin on my shoulder from behind and his arms slide around me, pulling my back tight against his front. 'Because he used to.'

I think about everything he's said over the weeks I've known him. 'Your father?'

He nods against my shoulder and I can feel the tension in him like this is some awful, monumental confession. The sense of sadness that floods through me is so overwhelming that I reach back blindly until I can get my hand around his hip and hold him there, making sure he stays while he explains.

'He moved back in after my mum died. Even though they were divorced and she'd thrown him out years before, he came back to "help" with my sister, and I let him, because I didn't live here either and I was completely lost in grief and I didn't know what I was supposed to do or what was right. I naively believed this tragedy had ignited some sense of family in him and he actually wanted to help, but I soon realised it wasn't about that. It was about getting his claws back into the house he'd lost in the divorce. This house is big enough that you can share it with other people and never have to cross paths with them. He spent most of his time at the office, and there were burnt rubber tyre tracks on the driveway from how quickly he sped away if we did need his help with anything. He just kind of existed in the periphery for about a year, occasionally trying to convince me that he should have a share in the house. And you know that feeling you get when you just *know* something isn't right? Eventually I found the transfer papers he'd had drawn up and discovered he'd spent the past few months trying to convince Dani she was too weak and stupid to have part share of a mansion and that she should sign it over to him to "look after". Thankfully my sister *wasn't* weak or stupid and hadn't fallen for it, and I found the courage to throw him out, and I've barely exchanged two words with him since.'

'But he's the monster of Buntingorden?'

He nods again. 'He's been writing those letters for as long as I can remember. Vicious, nasty letters to anyone who'll give him a platform. The local newspaper is his favourite, and he's got someone on the council in his pocket so any ridiculous thing he can find to complain about is taken seriously. It started when I was younger – he wanted to acquire a big chunk of land on the other side of the river, but the residents weren't going to let it be sold and built on. They got fed up of him harassing them, so they fought back and got some sort of landmark status declared, so he lost out on it. And he swore revenge. He wanted to make everyone in Buntingorden's life as miserable as possible. He started doing a bit of criminal damage but he got caught by the police and *they* wouldn't accept his bribes, so he started doing it all from behind anonymous poison pen letters and complaints about anything that made people happy.'

'He sounds like a lovely chap.'

My sarcasm makes Dimitri burst out laughing and his arms tighten and I feel the tension start to drip away.

'I didn't live here for years. I didn't care about Buntingorden or what was happening in it. Obviously I heard stories about The Stropwomble of Buntingorden when I came back, and it still took me a long while to realise it was him. And in the year he lived here after Mum died, it somehow came out that this was his house. I've always suspected it was deliberate – his way of making mine and Dani's lives that little bit more uncomfortable. And that's it, really. That's my terrible secret. You can hate me if you want to. There's a lot of people around here who would if they found out.'

'I could never hate you. You are the definition of unhateable.' I squeeze his hip so tightly that I start wondering how long the NHS waiting lists for hip replacements are around here. 'Why do people still think he lives here?'

'Because I never corrected them. There's the whole aspect that me saying something would've outed him, and no matter what he's done, he's still my father, and it's not my place to do that. There's a *lot* of anger towards him in this village and while people make jokes about monsters and use that cutesy name in front of kids, I think if the right powder kegs ignited at the same time, there'd be people who'd want to teach him a lesson. I don't want him to get hurt because of me. And another thing is that it makes people leave this house alone. I've been drowning in grief for a long while. Believe me, it's better if no one comes here.'

His chin is still on my shoulder, I can feel every movement of his jaw, and his voice is so quiet that I wouldn't be able to hear him if he wasn't speaking right next to my ear. His hand is on top of mine where it's holding on to his hip, and his other hand is on the window ledge in front of me. I reach out and drag my fingers across his gently, and when he turns his palm over, I slot mine into it and squeeze as tightly as I can.

'We became recluses. The garden overgrew, hiding us from the view of the world, and Dani was afraid of seeing people so when we had to go out, I'd pull the car round to the side gate and we'd sneak out that way. No one even seemed to notice that we were here. We were forgotten. Living ghosts. And that was fine.'

There must be finger-shaped indents in his hip from how tight I'm holding on to him. What I want to do is turn around and pull him into the tightest hug that mankind has ever experienced, but I also know that if I do that, one or both of us will break down in tears, and more than anything, I want him to keep talking.

'I never really grieved after Mum died. It was so fast, so sudden. Within the space of a morning, I'd left my life in Oxford and was back here, taking care of my sister because my dad and brother weren't interested. Dani didn't cope well with Mum's death and I had to be strong for her. And when she died last year, I was *so* alone. The grief completely crushed me. I needed to be alone to cope with it. I didn't want well-meaning neighbours popping round and people gossiping about me in the street. I was glad of the privacy that overgrown garden gave me, and if the price is a few kids throwing eggs at my house on Halloween and talking about the "monster" who lives here, then so be it.'

In my head, I do a calculation between that and the burn marks on the door when we came in. 'Why is the door burnt?'

'Because people are cruel. When my father got the fireworks display cancelled, one of the angry villagers chucked lit fireworks into the garden. A few patches of greenery burnt, but there was a doormat outside the door and one landed on it and set it alight.'

My hand must tighten around his hard enough to hurt, because he laughs and gently loosens it. 'Don't worry, I put it out before it did any real damage.'

Judging by the charred scars on his front door, I think he's being generous there.

'But that's why there are so many locks on the gate. I thought if they can do that kind of damage from outside, what would they do if they could get in? I didn't feel safe here and worried about someone uncovering my hidden gate. That's why it's locked. Nothing untoward, I promise. I should have told you about my father earlier, but I didn't want you to hate me, and I felt something in that river the other day that made me realise I had to tell you and I thought it might be best to show you first. I wanted to share every part of my life with you, even the bad parts.'

I don't know how he ever thinks I could hate him for anything he's just shared. All it does is show me how much he's been through, how much he's struggled, and how alone he's been, and how through it all, he's still come out the other side with an enviably positive outlook and a smile that never fails to brighten other people's days. How, even though he clearly has a fractured relationship with his father, he's still protecting him, even if it means putting himself in danger sometimes.

So *this* is what he was hiding. At least this explains the vague feeling I've been getting that he's holding something back. Nothing nefarious. Maybe it's time I let myself believe in real-life happy endings after all.

Without letting go of either hand, I do some twisty thing and turn around to look up into his blue eyes and the only thing I can think of to express the whirlwind of emotions swirling inside me is to kiss him.

He must feel it too because he lowers his head before I've even realised I'm going to reach up and pull him down, and I'm not sure which one of us moans louder as our mouths crash together. My hand slides into his hair, destroying the neat style it was in, and he backs me up until my bum hits the edge of the window ledge and there's no further to go. His arms are caging me in as my fingers wind in his hair and pull him closer, until our mouths, tongues, lips, are tangled in a frenzied mass of kissing and nothing is *enough*, and there are moans and grabbing, and panting, and somewhere in the depths of my mind, I know this isn't going to end at kissing if we don't slow it down. I force myself to loosen my grip on his shirt and start stroking through his hair rather than grabbing it, and I feel the way his mouth turns up into a smile against mine as he feels it too.

I feel him relax, letting out a sigh against my lips, and I get so lost in the kiss that I forget the hazards of kissing while both wearing glasses until our frames crash together with a plasticky crack.

'Well, it wouldn't have been us if a kiss didn't end with something breaking, would it?' He sounds breathless and his shivery voice makes me tingle all over.

He pulls back and I love how he has to lean against the shelf for support as he takes his glasses off and checks them for damage, and I turn away and do the same, and take a moment to compose myself because after that kiss, I'm feeling very *un*composed.

'Nothing broken?' he asks gently.

'No. You?'

He shakes his head when I turn back to look at him.

'I've wanted to do that since the moment I met you,' I tell him honestly.

'It was the giant flea that did it, wasn't it?'

The unexpected joke makes me giggle, and I reach up again and brush my thumb over his smooth jaw. 'Yeah. Between the giant flea and the crushed daffodils, you were irresistible.'

He turns into my touch and leans down to rest his forehead against mine. 'Thank you for listening. If I'd known this would be the reaction, I'd have told you weeks ago.' His whole face brightens and for the first time tonight, he looks like himself.

His hair flops forward and he's still so close that I can feel the weight of it against mine. I reach up and tuck it back, loving how his hair corresponds to his mood – when he's nervous, it's stiff as a board; when he's relaxed, it goes all floppy; and when he's being his usual clumsy, adorable self, it sticks out in all directions.

I can't hold back the hug any longer. There's something about Dimitri that makes me want to hug him, but it's different this time – this time, I *need* to hug him more desperately than I need to take my next breath. I feel like there aren't any words to get across how much he matters to me and how much it means that he's shared this part of his life.

I get one arm around his back and clutch him to me, and the other slides around his shoulders, caressing the shortish darker hair at the nape of his neck as I pull his head down to rest against my shoulder and squeeze him as snugly as I can without breaking any bones.

He cuddles me back so tightly. His whole body folds around me, and I can feel him sagging with the relief of telling someone. We stand there in silence for the longest time, just breathing, holding, letting my fingers card through his hair.

'And just so you know, I *am* trying to undo some of my father's damage.' His voice sounds blissful and far away. 'I've been in touch with the council and paid for the most spectacular Christmas tree to go up near the fountain this year. I've got the fireworks display reinstated for November. The bunting hasn't gone anywhere because I put an anonymous petition online about living in a village called Buntingorden without any bunting and enough people signed it. And at the end of October, I'm going to carve a load of pumpkins and go out one night and place them all over town with battery-operated tea lights in them. They won't be a fire hazard, and if I do it right before Halloween, it will already be over by the time he starts complaining.'

'So you're anonymously fighting your anonymous father?' I never thought the word anonymous could be so overused. I pull back and reach up to tuck his hair back, my hand staying on his neck and my fingers playing in his hair so he knows I don't want him to pull away. 'Why now?'

He closes his eyes. 'Because I feel like living again this year. Until now, I've been okay with hiding away, letting him get on with spreading his vitriol and telling myself it didn't matter, but since I started coming to the bookshop, I've realised how much I love this village. I was away for years. I associated the place with bad memories – I resented it because I'd been sent away. When I came back after Mum died, my focus was on Dani, and I got through each day on autopilot, from doctors to hospital appointments interspersed with trips to the library and the supermarket to collect groceries I'd ordered online. We spoke to as few people as possible. After Dani died, Robert literally pushed me back into life. I was sitting here one day and I heard a noise, and looked up to see him outside banging on this window.' He nods towards it, physically moving both of us. 'Somehow he knew about the side gate and he'd let himself in and come looking for me. He knew I needed to get out of the house, so he physically dragged me down to the shop, shoved me onto the sofa and poked tea and biscuits down my throat until I broke down and told him everything.'

I pull him down into another hug and my arms get impossibly tighter around him and if I didn't pull out a few handfuls of his hair during the kiss, I definitely do now. 'And let me guess, he found reasons for you to go there every day and made sure you stayed occupied and got out of your own head?' I say, because I know the kind of man Robert is. I know how concerned he was if I didn't seem as chirpy as usual, how encouraging he'd be if I went in there when I'd just lost a job or went in on the way back from my mum's endless lecturing about finding a husband. How he'd try to find me a book that fitted the situation and always offered me a cuppa and a biscuit.

'Exactly. Like the Peter Pan mural and refitting the children's section. He encouraged me to work on *Pentamerone*.' He smiles into my shoulder and lifts me up, turning us around until he can sit me on the shelf. 'I wasn't sure you'd let me do that again after the river incident.'

'Hah. You're okay as long as there are no bodies of water around. And no swans. They weren't too impressed.'

He presses his lips to my cheek. 'Hal … thank you. You're the best thing that's happened in my life for a very long time. I want this, I want you, but I'm so scared of messing it up. I mess everything up.'

'So do I.' I slide my hand up his jaw and lock eyes with him. 'But I've wanted to kiss you from the moment you landed on my floor. I've found every possible excuse to hold your hand, and every day has been a constant battle of wills not to inappropriately hug you. Nothing ever goes right for me, and if it looks like things *are* going right then I've obviously overlooked something and karma will catch up shortly. But I look forward to seeing you every day, Dimitri. My life is better because you came into it, and now we've done that, I don't want to go back to *not* doing that.'

Even as I speak, I wonder where I'm getting this confidence from. Nothing has ever worked out for me for long, from jobs to friendships, and especially relationships. 'So maybe we can try to not mess it up together?'

'I'd like that.' He steals another kiss and then grins again. 'Who knew going arse-over-tit could lead to this, eh?'

'Do you know how jealous Heathcliff's going to be? He's head-over-heels in love with you.'

'He's also head-over-heels in love with that little brown Cockapoo that walks past every morning, so I don't think the bar's set too high.'

'Well, it *is* a very handsome Cockapoo.'

He laughs, his usual laugh now, complete with twinkling eyes and smile that could light up the night. He leans in for a kiss, angling his head carefully to avoid another glasses crash, and I get lost in kissing him once again. My hands run over his shoulders, into his hair and back down his neck, constantly trying to pull him impossibly closer, to quell the butterflies that are zipping through me, the sheer excitement at being more than friends with this beautiful man who, honestly, I've felt more than friends with for a while now.

We're gasping against each other's mouths when we eventually pull back and his stomach lets out a huge growl of hunger.

'It wouldn't be a kiss if my body didn't betray me in some way.' He slips his hands around my waist and helps me down. 'We should eat. Come and see my kitchen.'

I follow him down the wide dark hallway, taking in the reminders of his sister at every turn – a wheelchair-sized stairlift on the huge staircase, wide hallways and enlarged doorframes, a shallow ramp that we go down into the kitchen. It's a huge room, bigger than the entire bookshop and flat upstairs put together, with a red-tiled floor, low-level wooden cupboards and low units at a height for someone in a wheelchair to reach. There are dusty vases of artificial flower arrangements, the kind that look like they were put there by his mum and have stood there ever since, and shelves lined with recipe books that I again guess didn't always belong to him.

In every flat I've lived in, I've always had tiny, cramped kitchens, and I can't imagine ever cooking – well, heating up microwave meals – in a place the size of this, and he *loves* baking. It should be a happy room, but once again, it isn't. This house is so overwhelmingly sad. Everything about it is the reverse of Dimitri's sunny, smiley, gorgeously positive personality.

I watch the way he bends over the sink to wash his hands, and then starts chopping vegetables, almost bent double to reach the countertops that are far too low for him. I can't shake the feeling of crushing sadness again. When I've imagined Dimitri cooking, I've imagined a warm and cosy kitchen, full of the music he hums in the shop when he forgets he's not alone, sizzling pans and beeping timers, and happiness, but actually seeing it … It's like he's living in someone else's house. Seeing him hunched over a unit that doesn't fit him, he looks like he's bowed under the weight of this house and everything that's happened in it.

'Can I help?' I ask.

'Of course not.' He looks up and grins at me. 'I invited you. Besides, how can I be sure that you haven't inherited your mum's cooking skills?'

'Oh, I assure you, my cooking skills make my mum look like kitchen queen. A smaller-boobed Nigella if ever there was one.'

The laugh echoes around the kitchen, tinkling into every corner before fading away, forgotten into the darkened corners.

I look up at the high ceiling, a cobwebbed hollow affair with two starkly bright bar lights hanging down, giving it the appearance of a hospital room, and I've never been so grateful for my tiny kitchen that's so small you trip over the living-room sofa if you take a step too many.

While he puts a pot on the stove, I wander over to the window, but we're on a slightly lower level now and the overgrown blackberry bushes outside have crept right up the bottom half of the window and their prickly branches are scratching against the glass.

Eventually I'm sitting at a table on the other side of the kitchen, sipping wine from Dimitri's father's abandoned collection, when he puts down the most delicious-looking spaghetti bolognese in front of me and sits down opposite.

'Cheers.' He leans across the table and we clink glasses and tuck in.

I thought I was so full of nerves that I'd never be hungry, but one mouthful of Dimitri's amazing food is enough to kick-start anyone's appetite. 'So your talent for cooking doesn't end at baked goods then?'

He blushes and mumbles something incoherent that's obviously a rebuttal of some kind, and all I wish about this meal is that it was something easier to eat as I splash the fifth tomato pip down the front of Nicole's dress and try to wipe it off without him noticing.

'So you and your brother both own this place?'

'Yeah. Mum left the house to me, Dani, and him in a three-way split. Now she's gone, my brother and I own it fifty-fifty. He wants to sell and I don't. We're in battle about it. The even split means neither of us can do anything without the other's agreement, and neither of us will give in. It's been in our family for nearly a century. My great-great grandparents lived here. I don't think it's right to wipe out so much history like that. I always thought I'd be passing it on to my future kids one day, not rattling around in it alone and having petty arguments with my brother that neither of us will back down from.'

'It must cost a fortune to run ...' If he notices I'm wheedling for more information, he doesn't say anything.

'And that's exactly why I haven't offered you a grand tour. I can't afford to keep up more rooms than I use. The kitchen and living room, and upstairs there's a bedroom and bathroom. The Aga heats this room, the fire heats the water as well as the living room, and the heat from that rises to the bedroom above it.'

I once again think about my tiny flat. It's been warm enough that I haven't put the heating on since I moved in above the bookshop, but no flat I've ever lived in has had more than a couple of electric radiators or been big enough that they weren't sufficient. This answers a lot about the financial situation he's mentioned a couple of times. I don't know anything about property, but even my untrained eye can tell that this house needs a lot of repairs, and it looks like the sort of place you could funnel money into for years and there would *still* be more to do.

'Everything else is closed off. I keep the doors shut to try to stem the draughts howling through, and as you've probably noticed, I spend most of my time taking advantage of your cosy bookshop rather than dealing with the problems here.'

I'd always thought there was a reason that he was never keen to go home, but I didn't realise it was because home was a crumbling, draughty, empty old mansion. He must be so lonely here. Living between only a couple of rooms, the rest of the vast building left to gather dust and conceal ghosts and belongings of people long gone. That feeling of sadness presses down on me again, and he must sense it too, because he reaches across the table and touches my hand.

'Enough about my woes. I've got some greeting card mock-ups to show you later, and I had an idea about your open day and how we can display these messages ...'

I want to know everything there is to know about his woes, but there's something vulnerable in his eyes, something that's begging me not to push it, so I squeeze his hand and let him change the subject. 'Go on ...'

'You've got a printer in the office, right?'

I nod, thinking about the clunky thing at the corner of the desk that I haven't had a chance to use yet. Robert must've replaced it fairly recently because it's modern by the other electronic items' standard.

'What if we scan them in and print them out – book cover on the front, message on the back, and display them somehow. It would save the books themselves being ruined by constant handling, and people could ask for them only if they want to buy them.'

'That's brilliant.' I grin at him. 'I feel like they should be hung up somehow, like a mobile or something ...' A blackberry bush blows in the breeze and scratches along the window with an ominous creak which draws my attention outside. 'Leaves!'

Dimitri turns around to look out the window behind him at my sudden outburst, but I grab his hand again. 'What if we print them out as leaf shapes and hang them up like leaves on a tree?

It would be a nod towards paper origins, and it couldn't be that difficult to cut a trunk and some branches out of cardboard … I could leave it up all the time then. Rather than one big exhibit on open day, it could be like an open*ing* day, and the messages could stay on display always … Why are you smiling like that?'

'Because you have no idea how radiant you are. And Robert has no idea how lucky Once Upon A Page got on the day he picked your ticket. That's *brilliant*, Hal. Both the tree and the opening day. I was thinking of a big one-day exhibit, but an opening day is so much better. Anyone can come and see the messages at any time then, and when you get in touch with local press and stuff to cover it, you can sell the "under new management" angle too.'

If I lay down on this tiled floor, my cheeks are so red that I'd be completely camouflaged.

'What about a real tree? I've got an old birch round the back that's as dead as a doornail. About six foot high, in a fancy pot. It didn't survive the winter a couple of years ago, so now it's just bare branches that I haven't got round to throwing away yet. If you tie each leaf onto it, it could look pretty spectacular …'

'Much better than what I was thinking of: cutting two trunks from cardboard and slotting them together so they stand upright akin to a primary school project. Are you sure you don't mind?'

'My mum planted it. It was a little seedling growing in the middle of something else and she rescued it and planted it up on its own, and it took years to be able to identify it. I've always felt awful that it died on my watch, but this would be a fantastic way of repurposing it. She'd like that.'

'She wrote the note that started all this … It seems right, somehow.'

'Like some sort of weird fate that we were meant to be here, and we were meant to pick up that book on that day …'

I nod because it's exactly what I've felt since the moment I saw that email from Robert. For the first time in my life, I've felt like things were going right – like I'm doing what I'm supposed to be doing, like I've got the job I was supposed to have, and most of all, like Dimitri was meant to fall through my door when he did.

'Thank you for an amazing evening.' Our joined hands swing between us, the tiles click under my feet and my voice echoes in the hollowness of the grand hallway. He's giving me a tour of the house, but there isn't much to see. Endless wide hallways, empty and dusty, the only surprise about them is that there *aren't* suits of armour that move of their own accord as soon as your back is turned.

He leads me up a staircase that looks like it should have Leonardo DiCaprio waiting under a clock at the top of it.

'Wow,' I say as he creaks open a huge double door, letting us in to a circular ballroom. 'This is where you work.'

I can't help letting out a breath as I look around the wide-open room. The faded walls were once red with gold accents, the scuffed floor must've been polished once, and a cobwebbed chandelier hangs from a ceiling so high that it must surely go all the way from the second floor to the very top of the house. But best of all are the array of easels that are stood around the edges of the room. An oak table in the corner bears sketchbooks and a display of cards in pastel-coloured mounts that I hope are what he's been making for the shop.

'Only in the spring and summer. I can't afford to heat it so it's too cold by the time autumn comes.' He walks across to open one of the lattice windows and let a breeze in, and I follow him so I can look out. The view from up here looks down on the overgrown mangle of a garden and the harsh-looking railings beyond. 'But if you're going to draw, you may as well do it in a ballroom, right?'

I can't argue with him there, and this is a seriously impressive room, but it shares the feeling of emptiness that the rest of the house has got. I close my eyes and try to imagine being here alone. What's a ballroom without a ball? Nothing more than an empty room whose sheer size only serves to make it feel emptier, and I have to shake myself to clear the feeling of hollowness that's settled over me. 'This even looks like the palace in *Anastasia*.'

'You know what that means, right?' He stands in a waltz position, one hand up and one hand out, and smiles that mischievous smile at me. 'Dance with me?'

After two glasses of wine, dancing doesn't seem like as bad an idea as it usually would, and to be honest, Dimitri could suggest going on a tour of a wasp farm with that smile and I'd probably agree.

I slip my right hand into his, and put the other one on his shoulder while his curls around my hip, and I let him lead us in whirling circles around the room, twirling me under his arm and spinning me away and pulling me back, and he's a couple of wine glasses down too because he sings 'Once Upon A December' quietly all the while, not seeming self-conscious at all, and it feels so much like the scene where the Dimitri in the film teaches Anastasia to dance on the boat that I almost start giggling. 'You can dance.'

'I can. I can't carry a cup of tea without spilling it, and I *definitely* can't sing, but I can waltz. My housemaster at school insisted on dance lessons. He thought it might improve my diabolical sense of coordination. You can guess how well it worked.'

It makes me giggle again because he's constantly full of surprises, and I love finding out all these little things I didn't know about him. He goes back to singing 'Once Upon a December' and I love that he trusts me enough to bring me here, to tell me about the life that he's clearly not shared with anyone for a long time. I love how he makes me feel like a princess as we dance around the room. The gold-leaf pattern running through the flooring twinkles when it catches the light from the chandelier as our feet move across it, and none of it matters because this is like something from a fairy tale. All that's missing is a yellow Belle dress and a teapot singing 'Tale As Old As Time'.

His eyes don't leave mine as we spin around, and I'm vaguely sure one or both of us should be getting dizzy by now, but everything has faded away except for the burning spots of sensation where his hands are touching me and that dazed, happy look in his eyes.

'Thank you for making new memories in this old house.'

'Thank you for letting me in.' I take the hand that's on his shoulder and pat it over his heart in case he thinks I'm literally thanking him for letting me in the door.

His arms slide around my waist and he pulls me closer until we're pressed against each other. I lean my head on his chest and his chin rests in my hair, and we're still moving around the room but it's more of a hug than a dance now.

'You think I'm mad, don't you?' he murmurs.

'I think you're many things, Dimitri. Kind, talented, brave, beautiful, and the loveliest person I've ever met, with an interesting taste in socks, waistcoats, and braces, but you'll have to elaborate on the mad part.'

'To stay here. I can see it in your face. You think I'm mad to keep this house.'

I suck in a breath. 'It isn't my place to judge anyone for how they handle grief. When my dad died, I became a teenage rebel and made my mum's life a misery for a few years. You can ask her, she'll be *more* than happy to tell you. This is your home. You grew up here. I can see why you don't want to give it up.'

'And now the honest, non-diplomatic answer?'

I smile against his chest because he already knows me well enough to hear the restraint in my voice. 'You're different here. I can see the weight of this place physically dragging you down,' I say in a rush. 'It's a beautiful house, but there are reminders at every turn. You can't get on with your own life because you're still living theirs. It's so sad here, and you're not. It's hollow and empty and isolated, and you're the opposite of all of those things. You're bright, and happy, and positive, and obviously I now know how much pain you've been hiding behind that sunny smile, but every inch of this place is shrouded in ghosts. You need …' I cut myself off because I'm out of breath from rambling, but everything I've thought since he opened that gate comes pouring out.

He's stopped dancing now but he hasn't pushed me away, and I press the side of my head closer to his chest. 'It's not my place to tell you how to live your life but if you ever want to spend the night in a bookshop instead of coming back here, I know one where you'd always be welcome.'

'It's that Waterstones in Cirencester, isn't it?'

We both burst out laughing at the exact same moment, and the tension that had shot through the room at my honesty dissipates instantly.

We pull apart and his hair has flopped over again and I can't resist reaching up to tuck it back, and even though I half-expect him to back away and tell me to mind my own business, he closes his eyes and turns into the touch, letting me cradle the side of his face and run my fingers through his hair.

When he opens his eyes, he leans down to kiss me, and far from the chaste nervousness of earlier, it's a *very* ungentlemanly kiss this time, and I melt into his embrace. In fact, kissing Dimitri is enough to knock anyone off their feet, and I don't realise how much I've melted into him until his knees start to buckle and we go crashing to the floor, hitting an easel on the way down. He lands squarely on a tube of yellow acrylic paint, which promptly explodes, sending out a huge splurt of paint straight onto Nicole's dress, his trousers, and the floor. I've bitten my tongue and Dimitri's got a hand to his lip and a pained expression on his face.

'And this is exactly why I don't buy nice dresses,' I gasp between fits of laughter. Nicole is going to *kill* me. I doubt even the winner of Dry Cleaner of the Year award could sort this mess out.

'Blame me for being a clumsy oaf. I'll pay the dry-cleaning bill.' He holds his hand out and lets me pull him into a sitting position.

I won't let him, but I think he's such a gent to offer. He laughs, looking tousled and uninhibited and … yellow. In trying to get the paint off us both, he's only managed to spread it further, and it sets me off giggling again. It takes everything I have not to dive on him, knock him onto his back and snog him senseless. I feel dizzy and it's not just from the wine or the dancing or possibly the paint fumes. I feel dizzy because I didn't think storybook romances like this happened in real life.

Chapter 16

The leaf idea was amazing. Over the past couple of weeks, Dimitri and I have worked every hour of the day and most of the nights to find as many messages as we can – between us, we've gone through a good fifty per cent of the shop, checking for messages and reorganising the shelves into proper order, and now it's the morning of the opening day. It's a sunny Saturday in late June, nearly two months since I got here, and for the past few nights, I've left Dimitri message hunting while I've been in the office, scanning book covers and messages, printing them double-sided, and cutting them into leaf shapes.

Della's tree has been installed on a platform in the prime position between the door and the stairs, and each leaf has been tied to its array of branches with green string. The door's open most of the time now it's summer, and the leaves rustle every time there's a breeze, gaining interest from people walking by.

Our online followers have gone up to a few thousand, and I keep getting messages asking when our online shop will be ready, and others have been messaging me and asking to buy a book with a message inside – any book, my choice. I'm getting messages of encouragement from people who love bookshops and don't want to see any more close down, and people like me who love the idea of the hidden love stories that can exist inside the cover long before the story starts. I've had people checking their own bookcases and sending me photographs of words scribbled inside their own books that they'd never noticed before.

Three local Cotswolds newspapers have done an article about the shop and the messages, and another one who ran a story about Robert's raffle has followed up with how the new owner's getting on. One of the viral news sites has got an article about the hidden inscriptions that's updated every time I post a new picture.

There's been an increase of customers coming into the shop too. Locals want to come in and chat about the books, and people have stopped by to look for inscriptions we haven't found yet and left with arms full of books, and there's been a few people saying they saw us online and a couple of selfies taken outside. We've turned the front window into a shrine to the messages too. Dimitri's chalked a tree at each side with heart-shaped green leaves, and pink hearts falling from their boughs to collect along the bottom of the glass, and the display is scattered with confetti and full of the books with the most romantic messages.

I still feel the same flitter of excitement when Dimitri knocks on the door, and I love that I can see the size of his smile even through the glass as I rush to open it.

'Hello!' He greets me with the same cheerful greeting that got under my skin from the very first day, but now he leans in for a kiss too, except he's so loaded down with bags that I can't reach him properly.

'What's all this?' I ask as I bundle him in and close up again because there's still half an hour until opening time.

'I told you I'd bake for the occasion.'

'Greggs wouldn't have baked this much for a new store opening. You must've been up half the night.'

'Nope, *all* the night, but let's not worry about that. I've already had so much coffee that I may not be liable for my actions.'

'Dimitri ...'

'I want this to be a massive success for you. You deserve this. Finding these notes was all down to you and your belief in love and happy endings. You deserve this shop to be found by people who love it as much as you do. Baking a few cakes was the least I could do.'

We've advertised this open day as far and wide as possible. I've gone over budget on social media advertising and promoting posts. We've printed out flyers and put them up everywhere that would let us, and other shops on the street have been massively supportive and put them up in their windows and on their counters. We're offering free tea and coffee and Dimitri offered to bake some goodies, although I didn't expect this much. I watch as he hoists cool bags up onto the counter and starts setting out piles of tiny book-shaped biscuits onto the fancy plates Robert left behind in one of the kitchen cupboards.

'These look amazing.' Obviously I pinch one of the tiny, artisanal delights that look like something you'd find in a fancy French patisserie. They're the most gorgeous little biscuits in the shape of books – chocolate-flavoured shortbread wrapped around sheets of marzipan that's scored to look like pages. I pop it into my mouth and nearly swoon on the spot because they taste even better than they look and they *look* amazing. I reach over and take another one. 'Is there no end to your talents?' I nudge my elbow against his arm, wondering how on earth I got so lucky. I've always thought men like him didn't exist, but sharing my life with him is a million times better than any fairy-tale romance book I've ever read, and I still can't believe I get to call him mine.

'How many people do you think are going to turn up?' I ask as he starts getting boxes full of cupcakes and trays of colourfully decorated gingerbread in the shape of tulips out too. 'You seem to be expecting Canada. All of it.'

'Hopefully a lot.' He shrugs. 'I was working on an "if you bake it, they will come" motto.'

'You didn't have to do all this. I didn't expect—'

'Actually, I wanted to thank you. Thank you for letting me stay on that first day. Thank you for letting me use this stupidly expensive book without buying it. Thank you for finding that note from my mum and turning your whole shop upside down to hunt for more. Thank you for giving me a home for my artwork.' He swallows hard. 'I think when you're caring for someone else, you lose yourself a little bit, but I've found myself again in this shop. It's reminded me of who I used to be and the things I loved. The only thing I ever wanted to do with my life was drawing, and that had faded in recent years, but being here has brought back my passion for it. I'm getting the joy out of it that I used to get. I'm one step closer to following my dreams because of you. You've made me believe that anything is possible.'

He nods towards the spinnable display stand near the counter, which is currently full of the hand-painted greeting cards he showed me in the ballroom the other day, featuring depictions of famous books and copyright-free quotes from them. They're the most gorgeous designs, from one of Peter Pan and Tinker Bell featuring the well-known flying instructions, to Alice falling down the rabbit hole and another one at the Mad Hatter's tea party with 'There's always time for tea' written in the cups on the table. There are the book versions of *Breakfast at Tiffany's*, *Mary Poppins*, *Robin Hood*, and the silhouetted characters from *The Wizard of Oz* with Dorothy wearing sparkly ruby slippers as they walk down a yellow brick road with 'There's no place like home' written above the sunset.

They're absolutely amazing, and I'm *proud* to have a display of them in the shop. 'People are going to love them.' I nudge his arm again, making him drop one of the biscuits he's still setting out, which cracks in half when it hits the plate, giving me a chance to lean over and snatch the two pieces away. Can't offer customers broken biscuits, obviously.

'I'm the lucky one, Dimitri,' I say with my mouth full of the most delicious melty book-shaped biscuit I've ever tasted. Not that I've eaten a lot of book-shaped biscuits, but I'm pretty sure I'll never again eat one as good as this. 'I'm getting to sell the work of a future best-selling author. When you're the next J.K. Rowling, I'm going to put up a plaque saying your first works were sold here.'

He laughs. 'It's not fair for you to say things like that when I'm this jittery from coffee.'

'Seriously.' I nudge him again, not for the purpose of stealing broken biscuits this time. 'You've done *so* much for me too. You've helped me with everything. You're like a second member of staff but you won't let me pay any wages. You've ignored your own deadline in favour of helping me, and I'm sure you're going to be in trouble with your publishers sooner or later, even if you say you aren't.'

'No, I—'

'You've made me feel normal with my book obsession. You've made me unafraid to be myself. I've always tried to hide how awkward and clumsy I am, and I've always tried to play down how many books I have and how much time I spend reading and living vicariously through book characters' lives instead of going out and actually living my own, but meeting you has … I don't know, it's like you've given me permission to be myself. You've shown me that there *are* people like me out there, people who will "get" me, and I've been looking in the wrong places and trying to be someone else until now. And I was totally out of my depth when I started here. I didn't even realise how much until the first day, and your quiet presence, constant reassurance, and your belief in me being able to do this has made me feel less and less out of my depth every day, and now it really does feel like I'm starting anew and opening a new shop today. I don't know what I'd have done if you hadn't been here …'

He cuts me off with a kiss, and even though I can hear the ticking of the clock counting down towards nine, it's impossible not to get lost in his closeness, his wood and charcoal aftershave mingling with the almondy scent of the biscuits and wrapping itself around me in place of his hands, which are still occupied with Tupperware containers and plates.

His forehead stays on mine. 'Hal, I need to tell you som—'

He's cut off by a knock on the door, and I look up to see a guy with a TV camera on his shoulder outside the window, waiting with other people.

'That's the local news!' I spot a logo on the camera through the window and start frantically trying to smooth my hair down and dash across to open the door and let in a journalist, producer, and cameraman.

Dimitri ducks into the office as they take photos of me behind the counter and start filming the tree of printed paper leaves, while I take the copy of *Les Mis* from the window display and show them the note to Esme. It's so close to nine that it isn't long before customers start filtering in too.

No one loves bookshops or love stories more than me, but even I'm surprised by the number of people who come in. Judging by the interest in the paper-leafed tree, it's not *just* for the free coffee and cake. People are wandering through the shop, pulling books off the shelves and searching them for messages. Some are regulars I've seen before and some are strangers. Some seem to be looking for something specific and some seem content to browse. Within five minutes of being open, I've made seven sales, which definitely deserves a spot in the Guinness World Records. I don't think I'd make that many if there was a new Harry Potter out and we were the only shop in England to stock it.

One of the first people to arrive is a man in his sixties who points to the copy of *Treasure Island* currently displayed in the window, along with the tin and toy car that Dimitri's cleaned up, and I beckon him over from where he's currently making a coffee and two orange squashes for a mum and daughters while they nibble on book biscuits. I think Dimitri would be less excited if

Long John Silver himself walked into the shop. I've never seen someone so happy to see someone else before.

The man cradles the rusty little car in the palm of his hand. 'I buried it when I was six years old. My father gave it to me on my birthday. My little brother was always taking my toys and I didn't want him to ruin it or lose it, so I hid it where only I'd be able to find it. My dad died later that year and we moved away from Buntingorden. I'd forgotten all about it until I saw the story on the sidebar of a news site and clicked on it because I recognised Once Upon A Page from when I was a lad.'

'Thank you for making me feel like a child again,' Dimitri says.

'How magnificent books are,' the man says. 'For my map to lead complete strangers to this all these years later is just wonderful.'

Dimitri hugs him like an old friend, and I give him the car, tin, and book that he kindly insists on paying for, which leaves me in no doubt that bookish people are the best people.

I'm so busy with customers that I don't notice the clock ticking towards eleven a.m. until a lady of roughly my age with strawberry-blonde hair around her shoulders comes up to the counter. 'Are you Hallie?'

I smile because I've already got an inkling about who she is. 'Mindy?'

'Hi. I was so excited when you called. Your shop is amazing, even better than it looked online.'

I still feel a jolt of excitement whenever anyone calls it 'my' shop because I still can't believe it *is* mine. Mindy knows we were trying to find Brandon on social media, but she doesn't know that he found us, or that when we asked her to stop by at eleven o'clock this morning, we've also asked him to do the same.

She clasps her hands together. 'I can't wait to know, did you find him?'

'You'll have to wait and see.' Dimitri appears beside me with such a huge grin that it instantly gives everything away.

Thankfully she doesn't have to wait long. As she pretends to browse the books near the counter, but I suspect is really just hovering, a man comes in and I recognise him from his Twitter profile photo.

He lifts a hand in greeting and it's almost cartoon-like how his hand stills in mid-air and he turns towards Mindy.

She jumps when he says her name.

My hand tightens around Dimitri's forearm as we stand back, and it's like watching a scene from a film unfold right in front of us.

Their eyes meet across the crowded room, and I can almost hear the love song reaching a crescendo in the background. It's just like when Kate Beckinsale and John Cusack meet again in the film. Minus the ice and gently falling snowflakes, obviously.

'It's you …'

'It's *you*. After all these years …'

They walk towards each other in slow motion. Well, it feels like slow motion, but really it's just regular motion because we're not actually in a rom com movie.

The journalists in the shop have clocked what's going on and camera flashes start going off. Mindy and Brandon both gave their permission to post their story online and the three newspapers have all picked up on it and the possibility of a reunion today was a huge draw for getting reporters down here.

'Are you sing …' Mindy starts, but her voice catches.

'You're both single,' Dimitri interjects. 'And you've both been looking.'

The relief that floods Mindy is visible, and Brandon's smile is wider than an advert for teeth whitener, and without hesitation, he marches across the shop, slides his hand up her jaw and pulls her in for a kiss.

It's gentle and respectful and they both look like they want it to carry on a lot longer than it does.

'I've been waiting fifteen years to do that,' Brandon says when they pull apart.

'I looked at every fiver. I made my friends empty out their purses every time I saw them. I was devastated when the notes were retired. I'd given up. I never thought ...' Mindy looks a bit overcome.

'I've been in every charity shop and bookshop looking for that book.' Brandon looks at me and Dimitri. 'And then it found me.'

'In my experience, books do that,' I say.

They smile at each other, almost drinking in every line on the other's face as Brandon's finger trails down Mindy's flushed cheek. They must lose all sense of time because they suddenly seem to snap out of it and realise they've got an audience.

'Can I take you for a coffee?' Brandon asks.

'I'd like that very much,' Mindy replies.

'For the love of all things bookish, exchange numbers this time, will you?' Dimitri says, making everyone nearby laugh.

They pose for a couple of photos for the journalists, and one of the four of us holding the copy of the book between us, before they come up to the counter to say goodbye.

'Thank you,' Mindy says. 'I can't believe you did this. All of this from one little book.'

'Thank *you* both.' I feel perilously close to tears at how lovely this all is. 'This is one of the most romantic things I've ever seen in my life.'

'You see? Books go on forever. Money is fallible but a book has saved the day.' Dimitri nudges me as Mindy insists on paying for the book and they take it with them, exactly where it's supposed to be.

After Mindy and Brandon leave for their coffee, with a joking promise to invite us to their wedding, a promise that I hope – and judging by the looks on their faces, *think* – won't be such a joke after all, I feel such a warm glow. I want to work in this lovely place forever. I never expected to get this far – nearly two months down the line, to not only still be here, but to also be celebrating my busiest day so far, with a man who makes me believe in happy endings, and for the main point of this day to be hidden messages inside books, something I've always had a low-level obsession with and never understood why. It feels like every moment in my life was meant to lead here.

I look around the bookshop and listen to the quiet soundtrack of a low hum of music from a customer's earbuds as he comes up to pay. There are people standing around everywhere, heads in books, fingers stroking over spines and tilting holographic covers. The book club have obviously heard rumours of biscuits because they arrive in twos and threes, Tilda, Hilda, Milda/Vilda, Pauline and Francine, trailing husbands and grandchildren behind them. Barbara and Percy follow, and I appreciate Dimitri's quick thinking in hastily hiding a batch of book-shaped marzipan biscuits before they decimate the lot.

One of the loveliest things is how every other shop owner on the street comes in and buys something. Either a book, or a mug, a notebook, a tote bag, or one of Dimitri's greeting cards. I've got to know them all by sight over the last few weeks, but I find myself tearing up a bit when they come in one by one throughout the morning, look at the tree, browse the shelves, and come over to pay for their purchases, and say things like, 'I've always known there was something special about this shop' and 'Good on you for bringing hope back to Buntingorden.'

The local news have gone, leaving only their cameraman behind, and someone reporting for BuzzFeed has turned up. There's a social media influencer taking pictures of each leaf on the tree, and someone from the local tourist information centre is considering adding us to one of his brochures and is sitting quietly in the corner, observing and occasionally scribbling something in his notebook, and just when it feels like every person in Buntingorden and a good patch of the surrounding villages too are squashed into the shop, Drake Farrer strides in.

I'm behind the counter with a queue of three customers so he joins the back of the line and starts looking around and sighing, tapping his foot like an annoyed Sonic The Hedgehog when you put the Sega Megadrive controller down for a minute as a child. I try to take as much time as possible with the customers to further add to his irritation because of all things someone like Drake Farrer deserves, being kept waiting is the least of them. Eventually I can't make small talk any longer and have to hand the last customer her paper bag and wait for Drake Farrer to approach.

As usual, he looks the epitome of sophistication, so smooth and well-kempt that you could say someone had pushed him through a hedge forwards. His navy suit doesn't have so much as a stray cat hair or bit of fluff on it, and his face is strangely absent of laughter lines, making it look as unnaturally smooth as his dark hair under all that wet-look gel.

'Mr Farrer.' I paste on my falsest smile. 'I should've known you'd be in today. Couldn't let readers enjoy something without coming to rain on our parade, could you?'

Instead of speaking, Drake Farrer holds up a book by a corner between his thumb and forefinger, keeping it away from himself like he might catch something from it. The rest of it is dangling down from the edge of the cover he's holding, having clearly been sliced almost completely through the middle, dropped in the river, and any remaining pages hacked into as many little pieces as possible. He drops it onto the counter where it lands with a clunk and scatters pieces of wet paper across the wooden surface. 'Returning your trash.'

I recognise it as one of the YA fantasy books Dimitri and I hid. All hope of remaining civilised and clinging on to sophistication fly out the window. 'You did this?' I say to his smug beady-eyed face. 'How can you be so proud of yourself for ruining a book? What did you do – go at it with a meat cleaver?'

'I told you exactly what I'd do if I came across any of your rubbish lurking around the village. If I was a nastier person, I'd have you done for fly-tipping. Littering at the least. That would come with a hefty fine that I'm *sure* you're earning enough to pay.'

'It's one book!'

'It's paper. It belongs in the recycling bin.'

'Oh, because *you're* all about saving the planet, aren't you?' I glare at him over the poor, limp mash of paper still dripping on the counter. 'How could anyone do that to a book? It was put there to give someone the enjoyment of finding it and reading it. Not that I'd expect someone like you to understand the joy of reading.'

'I enjoy reading. Contracts, mainly. And the accounts of failing bookshops. They always make for interesting stories, although they never end happily.' He looks around and clicks his tongue. 'And all this merchandise. Must've been a hefty credit card bill this month.'

The hairs on the back of my neck stand up and not in a good way. *How* does he know that? I glance over at Dimitri who has stopped with the teapot in mid-air in the middle of pouring a tea and is watching us with a ... worried expression on his face. He is the *only* person who knows I put the bookish merchandise on my credit card. And now Drake Farrer does too.

I trust Dimitri, I tell myself. It's not the first time I've had to repeat those words in my head. Drake Farrer takes over failing businesses for a living. He's just making some lucky guesses, like Dimitri said. Even as I hear my mum's words in my head about self-sabotaging relationships when they start to go well, a knot has formed in my stomach and I can't shake the feeling that something's wrong.

'Oh, why don't you get out?' I force the words through gritted teeth. 'I will *never* in a million years let you have this shop, and I don't want you in here, so just—'

'Oh, relax, princess. I'm not here for your shop today. I'm here for one of your daft little notes. My brother said there's one of 'em from our mother.'

I glare at him. 'It'll be on the tree. But don't touch anything. And don't ruin it. Or I'll have you done for criminal damage.' I give him a stern nod, quite proud of myself for thinking of that comeback on the spot. Usually I only think of great comebacks while in the shower three days later.

He looks between me and the tree like I've asked him to mount an elephant and ride up Kilimanjaro. 'You're not honestly expecting *me* to look through all that crap, are you?'

I don't make any move to help him, and eventually he gets fed up of me glaring at him because he rolls his eyes and saunters over to the tree.

I try to keep an eye on him, but another customer comes over to buy a book, and someone else takes a book from the window display and asks me if I know anything about the origin of it, and when I look back, Drake Farrer's got a grimace on his face as he looks through the tree leaves, crumpling them with his big fingers as he rejects each one. I catch Dimitri watching him too, half his attention on the tea he's making for an old man who's started telling him about his knee replacement and half on Drake Farrer looking through our carefully printed and cut leaf shapes.

I serve another couple of customers before Drake Farrer finally says 'Ah ha!' and reaches up to rip one of the notes from the string.

'Don't do that!' I shout at him, startling several customers, but it's too late; he's already bringing it towards the counter. All I've done is attract the attention of every customer in the shop, while Drake Farrer strides back over, holding the crumpled leaf aloft in victory. He barges past a customer who was about to hand me something to ring up.

'Excuse me, I'm busy.' I give him a scornful look and smile at the woman who's waiting for me to take a couple of books and a stack of greeting cards from her, but he waves the leaf determinedly in my face, and I catch a glimpse of the cover printed on it. It's *Pride and Prejudice.*

I go to take it from him but he pulls it out of my reach, and pure fury at his rudeness makes my reflexes much better than they usually are, and I feel almost cat-like as my hand catches his and curls around it like a claw as I pull the note from between his sausage fingers.

I drop his hand and smooth the leaf out, staring at the printed cover of *Pride and Prejudice* looking back at me. I turn the note over and read Della's writing on the back. Words that I've looked at many times now, memorising the handwriting so I'd recognise it again. Comparing it to the note in *Anne of Green Gables* to make sure I wasn't mistaken. The times I've watched Dimitri run his fingers over it.

I'm shocked by how quickly the tears come, and it takes every inch of strength I have to hold back a sob. 'Dimitri's your …'

'Brother, yes.'

No. No no no no. *No.*

'Did he not tell you?' Drake says sweetly. He knows exactly what he's doing. He *knows* that I didn't know. He obviously came here with the sole intention of telling me. That's why he made such a performance of it.

My stomach turns over like I've just been punched in the gut, and I cling on to the wooden counter to keep myself upright. Everything about the past two months goes rushing through my mind, like falling to earth with a parachute that won't open. Suddenly everything that didn't add up arranges itself into a painfully clear sum. Why Dimitri's been so vague. Why I don't know something as simple as his surname. Why he's an artist but he studied business and knows a heck of a lot about retail and property law. Why he doesn't seem to be on any form of deadline for his publisher. Why I've always had a vague feeling that he's hiding something and it didn't disappear after he took me to his house. How Drake Farrer knows so much about the shop. That weird hushed conversation I watched them have outside a few weeks ago. How can I have been so stupid?

'Hallie, it's not what you think.' Dimitri has come out of the office and is approaching the counter cautiously.

'You would say that!' I yell, attracting the attention of *every* person in the shop, Heathcliff, and a couple of people sitting around the fountain opposite. 'People always say it's not what you think when it's *exactly* what you think.' I try to regain some composure, but composure has never been my strong point, and tears spill out of my eyes, blurring the sight of him coming closer. It doesn't blur the flash of a camera as someone takes a photo.

I shake my head to try to clear it. 'Farrer and Son*s*.' I draw the 's' out until I sound like a hissing snake. 'You're the plural. You're the *other* son.'

'No, I'm not.' His hands touch the counter. 'My father wanted me to be, but I'm not. He named his company when we were kids, when he intended us both to follow in the family business, but I didn't. You *know* that.'

'I don't know anything! I don't know who you are, Dimitri! But I do know that *he* knows things about this shop that he has no right to know and they happen to be the same things I've told you privately. You must've been reporting back to him from day one!'

'That's not true. He knows exactly what to say to make people doubt themselves. He's trying to spook you because he thought you were new enough to fall for it.'

'Oh, come on, Dimitri. Don't add insult to injury too. You're obviously in it together. I didn't fall at his feet on the first day so he sent his brother in to gain my trust from the inside, spy on me, and learn my weaknesses so you can both swoop in and take advantage.'

'No. That's not true. I have nothing to do with their company.' Dimitri's voice is going higher and there's a look of panic on his face.

280

Complete silence has fallen in the shop, something you'd think would be impossible with this many people, but no one lets out so much as a sniff. Apart from me because I'm trying to sniff back some dignity, but more tears spill out of my eyes, and I shake my head, annoyed at myself for not being able to keep it together in public, and not just in public, but in front of the biggest public I've ever seen, including some journalists who are undoubtedly recording every inch of this for posterity.

'God, *how* can I have trusted you so much – and so easily, so quickly? I actually convinced myself that you were spending so much time here because you liked me.' That's more like it. Inappropriate oversharing. That's much more my style. 'Not a word you've said to me from the very first day has been true, has it?'

'*Yes*! Everything has. This is all a misunderstanding. Hallie, please …'

I intend to shut him up, but I'm crying so hard that my throat feels swollen and I can't get the words out, and he takes this as permission to carry on.

'Why would he tell you? Think about it, Hal. If we were in this together, why would he sabotage it? He's telling you this as a way of getting back at me. He was at the house last night, throwing his weight around, trying to bully me into selling. I couldn't stop myself yammering on about you because I'm so arse-over-tit in love with you, and he guessed you didn't know who my brother was and tried to use it to blackmail me into giving up the house.'

When I replay this conversation over and over in my head, I'm going to notice there's a sentence in there that I should probably pay attention to, but right now, my head is throbbing from the sinus pressure of crying and my mind is in such a knot that I can't hear myself think. 'That's not how blackmail works. You lose the edge if you tell someone what the other person doesn't want them to know. Then you have no leverage to blackmail *with*. That's the point. So either you're lying again or Drake Farrer is really useless at blackmail.' I look at the offending man. If someone put 'professional blackmailer' in the dictionary, his photo would pop up. 'And you don't honestly expect me to believe that Drake Farrer is inexperienced in blackmail, do you?'

'Why, thank you.' Drake Farrer has been silent up until now, except for his smirk, which is loud enough to hear. He actually has the nerve to bow like I've paid him a compliment.

'He's got nothing to gain from you knowing, but I've got something to lose – the only person who's made me feel worth something in years.'

A collective 'aww' goes through the shop.

I can't think about that. I can't think about the people watching or the words Dimitri is saying.

He sighs. 'Drake Farrer does things for one of two reasons – money or spite. And he certainly isn't getting any money out of me, so he came in here this morning with spite written all over his face.'

'At least Drake Farrer is honest. Dimitri Farrer is anything but.' His name actually hurts to come out of my mouth, like it physically burns the skin of my lips as I speak it. 'You're acting like *he's* done something wrong by telling me. *You're* the one who should have told me two months ago! There's no reason you wouldn't unless you didn't want me to know.'

God, I'm being melodramatic, aren't I? I've been reading too many books. I allowed myself to believe that, for once, something was going to work out for me. I should have known better. Things never work out for me – especially not relationships.

'Everything you've done, Dimitri. I thought you were an introvert, like me. Just a quiet reader who likes books more than most humans, like me. Just a lovely baker who gets me in a way no one ever has before.'

'I am. I am all those things.'

'You can't be all those things while also being the "s" in Farrer and Sons!'

'Do you know, it's very unprofessional to argue in front of customers …' Drake smarms.

'Get out!' Dimitri turns and bellows at him. He gathers up the destroyed book on the counter and shoves it at him, pushing wet paper into his pristine suit, forcing Drake to hold it against his chest. 'This is between me and Hallie. You've done enough damage.'

He gathers his suit by the scruff of his neck, wraps his fingers in it and uses the grip to march him towards the door, dodging past Mum and Nicole, who have just arrived and are standing open-mouthed in the doorway. Drake goes sprawling onto the pavement, catching himself on his hands but smooshing the ruined book between paving and chest. At least he'll have a hefty dry-cleaning bill to look forward to.

'You can go with him,' I say when Dimitri comes back towards me. I don't realise I'm crying again until water splashes onto the counter, and I duck down behind it to find a tissue before snot joins it, but mainly so I don't have to look at his soft face and how sad his blue eyes look.

'Not until you hear me out.'

I shake my head, my voice too thick with tears to speak, and one quick glance towards the door shows me that Mum and Nicole have linked arms and formed a human barricade. No way is Mum letting a man leave my life that easily.

I don't want to talk to him. I don't want to give him a chance to come up with a reasonable explanation and wheedle his way back in. I have to stay strong. I gained two things when I got here – him and Once Upon A Page, and I've only lost one of them. So far. And as much as I hate agreeing with Drake Farrer, it *is* unprofessional to argue in front of the customers.

A few have slipped out without buying anything, but most are still here. Some have got their noses buried steadfastly in books, and some have got headphones in and I see hands furtively flicking towards volume buttons to turn it up and drown us out. The others are not trying to hide their interest in the storyline. I can see people talking, nudging, whispering among themselves like this is a soap opera. *She should take him back. She should throw him out. She should hear him out. She should wallop him round the head with a book.*

The middle-aged woman who was waiting to be served and stepped back when Drake Farrer started talking approaches me again, holding out well-loved copies of Enid Blyton's *The Magic Faraway Tree* and a *Famous Five* collection along with a stack of Dimitri's greeting cards. 'So sorry to interrupt, love, but my bus goes in five minutes.'

I half-laugh and half-sob at the same time, beyond grateful for the distraction of a completely normal moment in the middle of this horror of a morning. I serve her with my brightest smile even though there are teardrops dripping from my chin that I'm trying to wipe off with my shoulder and my glasses have tear splashes drying on the lenses. After she takes her change from me and refuses a bag in favour of slipping the books and cards into her handbag, she reaches out and pats my hand. 'The path of true love never did run smooth, but these things have a way of working out. You'll see.'

As she leaves, Dimitri folds his arms. 'I'm not going anywhere until you talk to me.'

I sink down to my knees to hide behind the counter and blow my dripping nose with the wettest, snottiest, most undignified noise anyone has ever made in front of this amount of people before.

'Or let me talk to you,' he continues when I stand back up. 'Hallie, please, I can explain.'

My eyes are stinging again and I have to bite my lip to stop it wobbling, and when my voice comes out, it's shaky and thick from crying. 'Share every part of your life with me, eh?' I repeat the words he said to me at his house the other day. 'Is there any part of it that hasn't been a lie?'

'Everything. Drake is the only thing I didn't tell you about. Everything else was tru—'

'Even *Pentamerone*?' I cut him off. 'You've ducked every question I've asked you about your publisher. You've mumbled something non-committal every time I've mentioned your deadline. The whole thing is another lie, isn't it? There *is* no deadline because there is no publisher. An expensive book that you couldn't afford to take off the premises was just a way of worming your way in here, wasn't it?'

'That's not true.'

'Well, nothing you've told me so far *is* true. You used to read it to your sister in the library and followed it here when the library closed – bollocks.'

'Why would I lie about that? That *is* what happened. I used to read it to Dani in the library, the library closed and we didn't see it again, and then when Robert brought me here, I started telling him about it and he realised which book I was talking about and went and got it off the shelf.'

The problem is that everything Dimitri says sounds like a lie now. No matter whether it's true or not, and in fairness, that part probably is, how can I ever trust anything that comes out of his mouth again?

He knows I don't believe him. 'I made a mistake and told a stupid white lie.'

I swallow hard and blink fast in an attempt to ward off yet more tears.

'I haven't been commissioned to illustrate *Pentamerone*. I mean, I'd love to, and when I'm done, I *am* going to pitch it to a publisher, but I'm living on what little is left of the provisions Mum left, barely getting by and struggling to survive—'

Oh, this just gets even better. 'So your brother paid you to spy on me.'

'No.' He looks like he wants to say something else, but nothing comes out.

'Oh, so someone *else* paid you to sit in a bookshop and drink tea all day?' I almost laugh at the nonsense he expects me to believe. 'And yet, magically, Farrer and Sons know all my secrets, and it's just a coincidence that one half of the "sons" earned my trust, is it? You wheedled information about the shop's accounts out of me. You got yourself right in the middle of my future plans.' I don't add that I mean both professionally *and* personally.

I'd pictured a future with him. I could honestly see something going right for once. I could see me and Dimitri running this shop between us for years into the future. And this is nothing but a short, sharp kick in the metaphorical balls about what inevitably happens when I start thinking that something might go right.

Tears burn my nose again and I get out from behind the counter and stride into the shelves. I wonder if people can tell how much I'm shaking and how unsteady I am on my feet. I dodge around customers, who kindly give me a wide berth and a wary look or two, until I get to the Rare & Valuable shelf under the stairs. More tears spill over as I remember snuggling down here with my head on his shoulder, reading and talking and laughing. Back when he was still the person he pretended to be. I pull *Pentamerone* off the shelf and march back to the counter, stopping in the office on the way to grab his bag.

'Here, take it.' I shove the book into his chest so he has no option but to hold it.

'Hallie, I'm not taking—' He shakes his head, his hair drooped and flat now.

'I don't care how much it's worth. You've earned a salary for all the work you've done here. Call it a fee for reorganising thousands of books with me.' I'm shaking as I reach up and slip the strap of his bag over his head so it hangs around his neck. In any other circumstance, it's the way I'd have reached to hug him, and that's *still* the only thing I want to do.

I force myself to step back, banging into the counter and undoubtedly bruising my hip on the wooden edge. 'And now you can get out. I never want to see you *or* your brother in *my* shop ever again.'

He hesitates for a moment, like he's trying to think of something else to say, some other argument to put up, but I fold my arms and glare at him with the harshest expression I can muster while my face is still wet with tears, and then I turn away and stalk over to the office so I don't have to see him leave because I will *not* be able to hold it together.

I down a cold cup of tea like it's a shot and bite the inside of my cheek, and it's a good few minutes before I find the courage to turn around and look at the empty space where he was standing, and the array of open mouths staring at me.

'Hope you liked the entertainments, folks!' Nicole slams her hands together and walks into the middle of the shop. A few confused claps follow her. 'Come back next week for episode two of "People Acting Out Books In Real Life"!'

I might not always see eye to eye with my sister, but I love her for trying to cover this up and make it look like an intentional drama rather than my luck finally running out on the most important day of my career so far.

'That was from ...' She looks at me blankly.

'The Tale of the Loser Girl and the Gentleman, a love story that does *not* have a happy ending,' I finish for her as my voice breaks and I run upstairs.

Even though there's no one serving other than Nicole, I go up to the flat and hide in the bathroom. I've tried splashing water on my face five times now, but every time I do and take a deep breath and steel myself to go back down, I start crying again. The tears won't stop falling, and the harder I try to stop them, the more they flow.

Every time I picture his twinkly eyes and happy smile, I can't comprehend how he could've been lying all along. He always seemed so open, and even with the vague feeling that he was hiding something, I never had an inkling that it would be something so nefarious. The word makes hysterical laughter burst unexpectedly out of my mouth. How could I ever have laughed at the idea of Dimitri being up to something nefarious? How can he have stood beside me while Drake Farrer spoke and *not* mentioned they happened to be brothers? How can he have spoken so openly about his brother and *not* mentioned that he happened to be Drake Farrer? And worse still, how can I have fallen for it *and* for him? Why didn't I trust my instincts and the rest of my life experience that's always shown me that the perfect man doesn't exist, and the only type of happy ending I'm ever going to get is in the pages of a book?

'Hallie?' Nicole calls up the stairs. 'There's someone here asking for you. You posted her book on social media? Says her name's Esme.'

Esme! From the *Les Misérables* note! It's got to be! The excitement of hearing about the perfect relationship that must've sprung from that romantic note is enough to stop the tears in their tracks. I splash water on my face one more time, glad my T-shirt is black today otherwise it would be see-through by now from all the times I've missed my face. I smooth my hair down and dash for the stairs.

Nicole's obviously had a crash course in using the till because she's serving customers like her life depends on it, and I spontaneously hug her in the middle of putting money into the till. There's no sign of blood and she's still got the same number of fingers as before so it's obviously behaving itself. She has no idea how much I appreciate that, even though she's not a book lover and doesn't like shops in general, she's still willing to step up when I really need her.

'Don't worry about it,' she whispers back. 'We've all had bad break-ups, Hal, and I *do* know he was special. I don't know who's

288

more upset – you or Mum. Apparently she's been keeping in touch with him since he came for dinner and she's really going to miss his texts.'

'Yeah. He kept showing me photos of weird knitted things her group had been making. He had   ' The idea of how lovely Dimitri's been to my mum makes my voice crack again.

'Esme's over there,' Nicole says quickly and nods towards a fifty-something-year-old woman standing by the window and thumbing through the copy of *Les Mis*.

Mum intercepts me on the way and pulls me down into a hug, before saying, 'Plenty more fish in the sea, and we're going to find them *all*!' She's got a clipboard with a printed spreadsheet on it, and she's approaching all the men in the shop and asking them to fill in their age and relationship status.

She's going to be disappointed. I'd had enough of dating before I met Dimitri, now I never want to see another man again for the rest of my life. I might become a nun. It could be fun to live in a convent and sing songs like 'How Do You Solve A Problem Like Maria?' all day. I bet nuns get a lot of time for reading too.

'Esme?'

The woman closes the book and taps the cover with a long fingernail as she turns to me. 'That's something I haven't seen in many years.'

'I'm so glad we found it for you.' I give her my best smile.

'Found it?' Her face screws up in confusion. 'You think I want this crap?'

I can't hide my surprise. 'But … the note inside it …'

'Exactly. I'd have kept the book if it wasn't for that note.'

'So you didn't … date Sylvester then?'

'Oh, unfortunately, yes. I married him. I spent ten years with him – five of those believing we were gloriously happy, and another five believing he'd changed and wasn't going to cheat *again*. And again. And again. If you look closely enough around your shop, you'll probably find twenty other such "heartfelt" messages to twenty other girls he was trying to seduce. There's something about notes in books and being given books as a gift that makes it feel like so much thought and consideration has gone into it. It's something old-fashioned and inherently romantic, and it makes you feel so valued and important that you lose sight of what's right in front of you.'

Oh, tell me about it. Books erode a *lot* of common sense when it comes to men.

'And what was right in front of me was my husband sleeping with anything that had a pulse, including but not limited to, just about every colleague in his office both the female *and* male ones, our child's school teacher, one of my best friends, our regular taxi driver, and the florist who sold him the guilt-flowers he bought me every time he'd shagged someone else. I found that exact note, personalised to other poor, unsuspecting women, in many copies of many different books. He was churning them out like a factory line.'

Oh God. How can I have been so wrong? About *so* many things, but about this in particular? I was so convinced this was the most romantic thing I'd ever seen. Dimitri tried to tell me, but I couldn't comprehend that the dreamy note inside this book could've ended anything but happily.

'Anyway, I only came because I saw your post online that said you wanted to find me. I don't live far so I thought I'd drop by to let you know you can stop looking.' She hands *Les Mis* back to me. 'I assure you, I don't need any reminders of that relationship. I threw the book away for a reason.'

I stare open-mouthed after her as she whisks out of the shop.

This is *not* how I expected that to go.

I open *Les Mis* and read the inscription again, and it looks totally different now the rose-tinting is off my glasses.

I close the book and clutch it to my chest. All I want to do is tell Dimitri. He was right about it. I wouldn't even mind being wrong. I just want things to go back to how they were on the night we found this. Innocent. Flirty.

Not related to Drake Farrer and working for Farrer and Sons.

I realise that I'm standing here in a daze while the shop is so busy that Nicole's rushed off her feet and Mum's still accosting male customers with her clipboard and biro.

I take over from Nicole and go back to serving people, not managing to strike up my usual enthusiasm for selling romance books. Even books are different when you believe the stories in them might have a chance of coming true.

Because that's it, isn't it? That's all love will ever be – a fairy tale. Something to read about in books – because it never, ever happens in real life.

Chapter 17

'What an amazing start,' Nicole says. 'You've cleared loads of stock, you've earned more than enough to cover the business rates for the next few months, and can even go on that distributor's website you've been coveting – and you'll *still* have money to deposit into the bank this week.'

It's Sunday morning, the day after *the* day before, and because there were so many customers that I couldn't chuck them out at closing time, it got too late to clean up, so Nicole and Mum have come over to help me before I have to reopen again tomorrow.

The phone's been ringing off the hook with customer enquiries. The shop's gone viral but not because of the notes – because of the juxtaposition of me yesterday morning, talking animatedly about love, romance, and books, to me yesterday afternoon, my face red and my eyes swollen in the pictures as I try to summon up some enthusiasm for the notes again, and sandwiched between the two are photos of me shoving *Pentamerone* at Dimitri and throwing him out. The 'real-life heartbreak of romantic book-seller' posts have gone online far and wide, and the comments all say the same things about plenty more fish in the sea and being better off without him.

I don't want to be without him. I want this all to be a mistake, a misunderstanding. Every time I pick up the shop phone, I feel a little fizzle of excitement that it's going to be him, phoning with a perfectly reasonable explanation.

Could he have had a concussion or something and simply 'forgot' he was related to Drake Farrer after a terrible accident?

Could they have been separated at birth and he didn't even *know* until it was too late?

To be honest, I'm one step away from believing he was abducted by aliens and had his memory wiped by little green men – *that's* how badly I want this to be untrue.

'I don't understand it,' Mum says for the 48,528th time as she plumps up cushions on the reading-area sofas. 'What's so bad about being related to a property developer? He can't choose his family.'

'The point is that he lied about it, Mum,' I say through gritted teeth. It's not the first time I've explained myself this morning. 'The point is that he inserted himself into my life, into my shop, and I thought he was helping me, but what he actually did was get an inside look at my plans for the business and my accounts, and report back to his own firm whose sole purpose is to buy me out. Well, maybe not their *sole* purpose, I don't think I'm that important to them, but I'm certainly one of the key properties they want to acquire. He isn't who I thought he was.'

'What I don't understand is why no one knew,' Nicole says, also not for the first time. 'In a village this size, you can wave to someone in the street and they turn out to be your cousin. How did no one recognise him? Why didn't any of your customers know he was a Farrer brother?'

'I don't know,' I mutter, because it's also far from the first time I've asked myself the same question. 'I know he went to boarding school. I think they were both sent away at a really young age and Drake came back but Dimitri didn't. He said he never came back here until his mum died, and since then, he's ... spent a lot of time indoors,' I finish lamely. Even after this, I *still* don't want to gossip about the things he shared with me in private. I don't even know if any of it is true now.

'But he's so nice,' Mum carries on. 'And so funny. Do you know he offered to buy a hat from every single member of my knitting club for the charity sale next month? I've never even seen him wear a hat, let alone twelve. And the dick pics are hilarious.'

I don't think my head's ever spun round so fast before. 'Dimitri's been sending you dick pics?'

Either there's some miscommunication here or Dimitri is a *very* different person than I thought he was.

'Yes, look.' She gets her phone out and starts scrolling through it, and I hide my face behind a book because I'm not sure what on earth she's going to hold up. 'See?'

I peek over the cover of *The Book Thief*. 'Mum, that's … an Oxford English dictionary.'

'Yes! Isn't he wonderful? I was telling him about all the men who send me dick pics and he said it wasn't fair I had to see them so he'd send me something much better. Dic-*tionary* pics!'

'Oh my God.' I shake my head. I don't intend to laugh, but she holds up another photo of a Merriam Webster and then a Collins, and I can't stop myself. 'That's *so* Dimitri.'

She scrolls to another one of a Scrabble dictionary and then a thesaurus until Nicole and I are laughing so hard that it's a struggle to stay upright.

'How do you have Dimitri's phone number? *I* don't even have Dimitri's phone number.'

'He gave it to me. Said I could call him if I ever needed anything and that he wanted to hear all about how my allotment progresses.'

I suddenly feel more bereft than I have until now. He was *the* most amazing man. How can anyone have such a fun, childlike sense of humour, but still be the most perfect gentleman and treat my mum with such respect and kindness too? How can he have been so different to the person I thought he was? How can I have lost him?

Even Heathcliff looks devastated. His favourite greyhound has trotted past twice since yesterday and he hasn't even given it a glance.

Dimitri brought something to this shop. His easy cheerfulness calmed me when things were mad. His positive attitude made me feel like I could do even the most daunting of jobs. His sense of fun made every day whiz past in a blur of smiling eyes and cheeky grins. How can I open up the shop tomorrow morning and face the week without him?

No. This will just be another underhanded tactic. A way of getting my mum on his side and using her to get to me. 'Well, you can't. Don't ever call him, Mum, please?'

'Well, I haven't got much choice now you're so ticked off with him,' Mum grouches, sounding like an Enid Blyton character with her old-fashioned turn of phrase.

'Someone who does that can't be bad, can they? The dictionary pics, and *that*.' Nicole points to Mum's phone. 'You'd have to be a nutter to voluntarily give your number to our mum, *and* that was after The Dinner Incident. He knew what she was like.'

Mum pokes her tongue out at her. 'He was even complimentary about that. And he was the only one of you brave enough to try my pizza.'

'That wasn't pizza,' Nicole and I say in unison.

'And his oven cleaning tips were spot on. I never thought that cheese was going to come off, but it did.' Nicole goes back to slotting Fantasy books into the shelf alphabetically. 'I don't even mind about the ruined dress because he danced with you, knowing how clumsy you are. That's even braver than trying Mum's pizza.'

'Oh, don't remind me. Of the dancing *or* the pizza.' I think back to the day at his house. Dancing in that amazing ballroom, feeling like a princess. Feeling special and important and like it was the start of something wonderful. Like it must've taken a lot for him to let me see that side of him and share his secrets ... I can't connect the fact that *that* Dimitri is also the Dimitri who's been reporting back to Drake Farrer about my shop. 'Maybe I should give up now.'

'Nope, you lick your wounds and climb back on the horse. Metaphorically speaking. Well, unless the new man likes horses. But not too much. It's creepy when they like horses a bit too much.'

What kind of men is my mum meeting? Are they all sending her weird horse porn or something? 'I wasn't talking about men. I meant everything. The shop. The flat. The books. Sell it on to the Farrer brothers and be done with it. Cut my losses and get out.'

'You can't do that. Yesterday was an amazing day. Look at all those people who came. And look at all your followers and people who've signed up to be notified when the website opens. Look at how many comments there are on your pictures of the notes. Look at how many people are sharing them. Look at your Facebook group where people are finding books all over Buntingorden and hiding their own. It's become a real people's movement.'

'But it won't always be like that. There won't always be this many customers. There won't always be people hiding books, but there will always be people like Drake Farrer ripping them up. And how long until the wolves are door-knocking again? *Both* the wolves this time?'

'You can't do it anyway. Your old bloke said you had to pass it on to someone who wants it. Didn't you sign some sort of agreement to that effect?'

'I'll do that then. I'll have another raffle. I'll pick a winning ticket and maybe next time the winner will be a lot more capable than me. Somebody who's got a clue about how to run a business like this. Somebody who can see the property developers off.'

'Somebody who's not in love with one of them?' Nicole fixes me with a look that says she can see right through me.

'Love's a bit strong …'

'He said he was in love with you.'

Like I haven't thought about *that* 692,702 times since yesterday. 'He didn't *exactly* say that. And he was just rabbiting, rambling, trying to talk his way out of his lies.'

'I've never heard anyone say arse-over-tit in love with someone before. It's a nice way of saying head-over-heels, don't you think? Very fitting. Very him. Very *you*.'

'It doesn't matter now, does it?' I snap, because my nose is burning with the familiar feeling of imminent tears and neither of them are helping the situation.

Mum and Nicole share a look. 'You've changed since you started this, Hallie. For the first time in your life, you've been happy. You've never had a job you've truly loved before. You've never had a flat that was *yours*. This whole place was made for you. It's what you've been waiting for all your life.'

'And it's not just because of him,' Nicole adds.

'You've always loved this place. There's no way we're letting you give it up that easily.'

I had no idea that Mum or Nicole felt like that. For the first time in ages, I feel like I've got family support. They've always been disapproving of my string of dead-end jobs and mangy flats, but to feel them rallying behind me now – from the way Nicole stepped in and took over yesterday to the fact they're both here this morning – it gives me courage that they see the shop in the same way I do. As the thing I've been waiting for all my life. The thing I'd always hoped was in my future, but had given up on ever finding. Like love.

I have to push my glasses up and swipe the back of my hand over my eyes while holding *The Book Thief* out of the way. I want to tell them how much their support means, but I'm not going to be able to without sobbing. Instead, I turn around to look for the gap it came from on the Historical Fiction shelf and go to slide it back in, but there's something blocking it. I wriggle it around, but the spine still sticks out like there's something behind it. I crouch down and reach to the back of the shelf to straighten whichever book has got turned sideways.

'*The Princess Bride*,' I say as I pull it out. 'I've always meant to read this. It's got to be one of the top five movies of all time.'

Nicole makes a noise of appreciation. 'Has there *ever* been anyone hotter than Cary Elwes as Westley in the whole history of TV and films?'

'This was Robert's favourite book. He was always telling me to read it.' I turn it over in my hands, feeling the embossed title in the brown cover. 'This copy looks just like the one the grandpa reads in the film.'

I open the front cover out of habit, not expecting to find anything written inside the old book that's been forgotten on the shelf for God knows how many years.

And then I gasp in surprise.

'What?' Nicole and Mum chorus.

'It was him! The guy. In the books. With Della. It's him – *he's* the mystery guy.'

'Cary Elwes?' Nicole asks in confusion. They clearly think I'm bonkers.

'Listen to this.' I read out the note in smudged ink on the faded paper. '*My dearest Della, you are the most special thing in my life, and I look forward to every day that has you in it. There are two crowning days in my life – the day I took over the shop, and the day you walked in for the first time. Since then, every day has been an improvement. My love for you will never fade. Forever always, Robert.*'

'Well, that's sweet,' Mum says.

'No, you don't get it. Robert is the mystery man. Robert is the man Dimitri's mum was having an affair with. The notes in the books were to him. They shared their favourite books with each other! Hers were *Pride and Prejudice* and *Anne of Green Gables*, and his was *The Princess Bride*! He's the one we've been trying to find.'

They still clearly think I'm bonkers.

'This explains everything! Why the books are here – he didn't throw them away – he kept them near him, always.'

'And if they'd been sold?' Nicole asks.

'He's *Robert*. His number one belief was in passing books on. He believed that stories stay alive through the people that love them. With Della gone, he wouldn't have wanted to hoard them – he'd have wanted her favourite stories to be shared with new people and bought for new generations. *That's* why they're here – not because he stopped loving her, but because he wanted her to live on through these books. I have to tell—' I cut myself off. I *can't* tell Dimitri. That would mean I have to speak to him. And one handwritten inscription in a book isn't conclusive proof.

But Robert loved this book, and he loved the messages hidden in books like I do. It suddenly seems like all the hidden notes in the books in this shop aren't just a coincidence. Robert stocked this shop. I said weeks ago that all he'd bought lately were second-hand books. *These* books. Books with messages in them. Books that had meant something to someone once.

'The side gate!'

Mum and Nicole share another 'she's lost the plot' look.

'At Dimitri's house! He said Robert knew about the side gate. *This* is how he knew. And the love of his life! Robert lost the love of his life a few years back. Della died seven years ago. It adds up. It all suddenly adds up.'

I feel excited again. Finding this note ignites my enthusiasm for books, hidden messages, and this shop. This shop *is* special, and I will *never* give it up. This is why I love bookshops. There's a unique magic in them of never knowing quite what you might find, and that's always been what I loved most about coming in here. As the owner I've found some unexpected things here too. It's an honour to work here. It was the luckiest moment of my life when Robert picked my ticket, and I am not going to throw that away.

'No matter who Dimitri is and no matter what he's done, he deserves to know the truth. And I have to finish what I started with that first note.'

'What are you going to do?' Mum asks.

'I'm going to get to the bottom of this once and for all.' I glance at Heathcliff. 'We're going to Cornwall.'

Chapter 18

When I thought of returning the fish on that very first day, it was an omen. On Monday morning, I'm sitting on a train trundling towards Cornwall with the goldfish bowl on my lap. The bloke next to me is most amused and keeps looking over and sniggering to himself. He's already asked me if he can take a picture to post on Twitter. Thank God no dogs have got on yet or Heathcliff might hurl himself out of the bowl and make a break for freedom.

Nicole pulled a sickie with her own job and volunteered to cover the shop for me, so at least it's not closed after such a busy day on Saturday, because *this* seems like the place I'm meant to be today.

I probably could have had this conversation with Robert on the phone, but I thought if I turned up at the door of his flat and showed him the books I have in the bag by my feet, he might be more willing to tell me. Robert always was someone who thought things were better done in person and preferred real letters to emails, and face-to-face conversations rather than phone calls. And he did leave his fish behind. That's as good an excuse as any.

I don't know if it's really any of my business or not, and what

I probably should have done is given the book to Dimitri and let him make what he wants of it, but I feel like I started this and it has to be me who finishes it. And if I'm completely honest with myself, I'll admit that a good fifty per cent of my reasons for taking this journey are because Robert must know a lot about Drake and Dimitri Farrer and I want to know if I can trust *anything* Dimitri said.

Six hours after getting on the train, after a bus ride to the station that started before it was even daylight, I finally stretch my back out in the tiny coastal train station. I put Heathcliff's bowl down on a bench and sprinkle some fish food flakes in, gaining some curious looks from other passengers. I didn't know what to bring for him. It's not like taking a dog on a trip where you bring water, dog biscuits, a towel, and poo bags.

Robert left his address for mail forwarding and I thank my lucky stars that the train drops me off within walking distance of his retirement home because I don't think I can face any more trains or buses today. Well, apart from the ones home, because I've also got to get back today. I cannot expect Nicole to run the shop for another day.

I follow Google Maps on my phone – because if there's one thing I am guaranteed to do in this situation, it's get lost – and turn corner after corner of leafy coastal roads until I come to the right place.

One of the staff buzzes me in and directs me to his flat, giving Heathcliff a wary glance. Honestly, anyone would think it was weird to go travelling with a goldfish. When I finally knock on the door after a morning that feels like it's lasted forever even though it's barely lunchtime, the wild-haired old man who answers the door doesn't look even vaguely surprised to see me. I phoned this morning and spoke to a member of staff to make sure Robert was up to visitors, and I assume they let him know I'd be coming.

'Hallie!' He greets me with the same beam he always used to

greet me with when I went into the bookshop. 'What took you so long? I thought you'd have figured it out ages ago.'

'What? You know why I'm here?'

'I know why *you're* here.' His eyes fall on the goldfish bowl in my arms. 'I'm not quite sure why you've brought Heathcliff along, but I'm sure he appreciated the change of scenery.'

'He appreciated the two Pomeranians we passed on the way.'

Robert laughs and steps aside to let me into his flat, going to put the kettle on without even asking.

When he's made us a cuppa each, and retrieved the mandatory packet of biscuits, he invites me to sit in the garden. He excuses himself for a moment while I go outside and I'm sure I overhear a muffled conversation. Maybe I'm imagining it. Oh no, what if he had plans or something and now he thinks he's got to cancel them because I'm here?

I put Heathcliff's bowl under the shade of an open parasol above a wooden picnic table and take advantage of the sunshine and wander to the end of the enclosed communal garden to look out across the beach and breathe in the sea air. Robert wasn't joking about his flat being right on the sand.

'Did you have plans?' I ask the moment he steps out the door. 'I overheard you on the phone,' I clarify when he gives me a confused look.

'Oh, no, dear. Just checking on the progress of something.' He settles himself on the bench with Heathcliff's bowl on the picnic table beside him. 'You found the notes then?'

'Why are there so many of them?' The question spills out of my mouth before I can ask him anything else.

'Why do you think?'

I try to remember any of the things he's said to me over the years, but the truth is I've known the answer from the very first note we found. 'Because as a bookseller, you wanted to specialise in books that have meant something to someone. You wanted to pass on books that have been loved before.'

'Stories are timeless. They spill through ages, times, genders, races, religions, nationalities. They unite us. With the world the way it is at the moment, they're one of the only things we've got left that does. People are still reading books that were written hundreds of years ago. Children are still brought up with fairy tales that date back to centuries we can't even imagine living in. That's magic of a different kind.'

'So you hunt out only books that have inscriptions in them? You left me the details of local car boot sales,' I say because I can easily imagine him poring over boxes and boxes of books, painstakingly selecting only the ones that had words written inside them. Nothing was ever too much trouble for Robert when it came to books.

'I have done recently. I'm a huge supporter of new books too, but rereading old favourites brings a special kind of nostalgia that only books can create. If you reread a book you loved as a child, it transports you back to that time and place in a way that nothing else can. It's not the same as watching a film or revisiting a real place because it's somewhere that exists only in your imagination. So in the past couple of years, as I've sold books, I've started replacing them with second-hand books that have obviously meant something to the previous owner.'

'But not enough to keep them?' I ask. Dimitri would be proud.

He shrugs. 'I don't think of it as being thrown away. I think of it more as being sent out into the world to find their next person. A bit like when a relationship ends. No matter how much you loved that person for however long you had them, you pick yourself up and go back out into the world to find the next person you might fall in love with, but no matter what, there will always be a part of the previous person with you. Books are like that. I think you take a part of every book with you when you've finished it, because for just a few hours, you've lived another life. You've experienced what the character has experienced, felt what they've felt, and loved who they've loved.

I think the best thing you can do after reading a book like that is to share it.'

I'm once again reminded of how much I always liked Robert. 'I've always thought that you share a special kind of connection when you meet someone who loves a book that you love ...'

'There was a reason your ticket came out of that hat, Hallie.' Robert's toothy beam spreads slowly across his face. 'Books connect us in a world where a lot of connections are broken nowadays. They can help us, heal us, break us and put our broken pieces back together again. They can make us believe in magic. In love. In anything. That was my take on Once Upon A Page – that a book's life is never over, no matter how many years pass.'

I love that. A rush of love for my little shop back in Buntingorden floods me. It's always been a special place and I'm honoured to be in charge of it for the time being. And if I ever want to get back there, I'm going to have to ask what I came here to find out. 'What about Della?'

'Hallie, if you didn't already know, you wouldn't be here.'

We stare at each other for a long moment until he sighs. 'How many books have you found?'

'Three.' I flip up the top of my shoulder bag, get them out, and go across to the bench to sit next to him, handing them over one at a time as his aged hands take them from me, running shaky fingers over each one like it's something revered.

'I never got the chance to write my second one.' His watery eyes don't move from the cover of *Pride and Prejudice*. 'She was gone so quickly. One moment there, young, healthy, and happy. The next, I would never see her again.'

'Why didn't you ever tell him that you and Della were in love?' I ask gently.

He knows who I'm talking about without me needing to say it. 'It was private. She was gone and what we shared was the most special thing in my life. I didn't want it picked apart by a grieving family. She wasn't single when we started to fall for each other,

305

and if I'd said anything, they would have worked it out. I didn't want them to think badly of her.'

'They knew she was unhappy. They wouldn't have minded. Dimitri was happy when he found out. Glad she had something to live for. The love that she read about and wished for. The love she clearly didn't get with their father.'

'She had a hard life. She was married to a man who gave her about as much support as a blancmange. Dani's condition was challenging, but she never ever complained. Reading was her escape. I'd always known her in passing, but she started coming in regularly when Dani was in remission and went back to school and things were normal for a while. We talked, of course. Discovered we liked a lot of the same things, the same books, the same food, the same activities. I was a little older than her, but age doesn't come into it when you connect with someone on that level. She came in to buy books, then she started staying to read, and before long she'd come in and we'd just talk for hours in the afternoons before she had to pick Dani up. It became my favourite part of every day. We were in love before I knew it. Love was something I never thought would happen for me, but she blew in like a spring breeze and changed everything.'

I know that feeling.

My mind must wander, because when I blink myself back to reality, he's staring at me with a sympathetic look on his wrinkled face.

'Speaking of love,' he starts. 'You've obviously found out about our arrangement and come to get to the bottom of it ...'

I shake my head. 'The only thing I've found out is that Dimitri is the "s" in Farrer and Sons. I thought he was my friend ... and more. So much more. But he's been working for them all along, learning my weaknesses and reporting back so they can exploit them and swoop in to buy the shop when it fails miserably.'

Now it's Robert's turn to look confused. 'Dimitri doesn't work for Farrer and Sons. He doesn't even like them. He has almost no contact with his father and as little as possible with his brother. He isn't working for them, Hallie – he's working for me.'

I open and close my mouth a few times before anything will come out. 'What?'

'I didn't want you to be alone, but my health is failing and I couldn't do another month or so there to show you the ropes. I knew I was throwing you in the deep end, but at the same time, I didn't want to make you feel that I didn't have faith in you. You were the perfect person to take over Once Upon A Page, but the only person who didn't realise it was *you*. I wanted someone to be there for you, to support you, to help you if you needed it, without being heavy-handed enough to openly push a second manager or member of staff at you. Being a bookseller is a surprisingly lonely job sometimes, and you have no choice but to rely on yourself. *You* had to step outside of your comfort zone, but I wanted you to have a safety net – I just didn't want you to think I thought you needed a safety net. Does that make sense?'

It takes me a while to untangle the sentence in my brain. 'Kind of ...'

'He'd been playing around with illustrations from *Pentamerone* for a while. As a distraction after his sister's death, a way of remembering a book she adored, a way of keeping himself busy ... All of the above. He'd told me about the publishing deal he'd lost before, and I thought there'd be a gap in the market for a modernised *Pentamerone*, so I offered to pay him to sit there and finish the book he wanted to illustrate. He refused any money, of course, but he offered to help anyway. I knew he'd be the perfect person. That he'd keep to himself but he knew the shop well enough to answer any questions you had, and that he'd help if you needed it.'

'Then why does Drake Farrer know everything there is to know about the shop?'

'Because Drake Farrer hacked into my computer a few months ago.'

'It's Windows 98, it doesn't take much hacking.' I shake my head. 'I mean, what?'

'The cheeky blighter must've been watching the shop, and as soon as I went upstairs to answer a call of nature, he slipped in and got into the office. I'm not exactly speedy on the stairs, but I came down to find him sitting at my computer, feet up on the desk as bold as brass, laughing at me. And I know it's my own fault for not locking up, but I trust people. I think people are generally good, and no one's going to do anything untoward in a bookshop if they find it unattended for a few minutes, but unfortunately Drake Farrer is the exception to normal human decency.'

'Why is the company called Farrer and Sons then? Plural sons?'

'Because his father is a nasty bully who couldn't accept that one of his sons might not want to follow in his corporate footsteps and tried to manipulate them both from a very young age into believing that they had no choice but to join his company. You can't honestly have thought that Dimitri was going behind your back like that? *Dimitri*. He's the sunniest sunshine pot of personality. He hasn't got a dishonest bone in his body. I had to do some persuading to get him to go along with my plan because of that. He wasn't too happy about it.'

'Why didn't he just tell me that?' I say, more to myself than to Robert. 'The other day in the shop when I found out. Why didn't he say anything?'

'Are you sure he didn't?' he says in that way of a gently leading question that makes you think about the answer even if you didn't intend to.

'A little bit,' I stutter. 'He *did* say some of it, but I thought he was rambling because he'd been caught. Why didn't he just come out and say you'd sent him?'

'Knowing Dimitri, it would've been because he didn't want you to feel undermined. He didn't want you to think I doubted your abilities or left you with a "makeshift babysitter", which is how he put it when he was trying to talk me out of it.'

'So he'd rather let me think badly of him than admit you thought I needed help in the beginning? He would rather walk away from what we had than admit you had doubts about leaving your bookshop to someone completely unprepared?'

'I didn't have doubts, Hallie. I've never once doubted *you*, only your own belief in yourself. I worried that you'd feel overwhelmed and walk away, and Once Upon A Page needs you as much as you need it.'

An unexpected sob escapes my mouth and he reaches over to pat my hand. 'Dimitri doesn't do things without thinking them through first. He's very calm and he takes his time over things, and he doesn't argue. He doesn't raise his voice to be heard over a crowd. He probably thought you needed space and went away to work out the best way to explain things.'

All qualities I love about him. I keep going over all this in my head. It changes things a bit. But does it? He still lied to me. He still told me he was working on that book for a reason, although he's been so vague about his deadline that I have to question whether I ever really believed him in the first place. He's helped me so much, but now I don't know if that was only because he was fulfilling some obligation to Robert.

'It wasn't that well planned out,' Robert says when I put it into words. 'It was a casual arrangement between friends. I asked him to go to the bookshop as often as he could …'

'Every day?'

'No, not every day. He never came in every day. Has he been coming in every day with you?'

'There are too many "every days" in that sentence.'

Robert ignores my ignoring of the question and that beam breaks across his face again. 'If he's been coming in every day it's because he likes you as much as I knew he would. I always wanted you two to meet. I suspected you'd get on well. I kept trying to get you to come in when I knew he'd be there, but it never worked. And whenever I tried to get him to stay, he'd scarper. This was for him too, Hallie. I was worried that he'd go back to hiding away inside his ghost house after I left, never venturing into the outside world, alone with his grief. He wasn't in a good place, and I knew Della would want me to keep an eye on him. His father is a bitter, twisted, lonely old man, and people *still* think he lives in that big old mansion on Bodmin Lane. Dimitri needs to throw off those shackles, not withdraw further into them. He's got the strength of character to go against what his father wanted and to stand up to his brother, but he's stuck in this mansion full of beautiful ghosts. He needed someone to get him back into life, to make him want to live again, and if there's anything that can shake up a life, it's falling in love.'

'He's not in …' I realise it doesn't matter. I *am* in love with him, and every word Robert says makes me realise that I've got this all wrong. Another sob escapes and I try to disguise it with a hiccup but end up choking myself. I suddenly need to talk to him so desperately that I feel like I could teleport back to Buntingorden through sheer willpower alone. 'Do you have his number?'

'It'll be somewhere in my address book …' Robert gestures vaguely towards the flat behind us. 'Now where did I put it? Let me think …'

It's too long. It'll take too long.

'Mum!' I say suddenly, making both Robert and Heathcliff jump. 'She's got his number!'

My phone is at my ear in such record timing that it's a miracle I didn't drop it. 'Mum!' I shout the second she answers. 'You've got Dimitri's number, right? I need you to phone him, give him my number and tell him to phone me back *immediately*. Have you got that?'

'Ooh, Hallie, where are you? I ventured down to the shop

today so see how your sister was doing and if there were any men browsing the Relationships section—'

'Mum!' I cut her off. I'm desperately trying to undo the biggest mistake I've ever made and she's *still* going on about the Relationships section. 'This is important. Can you please phone Dimitri, tell him I need him to call me right now! I'll give you full credit for playing matchmaker!'

I hang up before she gets a chance to ask any questions.

It takes all eternity for my phone to ring. By the time it does, I think Robert's collected another week's pension, Heathcliff's faded into old age, and I've got seventy-five per cent coverage of grey hair instead of the few pesky ones peeking through I had before. In reality it's about five minutes, and when it does ring, it makes me jump so much that I nearly drop it into the lily pond in the corner of the garden. Knowing my luck, it'll be a telemarketer saying, "Have you had an accident recently that wasn't your fault?" Sometimes I start telling them about the accidents I've had recently that *were* my fault – they soon hang up.

Mum's number flashes up on the screen and I feel myself deflate.

'I couldn't get hold of him, Hal. I've tried three times but his phone rings out and then goes to voicemail. I'll text you his number so you can try, I'm sure he won't mind.'

I hang up, and save the number she texts me, but I get exactly the same response when I try to call it – ringing and then voicemail.

'Hallie, why don't you sit down and take the weight off your feet?' Robert's gently thumbing through the copy of *Pride and Prejudice* now and he pats the bench beside him without looking up. 'I'm sure he's busy and he'll answer when he can.'

'I should go. The last train's at four, but if I leave now, I could get the earlier one and still have time to get over to his house tonight. I *need* to see him. I need him to explain all this in person. I need to apologise. And you. He needs to know that you're the man who made his mum so happy.' I try his number again but only his voicemail picks up and this isn't something that can be left on an answering machine.

'Hallie, I really think you should stay awhile. Look at this place. Isn't it beautiful? Being this close to the ocean has a way of washing away all of life's greatest troubles.'

'I need to get back. The ocean will always be there, Dimitri won't.'

'Heathcliff needs a rest.' Robert picks up the goldfish bowl and holds it protectively on his lap. 'You can't go yet, he hasn't had time to recover his strength.'

'Yeah, he really exerted himself when that whippet chased its ball on the sand just now,' I mutter, wondering why he's so keen for me to stay.

There's a wooden park bench against the wall of his flat and I go over and flop down on it, resting my head against the back and turning my face to the sun, trying to let it warm me because everything inside me feels cold even though it's a warm June day.

It isn't long before Robert puts Heathcliff's bowl down in the shade of the parasol and comes to sit next to me. He starts telling me about Della and how they bonded over their love of books, how it was actually her who read the first book inscription out loud and how it made him start actively seeking them out, how much he always wished he could find some of the writers and receivers of these books lost in this house of time, and it's easy to lose myself for a while, only pressing redial every five minutes and getting the same response from Dimitri's number.

Robert keeps surreptitiously checking his watch when he thinks I'm not looking, and I'm convinced he had plans that he's cancelled because of me. I think about starting to move, but when I suggest there's still plenty of time to catch the two o'clock train, a look of worry crosses his face. 'How about a nice walk on the beach? I can't go far these days, but you can. Why don't you collect some seashells for your next summer-themed window display?'

I don't bother questioning how he knows that. Dimitri must've told him. Which is comforting in a way. It kind of proves that it was Robert he was reporting back to, not his brother.

I've given up on trying to guess why he's so keen for me to stay. Maybe he's lonely here? Maybe he misses Buntingorden and his little shop more than he lets on? If I stay much longer, I won't have a hope of getting that earlier train, but even the four o'clock one will get me back to Buntingorden at ten. It won't be too late to walk out to Bodmin Lane, and the beach does look tempting. It's been ages since I was on the coast and until now, I've been too tense to appreciate it, but as I get up and walk to the end of the garden and take a deep breath of salty sea air and feel my lungs fill and my shoulders droop as I exhale, I think it might not be such a bad idea. 'Fine.' I sigh. 'I won't be long.'

'Take your time,' he calls, sounding oddly victorious. 'Heathcliff and I are going to read together.'

I kick my shoes and socks off to leave them inside Robert's gate and step out onto the sand. It's a normal workday so the beach isn't too crowded, and most people are down by the water's edge, not this far up the sand, and I curl my toes into it, feeling the sun-warmed grains under my feet. I tell myself to relax. I've done everything I can for the time being, and apart from carrying on trying Dimitri's number, there's nothing I can do until I get home.

I see why Robert came down here. The waves are breaking gently in the distance and looking out at the ocean makes me feel small and free, like it's okay if I mess things up sometimes and make mistakes and drop things that aren't meant to be dropped. It doesn't matter if we're all specks of nothing in the grand scheme of things. Coasts have a way of making you feel philosophical.

I've only walked for a few minutes when I spot a *very* familiar

313

figure coming towards me. I recognise the long limbs and stance. But it can't be him. How long has it been since I last went to the optician? I take my glasses off and scrunch my eyes up before putting them back on again, like it might somehow reset my eyesight. The figure is still there in the distance and he's looking around like he's searching for something. And it still looks like him. 'Dimitri?' I call, expecting to be ignored because it *must* be a complete stranger, but he stops at my shout and puts his hand up to shade his eyes from the sun.

And it's definitely him. Or I'm hallucinating. The hallucination is more likely. I start running towards him, a bit like Bridget Jones chasing after Mark Darcy in her knickers while 'Ain't No Mountain High Enough' plays encouragingly in the background. But thankfully with trousers on. No one wants to see me running around in my knickers, not even in times of romantic crisis.

'Dimitri?' I repeat in confusion when I get near enough not to shout, almost certain that the horizon is going to waver at any moment and he's going to disappear like a mirage in a movie.

His hair is sticking half up and half down, looking like it's been worried by fingers pushed through it over and over, just like he does in the shop when he's hunched over his sketchbook trying to get the perfect curve to an ogre's claw.

'Hallie? Oh thank God, at least I'm in the right place. I thought I was going to wander right to the edge of the British Isles before I found you.' He speeds up, his boots sinking into the sand as he ambles towards me.

'What are you doing here?'

'I got lost. I took a wrong turn from the train station and somehow ended up on the beach. Robert said his apartment was right on the sand so I figured I'd eventually find it if I came this way.' He's quiet for a moment before he lets out a nervous laugh and his cheeks flare red. 'You mean in Cornwall, not on the beach itself, don't you?'

It makes me giggle, possibly with a slight edge of hysteria creeping in. 'I've been trying to call you.'

'I know. I didn't mean to worry you. Your mum texted that she'd given you my number so I guessed it was you, but I was already on my way, and on the phone in the middle of a crowded train carriage wasn't the place to say everything I need to tell you.'

'Did Robert know you were coming?' I ask as things slot together in my head. The hushed conversation earlier, the constant checking of the time, and why he was so keen for me to stay.

'Of course. Robert *made* me come. He phoned early this morning to say you'd spoken to one of the attendants in his building and were on the way down, and he had something he needed to tell us both, so I got the next train. I needed to see you, Hal. I'd been to the shop before that but it was early and you weren't answering. At least now I know why.'

'Robert's spent the past hour trying to stop me leaving to catch the earlier train so I could get back to you quicker. And now I know why too.'

I lose myself in his eyes and smile as we stand there staring at each other. My arms are sort of hovering in mid-air, about to hug him when I realise we do actually need to talk. The sight of him and the surprise of him being here has wiped everything else out of my mind and I can barely remember what went wrong between us in the first place.

I stutter a few times but I can't manage to get any words out, and Dimitri opens his arms and like most things lately, hugging him seems to be the answer to most of the world's problems, so I jump on him and, dodging all the laws of the universe, he manages to stay upright. His arms close around me so tightly that it would probably be painful if it was anyone else, and he lifts me up as my arms tighten around his shoulders and I bury my face in his neck.

'Are you crying?'

'No. Yes. I don't know, I've been in some permanent state of half-laughing and half-sobbing since I got here.' I involuntarily do a demonstration and have to inhale and exhale slowly, knowing he can feel every shudder of my breath.

'I know everything, Dimitri.' My voice is muffled against his sun-warmed skin when I can speak again. 'I'm sorry for getting it so wrong. You're the best thing that's ever happened to me, and I should've had more trust in you rather than waiting for the inevitable bad luck to follow me. Everything always goes wrong for me, and rather than enjoying the good things that were going right, I was waiting for the inevitable moment my luck ran out, and I thought that was it and I shut down.'

'I'm sorry about Drake. I thought you'd never talk to me again if you found out. I know I should have told you who he was at the first moment you mentioned his name, but I missed my chance, and from then on, it got weirder and weirder that I hadn't told you. It looked like I was up to something even though I wasn't, and then he came into the shop that day when I was there, and I thought that would be it, but he didn't say anything either, making it look like we were in it together. Which was exactly what he wanted. It gave him something to use against me.'

His arms tighten and he spins us around, still defying the odds and managing to stay upright. 'I couldn't bear the thought of losing you. I was head-over-heels and he knew it. Came over the night before the opening day and threw his weight around, tried to blackmail me into giving up my half of the house in exchange for his silence. I've had enough bullies in my life to have grown out of giving in to them, so I told him where to go. I was trying to find the right moment to tell you the truth, but it was so busy, and with the news people and the note writers who kept turning up ...'

'I know,' I murmur, thinking back to all the times he did keep trying to tell me something.

'I didn't mean for you to find out like that. I didn't think he'd do it because he'd be giving up the leverage he had over me. I thought I'd still have time after the opening day, and at least you'd finally know the truth even if you hated me for it.'

'I get it, Dimitri,' I say as close to his ear as I can get. 'And I wouldn't have hated you. I mean, it might've taken me a few days to think it through, but ... I *do* know you wouldn't do something like that.'

'I did lie to you about *Pentamerone* though.'

'I know. And Robert's told me you didn't want to, and it doesn't matter because I'm arse-over-tit in love with you, and—' Did I just say that out loud? Thank God the side of my head is still pressed against his so he can't see my face. If anyone asks, the redness is purely down to sunburn. Maybe the sound of the waves will have drowned my words out?

He wobbles on his feet and I start sliding out of his arms as he puts me down and leans forward so his mouth is next to my ear. 'Just so you know, I am many-arses over many-tits in love with you too.'

It does nothing to help the half-laughing half-crying situation. He pulls back and it would be impossible not to kiss him. I think I actually whimper as our mouths crash together, just as a gust of wind whips up, coating us in sand, and we both start choking and jump apart to spit out unwelcome grains.

'It was all going too well, wasn't it?' He says with a laugh, reaching out to take my hand as I try to shake sand out of my hair.

We start walking back the way I came along the beach, our entwined hands swinging between us, before I realise I haven't told him about *The Princess Bride*. 'Oh God, Dimitri, there's something else. None of that was the reason I came here. I found out who your mum's mystery man is. I found a book he'd given to her, and I couldn't tell you because it was yesterday and suddenly everything made sense, and ...'

'It's Robert, isn't it?'

'How do you know that?' I say in surprise.

'When he said you were on your way down and he had something to tell us both, things started to add up. I had a feeling that it was about more than the shop. He knew about my side gate. After Mum died, a box of books used to turn up on our doorstep every month – I thought it was a subscription or something she'd organised before she died, but since I've got to know him, I've realised it was obviously Robert's doing. He denied it, of course, but that's the kind of person he is. So I've spent the past few hours on the train adding up all these coincidences. I've guessed you found something that proves it?'

'*The Princess Bride.* Robert's favourite book. And I didn't find it, it found me.'

'I've always said books do that.'

'Me too.' Tears fill my eyes again and I try to blink them away. It must be all the salt in the sea air or something. No way am I actually crying this much. 'Are you okay with it?'

'It's … amazing, actually. He's one of my favourite people in the world. I can't think of anyone better to have made my mum happy.'

When we get back, Robert's sitting in the shade with Heathcliff's bowl on his lap, reading *Anne of Green Gables* to the fish. I thought he was joking when he said he was going to do that.

'Hallie …' Dimitri tugs my hand and pulls me to a stop outside the gate. 'You didn't really bring Heathcliff to Cornwall, did you?'

'I thought he might like to see Robert again.' I sigh. Why do so many people think taking a fish on a train is weird? 'And I think he's reconsidering his sexuality. There's a couple of seagulls on the roof that he seems *really* taken with. A Chihuahua walked past earlier and he didn't give it a second glance.'

He bursts out laughing and bends to press his lips against my cheek. 'I had no idea how empty my life was before you came into it. There is no one else in the *universe* who would take a goldfish on a train to Cornwall and make it seem normal.'

'That's not fair. I'm sure there are people who take their gold-fish out all the time.'

'Oh yes, five-star restaurants, Broadway shows, the cinema. Maybe they strap its bowl to a skateboard and pull it along on a lead ...'

'Oh, now that would've been an idea ...' I giggle, only half joking.

'Hello, you two lovebirds!' Robert calls when he looks up from the story and notices us. He nods towards our joined hands as Dimitri undoes the gate and lets us in. 'I've said for years that you two should meet.'

Robert returns Heathcliff's bowl to the table and gets up, tottering across to the bench that's in the sunshine and patting the empty space beside him. 'I think you already know, but it's long past time I told you something ...'

Dimitri hugs him as we both sit down, his fingers laced with mine. I don't let go of his hand while Robert tells him everything he's told me, and adds how proud his mum was of him for step-ping out of his father's shadow and putting his talent to good use.

We sit around talking about books and sharing stories about both Della and the bookshop for a good couple of hours, Robert sends out for the compulsory British seaside lunch of fish and chips, and even though it's been a long day and I'm looking forward to getting back to my little shop in Buntingorden, I'm reluctant to leave when half past three rolls around and we're going to miss the last train home if we don't get our skates on.

'Don't you want to keep these?' I ask him as I gather up our things, trying to make sure I haven't forgotten anything.

He holds the copies of *Pride and Prejudice*, *Anne of Green Gables*, and *The Princess Bride* out to me and shakes his head. 'You two should have them. Maybe one day, you can pass them onto your own children. Della would've loved that. For as long as these books exist, even when all of us are long gone, people

– be they future generations of family, or strangers who buy those books – will read those words and wonder who she was. That's a pretty special way of honouring someone.'

The tears come again as I take the books from him and slide them carefully into my bag.

'I chose you, Hallie.'

I know what he means without him needing to clarify. 'You picked a ticket out of a hat.'

'Did I? Or is there a certain type of magic in that shop that ensures the next owner is exactly who it's meant to be? The man who passed it on to me said exactly the same thing, and when I picked that ticket, I had you in mind. I wanted it to be you. Every page in that shop wanted it to be you. And it was you. Don't ever doubt that.'

I'm crying again as we both hug him goodbye, and get as far as the gate before he calls after me. 'And Hallie?'

I turn back.

'Heathcliff belongs to the bookshop. Take him with you.'

Dimitri dashes back and grabs the bowl. Well, it was worth trying, even though I've got quite used to having the goldfish around. And he's survived nearly two months in my care now. Maybe there is magic in that bookshop after all.

Chapter 19

It's dark by the time the bus pulls up at the end of Buntingorden High Street, and Dimitri's been *off* all the way home. Quiet, lost in thought, and secretively texting someone while clearly trying to hide his phone from me, and I can't work out what's going on.

As we approach the shop, I realise the chains have gone from the stairs leading to the roof terrace and the stairway is open, and when we get even closer, there's a glow coming from up there, like some sort of candle or lamp.

Or the building's on fire. That would be just my luck.

'What's going on?' I ask Dimitri.

'You'll see.' He winks at me, seeming devious and confident as I follow him up the narrow stairway.

'You took your time.' Drake Farrer is leaning back in a chair with his feet up on one of the tables next to a glowing oil lamp that's supposed to keep midges at bay.

'What the hell are you doing here?' I snap. Of all people I'd have been happy never to see again.

'Oh, relax, princess. It was his idea, not mine. It's past ten o'clock at night, do you think I *want* to be sitting up here freezing my bits off with all these midges?' He slaps at the side of his neck.

I thought even midges would have more discerning taste than him.

'It's June! It's a lovely warm night.' I'm instantly annoyed by his distasteful tone.

'Hal, it's okay, I asked him to meet us here,' Dimitri says. 'He's who I've been texting since we left Cornwall.'

Oh, great. 'So we can dredge up the other day all over again? I don't need him to confirm anything, Dimitri. I trust you.' I'm distracted from Drake's usual smarmy grin by his shoes, which are so abnormally shiny they reflect the moonlight.

'I know. It's not about that. He and I are going to do a business deal.'

Drake uncrosses his ankles and finally deigns himself to put his legs down and sit upright. He swings his briefcase onto the table and snaps it open, Dimitri pulls out a chair and sits opposite him, and I go to put Heathcliff's bowl safely on the other table and wonder what on earth is going on. Dimitri doesn't seem like himself. He seems calm and confident which is not a feeling Drake inspires in many people. 'Did you bring the paperwork I asked for?'

Drake Farrer looks almost as confused as I am. Whatever this is, he clearly isn't sure about it either. 'Yes, but I don't know what you think you've got that *I* want.'

'My half of the house. My half of the house in exchange for the ex-bakery downstairs, enough cash to do the renovations, and a clause to ensure it can never be turned into something that would cause the village to lose its charm and unique spirit.'

'What?' I say.

'What?' Drake Farrer says.

'I have something you want and you have something I want. It's a fair swap.'

'Dimitri ...' I take a step towards them. 'That is *not* a fair swap. He was being generous when he offered me thirty-five grand for my shop. That *mansion* is worth a heck of a lot more than that.'

322

'Listen to your missus, brother,' Drake says. Even though it's meant as an insult, there's something quite nice about being called Dimitri's missus.

'That's exactly why he's going to take the trade.' Dimitri turns to me. 'Because I don't care about the money and Drake does. Whichever way you look at it, he's going to do *extremely* well out of this, and Drake's a businessman. Good business decisions are what he does.'

'Dimitri, we might not always see eye to eye, but you're still my brother. It's my duty to warn you this is *not* a fair trade.'

'I'll have quotes for the building work with you by the end of the week, so factor that into your price.' Dimitri ignores him. 'I want a couple of weeks to get my stuff out of the house, I want that clause put in the contract, and I want you to leave Hallie's bookshop and the rest of this street alone. You *and* Dad. He will undoubtedly benefit from you having full ownership of the mansion. Get him to stop his letters, stop his complaining, and end this campaign of hatred that's gone on for far too long, and it's yours.'

For the second time in recent weeks, I am utterly convinced that Dimitri has magic powers because he's managed to render Drake Farrer speechless too. He seems like a different man tonight – far from the stuttery awkward guy I fell in love with, he seems like a student of the property law he once studied, the suave businessman that his father wanted him to become, a cut-throat entrepreneur who can duck and dive just as smoothly as his brother can.

Even Drake looks to me before looking back at Dimitri and shaking his head. 'You're a lunatic but you're right. You're making me an offer I can't refuse. I'm not going to turn that down. I accept.' He holds his hand out and they shake on it before I have a chance of trying to talk sense into him again.

'And I know you both think I'm the worst person in the world,' Drake continues. 'But I do know our mum wouldn't have wanted me to treat you unfairly, so you can get your building quotes to me, but I have a rough idea of how much it's going to cost to do these places up, and I'll double it. Make sure you've got enough leftover to knock the flats into one if you're going to be living together. A buffer while you finish your book or whatever it is you do.' He waves a perfectly manicured dismissive hand in typical Drake Farrer style just so we know he hasn't had a complete lobotomy and become a decent person overnight.

'I'm an illustrator, Drake. No matter how many times you and Dad try to belittle me because I didn't follow his planned career path, I'll still be an illustrator, and I'll still be happy doing something I love, no matter how much it pays.'

Drake mutters something unintelligible and rifles through the papers in his briefcase until he pulls out a sheaf of official-looking documents and starts writing on them.

I watch in silence until he eventually scribbles his name in a couple of places and hands the pen and documents to Dimitri. 'This is only a commitment. You'll have to come into the office next week to sign the official paperwork.'

'I know.' Dimitri signs his name, takes one copy for himself and hands one back to Drake. 'Nice doing business with you.'

I notice the tremor in his fingers as he hands Drake's pen back too, and I realise he might not be quite as composed as he's coming across.

Drake snaps his briefcase shut and stands up. 'Miss Winstone.' He nods to me and then Dimitri. 'Enjoy your new cramped lives together. I'll leave you and your fish to it.'

It almost makes me laugh out loud because I'd momentarily forgotten Heathcliff on the table behind me. I expect Dimitri to get up and walk him downstairs, but he doesn't look like he can move, so I let my hand brush across his shoulder as I quickly follow Drake, feeling a bit like a guard dog, seeing him off one last time. The smile I give him as he walks away is certainly closer to 'bared teeth' than an actual smile. I watch until he disappears into the distance before I go back up to the roof terrace.

Dimitri is standing now, leaning over the table and looking like he might be about to hyperventilate.

'You were amazing,' I say, even though I still can't get my head around what just happened. 'Suave and sophisticated. As much of a businessman as Drake will ever be.'

He laughs. 'Oh God, sophisticated and me don't go together at all, do they? I thought I was being all debonair like Marlon Brando in *The Godfather* then, and just as I was thinking all I needed was a cat to stoke menacingly, one of my braces pinged off and knocked my glasses sideways, and then I looked down and realised I'd put on my sprout socks this morning.' He leans against the other table and wiggles a foot at me, showing off a pair of navy and white striped socks with grinning green vegetables all over them, sticking out of his matching boots today. I kind of like the dual-coloured ones.

I go over and stand next to him, reaching up to lift his hair where it's flopped over and tuck it back. 'Are you okay?'

'Yeah. I knew I had the upper hand there. And it's been a while since Drake and I had a civilised discussion – that's enough to unnerve anyone.'

'Do you think he'll do it? Stop your father complaining about everything?'

'I think so. All that matters to my father is money. He and Drake will either flatten the house and build something there or restore it and turn it into a hotel or something. Either way, it'll be a big enough project to keep him busy, and it's what he's wanted for years. I think he'll see that it's worth giving up his campaign of nastiness for.'

I can feel joy bubbling up inside me, popping at the surface, trying to get out. 'Why did you do that?' I ask when it eventually bursts. 'The house must be worth a fortune, and the shop is *not*.'

'Because you were right,' he says eventually. 'You were right about the house. It *was* dragging me down. Every time I go back there, it's like stepping back in time, and the emptiness closes around me like a tomb. I don't want to live there anymore.'

'But the money ...'

'It's not about the money. If I cared about money, I wouldn't draw pictures for a living.' He lifts his head and meets my eyes. 'The house makes me feel dead inside and being here makes me feel alive. I'm different here. I've found myself here. I'm who I want to be here, and I lose that when I go home every night. You've reminded me how much I love Buntingorden. The house is just a building, but my mum and sister will always live on in this village because places like Once Upon A Page exist, and I had a chance to exchange the past for the future.'

It makes me well up again and he ducks his head. 'You changed my life, Hal. You made me remember who I used to be and what I used to love. In the past few years, I've hidden away in that house and given up on living, and you've reminded me that I used to have dreams. Seeing you throwing your all into the bookshop has reminded me that it's never too late to follow them.'

'You haven't even seen inside. It could be rotting away. It could be tiny. You're used to a massive kitchen.' Even as I'm saying it, my voice is going high with excitement. 'Do you have any idea—'

His arms slide around my waist and he picks me up and spins us around, hugging me to him.

'—how amazing you are?' I say against the skin of his neck.

He laughs. 'They must have a good-sized kitchen. It used to be a bakery.'

I squeeze my arms tighter around him. 'And now you own it ...'

'I own a shop. And half a roof terrace.'

I giggle and he spins us around again before finally putting me down, his hands on my waist, holding me steady as my hands drift up and down his bare arms to his T-shirt sleeves and back. 'What are you going to do with it?'

'It's going to be an art gallery. I'll display some of my stuff there, but mainly I want to showcase young, local artists who need someone to believe in them. And there's this little bookshop next door that I think deserves to be bigger, so I thought we could knock the walls through and expand, and maybe add a few tables for a café and a little bakery counter ...'

I reach up and fit my hand over his mouth because his talking has turned back into nervous rambling. 'It's exactly what Buntingorden needs. Especially the art gallery part.'

His eyes are watering as he laughs, and I let go of his mouth because accidentally suffocating the man I love would be the unwanted icing on the cake of a day that has turned out nothing like I expected it to. I lean up on my tiptoes to press my lips against his instead.

'It's what I've always dreamed of for this place,' he says when we pull back. 'More books, a café, an art gallery, and an open roof terrace where people can bring their cakes and books and sit in the peace up here watching the river trickling by.'

'It sounds perfect.' Up here in the darkness, lit only by the bright crescent moon and the warm orange glow of the oil lamp on the table behind us, I can't imagine anything nicer than sitting here on a warm sunny day with a pot of tea, a good book, and a pretty cake, listening to birds chirp and watching the swans float by on the river below.

'Your belief in the love in those notes made me believe in love again,' Dimitri murmurs. 'It made me want to prove to you that love exists in real life too. It made me realise that *I* still believed in love. I'd been alone for long enough to convince myself it was better that way because I didn't have anyone to lose. I never thought I'd let anyone in again, but I had absolutely no choice with you. Not from that very first day when you didn't make me feel like the clumsy oaf I am ... I felt like I'd found a part of me that I hadn't realised was missing until that moment.'

'Me too,' I mumble, trying not to cry again. 'And what about you? You've made me believe I can run a bookshop. I don't know what I'd have done without you. You've brightened up my life every day you've been in it.'

'This is what I want, Hal. All that matters is how being with you makes me feel. And that's like I can live again for the first time in years.'

I rest my thumb in the gorgeous dip in his chin and let my fingers stroke his face, tucking the ends of his hair back. 'And you make me feel unafraid to live. For the first time in my life, it doesn't feel like everything's about to go wrong.'

One of the railings behind us creaks ominously, and Dimitri leans his forehead against mine and laughs.

His hand slides down my jaw and tilts my head up until his lips press against mine, softly at first, like he's waiting for me to object, and I push back, silently letting him know how desperate I've been to kiss him, and it's all he needs. The kiss gets stronger as we clutch at each other, and he picks me up and sits me on the table, and some part of me is almost definitely about to catch on fire from the lamp but none of it matters when his hands are everywhere, holding me, pulling me impossibly closer, tangled in my ponytail, my T-shirt, as my fingers wind in his hair and the other hand curls into his shoulder hard enough to leave nail-shaped indents in the skin under his T-shirt, and I feel light-headed and dizzy and like I never want it to stop.

Time disappears as we kiss – a kiss that feels like not just a kiss but a promise of forever. A kiss with no holding back, no secrets between us now.

Somehow two people as awkward as us can have the most perfect kiss ever.

When we pull back, I can't bear to take my hands off him. He hugs me from behind and I hold his arms around me as we stand next to the railings at the edge of the roof terrace, looking out over the darkened river and the grassy bank, and there's only one thing I can think – how did I ever get this lucky?

His arms tighten around me as his chin rests on my shoulder and we stand there looking out, the rustle of summer trees and the gentle lap of water below. Above us, the stars are out in the clear night sky, twinkling brighter than usual in their thousands.

It feels like a scene straight from a romance novel. And the best thing about romance novels is that they always end happily. For the first time, it feels like real life is better than any book I've ever read, and like all love stories, even the unlikeliest ones, deserves a happy ending.

Swept away by Hallie's story and the Once Upon a Page bookshop? Don't miss *The Little Vintage Carousel by the Sea*, another gorgeously uplifting romance by Jaimie Admans. Available now!

Acknowledgements

Mum, this line is always the same because you're always there for me. Thank you for the constant patience, support, encouragement, and for always believing in me. I don't know what I'd do without you. Love you lots!

Extra special thanks to an amazing author and one of my very best friends, Marie Landry, for being wonderful in general and brightening up my life every day, and particularly in this book for sharing her love of *Anne of Green Gables* with me and letting me shamelessly borrow her gorgeous descriptions! Caru chi!

Bill, Toby, Cathie – thank you for always being supportive and enthusiastic!

An extra special thank-you to Bev for always asking about my writing, and being so caring, kind, encouraging, and for all the lovely letters – a bright spot during dark times!

Thank you, Charlotte McFall, for always being there for me, a tireless cheerleader and brilliant friend.

Thank you, Jayne Lloyd, for all the fantastic emails that make me smile, whatever the weather!

The lovely and talented fellow HQ authors – I don't know what I'd do without all of you!

All the lovely authors and bloggers I know on Twitter. You've all been so supportive since the very first book, and I want to mention you all by name, but I know I'll forget someone and I don't want to leave anyone out, so to everyone I chat to on Twitter or Facebook – thank you.

The little writing group that doesn't have a name – Sharon Sant, Sharon Atkinson, Dan Thompson, Jack Croxall, Holly Martin, Jane Yates. I can always turn to you guys!

Thank you to all the team at HQ and the two fabulous editors who worked on this book – Charlotte Mursell and Belinda Toor!

Thank you to all the friends and family who shared their favourite books with me for this project because I wanted to make sure that every book mentioned meant something to me or the people I love!

And finally, a massive thank-you to *you* for reading!

Dear Reader,

Thank you so much for reading *The Little Bookshop of Love Stories*. I hope you loved getting lost in books with Hallie and Dimitri as much as I did while I was writing it, and enjoyed a spring escape to Buntingorden too!

The idea for this story sprung from a news article about a bookseller who gave away his bookshop to a customer, and I couldn't stop thinking about what it would be like to suddenly find yourself in charge of a bookshop – surely every book lover's secret dream? It's definitely mine, and I loved getting to fictionally play with the idea through Hallie. As I'm generally unlucky myself, I also loved the idea of this character who never has anything go right for her suddenly winning the best prize she can imagine. Everyone's luck has to change sometime!

If you enjoyed this story, please consider leaving a review on Amazon. It only has to be a line or two, and it makes such a difference to helping other readers decide whether to pick up the book or not, and it would mean so much to me to know what you think! Did it make you smile, laugh or cry? What would you do if you suddenly won a bookshop? Have you ever found a secret message hidden in a book or written one yourself?

Thank you again for reading. If you want to get in touch, you can find me on Twitter – usually when I should be writing – @ be_the_spark. I would love to hear from you!

Hope to see you again soon in a future book!

Lots of love,

Jaimie

Dear Reader,

We hope you enjoyed reading this book. If you did, we'd be so appreciative if you left a review. It really helps us and the author to bring more books like this to you.

Here at HQ Digital we are dedicated to publishing fiction that will keep you turning the pages into the early hours. Don't want to miss a thing? To find out more about our books, promotions, discover exclusive content and enter competitions you can keep in touch in the following ways:

JOIN OUR COMMUNITY:
Sign up to our new email newsletter: hyperurl.co/hqnewsletter
Read our new blog www.hqstories.co.uk
🐦 : https://twitter.com/HQDigitalUK
f : www.facebook.com/HQStories

BUDDING WRITER?
We're also looking for authors to join the HQ Digital family!
Find out more here:
https://www.hqstories.co.uk/want-to-write-for-us/
Thanks for reading, from the HQ Digital team

Keep reading for an excerpt from
The Little Vintage Carousel by the Sea …

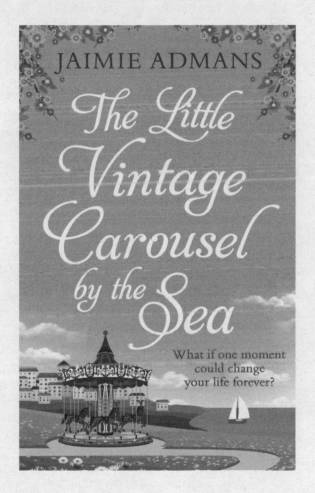

JAIMIE ADMANS

The Little Vintage Carousel by the Sea

What if one moment
could change
your life forever?

Chapter 1

Why does every man in London think that eight o'clock on a warm June morning is the ideal time to remove their shirt and get on the tube? I consider this as I peel myself away from a sweaty back and turn around to find myself face to face with someone's wet armpit. There's often a good time for shirtlessness, but the middle of rush hour on a crowded train is not it.

I sigh and stare at my feet. Every morning I get on this train and get off feeling like a floppy sardine that's just been let out of a tin and probably smelling worse. All to go to the soulless office block of the women's magazine where I work as a fact-checker, and then do the exact same thing at half past five with all the other sweaty, irritable commuters who would really love nothing more than to poke their boss in the eye and run away to a beach somewhere.

Someone stands on my toe and a handbag hits me in the thigh as someone else swings it over their arm. Ow. Only four more days to go until the weekend, and then I can have two whole days of not having to leave the flat and face the crowds of London. Two whole days of uninterrupted Netflix, apart from when Mum calls to update me on my ex-boyfriend's latest news, which she knows because they're still online friends even though I deleted him over two years ago.

I jump back as a briefcase threatens to take out my kneecaps. There's got to be more to life than this.

I look up and my eyes lock on to a man near me. Train Man is going somewhere today. Usually he only has a backpack with him, but today there's a huge suitcase leaning against his leg, rucksack straps over both shoulders, and a holdall bag hooked over one arm. He's standing up and holding on to a rail like I am, his attention on the phone in his hand, the lines around his eyes crinkled up as he looks down at it, and the sight of him makes something flutter inside me.

I see him quite often, but he's always already on the train when I get on, and we're usually much further apart. Up close, he's even more gorgeous than I'd always thought he was. He's got short brown hair, dimples denting his cheeks, and the kind of smile that makes you look twice, which I know because he's one of the rare London commuters who smiles at others.

The noisy tube train full of other people's body parts in places you don't want other people's body parts, the noise of people sniffing and coughing, an endless medley of beeps as people play with their phones, snippets of conversation that aren't meant for me … they all fade into the background and the world turns into slow motion as he lifts his head, almost like he can feel my eyes on him, and looks directly at me. If it was anyone else, I'd look away instantly. Staring at strangers on the tube is a quick way to get yourself punched or worse, but it's like a magnet is holding me, drawing my gaze to his, and his mouth curves up a tiny bit at each side, making it as impossible to look away now as it is every other time he smiles at me.

I feel that familiar nervous fluttering in the deepest part of my belly. It's not butterflies. My stomach must have disagreed with the cereal I shoved down my throat before rushing out of the flat this morning. Even though it's the same fluttery feeling

I get every time I see him and he sees me. Maybe it's because I'm never usually this close to him. Maybe those dimples have magical powers at this distance. Maybe I'm just getting dizzy from looking up at him because I'm so short and he's the tallest person on the train, towering above every other passenger around us.

His smile grows as he looks at me, and I feel myself smiling back, unable not to return his wide and warm smile, the kind of smile you don't usually see from fellow commuters on public transport. Open. Inviting. His gaze is still holding mine, his smile making his dimples deepen, and the fluttery feeling intensifies.

I feel like I could lean across the carriage and say hello to him, start a conversation, ask him where he's off to. Although that might imply that I've studied him hard enough on previous journeys to work out that he doesn't usually have that much luggage. And talking to him would be ridiculous. I can't remember the last time I said hello to a stranger. It's considered weird here, not like in the little country village where I grew up. People just don't *do* that here.

He's wearing jeans and a black T-shirt, and he tilts his head almost like he's *trying* to hold my gaze, and I wonder why. Does he know that I spend most journeys trying to work out what he does, because there's no regularity to his routine? I'm on this train at eight o'clock every morning Monday to Friday, I look like I'm going into an office, but he's always in jeans and a T-shirt, a jacket in the winter, and sometimes he's on this train a couple of times a week, sometimes once a week, and other times weeks can pass without me seeing him. I don't even know why I notice him so much. Is it because he smiles when our eyes meet? Maybe it's because he's so tall that you can't help but notice him, or because London is such a big and crowded place that you rarely see the same faces more than once.

His dark eyes still haven't left mine, and he pushes himself off the rail he's leaning against, and for a split second I think he's going to make the move and talk to me, and I feel like I've just stepped into a scene from one of my best friend Daphne's favourite rom com movies. The leading couple's eyes meet across a crowded train carriage and—

'The next station is King's Cross St. Pancras.' An automated voice comes over the tannoy, making me jump because everything but his eyes has faded into the background.

I see him swear under his breath and a look of panic crosses his face. He checks his phone again, turns around and gathers up his suitcase, hoists the holdall bag higher up his arm, and readjusts the rucksack on his shoulders.

I feel ridiculously bereft at the loss of eye contact as the train slows, but I get swept along by the crowd as other people gather up their bags and make a mass exodus towards the doors. He glances back like he's looking for me again, but I'm easy to miss among tall people and I've moved from where I was with the crowd. He looks around like he's trying to locate me, and I want to call out or wave or something, but what am I supposed to say? 'Hello, gorgeous Train Man, the strange short girl who's spent the entire journey staring at you is still here staring at you?'

I'm not far behind him now, even though this isn't my stop and it's clearly his. I can see him in the throng of people, his hand wrapped around the handle of the huge wheeled suitcase he's pulling behind him as the train comes to a stop.

As if the world turns to slow motion again, I see him glance at his phone once more and then go to pocket it, but instead of pushing it into the pocket of his jeans, it slides straight past and lands on the carriage floor at the exact moment the doors open and he, along with everyone else, rushes through them.

He hasn't noticed.

Without thinking, I dart forward and grab the phone from the floor before someone treads on it. I stare at it for a moment. This is his phone and I have it. He doesn't know he dropped it. There's still time to catch up with him and give it back.

Zinnia will probably kill me for being late for work, and I'm

342

still a few stops away from where I usually get off, but I don't have time to wait. I follow the swarm as seemingly every other person in our carriage floods out, and I pause in the middle of them, aware of the annoyed grunts of people pushing past me as I try to see where he is. I follow the crowd off the platform and up the steps, straining to see over people's heads and between shoulders.

I'm sure I see his hair in the distance as the crowd starts to thin out, but he's moving faster than a jet-powered Usain Bolt after an energy drink.

'Hey!' I shout. 'Wait up!'

He doesn't react. He wouldn't know who I was calling to, if the guy I'm following is even him.

'Hey! You dropped your—'

Another passenger glares at me for shouting in his ear and I stop myself. I'm already out of breath and Train Man is nothing more than a blur in the distance. I rush in the same direction, but those steps have knackered me, and the faraway blob that might still be the back of his head turns a corner under the sign towards the overground trains, and I lose sight of him.

I race ... well, limp ... to the corner where I saw him turn, but the station fans out into an array of escalators and glowing signs and ticket booths, and it's thronging with people. I walk around for a few minutes, looking for any hint of him, but he's nowhere to be seen. In the many minutes it's taken me to half-jog half-stumble from one end of the station to the other, he could be on another train halfway across London.

I pull my own phone out and glance at the time. I'm twenty minutes late for work, and still three tube stops and a ten-minute walk away. Zinnia is going to *love* me this morning. I put my phone back in my pocket and slide his in alongside it.

I'll have to find another way to get it back to him.

I could just hand it in at the desk in the station, but he'll probably never see it again if I do that. If I dropped my phone,

I'd like to think that a stranger would be kind enough to pick it up and attempt to reunite it with me, rather than just steal it. Why shouldn't I do that for Train Man?

There's something about him, there has been since the first time I saw him standing squashed against the door of a crowded train, right back in my first week at *Maîtresse* magazine. I know Daphne's going to say that this is the universe's way of saying I'm supposed to meet him after all the smiles we've exchanged, although she regularly says that when she's trying to set me up on dates, if she's not too busy reminding me of how long it's been since my last date.

But it doesn't mean anything. He isn't even going to know that I'm the girl he smiles at sometimes. I'm sure I can just get an address and pop the phone in the post to him.

Simple as that. It won't be a problem.

Want to read on? Order now!

DIGITAL HQ

If you enjoyed *The Little Bookshop of Love Stories*, then why not try another delightfully uplifting romance from HQ Digital?